STAN BARSTOW

'The only novelist of substance writing from within the north'

KEITH WATERHOUSE

'The affair between Alderman Simpkins and Mrs Moffat, one of his constituents, would have made an interesting tale in its own right. So would the awakening of Andrea Warner by Philip Hart, grammar school teacher. Stan Barstow dovetails these together without skimping on plot, characterisation or theme. This is the core of his power as a writer; he *cares* about people. It needs more than narrative skill to manage this: it takes imaginative warmth and a rare balance of sensibilities.'

TRIBUNE

A Raging Calm

Stan Barstow

CORGI BOOKS
A DIVISION OF TRANSWORLD PUBLISHERS LTD

A RAGING CALM

A CORGI BOOK 0 552 09475 7

Originally published in Great Britain
by Michael Joseph Ltd.

PRINTING HISTORY

Michael Joseph edition published 1969
Corgi edition published 1970
Corgi edition reprinted 1971
Corgi edition reissued 1974
Corgi edition reprinted 3 times 1974
Corgi edition reprinted 1975

This book is set in Times 10/11pt.

Corgi books are published by Transworld Publishers Ltd.,
Cavendish House, 57–59 Uxbridge Road, Ealing,
London, W.5.

Made and printed in Great Britain by
Richard Clay (The Chaucer Press) Ltd, Bungay, Suffolk

Oh these deceits are strong almost as life.
Last night I dreamt I was in the Labyrinth,
And awoke far on. I did not know the place.

EDWIN MUIR. The Labyrinth
COLLECTED POEMS, Faber & Faber

In tragic life, God wot,
No villain need be! Passions spin the plot:
We are betrayed by what is false within.

GEORGE MEREDITH: Modern Love

This is a work of fiction. The characters and incidents in it are imaginary

Thanks are due to Faber & Faber Limited for their permission to reproduce three lines of THE LABYRINTH by Edwin Muir from *Collected Poems* published by themselves

PART ONE

Simpkins, alderman, ex-mayor of this town, engineer by trade, longtime widower in public, longtime lover of a married woman in private. (Simpkins was discreet, never gossiped about this relationship and people were better at live-and-let-live than they sometimes got credit for.)

Simpkins on this November morning opened the door of his house on Beacon Hill and saw the first snow of the winter; saw it now for the first time because he had ignored, bloody-mindedly, his sister's request that he turn his head from the breakfast table and look out at the unbroken layer on the lawn. His bedroom curtains were still drawn when he got up. White light striking through the slats of the venetian blind in the bathroom had told him that last night's silent, freezing cold had given way to snow, but his preoccupation with a slight hangover, his rankling memory of Bess's sharp words and the disquieting knowledge that he couldn't actually *remember* the drive home kept his thoughts occupied during the vigorous exertion of his shower, then his shave. The mirror over the washbasin gave him his face: a little jowly now, but still pleasantly square-jawed, and the blue eyes that Norma had once told him could survey people in a disturbingly direct and piercing way seemed to become more piercingly blue with age. His hair was completely grey, at fifty-five, but thick and healthy and likely to last him his time out, thank God. His height was indicated by the slight stoop with which he faced the mirror. The glass was adjustable but its basic position favoured Bess who had their mother's shortness of stature while he had inherited his father's height.

Out of the car-park of the White Horse, left and along Corporation Street, across the Market Place, left again into Market Street and round the island at the end, half a mile along Huddersfield Road and right into Heights Lane, with a pull up the last three-quarters of a mile. Six or seven minutes, door to door. He knew it all, knew it well. Why should he remember the details of a drive whose every yard he had traversed hundreds of times (nay, more like thousands) before? He'd had nothing important on his mind, either, so far as he could remember. He was just relaxed in the after-glow of drink and good fellowship with Baden, Bobby, Arthur and the others, on one of those occasional evenings when, in the company of men he'd known for most of his life and drunk with many times, the talk flowered in an unusually vivid way. Not that they'd drunk much—or *he* hadn't, anyway. He ducked his head to sluice his face. Too quickly—his brain seemed to slip forward and gently col-lide with the inside of his skull. That last brandy and soda had done it: that final shot of spirits after the pints of bitter, served by a tolerant landlord when the towels had gone over the beer-pumps and he was legally out of order. But dammit, he was safe enough with half the Watch Committee on his premises and their cars—makes, models and licence numbers known to any passing policeman—in the car-park. A brave bobby, or an ignorant one, who would dare that barrier of privilege. They didn't abuse their positions, that was the point. Edgar knew they wouldn't put him in a spot. One quick last one and out into the gripping cold, with Baden hanging back for a special goodnight after the others had got into their cars.

'Snow before morning, Tom.'

'You think so?'

'I know it. Early this year.'

'Aye ... How's Maude?'

'Oh, fair to middling, as usual.'

'I haven't seen her lately.

'It's your own fault '

10

'Aye. Well, give her my regards.'

'Running off, are you?'

'Why, had you something else in mind?'

'No, no. Just thinking, though; you're as careful as the married 'uns in hurrying home.'

'No point in upsetting 'em for nowt, Baden.'

'I allus thought him that paid the piper called the tune.'

'There's no good tunes played on a sour instrument.'

Baden chuckled as he made off heavily across the yard. He couldn't be much heavier than Simpkins, but being shorter and portly with it seemed to make him put down his feet with twice the weight. And about twice the lack of tact, too. Many a time Simpkins had groaned in the council chamber when a passage of at least semi-diplomatic man-oeuvre had been turned by Baden's headstrong advocacy into an obstinate clash of wills and personalities.

Simpkins sulked over his breakfast. If Bess preferred any kind of talk to silence and had apparently relegated their encounter of last night to its place as an incident in the past (but forgotten only until it could be unearthed to best effect), it didn't mean he had to kowtow to her moods. The overnight fall of snow had given her a fresh subject for her chatter. That and a robin which was asserting sole owner-ship of the bacon rind she had thrown out.

'Bad 'uns, they are. Pretty to look at, but real bullies.'

Like some women I could name, Simpkins thought sourly. He had opened the front door with his latchkey and the next moment found himself flat on his back as the hall rug shot out from under his feet on the polished boards. Bess, still up, ran out of the sitting-room and put her hand under his elbow as he stood upright.

'I've told you before that polishing under that rug is dangerous. I might have broken something.'

'If a man's not steady on his feet,' she said.

The phrase he'd uttered before she appeared and the brandy on his breath were enough for her. The widow of a man who had drunk too much, she hated alcohol even in moderation and saw any evidence of it as a sign of excess.

11

'What the devil are you on about?'

'You're late and you've been drinking.'

'I'm not particularly late and I'm certainly not drunk.'

'There are stages of drunkenness, Tom, and if you can't come into your own house without falling down...' That way she had of leaving accusatory sentences unfinished.

Simpkins was angry. 'And if you can't stop filling the house with blasted booby traps. If anybody from outside falls like that I might well find myself forking out compensation.'

'And that would touch your pocket.'

'Now look here, Bess, that's just not fair.'

It wasn't and she knew it. 'You tell me I don't look after this place in a proper manner. If you think so, you just tell me.' Blue eyes blazing, small slim body rigid with what was to him illogically outraged pride, she challenged him to do what he knew he never could do.

'Don't talk daft, lass. You know I can't say that.'

'Then consider your words with more care, if you please.'

His next words died in his throat. She was beyond arguing with in this state. They rarely quarrelled and the concessions he was in the habit of making to her were a minor price to pay for a well-ordered and usually peaceful home. He wondered if something out of the ordinary had happened to create her corrosive mood and decided not to ask now.

This morning he was inclined to put it down to 'the change'. He'd an idea she was going through the menopause and he knew it was supposed to make women irritable and hard to live with. Be that as it may, she would know, if she wasn't too self-centred to perceive anyone else's mood, that he still wasn't pleased by what had happened.

He exchanged a couple of words about lunch and got his coat. The rug was still there in the hall. He kicked it to one side, leaving it conspicuously crumpled against the skirting board and opened the front door.

Simpkins' house stood majestically on the hill. Four-bed-

roomed, stone-built, Victorian, it looked unusually impos-
ing from some way off. His father had bought it at the turn
of the century and Simpkins had lived in it all his life. It
stood sideways to the road and a gravelled drive swept
round past the front windows, which commanded a view
across steeply falling ground of the town. A thin pall of
industrial haze was already hanging over the wide basin
and white plumes from the twin cooling-towers of the
power station by the river trailed off dispiritedly against the
leaden sky. There was some demolition of terraced cottages
going on down the hill and the transformed vista under
snow of the straggling lines of houses and the newly cleared
spaces reminded Simpkins unexpectedly, as he lifted his
eyes from the lighting of the first pipe of the day, of Scarborough and Nell, thirty years ago. The impression was
gone in a moment, but the memory had surfaced vividly:
the flat on the top floor of a house by the church with a
view from the high window of rooftops stepping hap-
hazardly down to the harbour. A room and the two of them
in a town which, in that magical summer, had somehow
after their tentative first coming-together brought about the
flowering of a sensuality they spent wondering delighted
hours in exploring and savouring.

'Ah, this town,' she said. 'I shall always love it.'

'We'll buy a house here when I retire,' he said.

'Yes, when we're old and grey, and we only want each
other once a day.' She rolled away from him, laughing, the
high, dangerous colour flushing her cheeks. 'Do you think
I'm too brazen?'

'No.'

'No, and it doesn't matter. I love you, Tom Simpkins. I
love you, I love you, I love you.'

Now he was grey, if not old; and she ... Nell, the golden
girl of his youth ... she had given him love and a sexual
confidence which, after her pitiful tubercular decline and
merciless end, he'd used at any opportunity that arose to
satisfy his immediate appetites and numb the desolation of
her death. Odd, he had thought, for him—after a puritani-

13

cal upbringing and sexually timid youth—to find how much sensuality was bottled up behind the respectable exteriors in this town; how many women were lonely or neglected in some way or other and ready, with the right kind of approach, to look for comfort in irregular unions however fleeting. He exaggerated: there had been no more than three or four. Still, he couldn't have found them all, and the identity of some of them was surprising. He made no excuses. There had been times when he wanted the open thighs of a woman and he'd looked for them. At other times he accused himself of exploiting his bereavement for his own ends. Everyone said how tragic it was. Sympathetic women were at least less likely to rebuff him sternly and in the event of a scandal his emotional state could be cited in mitigation. But no: the real answer was that for the first time in his life he was free of all kinds of inhibitions, both personal and social, which had hampered him before. He was unhappy and he didn't care what anybody thought about him.

It was the unfamiliar aspect of a familiar view which had started all this off. That and the unusually introspective mood in which he'd begun the day. He was restless, had looked at the feeling and acknowledged it by the time he braked the Austin at the bottom of the lane. He went farther and acted upon it when with no more than a second's indecision he turned the car right towards the town and away from the Works. They could manage without him for a few hours.

There was hardly any sign of snow in the town centre. The wheels of the early traffic had turned it to water and the streets were wet and black in the cold. He left the car in the Town Hall park and walked down the road and across the square to Fenwick's. He still wanted to call it Van Huyten's, though the old man had been dead two or three years and the new owners had changed the shop beyond recognition. The young fellow who had managed it during the last years of the old man's life, and with whom Simpkins had often chatted about music and records, had gone

14

too when the business changed hands and now he encountered a series of faceless youths and girls who might be familiar with the top twenty but didn't know a Beethoven symphony from a Strauss waltz. He could see one through the plate glass as he pushed open the door and stepped thankfully into the warm interior of the shop.

The lad looked up from a sheaf of invoices as Simpkins walked the length of the fitted carpet. 'Good morning.'

'Morning. I ordered a couple of records last week. Simpkins, the name is.'

'Did you have a card notifying you they'd arrived?'

'No. They mightn't have come yet but I was passing so I thought I'd call in.'

'I see. Mr Simpkins ...' The boy consulted a book and turned to look on the bottom row of the record racks behind him. 'Yes, here we are ...' He read from the sleeve: 'Bruckner. Symphony number Seven.' He made it sound like a foreign language and the identical design of the second sleeve baffled him for a moment. 'They're both the same.'

Simpkins shook his head. 'No. It spreads on to two records.'

'Oh yes! I see. No just running through that while the kettle boils.'

'No, you need an hour or two.'

'Would you like to hear part of it?'

Why not? He knew it, but there was more justification for listening to it than there was for the Saturday-afternoon jingle, jangle madhouse row of records which the people buying them had heard dozens of times in the past few days on the wireless. He asked for the beginning of the first side and went into one of the listening-booths.

A crackle and a hiss were the mechanical heralds of that glorious soaring rainbow of sound. Old Bruckner, the peasant, laughed at by many of his contemporaries; neglected for half a century and more for being long-winded and overblown. Bruckner dedicating the glory of his art to the Maker he believed in with simple fervour. And whether you believed in God or not a love of this radiant music was surely in itself a passport to whatever heaven existed. Perhaps it brought it momentarily within reach here on earth. Here in a listening-booth in a record shop in Cressley on a cold November morning, heaven lay briefly around him. But, far from all-embracing, a hint of an unattainable state; beauty that in its very loveliness enfolded the heart in melancholy. It was a long time since music like this had formed a communion between himself and someone else, and in his happiness made him happier still.

Nor, on the other hand, did it usually make him miserable. If he hadn't the positive joy he'd known with Nell, he still kept a sane and reasonable grip on life. He filled his time usefully, took the pleasures he liked and indulged little in the kind of morbid restlessness that was pestering him this morning. Anxiety nagged at the periphery of his mind as he went out and paid for the records and left the shop. What the hell *was* wrong with him today? Was it something someone had said last night? Had he himself been indiscreet in a way he'd thought little of at the time but which was nudging away at him now like guilt? If it was something he'd contemplated on the drive home it had occupied him only absentmindedly and hadn't been a worry then. The incident with the rug and Bess had pushed it back under the surface of his thoughts and he'd had enough to drink to make him sleep within a few minutes of getting into bed.

Mirrors on opposite walls of the listening-booth, surrounded by record sleeves, had given him an unaccustomed view of the back of his head. He could do with a haircut and, since he was playing truant, he might as well see to it now. He returned to the car and put the records on the front passenger seat. How much more interesting and convenient it was buying gramophone records now than in the days, fifteen years ago, when the Bruckner would have come, laborious with irritating side-breaks, on nine or ten heavy shellac discs. If it had come at all, that was, in those austere days when performances even of favourites from the orchestral repertoire were limited in choice. He had a long cupboard of old 78s—there must be four or five hundred of them—which he hadn't played or even looked at for years. He could spend an interesting few hours glancing through them, weeding out pieces he had duplicated, perhaps recapturing a little of the thrill of first familiarity with those works which had introduced him to the abiding pleasures of music. He never, for instance, went out of his way to hear the Tschaikovsky symphonies nowadays but it might be exciting to renew acquaintance with the Koussevitzky Fourth and the Furtwängler *Pathetique*—both classic performances which he doubted had ever been surpassed in the past fifteen years' proliferation of LP issues. Then there was Weingartner's Beethoven; but Beethoven being a never-ending joy he had duplicated the nine symphonies in modern recordings. Kleiber, Klemperer, Karajan. KKK—the initials *could* stand for something constructive in this most destructive of centuries.

That was a condemnation he usually resisted. He had to admit the dreadful tally: two world wars—the second including the deliberate extermination of six million Jews—Hiroshima, Nagasaki; Korea, Kenya, Cyprus, Suez, Hungary, the Congo, Vietnam ... Man's place in the sun was still being forged in blood and death. And yet, weren't men's consciences nearer the surface? In an age of doubt and anxiety wasn't the other side of the coin a healthy questioning of values and standards and an urge towards reform? Simpkins believed this. While the stupidity of human beings constantly saddened and angered him, he believed in the presence in the world of a greater moral concern than ever before. And if a great deal of it was hypocritical then it wasn't a bad norm to pay lip service to. To his Tory friends things just went from bad to worse. The virtually unrestrained individualism they called free enterprise was being curbed by legislation and restrictions they abhorred and branded as crippling; whereas Simpkins saw it as an inevitable development in the search for the greatest good. When he argued in this vein he was accused of

17

preaching Socialism. He would smile then and talk of historical inevitability, while most of them argued from the particular, their context limited to Cressley, their standard of right and wrong thinking based on the success or failure of their own affairs. Not that there weren't reactionaries on the other side, men to whom Socialism was expediency, who saw employers as the enemy, men who would tell you openly that they were working men and as such could not afford to be anything else but Socialist. Simpkins had always been a radical but, elected as an independent member, he took his seat on the majority side of the chamber along with men who occupied varying positions right of centre. His presence there tended to make his colleagues regard him as one of them, while his occasional advocacy of a measure raised on the other side of the chamber brought him under pressure from both groups. Walter Whitehead, the leader of the Labour minority on the council, had more than once hinted that a place with them would not be too hard to find and wasn't it time he crossed over and left his present company? It was simple, Simpkins told him; every issue was one of conscience to him and he would be in trouble from the start for not toeing the party line. Besides, he added with a twinkle, wasn't it better for there to be somebody a bit radical in a position to inject occasional doses of common sense into the more outlandish Conservative measures? In truth, Simpkins disliked politics and all the strategy, concessions and compromise inherent in 'the art of the possible'. Economics bedevilled everything. It must surely be possible to arrive at some economic system which would be flexible enough to suit the majority and efficient and stable enough to stop being the prime bone of contention. Then the parties could regroup themselves round the moral and spiritual issues through which men might find their real happiness and fulfilment. It amused him to think just how drastic that regrouping might be. And oh, what superstitions and prejudices would be given airings then! But, Simpkins thought, we'd seen enough since the war to know that when you removed a man's obsession with keeping body and soul together you left a gap that must be filled with something else. Well—he shrugged—some people liked Bingo; he liked Bruckner. Who was happier for which, was another question.

The great tune soared in his mind as he climbed the bare wooden steps to Henry Waterman's barber's shop. There was a new ten-chair saloon in modern premises a couple of streets away but Simpkins had always been loyal to Henry in his bare shabby shop over the confectioner's by the market. It was market day; the traders had set out their wares and already now, at not yet ten o'clock, the streets were lined with parked cars and women with shopping-bags and baskets jay-walked with the apparent disregard that made driving in the area a hazardous stop-go progression with potential damage to life and limb along every yard.

A pile of cardboard cartons almost filled the vestibule at the top of the stairs. Simpkins pushed open the door and went into the shop itself. There was an old man sitting on one of the half-dozen bentwood chairs under the window, his arthritic hands resting on the handle of a walking-stick standing upright between his knees. Sitting on the other row of chairs along the side wall was a young housewife, watching a little apprehensively as Henry cut the hair of her small son. The second barber's chair was empty and there was no sign of the lad who was Henry's assistant.

Henry looked up from the head of the boy as Simpkins entered.

'Morning, Tom.'

'Henry.'

'A cold 'un this morning.'

'It is that.'

'I thought it might have come a bit warmer after that fall of snow, but it hasn't.'

'No, not yet. It might if the sun comes out later on.'

'You don't think there's any more to come, then?'

'No, I think that's the lot for a while.'

'Hmmm.'

Simpkins took a seat near the old man as Henry limped round to the other side of the boy. He wore a boot with a built-up sole to help compensate for his left leg which was several inches shorter than the right. Simpkins thought that the contorted energy of his walk pulled his internal organs about, resulting in digestive troubles which accounted for the yellowish colour of his face. But he was always cheerful in his way; if you could describe his often sour comments on humanity and his endless curiosity about people and their affairs as cheerfulness.

'On your own this morning, are you, Henry?'

'Aye, the lad's got flu.'

'Hmm. It'll make it harder for you.'

'Oh, I don't know. In this kind of weather people let their hair grow a bit longer. It helps to keep 'em warm.'

The child sat rigidly on the stool in the chair, watching Henry warily in the mirror as he snipped at his hair. He jerked his head suddenly as some clippings fell on his face.

'Just shut your eyes, young man, while I trim your fringe,' Henry commanded him.

The boy's eyes opened wide at the loud abruptness of Henry's voice and his mother said, 'Do as the gentleman says, Neville. He'll soon be finished.'

'That's right,' Henry said. 'He does want a fringe, doesn't he, or do you want him with a parting?'

'Oh, he's a bit young for a parting,' the woman said.

'Aye, he'll not be chasing the lasses yet, eh?'

'Give him a chance. He's not going to school yet.'

'Not going to school—a big lad like you? How old are you, sonny, eh?'

The boy sat mute, eyes tightly closed, as Henry tried to coax him into conversation. Simpkins turned over the papers on the chair beside him. There was the *Daily Express* with yesterday's *Yorkshire Evening Post* and a couple of copies of a weekly magazine which contained little jokey short stories and bits of show-business news but was mainly devoted to pictures of bosomy girls in various states of undress. He flipped the pages, feeling no response to the abundance of breasts, bellies and thighs. Was he getting past it altogether? he wondered. He'd always preferred the imperfections of reality to this kind of remote titillation but it struck him now that it was a long time since anyone had stirred him to more than a momentary sexual curiosity; a long time since he'd felt the rage of real urgent desire in his flesh. He didn't even regret it. There had been pleasure in both pursuit and kill but there was no point in trying to eat when he wasn't hungry. He felt no necessity to prove anything to himself.

Henry's eyes glittered behind his glasses as he saw Simpkins put the magazine aside. 'A bit of summat to take the young fellers' minds off waiting, eh, Tom?'

Simpkins started. 'Oh, aye. Yes.' He shot a sudden half-embarrassed look at the young woman, but her attention was still fixed on the boy in the chair.

'Does he want a drop of cream?' Henry asked her.

She said, 'I don't think——' and the child, speaking for the first time, broke in with a clear, firm 'Yes, please.'

Henry laughed and glanced questioningly at the mother.

'All right,' she said. 'Just a bit to satisfy him.'

'I'll give him a drop of my special, eh? How's that, young man?' The boy watched as Henry picked up a bottle and shook a blob of glutinous liquid into his palm. He rubbed it into the boy's hair and brushed and combed the fringe a little to one side. 'There we are. He's a real bobby dazzler now.'

The mother fumbled in her purse as Henry whipped the sheet off the boy, lifted him down out of the chair and put the stool away. She paid and they left, the boy suddenly releasing a flood of pent-up chatter as they passed through the door.

Henry shook the sheet, 'Right, Tom, I think we can take you next.'

Simpkins motioned to the old man. 'What about . . .?'

'Oh, old Bob'll let you go out of turn.' He raised his voice to speak to the old man. 'You'll let Mr Simpkins go next, won't you, Bob?'

The old man lifted his eyes and focused them vaguely on Simpkins. 'You carry on. I'm all right here awhile.'

'He's in no hurry,' Henry explained as he tucked the sheet in round Simpkins' collar. 'He's a pensioner, living on his own. He won't have lit his fire this morning and he's warm enough here, and saving coal.'

'I see. He doesn't say much.'

'No. He comes in every few days. Sometimes he wants a shave, occasionally a haircut. Sometimes he just wants to sit where it's warm and there's a bit of life going on round him. He's all right. He doesn't do any harm and he knows not to take up space when we're busy. On your own, nowt to look forward to, in people's way. It's funny to think it could come to any of us.'

'I hope not,' Simpkins said.

'Ah, well, we're lucky, you and me. We'll be cushioned a bit. You more than me, of course.'

'Come on, now, Henry,' Simpkins said. 'You've had this place as long as I can remember. You must have a bit tucked away.'

Henry laughed. 'Oh, I can't grumble. I've had to be careful, though. I mean, folk coming in here when it's packed, they count heads and seem to think I'm coining it as fast as I can fill and empty the chairs. They forget the quiet times when I'm twiddling my thumbs and I've the lad to pay for doing nowt.' He flourished his scissors. 'How do you want it?'

'Same as usual,' Simpkins said. Henry always asked and he always gave the same answer. 'I'm not going in for anything new.'

'There's that other place round the corner,' Henry said, switching on the trimmer and touching it to Simpkins' neck. 'They're charging all sorts of fancy prices for what they call re-styling. Me, I have one price whether a chap wants a lot off or a little. And you get some rum customers these days. Sometimes you think you're in a woman's salon, the types you get in. And the funny ideas ... They see some beat group on the telly, or a wrestler they fancy, and they want to be like them. I had a young lad in only yesterday. He wanted me to give him some kind of bloody Red Indian cut—all shaved off bar a strip down the middle.'

'What did you do?'

'I told him I'd do it if he brought a note from his mam. I've had enough trouble that way. I once cut a lad's hair off and gave him a crew cut—about half an inch long all over. Next thing I knew I had his mother up here raising hell. No, owt out of the ordinary and they have to be over the age of consent before I'll touch it.'

He switched off the buzzing trimmer and got to work with scissors and comb. Simpkins closed his eyes. He actually liked having his hair cut. There was something in sitting there and hearing the snip-snip of the scissors which relaxed him. Perhaps he'd let Henry give him a shampoo afterwards. The thought of the warm water on his head and Henry's fingers lathering the grime out of his hair took him to a memory of the Turkish Baths. It was a surprisingly tempting image. He promised himself he'd go again soon, steam the grease and dirt out of his pores and have his flesh toned up under the kneading hands of the masseur.

'Are you having the morning off or did you just pop out for a trim?' Henry asked.

'I'd one or two things to see to in town so I thought I'd call in while I was here.'

'It'll be busy in the streets.'

'Aye, and busier still this afternoon.'

'Trouble is finding a place to park your car.'

'Oh, I left mine by the Town Hall and walked round.'

'Aye ... It gets worse, this traffic business. One thing, if it all chokes up solid it'll solve the accident problem.'

'Hmmm.'

'That was a nasty do up Greenbank the other night.'

'Oh?'

'Didn't you hear about it?'

'No.'

'One of them big articulated lorries skidded and went straight down the banking side. It was in last night's paper.' Henry left Simpkins' hair and went to get the *Evening Post*. He turned the pages. 'Aye, here. Local feller as well, the driver. Gives his name here. Moffat. Sidney Moffat.'

Simpkins' heart gave a jolt. His ears burned as colour flooded up to them.

'Does it say how badly hurt he was?'

'No. Just that they got him out and took him to hospital. There's a picture as well. It looks a rare old mess.'

Simpkins struggled his hands free from under the sheet. 'Can I see it?'

Henry passed him the folded newspaper. 'I can't say I know the feller, but you might. Says he lives up Edgehill. You've got a bit of property up there, haven't you?'

Simpkins' eyes took in the picture of the huge vehicle with spilled load lying on its side and went to the paragraph. 'Yes, I know the family. They live in one of my houses. The wife used to work for me at one time.'

'You can't make out from that whether he's really hurt or he got off with shock and bruises. They took him to hospital, though.'

'Yes.'

Henry stood behind him and clicked the scissors. 'Shall I carry on?'

'Yes, please, Henry.'

He read the paragraph once more then drew his hands in under the sheet again, letting the paper slide to the floor. Henry was saying something but he wasn't listening. So that was it. That was what had been worrying him all morning. He remembered now that someone near him in the White Horse had mentioned Sid's name. It had come to him indistinctly through the rumble of conversation and there must have been mention either immediately, or more likely some moments before, of the accident. He was talking to somebody and he had long ago trained himself not to react too quickly to that kind of reference; so it had somehow bounced tangentially off the surface of his mind and lodged itself in his subconscious, plaguing him till what Henry had told him released it into the light. His heart was beating fast. He wondered if Henry could judge the extent of his agitation. What was Norma thinking and doing now? He must go and see her.

Two more customers came in and distracted Henry from further conversation with him. He was thankful when the sheet was removed. He suffered Henry to brush his shoulders and asked for some threepenny bits in his change.

'I want to make a phone call.'

He wasn't far from the General Post Office. He walked there and stepped into one of the telephone booths. They would probably have taken Sid to the Infirmary. He found the number in the directory and rang it.

'I wonder if you've any news of a patient called Sidney Moffat. He'd be brought in on Monday night after an accident in a lorry. I'm a friend of the family.'

The woman at the other end asked him to hang on. He waited, picturing thin, mild-mannered Sid. Sid the amiable cuckold, being pulled from the wreckage of one of the huge lorries he didn't look to have the strength to drive. And why hadn't Norma let him know something? There hadn't been a word from her.

'Hello.'

'Yes?'

'Mr Moffat is as well as can be expected.'

'Is that all you can tell me?'

'I'm afraid it is. He was operated on yesterday and he's as well as can be expected.'

He might have lost a limb, or his sight, or be at death's door. There was nothing else to be got from the woman, though. It was probably all she knew; what she had been instructed to say. He thanked her, then rang off and dialled the number of his office. His secretary, Miss Warner, sounded relieved to hear his voice.

'Oh, Mr Simpkins, I was wondering where you'd got to. I spoke to Mrs Hargreaves but she said you'd set off for the office an hour before.'

'You rang my sister?'

'Well, yes. When you didn't turn up I thought I'd better. I didn't know of any outside appointments you had for this morning and I knew Mrs Hargreaves would have rung me if you'd been unwell.'

'Yes, that's all right.' Now Bess would be wondering where the devil he'd got to. 'Look, Miss Warner, I've got one or two things to see to here in town. I'll be in this afternoon, all being well. I haven't got anything in the book, have I?'

'No, no appointments at all. One or two people have been wanting to see you.'

'They can wait till later. Will you ring Mrs Hargreaves, tell her that you've heard from me, and that I shan't be home for lunch?'

'Righto, Mr Simpkins.'

'Is there anything else?'

'No, not at the moment.'

'All right, then. You hold the fort till I get there.'

She chuckled over the line. 'I'll do my best.' She was a nice girl and he thought she liked him.

He put the phone down and filled and lit a pipe before leaving the booth. He pulled at it greedily, drawing the smoke down into his lungs. It occurred to him now that he should have asked if Sid was being allowed visitors, which might have given him more of a clue to his condition. But he would find out when he saw Norma. He went out of the building and walked briskly to his car.

2

The sky had brightened by the time he reached Edgehill. The sun blinded him in the moments when he drove directly into it and he was too warm in his thick overcoat with the heater on as well. A powdering of snow lingered on grass plots and in the untrodden corners of yards and entries. On the roads it had been ground into a thin salty paste which was flung in a spray on to his windscreen by the vehicles he was trailing up the hill.

Edgehill had been an independent village fifty years before. Now it was only the grouping of the older houses in the streets round the parish church and the relative newness of the property flanking the road up to it which gave any feeling of a once separate identity. The houses Simpkins owned there were half a dozen stone-fronted three-bedroomed villas in a terrace. They were his and Bess's, left to them jointly by their mother. Simpkins' father had owned property in several parts of the town and it was for many years a lucrative investment. But after the war and a decade in which the capital value of the houses had increased appreciably, he had decided that now was the time to sell and re-invest the money. Old Simpkins, seeing the cost of maintaining the property rising all the time, and envisaging the programmes of redevelopment which were bound to be implemented in the next ten or fifteen years, sold as fast as he could, with vacant possession where possible and to sitting tenants where death or a move away seemed unlikely for a long time. The building societies' terms for the purchase of that kind of semi-obsolete housing were harsh where they weren't non-existent and old Simpkins made it easy for buyers by having his solicitors draw up his own mortgage schemes. There was a severe housing shortage and young couples who could neither rent accommodation nor afford to buy modern semis were happy to put down small deposits and pay weekly sums against the purchase of two- and three-bedroomed terraced houses in which to start their married lives. The best of these owners, the ones with pride, improved the property, fitting cupboards and water-heaters, ripping out and replacing old fireplaces, hanging modern wallpaper and replacing a dingy tradition of grained and varnished woodwork with a new one of bright shining paint. In those years there were 'little palaces' to be found in many unlikely streets and despite the absence of bathrooms and indoor lavatories more than a few couples, Simpkins knew, could look back at that period, before the coming of children threatened overcrowding and necessitated a move on to better (and more expensive) accommodation, as the cosiest and most contented of their lives. Now these six houses in Edgehill were all that remained and Simpkins, burdened by rent control and still more expensive repair costs, found ownership of them a nuisance. But Bess, clinging to an understandable belief in the everlasting security of bricks and mortar, hung on and refused to let him sell.

The houses stood in a row at the end of a roughly surfaced road, laid out when the property was built but since allowed to fall into disrepair. It led nowhere anyway, petering out on to a flat patch of grassy waste ground fenced off from the drop at its farther end by iron railings. Simpkins considered the view from these railings to be among the finest in the district. You looked at an angle along the valley. The town lay down in the basin on the left. The far horizon was bounded by hills, with buildings straggling up their lower slopes. In the middle distance a great high spur of land thrust sideways into the valley, seeming, in certain lights, from its loftiness and the houses strung out on its summit ridge to be almost suspended in the air. In the valley bottom smoke curled up from a thousand domestic chimneys. Simpkins loved it. It was his country and had always been part of his life. He could never make up his mind if it was the dour uncompromising character of its industry which gave it its special drama, or whether it would have been equally, though differently, magnificent before the coming of the mills and factories, and the houses which were their necessary appendage.

The Moffats lived in the end house and Simpkins could conveniently park his car on the waste ground; something he had found helpful to discretion in times past. He did this now, jolting slowly along the street in bottom gear then turning gingerly at the end in case the thaw had softened the ground enough to trap his wheels. He went round the back of the house and tapped on the kitchen door before pushing it open and stepping inside. The house was quiet. He called out, 'Anybody home?', opening the door to the hall and standing there. In a moment he heard a sound from upstairs and Norma's voice said, 'Who is it?'

'It's me, Tom.'

'Oh! Just a minute.'

A door closed on the landing and he turned and went back into the kitchen. It was furnished as a day-to-day living-room with a couple of wooden-armed easy chairs before the tiled fireplace. He sat down in one of them, still in his heavy coat, and felt for his tobacco pouch. Water gurgled in the waste-pipe as the washbasin in the bathroom was emptied. A few moments later he heard feet on the stairs and Norma came in. He guessed she had washed her face and put some fresh make-up on. She was in her working clothes, but clean and neatly shod. There was nothing of the slut about Norma—none of the haircurlers, matted woollen jumpers and toe-burst slippers some women thought good enough for about the house. She had always had her own pride. He got up, thinking that although she had put on weight and thickened round the waist since he first knew her, she was still a firm-bodied handsome woman. She had no smile of greeting for him; but then, she had never smiled easily, though her laugh was rich and full when she was really amused; and this was, after all, a serious occasion.

He said, 'Norma, I just heard about Sid.'

'Yes.'

'I was in the barber's this morning and he mentioned it. Then I saw last night's paper. I don't know how I didn't come to hear about it before.'

'It was late on Monday night when it happened. He was on his way back from Liverpool.'

'How is he, though, Norma?'

'They operated on him yesterday.'

'Yes, they told me when I rang up.'

'You rang, did you?'

'This morning, as soon as I heard. They told me nothing, though. Just that he's as well as can be expected.'

'Aye. That's about all they'll tell me.'

'But how badly hurt was he?'

'He's got a broken leg, a broken arm, two broken ribs and internal injuries.' Her voice was flat, emotionless.

Simpkins said, 'Oh, dear . . .'

'It's the internal injuries they don't seem to know about. Whether they'll leave any lasting damage.'

Simpkins absently tamped tobacco into the bowl of his pipe, looking all the while at Norma. 'Poor old Sid.'

'Aye. It's the story of his life.' She moved past him to the sink and picked up the kettle. 'Have you time for a cup of coffee?'

'I think so.'

'Don't think you've got to stop if you're busy.'

'Surely I can spare the time for a cup of coffee, Norma.'

'I don't know what you can spare.'

'Norma, I really didn't hear till this morning.'

'I know. You just said so.'

She ran water into the kettle and put it on the gas stove.

'If it comes to that, I think you might have let me know.'

'What could I have said?'

'You could have said what had happened.'

30

'And that would have brought you round, after a fortnight without a sign of you?'

'I've been busy with this and that. I hadn't realised it was so long.'

'No.'

'There's nothing in it, you know, lass.'

'Nothing except you haven't bothered showing your face for two weeks. I can remember when you used to be here twice a week. As soon as Sid's back was turned.'

'Is that fair, love?'

She stood with her back to him, putting Nescafé into the cups.

'I don't know what is fair any more.'

'How have the kids taken it?'

'Nick came up yesterday but there was nothing he could do so I made him go back. He seems to take it in his stride. I don't mean he isn't upset; but it's Shirley who's really taken it bad. I've sent her to school but I don't think she'll keep her mind on much.'

She turned and looked at him. 'It's funny, that, isn't it? And they say blood's thicker than water.'

'Different temperaments,' Simpkins said. 'And Nick's older, and a man already.'

'He's the one who should have been ours, mine and yours. Shirley's so much like Sid in her ways I can't believe it sometimes. Highly strung, nervous, catches cold as soon as the sun goes in.'

'You've always thought I was the confident one, haven't you, Norma?' Simpkins said. 'No cares, does what he wants to do, doesn't worry about what he can't cure; sees the world as all of a piece, quite a cosy place to be in.'

'Well, why not? You're kind and considerate when you want to be, but...'

'But that's not like being sensitive, eh?'

In all the years of their relationship she had never got through to the real him. It saddened him to know what in fact he had always known. She saw his money, his success, his place in local affairs as everything. His deepest thoughts about life and the world he had never communicated to her because he had thought she wouldn't understand them. She herself, after all, was a practical one, and sensitivity and nervous energy were to her the trappings of inadequacy and failure. Now, in some way, she was using these judgements with which to whip him, as though all she had admired in him in the past was now seen to be spurious and superficial, incompatible with any real depth of feeling.

But she was overwrought. He must allow for her state of mind. He moved towards her as she lifted the kettle off the gas and poised it over the first of the cups. 'Norma . . .' She suddenly dropped the kettle with a clatter. 'Blast! I nearly scalded meself.'

He said again, 'Norma,' and put his hand on her shoulder. A second later he knew she was crying.

'Come on now, Norma. Come on, love.' He turned her round and drew her head into his shoulder, holding her. 'He'll be all right, love, you'll see. It'll take a bit of time, but he'll come through.'

'The poor bugger,' she said. 'He never has any luck.'

'Only with you,' Simpkins said.

'God, that's a laugh!'

'You know it isn't.'

Perhaps the only luck Sid Moffat had had in his life was in her, the wife who was physically unfaithful but who had kept a home for him and succoured him with another kind of loyalty when she might well have long ago packed-up and gone.

'Oh, it's all gone wrong,' she cried suddenly, her voice thickening through the sobs in her throat. 'There's nowt right with any of it.'

He patted her back. 'Steady on, steady on. It'll all look better this time next week.'

She trembled in his arms and abruptly drew back her head to look into his face. A fierce intensity blazed through the tears in her eyes. He tried to meet and fathom her gaze in the moment before she almost savagely fastened her mouth on his. He was astonished by the ferocity of her kiss.

Passion of this kind was the last thing he had expected. When she pulled away her mouth was still near enough for him to feel the heat of her breath on his cheek as she said, 'Take me upstairs, Tom.'

He was totally unprepared for both her words and the dismay that filled him.

'But——'

'For pity's sake, Tom, I want some comfort. Take me upstairs.'

He had to respond. He turned away without speaking and took off his overcoat. When he looked at her again she was by the door, her back to him, as though waiting. But when he moved towards her she went through the doorway and on ahead. He followed, finding her in the big bedroom, looking out through the lace-curtained window. The bed was made, the cover drawn up taut and creaseless.

'Do you want to——?' he began and she interrupted him as though knowing exactly what he had been about to ask. 'No.' She walked to the bed and lay down on the edge of it, her arm across her face, like someone resigned to rape. He was reminded of the first time, except that then he was afire for her and she had watched him with questioning, almost challenging eyes. He placed himself beside her and slipped his arm under her head before lowering his face to hers. She took her arm away and let it fall across the bedspread, kissing him now with soft open lips. They lay like that until she pulled him over on to her and began to stir under him with an increasingly urgent movement of her hips. He wasn't ready. He knew it with something like panic and when, a moment later, she took him to draw him into her the slackness of his unresponsive flesh tapped a level of hysteria he had never seen in her before. She moaned, her head rolling to one side.

'Oh no, oh no! Oh God, no!'

She began to sob uncontrollably. The tears seemed to wrench up agonisingly out of her, racking her whole body.

'Norma,' Simpkins said. 'I'm sorry, Norma.' He stroked her hair and she twisted her head away.

33

'Now it's you,' she said.

If she would just give him a little time. He couldn't cope with the urgency of her need. Just a little time ... tenderly, slowly, with gentleness. But there was no containing her, no way of curbing the rage that possessed her. Nothing would do now but an answering rage. He felt her rear up under him. Then she struggled out and was stumbling from the room. He was left there, kneeling on the carpet, his face buried in the bedspread, as though in an attitude of desperate prayer. She was like someone drowning, he thought. The more wildly you thrashed about the less you were able to save yourself.

He got up and went into the bathroom to rinse his face with cold water before going downstairs. Norma was sitting in one of the easy chairs in the kitchen, leaning forward, elbows on knees, her hands covering her face. She didn't move, though she must have heard him come in. He sat in the other chair and watched her for a time without speaking. Eventually he said:

'I'm sorry, Norma. And I'm ashamed.'

'Of me?' she asked from behind her hands.

'No,' he said. 'Of myself.'

But he was ashamed *for* her. Was there anything more abasing than a sexual rage that couldn't find a response? He would have given anything rather than see her like that.

'I feel I've let you down.'

'Is it the thought of him helpless in hospital that's touched your conscience?'

'Maybe it's partly that.'

'I was thinking about you all yesterday,' she said. 'Wanting you to come. Then I go for you like a bitch on heat the minute you walk in.' She rubbed her face with her hands then lowered them, keeping her eyes averted. 'God, I never thought I'd grovel in front of any man like that.'

'Stop chastising yourself,' Simpkins said. 'If it comes to that,' he went on wryly, 'I never thought I'd see the day when I couldn't come up to scratch. There's a big difference between not wanting and not able.'

34

'It's not that I don't think anything about him,' she said fiercely, turning her head now to look at Simpkins.

'I know that, love.'

'It's just that . . .' She clasped her hands together, looking for words. 'I just wanted to know I hadn't lost everything.' Her voice broke before she had finished and suddenly she was in tears again. Simpkins got out of his chair and crouched beside her, taking one of her hands.

'It's going to be all right, Norma. You'll see.'

He was beginning to understand her state of mind. Her cry of 'Now it's you' had given him the first clue. Sid's accident, so characteristic of the bad luck which had dogged his ineffectual life, could be seen by Norma as something she had almost brought about herself. For since the coming of Simpkins she had stopped trying to change him; she had stopped railing against his inadequacies and settled for what there was. She had become, in fact, grateful for his own knowledge of himself which allowed acquiescence in the matter of her relationship with Simpkins. Now, guiltily, after the years of indulging in his complaisance, she had needed to know that it had all been worth while; that what she had taken from Simpkins to fill the barren spaces in her marriage could be measured against the bruised and broken body of Sid and not fall short. 'Now it's you!' she had cried, meaning 'If you don't want me now, there's nothing.' His failure to take her was to her an inability to celebrate her as a woman, to justify her at a moment when she needed it most.

3

She had come to Simpkins seventeen years ago, knocking on his door one evening while he was having dinner and asking Bess, who answered, if she could see the councillor.

'A Mrs Moffat,' Bess told him.

Simpkins looked up from the steak-and-kidney pie Bess had only just placed in front of him. 'What's she like?'

Bess pursed her mouth. 'Cheaply dressed, but clean and respectable-looking.'

Simpkins grunted.

'Shall I tell her to come back later?'

'What will she do while she's waiting?' Simpkins asked. 'Walk the streets? No, you'd better ask her to wait in the sitting-room.'

When, ten minutes later, and with coffee postponed, he walked through into the other room, Simpkins found a fair woman in her late twenties with a handsomeness of face and sturdy body which took him pleasantly by surprise. She got out of her chair as he went in.

'No, no. Please sit down.'

She did as he said, clasping her hands over the bag on her knee. Simpkins fiddled with pipe and tobacco.

'It's a cold night. Did you come up by bus?'

'As far as the bottom of the lane. Then I had to walk.'

'Yes, of course. It's a bit of a pull up that last half mile.'

'Oh, I'm healthy enough. There's worse things than that in a day's work.'

'I suppose so.' Simpkins was standing looking down at

her, his back to the fire. To put her more at ease he moved from this dominating position and sat down on the other side of the hearth. 'Well, what can I do for you, er, Mrs Moffat?'

It was about the council house they lived in, she told him. She sat upright in the chair as she talked, with her knees and ankles neatly together. Her husband was a lorry driver but he spent a lot of his time off work with a stomach ailment that the doctors didn't seem to be able to cure. In fact, she said, his constitution as a whole had been damaged while he was a prisoner of the Japanese in Burma. Just now he'd been playing sick for several weeks and with her trying to keep things decently going on the dole they'd got behind with their rent.

'There is a department for this kind of thing,' Simpkins told her.

'Aye, I know. The rent collector advised me to go and see them. But I don't want to tell all my affairs to a clerk or a bit of a lass in the Town Hall. You're our councillor. We voted for you. So I thought you were the best man to see.'

'Just what is it you want me to do?'

'Get me a bit of breathing space so I don't have to make excuses to that rent man every week, or find meself with an eviction order.'

'Oh, it won't come to that where there's genuine hardship. If the facts were put forward you might well get a reduction in your rent.'

'No.' She shook her head and her mouth set firmly. 'I don't want charity. We can pay our way if we're given a bit of time.'

Simpkins sucked the stem of his pipe. She was stubborn. It must have cost her something in pride to come to him, a stranger whom she knew only through the message in his election leaflet, newspaper reports of council meetings or by reputation. He thought that they couldn't have met while he was canvassing or he would have remembered her. She was a very attractive woman.

He cleared his throat. 'Well, you know, Mrs Moffat,

that's all very well, but the longer you go on like this the more money you'll owe. You don't want to get yourself permanently into debt, do you?'

'I don't want to be sitting here asking for help, either,' she said bluntly. 'But sometimes you've got no choice.'

'No. Quite.'

Her glance flickered round the room and Simpkins felt momentarily guilty, less about its solid comfort than the touches—the original oil painting over the fireplace, the china figurines that Bess collected on the mantelshelf, the expensive radiogram, the standard lamps—which spelt luxury, money to spare.

'I'm looking for some kind of part-time work for meself,' she said, 'but it's not all that easy with a baby.'

'How many children have you got?'

'Just the one. A boy. He's going on two.'

'He'll be a bit of a handful.'

'Aye. It's not easy to find somewhere to leave 'em at that age.'

'No ... Well, I'll do what I can for you, Mrs Moffat, but you realise that I've no power to act on my own and I shall have to have all the details before I can present your case.'

'Yes, I don't mind that.'

Simpkins got up and went to his writing-desk. He let down the flap and sat up to it, reaching for a sheet of paper and unscrewing his fountain pen.

'Now, we'll start with your husband's name and the address of the house ...'

One evening a couple of weeks later Simpkins called at the Moffats' house to tell them that the Housing Committee had considered their case and were prepared to give them a couple of months to find their feet. He did not tell them of the argument there had been about the wisdom of the decision and the precedent it might be thought to establish if the facts became general knowledge. There was mention from one Labour member of machinery designed to alleviate this kind of hardship but Simpkins argued persuasively about the Moffats' pride and Mr Moffat's war service.

The war was not long over. Some members had seen active service themselves; others who had been exempted to run businesses dealing in essential supplies and had made good profits were sometimes sensitive about the subject. At one point Simpkins was foolishly tempted to guarantee the authority against any real debt the Moffats might incur. Foolishly because, though he wondered why Mrs Moffat had made such a strong impression on him at one meeting, it had struck him that someone on the committee might already suspect him of undue bias in her favour. Thoughts like that flitted through his mind. It was his first term on the council. He knew little yet about lobbies and pressure groups but enough about personal patronage and protection to realise that if he had in fact more than a merely dutiful interest in the Moffats' welfare he would have settled the matter privately without bringing it into the daylight of official scrutiny. He hoped others realised this as he dug in his heels against the dour common sense of those who opposed his plea. Years afterwards he was to look back on those fleeting thoughts as something of a premontion of the rôle he would come to play in the Moffats' lives.

The house was on an estate built during the 'thirties. Moffat had lived there with his parents before the war. His father was dead when he came back. He married and brought his wife into the house. His mother had died a couple of years ago while Norma was carrying the baby. Since then his health had deteriorated. He was troubled by this mysterious stomach ailment and a general feeling of debility. He blamed it on what he'd gone through in the war, though, he had to admit, he'd never been particularly robust as a boy and was vaguely surprised to get a grade-one pass in his medical and find himself an army driver. Simpkins asked him if he had no chance of a disability pension.

'What proof is there that it was that?' Moffat shrugged. 'Anyway, anybody who fought the war in them jungles deserves a pension, even if the Japs didn't get their hands on him.' He glanced at Simpkins. 'Did you ever get out East?'

'No farther than Egypt,' Simpkins said. 'I was an engineering officer in the RAF. I seemed to spend most of the war training recruits.'

'You didn't fly?'

'They said I was too old.'

Simpkins sipped the tea that Mrs Moffat had insisted on making for him. Moffat sat forward in his chair by the fire, one foot on the kerb, his elbows resting on his knees. Simpkins could detect the lack of flesh on his thighs from the way his trousers hung baggily on them; and his wrists protruded bonily from the cuffs of his cardigan. His sunken cheeks made his eyes look dark and enormous. 'All teeth and eyes,' Bess would have said of him. He was younger than Simpkins but already going bald. Moffat was polite, and seemed to Simpkins to be intelligent, but his manner was vague and withdrawn. He said little. It was obvious who was the driving force in the two of them. He looked like a man who was baffled by the world and on the point of giving up. Simpkins wondered what could have made Mrs Moffat marry him.

She was as firm and direct as at their first meeting, thanking Simpkins clearly but without effusiveness. 'It's nice to know there's somebody who can get things done,' she said. The room was clean and tidy and Mrs Moffat was ironing clean washing, most of it babies' nappies. 'I'll be glad when that young scamp learns to control himself and we can get rid of these things.'

'What do you call him?'

'Nicholas.'

'That's nice.'

'I suppose he'll get "Nick" when he's older, but he'll have to put up with it.'

'It sounds manly, anyway. I shouldn't think he'll mind.'

She was to the side of Simpkins and a little behind him as she stood at the ironing board and he couldn't look at her without turning his head. He realised he wanted to and was glad of another subject to broach.

'I was wondering, Mrs Moffat. You said something about trying to find work.'

'Yes.'

'We could do with some more help in our canteen. The women who work in there come and go; the young ones getting married, the older ones deciding they want a bit more time to themselves.'

'Well, it's the baby, you see. I've nowhere I could leave him all day.'

'It would only be for three or four hours around lunchtime. It's not heavy work and the pay's decent.'

'Oh, I'm not scared of a bit of work.'

'No, I'm sure you're not.'

She put down the iron and spoke to Moffat. 'D'you hear what Mr Simpkins is saying, Sid? How would you feel about seeing to Nicholas in the middle of the day?'

'I can manage that.'

'If you'd rather I waited, to see if you're fit to work in a week or two...'

Simpkins wondered how much of her deferring to her husband was because of his presence.

Moffat shrugged. 'Who knows? I shall have another job to find as well.'

'Won't Dalby's take you back?'

'Not if they've got another driver to take my place.'

'Well, what do you say, then?'

Simpkins said, 'Look, if you'd rather talk it over when I'm gone...'

'No, that's all right.' She spoke to Moffat again. She was like a mother addressing a grown-up son. 'We shall have to do something, Sid. I mean, the rent's not going to go away just because we've got a breathing space.'

'Now I can't support my family,' Moffat said, but quietly, with more in it of resignation than bitterness.

'Don't talk daft. There's many a thousand women go out to work.'

'Well, you do as you think fit, Norma. I'll see to Nicholas all right.'

She shot a quick glance at Simpkins but he could read nothing in it. How many decisions, after the deferring, did she have to make herself?

'It looks as if we're in your debt twice over, Mr Simpkins,' she said, resuming her ironing.

'Nonsense,' Simpkins said. 'You don't owe me anything at all.'

'If it's all so easy I wonder why more people don't stretch their hand out.'

'It just happens that I'm in a position to help on both counts,' Simpkins said. He was appalled as he glanced at Mrs Moffat to see what might be the sparkle of tears in her eyes and he turned his head quickly and took out his wallet.

'When can you call round?'

'Anytime. Will tomorrow morning do?'

'That's fine. You take this card and ask for Mrs Hartley. She's the cook. She'll show you what the job involves and if you fancy it you can start on Monday.'

In the spring of 1948 Simpkins' father died. Ailing for some time, he had spent a couple of winters in Spain, away from the damp and fog of the West Riding. The cold close of an English February did for him and after taking to his bed for a few weeks he passed away quietly in his sleep. Simpkins and Bess sat alone in the house when the funeral guests had gone. The family business had gone public before the war, but he and Bess now owned the controlling shares and, at thirty-eight, he was chairman and managing director.

'Well, Bess?'

'Well?'

She had cried in church and at the graveside but now her eyes were dry and her features composed.

'Here we are on our own, like a couple of old maids.'

'You've always thought of me more as a natural spinster than a wife, haven't you, Tom?'

'What makes you say that?'

'Because I suppose it's true in a way.'

'You've plenty of time to get married again.'

'No, I don't think I shall. Oh, I like having men around, and looking after them. All that. But marriage ... it ... it violates something in me. I can't bear to be that close to anybody. You know what I was like as a girl...' Simpkins made a vague movement of his hand. 'I was proud, touchy, stand-offish. People used to say I was a little snob. There was more to it than that. Perhaps some other man than Arthur could have won me round. He had his own kind of pride—and weakness—and he soon gave up trying. Oh, I was ... dutiful. But it wasn't enough. So he drank. It must have hurt him to know that other people thought that was the fly in the ointment ... I do very much regret, though, that we didn't have a child. I have some maternal instincts, you know.'

She had confessed with her back to him. Now she turned from the window. Her face was in shadow, the strong evening sunlight behind her. He thought she blinked her eyes several times rapidly, and there was a tight little smile on her lips.

'What about you?'

She had never talked to him so intimately. About her marriage to Arthur Hargreaves, and his drinking, she had maintained an aloof silence that was characteristic of the proud girl Simpkins had always known. Now he felt moved to be self-revealing in his turn. He wanted to tell her the truth but not in a way that would hurt her because it was a different truth from her own.

'Marriage? It's doubtful.'

'Not for the same reasons as me, though?'

He shook his head. 'No.'

She said, with a strained tightening of her face in embarrassment, 'Did Nell ever make you feel like ... like a dirty old man?'

Simpkins was almost equally embarrassed. 'No.'

'That's what Arthur once said to me. I expect you can understand what he meant.'

'Yes ... It must have been awful for both of you.' Oh, what miseries the union of two unmatching personalities could cause! Smooth-functioning enough on their own they were abrasive when come together, reducing each other, not complementing. But he and Nell, they had searched out the good things in each other, releasing potentialities to flower in an abundance of joy.

'I don't think I ever really analysed it till Arthur went away,' Bess said. 'Then, and particularly after he was killed, I had time to think. I tried to be fair, to allocate the blame truthfully. I was forced to accept that I never should have married him; perhaps never married at all. It was a thought that took a lot of coming to. Polite people don't talk about these things—not polite people like me, anyway. And without real means of comparison you take the pattern of your own affairs as normal.'

'Don't you think that's what might have thrown Arthur?' Simpkins said. 'It's as easy for a man to be without experience as it is a woman. And it could be horrifying for such a man to find himself caught inside a marriage where all his fears and inhibitions are encouraged.'

'You mean if he'd had more experience he would have known how to judge me and keep himself more intact?'

'Perhaps ... But the final disaster for him could have been quite simply that he loved you.'

'Oh, Tom...' He thought she choked slightly on the words. She clasped her hands together and walked across the room to stand looking at the sideboard. There was a photograph there of Hargreaves, along with others of Nell and their mother.

'This is becoming morbid,' Bess said after a moment. 'Like a shrine to lost hopes and fears.'

'Yes. I only kept Nell's picture there because Mother wanted it.'

'Now there's Father's to add ... The land of the dead multiples while that of the living dwindles ... Oh, Tom,' she said again, bursting out with it this time and spinning round to face him, 'why don't you get married and bring

44

children into the house?'

Simpkins stirred in his chair. He wanted to smoke but was tired of his pipe. He got up and went to the little round walnut table on which was the box of cigars he had offered to their guests. He took one out and toyed with it.

'I couldn't get married just for that, Bess. Nell and I had too much together.'

'But you've...' Bess hesitated. 'You've had some little adventures, haven't you?'

He was surprised, thinking he'd hidden that.

'That's different. You don't build a lifetime with a person on that kind of thing.'

'Oh, I'm not sitting in judgement on you. I might have at one time.' Again the tight strained smile. 'I might again. But not now. I just want to know what's happened to all of us. Where we've all gone wrong. What kind of a future we can hope for.'

'Unhappiness breeds in all sorts of ways, from all sorts of situations,' Simpkins said. 'I just found that despair finds echoes in more people than I'd have thought...'

'Was it as bad as that for you, Tom?'

'Yes. Finding Nell seemed like the most enormous piece of good fortune. The incredible thing was she wanted me as well. There was a marvellous instinct between us, an understanding of mind and body and emotions. We loved each other without reserve or shame or inhibition. It's impossible to describe to anybody who's never experienced it. It was like a splendid madness in which there was all the sanity in the world. When she died and it was all taken away from me I felt another kind of madness. You'd have to have known my joy to understand my despair. Luckily, I'm not a naturally melancholy man. I'm fairly level-headed and self-sufficient. The years slip by. You don't forget but you learn to remember without the awful pain. The war helped by forcibly taking me out of my surroundings and putting me among new people.'

'It's still strong enough to stop you marrying again?'

'Shall we say I've never met anybody else I wanted to tie

myself to.'

Bess sighed. The black frock she wore suited her pale colouring. Her face was still virtually unmarked, her figure slight and girlish. He felt sorry for her and in doing so discovered pity for himself. She was right. There should be children about the house. How ingrown and unproductive their lives could now so easily become.

'Well, I'm financially independent,' she said in a moment. 'I've got you to look after and you've got me to look after you. So neither of us needs to do it for the wrong reasons.'

'No.'

'So I suppose we just pick up the threads and carry on.'

'Yes.'

'Yes,' she said after him. She turned to the sideboard again and put the photographs in a pile. 'But I'm clearing these off here for a start.'

Norma Moffat had been working for Simpkins for some months. He occasionally contrived, without conspicuously singling her out for attention, to have a word with her and ask how things were going. Moffat's health had improved enough for him to find another job and he was long-distance driving now, which kept him away from home on two or three nights in a week. Mrs. Moffat, feeling the benefit of the extra money, had found a neighbour who would look after the baby so that she could carry on working.

One Friday evening, after the factory had closed, Simpkins caught sight of her in town, hurrying towards the bus station in pelting rain with a full shopping-bag in each hand. He managed to ease the car out of the flow of traffic and pull in to the kerb, where he could call out to her.

'Mrs Moffat ... Over here.'

He held the door open for her. 'Can I give you a lift?'

'I don't think it's on your way.'

'You'd better get in without arguing or you'll get soaked.'

He took the heavy bags from her and lifted them over on

to the back seat. She got in beside him and he leaned past her to make sure the door was secure.

'It wouldn't do to lose you before we get there.'

'You're not that kind of a driver, are you?'

'What?' He laughed. 'No, I've never lost a passenger yet.'

'Steady.' She reached out and touched the walnut fascia. 'It doesn't do to tempt providence.'

'I didn't think you'd be the superstitious type.'

'Life's full of surprises,' she said. He didn't know whether this was offered as a reason for her superstition or a comment on his misreading of her character. He let it go, asking after a few moments, during which he'd reached the edge of the shopping centre:

'You *were* going home, weren't you?'

'Yes, I'd finished. But look, why don't you drop me at a bus stop instead of going right out of your way?'

'It's still raining hard,' Simpkins said. 'You'd be wet through in no time and it only takes a few minutes by car.'

'Well, thank you, anyway.'

She sat with her hands clasped loosely in her lap. He was aware of her taking little sidelong glances at both him and the fittings in the car as they drove out of town in the rush-hour traffic. Once he felt her turn her head and for several seconds gaze with frank curiosity at his profile. When he twisted his own head slightly and gave her a quick smile she lowered her eyes and looked away, but without embarrassment at being caught in her candid appraisal of him.

'Did you like living on the estate?' he asked her.

'Not particularly,' she said frankly. 'It's noisy with all the kids playing, and as soon as Nicholas gets running about a bit I shall be scared to death of him getting on to the main road at the end of the street. Still, it's a home of our own and beggars can't be choosers.'

'And everybody who can't find the deposit to put down and buy a place is a beggar nowadays,' Simpkins said.

'Yes. We were lucky that Sid's mother was on her own and could find room for us.'

Simpkins slowed down and stopped some way behind a

47

bus which was taking on passengers, and let oncoming traffic pass by.

'I've got a house coming vacant in a few weeks' time,' he said. 'Up at Edgehill. The tenants are moving south.'

She turned her head and looked at him again, but didn't speak. Simpkins beat a little tattoo on the rim of the steering wheel with the fingers of his right hand. The road ahead of the bus was clear. He moved up to pass and as he did so the driver pulled the double-decker away from the kerb and forced him to drop behind again. Simpkins sighed but suppressed his inclination to swear.

'I wonder if you'd be interested,' he said. 'Three bedrooms, no through traffic and the rent's less than you're paying now.'

'Isn't it spoken for already?'

'Oh, I could let it twenty times over, just to the people I know about.'

'Is it fair to let somebody jump the queue?'

'Your sense of justice does you credit,' Simpkins said. 'But I'm not the Corporation. I don't have to work to a scrupulous order of points and priorities. It's my house—or at least, mine and my sister's—and I can let it to whom I like.'

'But why us?'

'I thought it might help you over some of your difficulties. You managed to scrape through your last trouble but if your husband should fall ill again you might not be so lucky.'

'It might be you we owed back rent to,' she said. 'What then?' Again she looked at him, summing him up, but with justification this time. He'd made the offer on an impulse born of her presence beside him in the car. There were no strings but he expected her to wonder.

'You'd better let me worry about that.'

She was quiet for a moment, thinking. Finally she said, 'Look, you can say I've got a cynical mind, if you like; but I've given up expecting something for nothing in this world. Why should you do this for us?'

48

Simpkins shrugged. 'Why not?'

She was silent again before she said, 'I don't want to be rude, but have you taken some kind of a fancy to me?'

It was the momentary failure of her courage, making her phrase the question in less than unmistakable terms, that diverted Simpkins' embarrassment and allowed him to laugh.

'You're a very direct woman, Mrs Moffat.'

'If you don't ask you often don't get to know.'

'And does a direct question always get a straight answer?'

'Not always.'

'Well,' Simpkins said, appearing to choose his words with care, 'you're an attractive woman. I like and admire you, and since you first came to see me I seem to have taken an interest in your welfare. Does that answer your question?'

She peered out of the car. 'We're here.' She pulled up the collar of her raincoat and looked round for her bags. 'If you drop me at the corner you can turn straight round.'

'It's still raining hard, you know,' Simpkins said. 'You'll get very wet even over that short way.'

'I'll be all right. I shan't melt.'

He lifted over the bags as she prepared to get out. 'Will you think about the house and let me know.'

'When would you like me to tell you?'

'As soon as possible. You can see it, of course, before you finally decide.'

'If I let you know on Monday?'

'That'll be all right.'

She got out and bent to look directly at him before closing the door. 'Cheerio, then. Thanks very much for the lift.'

He watched her walk away with quick steps, her head bowed before the rain. She swung one bag round so that she held the dragging weight of both of them in one hand, and her other hand went up to hold her collar close round her throat. He felt the quiver of excitement in his stomach as he turned the car.

She telephoned him at home on Sunday afternoon

apologising for intruding on his leisure time but pointing out that it was easier than approaching him at the Works. He didn't recognise her voice at first; the telephone altered its timbre and thickened her accent slightly. She and Moffat would like to see the house, she said. Simpkins asked when Moffat would be free and arranged to call for them on Monday evening.

'Couldn't you tell the people we're coming and let us go on our own?' Mrs Moffat said.

'It's just as easy for me to pick you up.'

'Yes, but . . .'

He waited. 'Yes?'

'It's just that you've put yourself out too much already.'

'Can't you let me be the judge of that?'

'Well . . . all right, then.'

'Your protest has been noted,' Simpkins said, 'and it will be recorded in the minutes.'

The neighbour Mrs Moffat relied on was out so they took the baby with them. He was boisterously noisy as they looked round the house. Simpkins apologised for disturbing the Naylors and perhaps it was his presence plus Moffat's knowledgeable way of tapping on walls and woodwork and asking questions about dry rot, damp and the electric wiring which led them to believe the Moffats were prospective buyers of the property. Simpkins didn't correct their impression. In the presence of the Naylors, realising how fortunate they would count the Moffats who had a house and were now being offered another one to rent, he became suddenly sensitive about outsiders' possible interpretation of his patronage. He wondered, remembering their conversation in the car, if this had been in Norma Moffat's mind also when she suggested they might visit the house without him.

They got Nicholas away from the Naylors' patient dog whose skin and hair he was crowingly grasping in small but hard handfuls and drove back down through town.

'Be a bit handier for shopping, p'raps, Norma,' Moffat said.

'There are shops there, and a regular bus service from the end of the street,' Simpkins pointed out.

'It's high as well,' Moffat said. 'It's healthier living high up in an area like that. Up above the smoke, where you can breathe.'

Yet when his wife put the question to him straight Moffat began prevaricating again as he had about her taking the job. Once more, it seemed to Simpkins, the decision was left to her. When they reached the estate she asked Simpkins in for a cup of tea. He pleaded another engagement. He was tired of Moffat's company. Norma Moffat was a vital woman who gave off an air of pride and durability. All that came off Moffat was the smell of failure and defeat. Simpkins was sorry he felt that way. The man had had a hard time and ill luck had no doubt added to it. But with a woman like Norma to fortify him he shouldn't have let it get through to the heart of him. He was a hollow man and depressing to be with.

'You'll give us a day or two to talk things over, Mr Simpkins?' Mrs Moffat said. There was, for the first time since he'd known her, a note of real apology in her voice. 'I mean, it's not just a matter of picking up and going. There's all sort of things to think about.'

'It's all right,' Simpkins said. 'I quite understand.'

He sat that night, after Bess had gone to bed, over a glass of whisky by the fire and thought about them. He had become used by now to influencing people's lives. He was a long way from the timid, chapel-haunted boy with his masturbatory sex-fantasies and the youth who kept his first smoking and drinking secret, repressed by that irascible, perfection-mad father who later depended upon him with an assurance that seemed cruel in contrast to earlier reiterated expressions of no confidence. He had developed late and the Old Man was responsible for the delay. Yet he had come through. His lost marriage to Nell had brought him to one kind of maturity; his war service and increasing authority in the Works as his father's health failed produced another. But he had not for a long time felt so keen a sense of responsibility towards anyone as he did now to Norma Moffat. He was concerned that she should fare well; and to share in some way the strength and vitality at the core of her was what he wanted in return.

4

When the Moffats took the house Simpkins passed on the keys as soon as the Naylors handed them in, then kept away for several weeks.

'Let me know if there's anything you think I should see to,' he said. 'I hope you'll be comfortable.'

He didn't speak to Norma Moffat and saw her only once or twice, at a distance, during the next month. It was a heightened sensitivity to the situation that held him back. He had helped the Moffats because he was interested in Norma. Other people might not be aware of it, but she was and he was not going to dash up there the minute they moved in to prove it to her.

But at last he went.

She came to the door wearing an overall and a headscarf covered her hair.

'Hello, I thought you'd have been up before this.'

'I'm sorry if I've come at an inconvenient time.'

'That's all right. You don't expect the red carpet, do you?'

There was a new boldness added to her customary directness of speech. He felt dismay. Did she believe she had so easily taken his measure?

She led him inside, wiping her hands on an old piece of towel. Their furniture looked somehow incongruous in these rooms; not because it was mostly old pieces, inherited from Moffat's mother, but because Simpkins associated it with another place and this house with the clutter the Naylors had gathered round them.

'I'm doing a bit of decorating,' Norma Moffat told him. 'Sid's away.'

'Do you usually do it on your own?'

'Oh, no; he gives me a hand when he's at home, but I thought I'd knock on a bit with the donkey work while I was by myself.'

'This paper isn't too bad,' Simpkins said. 'Are you going to do it right through?'

'Eventually. It's not like home, is it, living with some-body else's choice of paper? I've started at the top and I shall work down, one room at a time, as I can afford to buy the stuff. There's a patch of damp upstairs I'd like you to look at while you're here.'

He followed her into the passage and up the stairs.

'I've just got Nicholas to sleep, by the way, so we can't make much noise.'

The bare dusty floor of the larger of the two main bed-rooms was littered with big and small pieces of the paper that Norma had stripped off the walls. A yellow plastic bowl of grey water stood on a stool, with a broad-bladed scraper and a wide brush she had used to wet down and soften the paper. Simpkins saw the irregularly oval stain of damp as soon as he went in.

'Yes,' he said, 'that wants seeing to. I wonder the Naylors never mentioned it.'

'They had a bedhead up against the wall there, if you remember,' Norma pointed out. 'They probably never no-ticed it till they were moving.'

'It must be the pointing that wants touching up,' Simp-kins said. 'If you'll wait here, I'll just pop out and have a look.'

He went downstairs and out of the house. He peered up at the gable end which took the full force of the wind and rain sweeping across the open valley. There was little he could see.

'I can't really tell,' he said when he'd gone back in and up into the empty room. 'I'll send the builders up with a ladder. They'll find it.'

'I don't want to spoil new wallpaper till they've been.'

'I'll get 'em here as soon as I can,' Simpkins said. 'But you know what they're like these days: busy and picking and choosing which jobs they'll do. In the meantime, though, there's some damp-proof lining paper you can buy. If you stick a piece of that under your wallpaper just there it'll stop it coming through till we can get you fixed up outside.' He moved across the room. 'It's a lovely view from up here.'

She joined him at the uncurtained window. Some children were playing with an old pram on the waste ground.

'You haven't got rid of the kids after all.'

'Oh, there's not so many of 'em and they have to have somewhere to run about.'

She was very close to him, her shoulder almost touching his. The evening sun was bright and warm on this side of the house. There was a thin film of perspiration on her nose and the heat of her body inside the thin overall was an almost palpable thing. He moved away as he felt his flesh stir.

'Is there anything else you'd like me to look at while I'm here?'

'I can't think of anything.'

'You're sure you're quite comfortable?'

'Yes, thank you.'

He strolled out of the room and waited for her on the landing. Following him, she stopped and lifted her foot to detach a curl of damp wallpaper from the sole of her shoe. He often wondered afterwards what the course of events would have been without that tiny incident. There would probably have been another moment, though perhaps not one which led quite so easily into what was to come. As it was, she swayed as she balanced on one foot and he automatically reached out and steadied her elbow.

'It treads all over the place if you're not careful,' she said.

He found himself still holding her arm as they faced each other. Foolishly, no words came as the moment lengthened and took on meaning. He was on the point of blurting out something, anything, and leaving her, when she said quietly, looking directly at him,

'Is it rent day, then?'

He felt it like a slap in the face. He let go of her and started to turn away.

'I'm sorry.'

She took his arm and restrained him. 'Just a minute.'

He turned to her again. 'Is that what you've been thinking?' he said stiffly.

'Have I hurt your feelings?' He said nothing. 'You do want to, though, don't you?' Her hand slipped down his arm till she held his fingers. With the other hand she pulled out the knot of the headsquare under her chin and shook her hair free. It was like a spoken understanding. He drew her to him and they kissed. He wondered if she could feel the pounding of his heart next to her.

'We shall wake the baby,' she said, her face against his. She stood away from him and pushed open the door behind her. 'In here.' She led him by the hand into the other room. As she shut the door he took her again and held her tightly kissing her till her body moved against him. He trembled at the sweetness of her and with gentle pressure laid her back across the bed. In silence they lay together. She didn't speak as he unbuttoned her overall and spread it out on either side of her like turquoise wings on the counterpane. Her white body lay long and supine under him. He realised he had always known just what it would look like and now its enfolding warmth excited him to a feverish response. He touched his mouth to the cleft of firm flesh in the vee of her brassière. He was too impatient to release it and enjoy her freed breasts. 'Another time,' he thought. 'Another time...' She sighed as his hand moved between her parted thighs and sighed again, long and shuddering, when, a little later, he went easily into her.

He was surprised at the urgency of her answer. She gasped 'Oh!' as they came together, the tension ebbing out of her body in the spasms of her climax. They lay still.

Simpkins, his head beside hers, put his lips to the lobe of her ear while his hand gently caressed her belly. Some time passed. The cries of the children came faintly up to them. Norma moved suddenly. 'I must get up.' She slipped out from under his arm. He heard her in the bathroom and he got up himself and adjusted his clothes. He was waiting on the landing when she came out. She passed without looking at him.

'We'd better go down.'

He went after her. The back door stood wide open as he had left it. 'Look at that.' She closed the door and turned to face him, her hands fussing at her hair.

'Well,' she said. He returned her gaze without speaking. 'Are you all right now?'

'What?'

'It was what you wanted, wasn't it?'

'Were you so sure you knew?'

'Oh aye. I could see the way you looked at me. And I've heard you like the women.'

'You've heard what?' Simpkins said.

'Oh, it's nowt. Just a bit of talk here and there.'

'D'you mean to say I've got a reputation?'

'No, nothing like that. But you're a widower and you're not a pansy.'

'Thank you.'

'Give over,' Norma said. 'Most people like somebody who's a bit of a lad.'

'Oh, well then.'

She took a brush out of a drawer and began to drag it vigorously through her hair. It was all so casual now after the intensity of a little while ago.

'So,' she said. 'You've been good to me and now I've given you something back.'

He was disappointed. 'Is that all it meant? Just a payment in kind? Is that what you've been thinking all along? That I was helping you for that?'

'No, I wouldn't say I'd thought you'd planned it just like that. But you're not making out there's any big thing between us, are you?'

It was all too direct for him. He shrugged. 'I suppose not.'

'So you don't have to feel under any obligation, just because of what's happened.'

'If you consider the debt paid in full,' he said distantly.

She pushed hairclips into place and looked at him, speaking after a pause.

'Are you trying to say you'll want to come again?'

'You haven't put me in much of a position to do that, have you?'

'I'm a married woman, you know.'

'You needn't remind me of that.'

'What is it you want, Mr Simpkins?'

He winced. 'Look, we've just been in bed together. You might relax enough to call me Tom.'

'Well, here—on our own—all right. Tom. What is it you're after? Did you like it that much or do you just want to know where you can get it reg'lar?'

Simpkins flushed. He fastened his jacket and glanced about.

'I didn't bring a coat, did I?'

'What's up?' she said. 'Have I offended you now?'

He rounded on her. 'For God's sake, woman, do you have to say everything that comes into your head? You weren't under any obligation to me and I don't like it turned into some kind of transaction. I don't buy women, with money, presents or anything else; and it never occurred to me that you were for sale.'

'Don't be so touchy. I just like to clear the air.'

'Well now that it's well and truly cleared, I'll go.'

She moved towards the sink. 'Sit down and I'll make a cup of tea.'

'I'd better be off.'

'No, look, I said sit down. If you go now you'll never come back again. You know that.'

Yes, he knew it. He sat down, still ill at ease, as she ran water into the kettle and put it on the gas. She took cups from the cupboard over the sink and set them out. Standing there then, across the room from him, she said quietly.

'*Did* you enjoy it?'

'Very much.'

She turned her head. There was a softness in her face that he'd never seen before. 'We did well together, didn't we?'

He couldn't stop himself smiling through the tenderness her words roused in him. 'Very well indeed.'

Her lips twitched in return. 'Yes ...' Then suddenly she was solemn again. She rubbed her hands over her face. 'I haven't forgotten I'm married,' she said.

'No.'

'Only ... there hasn't been much of that for a long time.'

When she didn't go on, Simpkins said, 'I had wondered if——'

'He was never much interested,' she said, 'even at first. Once Nicholas was on the way he seemed to think he'd done his duty by me ... Did you think it only happened with women?'

'More often, perhaps.'

'Aye, but a woman can just lie there and put up with it. A man's got to do more about it. Most of the time Sid's impo-tent.'

'Impotent,' Simpkins said, and was immediately sorry he'd corrected her.

'However you say it ... I know what it's like in practice. I was brought up respectable. You don't find out that sort of thing about a man till after you've married him and it's too late. You're supposed to make the best of it then. You're the only other man I've ever done it with. Do you believe that?'

'There's no reason why I shouldn't,' Simpkins said.

'Except the brazen way I took you into the bedroom and let you have me.'

'Oh, now——' Simpkins began.

'But I don't care,' she went on quickly. 'It was bloody marvellous and I don't care what anybody says.'

59

'Nobody else need know.'

'You know what I mean. I'm talking to you and my conscience.'

Simpkins glanced briefly in at his own conscience and was at present unmoved. He felt about himself a curious peaceful detachment. Emotions could be deceptive and the act of love had a way of stripping off the disguises lust gathered round itself. His detachment set him free to look outwards to her; it left his concern for her untrammelled by guilt for his ready yielding to the temptation of her body.

'Did you know your husband before the war?'

'Oh yes. I was only a bit of a lass then, of course. Plenty old enough to be married and starting a family, but still not grown-up in my feelings, somehow. I went out a few times with Sid. There was something about him that appealed to me. A kind of delicacy. It's the only way I can describe it. You somehow got the feeling he was cut out to be different from the others. Even though the jobs he'd had were nothing special and he'd taken up driving for a living, you thought he might suddenly find his feet and do something good. Or at least, I did. Then the war broke out and he was called up into the army. It was a feather in your cap to have a man away fighting, somebody to write to and go about with when he was home on leave. After the first twelve months he went out East and I didn't see him again till he was repatriated after it was all over.'

'He wouldn't be in such good shape then.'

'No. But he had a spell in a rehabilitation hospital and got some of his weight back and he didn't seem to have had any lasting damage done to him. I didn't know what I felt for him then. I suppose I hardly thought about it. I'd waited for him all that time and I was all caught up, like everybody else, in the excitement of the war being over and the men coming home. We got married nearly straight away. It wasn't so bad at first. Sid's father had left a few debts and he made 'em good out of his back pay and gratuity. Then he had a spell when he got on gambling and that more or less took care of the rest. We'd seemed to be

60

quite well set-up before that. I put it all down to him finding his feet and I couldn't deny him his pleasure after all he'd been through.'

The kettle came to the boil and she made the tea. Then she stood with the pot cradled in her hands, her head cocked at the ceiling. 'That's Nicholas.' She put the pot down and made for the door. 'It'll be mashed by the time I come back.'

Simpkins had heard nothing. He filled and lit his pipe. She returned in a few moments. 'He must have been dreaming.' She sniffed at the air. 'Oh, it's your pipe.'

'I hope you don't mind.'

'Oh, no. It smells lovely. I like to see a man with a pipe. Sid used to smoke one a bit before the war. He can't manage with it now; it upsets his stomach.'

Simpkins saw a mental image of the young Moffat, clean and meticulous in his leisure hours, probably sporting a hairline moustache, and puffing on a pipe with a long stem and small bowl. The kind of pipe, over-neat, almost dainty, that he had never smoked himself. And Norma, fresh faced, unawakened in her emotions beyond adolescent admiration, perhaps vaguely wondering why Moffat never touched her but attributing it to his gentlemanliness, his sensitivity, his difference.

And now what?

They entered upon a period in which, despite the anxiety and deceit which lay under the surface, there was a certain contentment for both of them. Simpkins was careful to visit the house on some occasions when Moffat was at home. He would have preferred not to have set up any relationship with the husband of the woman whose lover he was—he wished, indeed, that they need never have met at all—but it was desirable for the sake of inquisitive eyes outside to establish a rôle as a friend of the family. He undertook an expensive programme of not strictly necessary improvements to all the houses, which gave him a further excuse for being seen about. Even so, he knew there would be talk and he was concerned to be as discreet as possible for Norma's sake. He was glad when summer was over and, the days steadily shortening, he could arrive under cover of darkness.

He felt for Norma a tender protectiveness which was deepened by their lovemaking. Romantic moments were tempered by her habit of candid speech and her cool dispassionate view of life, but he knew she was grateful for his care in satisfying her and nurturing the sensuality frustrated by Moffat's inadequacy. She looked well. Her skin took on a youthful bloom and the faint but distant signs of strain he had seen constantly on her face at the beginning of their acquaintance disappeared. She began also, almost imperceptibly at first, to put on weight, and was self-conscious about it as he teased her, clutching at the flesh of her hips or weighing her breasts in his hands as she lay with him.

'Give over,' she said. 'I know I'm getting fat without you always drawing attention to it.'

'I think it's lovely,' Simpkins assured her, straight-faced. 'I've always wanted a Rubens lady with mountains of white flesh I could wallow in.'

'I haven't got to that yet, but I shall have to do something about it. I can't get middle-aged spread at my time of life.'

'There isn't one ample square inch of you I don't want to kiss.'

'Oh, you devil,' she said. 'You must have learned your tricks from an Egyptian whore.'

'They used to run crash courses for servicemen in Alexandria.'

'I'll believe anything you tell me.'

'I'll bet you would as well. As it happens, I've never been with a whore in my life.'

'Then there's some women round here who ought to be locked up.'

Simpkins laughed. 'Do you really believe you're the latest in a long line of conquests?'

'I'm not the first woman you've been with since your wife died.'

'I have souvenirs of them hanging across my bedrail,' Simpkins said. 'Each one is a pleasant memory stored away against a lonely old age. My plan is to get to three-hundred and sixty-five, then every day of the year will be a kind of erotic anniversary.'

'You mucky old man. What number am I?'

'Eighty-nine or ninety. I can't remember off-hand.'

She dug him in the side with her elbow. 'Give up.'

'It was you who suggested I'd got a reputation.'

'Oh, that. No, it was just a bit of talk among the women at work. They see an attractive man of your age and wonder why you don't get married again. Then they say, "I'll bet he's a bit of a boy on the quiet." You know the sort of thing. I expect with one or two of them there's a bit of wishful thinking in it.'

'Get me their names,' Simpkins said. 'I might make my century before the year's out.'

'It is some time since your wife died, though, isn't it?'

'Ten years.'

'How long were you married?'

'Three years.'

'Somebody said it was TB.'

'Yes.'

'It's a shame.'

'It was more than that. It was tragic. Because before long they'll have it under control and nobody need die of it any more.'

'Do you . . . do you think about her a lot?'

'Every day.'

It was hardly, he thought, the most appropriate moment to confess love for somebody else, even if she lived only in memory; but Norma had asked and he'd given her an honest answer. He moved his hand gently up under her breast as if to reassure her that it was she whom he'd made love to and not a ghost invested with her flesh.

'You learn to live with these things,' he said.

63

'Aye ...' She sighed and shifted her position, turning on her side to face him. He felt the weight of her breasts against his chest and murmured, 'Fatty...' It was a joke, her putting on a little weight. She had a magnificent body, slightly thick in the waist, perhaps, but with a lovely curve of hips, and breasts that were firm and high. He tucked in closer to her and fought off the desire to drift into warm and sensual sleep. He couldn't stay much longer. It was already quite late.

'Tom.'

'H'm?'

'Tom, we don't talk a lot of silly slop and we don't have to make a lot of fuss about love and all that, but...'

'But what?'

'There is something, isn't there? I mean, even this wouldn't be like it is without something else, would it?' She sped on now without letting him answer. 'What I want to say is, you're a fine man, Tom. A good man, I think. And I'd like to believe that you won't get tired of ... of this, and suddenly stop coming any more. Because even if you stopped wanting me like this I'd still hope to see you now and again.'

It was probably the most open statement of its kind she had ever made. He knew it had cost her an effort and he was moved by it. He kissed her hot flushed cheek and then her lips.

'I shall keep coming, love, as long as this powder keg we're sitting on doesn't blow up under us. It's not altogether up to us, you know.'

Norma was silent for a time. Then she said, 'A woman in the street said something to Sid the other day.'

'Oh, lord,' Simpkins said. 'Who was it?'

'That Mrs Crutchley on at the end.'

'And what did she say?'

'He came in and told me she'd stopped him. "Your landlord seems to be a regular visitor while you're away," she said. And Sid said he said back to her, "If it's Mr Simpkins you're talking about, he's been a good friend to us and he can come to my house any time he likes." He hardly ever gets mad but he was blazing when he came in. "Bloody nosey bitch," he called her.'

Simpkins said nothing, trying to work out the implications of this incident. He felt suddenly exposed; not for the moment master of his own life but at the mercy of the schemes and desires of others.

'He said something else, then, a bit later on,' Norma said.

'Oh?'

'He said, "I know I haven't been all I should have been to you, Norma, but I'm fond of you and I hope you'll stay fond of me." '

'He said that?'

'I'm telling it to you word for word.'

'But,' Simpkins said in surprise, 'it sounds as if——'

'Yes, it does.'

'There was nothing else?'

'No, just that. I'd have liked something a bit more plain than a hint, but I let it drop.'

'You did right. You couldn't expect him to spell it out for you.'

Simpkins had read novels about Society in which inadequate husbands (usually old men who had acquired young beauty like buying another desirable possession) had tolerantly acquiesced in the matter of their wife's lovers; and in real life he'd known at least one marriage where a reciprocal arrangement of live-and-let-live seemed to operate; but this apparent complaisance of Moffat's made him uneasy. Probably because he couldn't see himself in a like rôle, he thought wryly, he was mainly at the moment concerned about Moffat himself.

'So you see,' Norma was saying, 'it might be all right after all.'

'The bomb has been de-fused,' Simpkins murmured.

'What? Oh, yes, I see what you mean.'

'We've got to go on being careful and discreet,' Simpkins said, 'if only for his sake.'

'You don't think I'm either daft enough or cruel enough

to flaunt it in his face, do you? I admitted nothing—there was no reason to—and I shan't bring it up again unless he does.'

'Let's hope that old gossip at the end has said enough to satisfy her.'

'I'll give her a mouthful if she as much as looks sideways at me.'

'Just be careful,' Simpkins warned her. 'Don't surrender your position for the sake of a good row.'

'It might stop her mouth for good.'

'I doubt it. Women like that thrive on scandals and feuds. It's hard to cure them without exposing yourself. And we *have* got something to hide.'

'Perhaps you're right.'

'I'm sure I am. We shall just have to outlive their curiosity.'

'What d'you mean?'

'I was thinking just now that the decisions weren't in our hands. Now it looks as though there won't be a blow-up unless we make it ourselves. People watching for it will get tired of waiting.' He turned to her again. 'We were talking just now about this going on for a long time.'

'Yes. Yes, we were. And I want that, Tom. I do want that.'

When, in the summer of the following year, Norma told him she was pregnant, they both knew without doubt that the child was his.

'It was always a possibility,' she said. 'It's a risk you take.' She seemed calm about it, even in a way pleased and satisfied.

It made things different. Simpkins asked her to marry him. He asked her, choosing his words with care, but she knew he was only really offering her a choice.

'No, Tom. In the first place, I can't leave Sid. And in the second, fond enough as I think you are of me, you'd never have asked me but for this.'

66

'Suppose he throws you out? I mean, it's bound to alter things a bit.'

She shook her head. 'I don't think he will.'

'But how will you tell him?'

'I shall just have to try to bring him up to scratch first,' she said calmly.

'You mean make him think it's——?'

'I shall give him the chance to think so. I can't alter what's happened—I wouldn't if I could—and I shall give him the chance.'

'You're not considering me, are you?' Simpkins said. 'I haven't got a child. Now I'm going to have one and I can't acknowledge it.'

She regarded him steadily. 'I've told you I won't leave Sid, Tom. If you force him to throw me out by claiming this baby it'll come to the same thing. What will he do without me? Who else will marry him? Where will he find another home? And what about Nicholas? I've said what I'm going to do, Tom, and I'm going to do it.'

He saw in her a determination that nothing could budge, and he gave in. Months later, when Norma was nearing her time, Moffat asked him to be godfather to the child. Simpkins, often uneasy, was for the first time visibly embarrassed before Norma's husband.

'There's nobody more right to it than you, Tom,' Moffat said. 'I must warn you, though, that I take it seriously. I like godparents to be people who'll remember their responsibilities if the need ever arises.'

Simpkins was astounded by the complete absence of irony in Moffat's voice. Of a sudden he found himself warming to the man. He had thought of him as hollow, and so he was in many ways; yet there was in him a kind of character and pride he could only admire.

So Shirley was born. It might be said in all innocence in years to come that Simpkins loved her as if she were his own. Just now he curbed in himself any desire to make too much fuss of the crinkly faced sweet-smelling bundle he found himself holding for a moment in the church. The boy,

Nicholas, had held his hand on the way in and called him 'Unka Tom'. Simpkins stood in the tiny group round the font as the parson intoned and reflected that his own daughter would grow up doing the same.

5

As he'd sent a message to Bess saying he wouldn't be home for lunch, Simpkins stopped off at the White Horse. There was a bright fire burning in the carpeted lounge and he made straight for it, rubbing his hands together in the heat then turning to stand with the skirts of his coat held up as he gently stroked his buttocks and the backs of his thighs.

'Pleasant enough in the sun but damn' cold when you get out of it,' the landlord said.

'It is that, Edgar.' He ordered a double Scotch and glanced at the two men eating at a table under the window and discussing the contents of what looked like catalogues of clothing. 'You're a bit quiet today.'

'It varies, you know. And it's early yet.'

'What can you offer me to eat?'

'Chicken, a bit of steak, or a pork chop.'

'H'm.' He ought to be hungry but the emotional upsets of the morning had robbed him of any real appetite. 'I'll have a steak sandwich—in teacake—with a few onions. Just a few—don't swamp it. And a cup of coffee when I'm ready.'

'Right you are, Mr Simpkins.'

He had moved away from the fire for fear of scorching his clothes and was standing at the bar counter sipping his whisky when the door opened and Matthew Whittaker came in with another man. Simpkins had known Whittaker for many years without their becoming much more than acquaintances. His father and Old Dawson had been two of a kind: hard-headed, forceful, blunt, temperate in their personal habits and supporters of the same chapel. Simpkins regarded Matthew as being a bit of an old woman, a man who looked askance at a glass of whisky, as though it might lure him into some scandalous loss of dignity and reputation. He seemed to have inherited all his father's sense of restraint and not much of his vigour and drive. A few years younger than Simpkins, he was shorter and less robustly built, and his hair was still dark. His slight smile was taken at first as an expression of a pleasant disposition, and was then seen in the way it perpetually lingered to have little positive meaning. Simpkins was surprised to see him and said so.

'Hello, Matthew. I didn't know this was one of your haunts.'

'Tom. How are you? It isn't, but Sir Walter fancied eating in a pub and somebody told me the food here was good.'

'Oh, Edgar 'ull do you something simple and tasty. None of your fancy trimmings, mind, but plain and wholesome.' He grinned. 'It's a job when you've got those posh dining-rooms up there and you have to eat at the White Horse.'

'You know how it is, Tom. If you dine in you've got your executives for company and you can't always talk freely.'

'Perhaps so. But don't let me butt in either. I'll just get my sandwich and leave you on your own.'

'No, no. You're all right there. Let me introduce you. Sir Walter, this is Tom Simpkins. Sir Walter Tyler of Hartley, Rumbold.'

Simpkins shook the hand of the tall man in the dark pin-striped suit. He was one of those men who shine with cleanliness and good grooming. His white collar gleamed with starch and he wore the striped tie, fastened in a neat small knot, of a regiment Simpkins couldn't identify. Nor, at the moment, could he bring to mind what line Hartley, Rumbold were in.

Edgar came out of the back place with his sandwich, paper napkin and a knife.

'Here's my lunch. Let me get you a drink before you order yours.'

'That looks about as plain and wholesome as you can get,' Tyler said. His voice was deep and his enunciation clear, in an accent that was completely regionless.

'It's enough for me just now.'

'I suppose we've all reached an age where we've got to watch the waistline a bit. I sometimes think it's as well that expense-account luncheons have been curbed.'

'Well, Matthew will find this a bit easier on the pocket than taking you to the Queens in Leeds,' Simpkins couldn't resist saying. He glanced at Matthew who was blinking his eyes behind his glasses as though not knowing how to take the remark. His smile reasserted itself as Tyler gave a snort of agreeable laughter.

'What will you have to drink, Sir Walter?'

'No, no,' Simpkins said. 'I offered.'

Tyler asked for a Scotch. 'I'm tempted to try the draught bitter,' he said, 'but I'm afraid it would only make me sleepy.'

'Me too. I can't take it at lunchtime. What about you, Matthew?'

'Oh, I don't know. A medium dry sherry, perhaps.'

Simpkins took the knife and cut into his sandwich. 'You won't mind if I get on with this?'

'Tom's one of our occasional suppliers, you know, Sir Walter,' Whittaker said. 'He has a factory not far from ours.'

'I wouldn't call it a factory,' Simpkins said. 'More a glorified machine shop.'

'You don't cover as much ground as Whittaker's?'

'Good lord, no. We're in a much smaller way of business. Matthew's got a generation's start on me. And anyway, I've always tried to keep it manageable and under control.'

'I've always found expand or die a pretty sound rule of business,' Tyler said.

'You do hear it,' Simpkins agreed. 'But there's also a rule in swimming and that is don't get out of your depth.'

'What's your main output?'

'Smallish machined parts and pressings. We can manage a bit of fabrication as well.'

'We're always interested in machining capacity,' Tyler said. 'Perhaps I can push something your way one of these days.'

Simpkins took a business card out of his wallet and handed it to Tyler. ' "Assuring you of our best attention at all times." '

He left them soon after and drove out to the Works. The lunch period wasn't yet over and the clang and clatter, whine and rumble of working hours was stilled. There was no one about in the office corridor. Through the glass partition he could see instruments left on the two boards in the drawing office. A man slept on a chair in the corner, his feet upon another chair and an open newspaper covering his face. Simpkins went into his own office. There was a pile of opened mail on his desk along with two or three slips of paper on which Miss Warner had typed messages about people who had telephoned. He glanced at everything briefly then stood at the window and filled his pipe. The brightness of the day had gone. The sky was sullen now over the rooftops. There would probably be rain later, slashing sleety rain which would wash away what was left of the snow and then freeze in the night. Winter was coming early and he was uneasy and depressed.

He had left Norma still upset. She had stopped crying and was talking rationally about practical matters, but lingering distress could be seen in her eyes and the unnaturally nervous movements of her hands. That she should have chosen that particular way of testing their relationship dismayed him. The fire and urgency had long since gone out of their lovemaking, but over seventeen years they had grown steadily into each other's lives. This seemed to Simpkins a much more positive and lasting proof of his loyalty and the durability of what they had started so long ago than his ability to make love to her at the drop of a hat. Still, he had failed her and his sorrow and shame were no substitute. He wondered if he had been unthinkingly letting her down for some time. In the gradual transformation of their relationship from its basis in passion to one of companionability she might have seen herself relegated to mere habit. She could be thinking that only Shirley took him there at all now.

His pipe wouldn't draw. He scraped the tobacco into the biggest of the clean ashtrays on his desk and rummaged in a drawer for a pipe-cleaner. The big head-and-shoulders photograph of his father stared down at him from the wall. It had once hung facing Simpkins as he worked but he could not stand the unnerving glare of those uncompromising eyes every time he looked up. A position on the side wall was little better. The eyes, like Kitchener's pointing finger in the famous World War One recruiting poster, followed him everywhere. Now he sometimes felt the glare on the back of his neck, but he couldn't bring himself to remove the portrait altogether.

'You old bugger,' he said out loud. 'You with your clearcut principles. You always knew your duty and lived according to it, no matter how much it hurt anyone else.' After the birth of their two children, Simpkins' father discovered his wife in an indiscretion. Her infidelity was never proved. A judge would perhaps not have considered the evidence sufficient but it was enough for Simpkins senior. He didn't believe in divorce but from then on they occupied separate bedrooms. The passing years thawed some of the ice in old Simpkins' heart but that politeness rather than affection was the principal characteristic of his attitude to his wife was something his son had long accepted without knowing the real reason for it. It was only after his mother's last illness, during which she confided in Bess, that Simpkins learned the truth.

'I wonder what you'd think of me now. Not much, I'll be bound. You might say I'd had it too good for too long, and you'd be right. The day of reckoning draws near.'

Several pairs of feet passed along the corridor. He heard the door of the office next to his open and close. The bell rang for the end of the lunch break and a hum of power emerged out of the silence it left behind it. He pressed a key on the dictaphone and called Miss Warner in.

'You did ring Mrs Hargreaves and give her my message about lunch?'

'Yes, I did.'

'What did she say?'

'She thanked me for letting her know.'

'Is that all?'

A discreet but perceptible gleam of amusement lit Miss Warner's dark eyes. 'She sounded just a little testy.'

'Ah.' Probably thinking he was paying her out for last night. 'Well,' Simpkins drew his chair forward, 'let's see if we can get rid of some of this mail.'

Miss Warner sat down alongside the desk. She crossed her legs, exposing an amount of thigh that would have been thought immodest twelve months ago and resting her short-hand notebook on it. She was twenty-eight, had been with Simpkins for four years and was attractive enough to make you wonder on first sight why she wasn't married. Simpkins had wondered about it for years, but he never probed. They had a relationship of easy business familiarity, with little formality beyond his way of addressing her. His previous secretary, Miss Raven, was a *real* spinster, older than he was, whom he would never have dreamt of addressing by her first name, and the habit had stuck with this one.

Simpkins dictated for half an hour, clearing what he could deal with immediately. The rest he would pass to someone else or take advice on. It gave Miss Warner something to be going on with and it would ease for her the last hour or two of the day. He had never been one for holding everything back till four-thirty and expecting it miraculously to appear, ready, at half-past five.

'I think that's all for now.'

'Oh, by the way, Mr Batchelor tried twice to get you this morning.'

'Righto. He'll try again if it's anything important.'

She hesitated in the open doorway. 'There was something else.'

'Yes?'

'I wasn't going to mention it because you've been out this morning and you might want to do some extra work to catch up. But if I could possibly get away on time I'd be grateful. I've got a rather special engagement this evening.'

'I shouldn't think it's beyond the bounds of possibility.'

She smiled. She had a rather fetching smile. There was charm as well as shrewdness and intelligence in it and it opened a tiny dimple at each corner of her mouth.

'Thank you.'

The door closed behind her. Was she going to drive some poor adoring devil half out of his mind tonight, holding on to her virginity for a special person who had yet to turn up; or was she a modern miss who gave in gracefully, taking her pleasure as it offered itself? Might her 'special engagement', on the other hand, be one in a hazardous series of carefully planned and prayed-for illicit encounters, with unbearable expectancy before every meeting and agony to carry home afterwards? Simpkins, who had concealed things, wondered.

His Dictaphone buzzed. He pressed the switch under the green light and Horace Batchelor's voice came through the speaker.

'Oh, Horace. Miss Warner said you'd been trying to see me.'

'I would like to. I ought to be able to handle it meself, but it appears I can't. It's the Bedford lad. It's gone beyond a joke with him.'

'What's he been up to?'

'What hasn't he been up to, except a decent day's work. I've never said owt before, though I've given him a warning or two. His timekeeping's been a disgrace for months, and so's his general attitude to everything. Bill Evans came to see me about him this morning. He said he couldn't put up with him any more. He's like a rotten apple in a barrel. Seeing him get away with murder has a bad effect on everybody else.'

'Why haven't I heard about this before?'

'We thought we could handle it. In fact, I'd have sent him packing a long time ago but I knew you'd a special interest in him so I've bent over backwards to give him every chance I could. Anyway, I'm not having any more of it. When Bill brought him to me he got real nasty.'

'Oh?'

'Aye, he——' Batchelor stopped. 'You haven't got Miss Warner in the office, have you?'

'No, I'm on my own.'

'Well, he turned straight round and told us both to fuck off. Said I couldn't sack him without your say-so and he wanted to see you. It'll get to summat if every fellar I give his cards to starts demanding to see the boss first.'

'It won't get to that, Horace. This is something of a special case.'

'Oh aye, he's got more rights than fellers who've stayed honest and kept out of trouble. Ask me, he'd be better off back where he was before.'

'Idleness and indolence aren't crimes, Horace.'

'Crimes or not, a feller who gets away with 'em creates bad feeling about a factory and I'm not having my authority undermined any longer. He's got to go.'

'I suppose I'd better have a word with him.'

Batchelor's voice was stiff with disapproval. 'Just as you like.'

'Look, Horace, I did the starting and I'll do any finishing that's got to be done. You get hold of him and come up here. Bring his time sheets with you and leave him in Miss Warner's office when you arrive.'

Simpkins tried to carry on working but after a few moments he dejectedly pushed his papers on one side. He'd been on the local bench when Don Bedford was brought up charged with stealing a car and breaking into a working men's club. He and his two mates had crashed the vehicle with several thousand cigarettes in it after a seven mile chase with a police car along the A1. They were sent to

Quarter Sessions. Albert Bedford, the boy's father, had worked for Simpkins at one time. He was in the magistrate's court and Simpkins spoke to him afterwards. He'd been a full-blooded hard-living man in his prime but ill health had forced him into an early retirement. His body had lost its flesh and his authority had apparently followed his physical decline. He made no plea for his son, but said harshly, forcing the words through his gasping breath, 'It's a pity they can't flog some sense into him. To think a son of mine . . .' He wheezed and the rest of his words were lost in a rasping cough.

'Do you think a lot of it might be due to him getting into the wrong company?'

'I sometimes think he's too bloody stupid to go t'last. They couldn't make owt out of him at school and he's never learned a trade since. Just messed about at one job after another.'

'It's not a good time to wash your hands of him, is it?'

'What can I do? It's out of my hands now.'

'Not for ever, though.'

'What d'you think they'll give him?'

'He might be lucky. He's the youngest of the three. He wasn't driving the car, and it's his first offence.'

'Let's hope they give him long enough to think about things.'

'What about afterwards?'

'We'll have to wait and see what frame of mind he's in then, won't we?'

The magistrate at Quarter Sessions took the view Simpkins expected. Bedford's accomplices received prison sentences; he was given a period of Borstal training. When he came home Simpkins gave him a job.

Horace Batchelor tapped and looked round the door from Miss Warner's office, coming in when he saw Simpkins sitting there alone. Batchelor was Simpkins' works manager, a smallish, bald, outspoken man with a big nose and red bony hands. There was grease on his overall. He could have sat back and supervised from his office downstairs but he still liked occasionally to get in among the work and exercise his old skills. He dropped a sheaf of time sheets on Simpkins' desk. Simpkins riffled through them. They were, as Batchelor had said, a bad record.

'You know, you really ought to have put me in the picture before, Horace.'

'It's my job to handle the people downstairs and when I think I can't do it any longer I'll pack it in.'

Simpkins sighed. There was an obdurate streak in Batchelor which sometimes led to unnecessary awkwardnesses. But he was a fair man in his way and though he had never approved of Bedford Simpkins didn't doubt that he'd given the boy every chance to prove himself.

'Is there anything else I ought to know before I see him?'

'I should think what I've told you's enough.'

'All right, then, let's have him in.'

Bedford was about the same age as Nick Moffat, but his face was habitually sullen and his eyes reflected none of Nick's lively intelligence.

'I understand there's been some trouble downstairs.'

Bedford didn't speak but moved his shoulders in a gesture that was almost a shrug and put his hands in the pockets of his jeans, standing with his weight on one foot. It was hard in him to tell the difference between insolence and *gaucherie*.

'All this, you know ...' Simpkins indicated the time sheets. 'It's something no firm can put up with. What's it all about?' He waited for Bedford to speak.

'Well, come on, lad,' Batchelor said. 'You wanted to see Mr Simpkins and now's your chance to have your say.'

The boy's jaw moved as though the words were jammed somewhere. Simpkins realised he was chewing gum.

'They don't like me down there.'

'Who doesn't?' Bedford moved his shoulders again. 'Why don't they like you?'

'People get against you when you've been in Borstal.'

'Oh, come on,' Simpkins said. 'Don't you think they're more likely to take against you if you walk about with a chip on your shoulder and don't pull your weight?'

'It's borin' an' all,' Bedford said. 'Just carryin' stuff about all day.'

'But what else can we give you to do except labouring? You haven't got a trade. You're not even semi-skilled and you're not making any effort to learn anything. Nobody owes you a living, you know. I gave you a job to help you find your feet and because I knew your father. I didn't have to. I could simply have forgotten all about you when you were sent away.'

'It was you who helped to get me sent away.'

Batchelor said, 'Bloody hell!' under his breath and turned to look out of the window in exasperation.

Simpkins felt himself battering against an impenetrable stupidity.

'Do you mean to say you should have been allowed to get away with it?'

'You knew I'd been led on by them other two. You told the old feller so.'

'I told your father that bad company might have helped to lead you astray. That's why I wanted you to have another chance when you came home.'

'I don't call humping stuff about much of a chance. It's the worst job in the place.'

'What's the best, then?' Simpkins asked.

The youth's face twisted in a grin that was almost bashful.

'What d'you mean?'

'If you've got the worst job, who's got the best?'

'You.'

'All right.' Simpkins got up and walked round the desk. 'There's the chair. Do you think you can fill it? Do you think you can do what Bill Evans does? And what about his job—Mr Batchelor's? How do you think he got where he is? I'll tell you—through hard work and learning something when he was your age instead of walking about moaning. Do you know he can do practically any job on the shop floor, including yours?'

'This conversation's as stupid as he is,' Batchelor said. 'I don't know why you waste your breath on him.'

'What do you expect me to do?' Simpkins said to Bedford. 'Give you a cushy little number with no work attached to it?' He was losing his patience, felt he ought not to, but found it a luxury after the tensions of the morning. 'Who the bloody hell do you think you are?'

'I'm as good as anybody else here.'

'You've done a lot to prove it, haven't you?'

'There's not much chance, is there, on that job?'

'Chance? There's a chance to show you can do an honest day's work. How many chances do you want? Do you think people have nothing better to do than keep looking after you? You've a bit of leeway to make up, lad.'

'I've done my time.'

'Well, God bless you,' Simpkins said. 'You've done your time so we all have to fix things so you can spend another twelve months doing bugger all. No wonder your father loses patience with you.'

'Oh, him . . .'

'Yes, him. He liked his ale and a few bob on the horses but he knew how to do a good day's work as well.'

'He's not working now, is he?'

'No, he's had some bad luck. It can happen to anybody.'

'Some folk get more than others.'

'Aye, and some folk go round begging for it.'

Simpkins walked back round the desk and sat down. Bedford waited, his jaw moving almost imperceptibly on the gum.

'Am I finished, then?'

Simpkins looked up at him. Bedford stared back. It was too late. Horace had kept it all bottled up and had now delivered his ultimatum. Simpkins couldn't undermine his authority. The stare, held on Simpkins' face, turned into a sneer. The bloody fool, Simpkins thought. He wanted to hit him.

'There's nothing I can do about it. Mr Batchelor's warned you before. There's also the matter of what you said to him and Mr Evans. I hoped you'd find your feet here, but it hasn't worked out. I'm sorry.'

'Why should you be sorry?'

'Yes, lad. Why should I be?'

Batchelor moved across the room and opened the door. 'Come on, I'll get you fixed up with your cards.'

The room was quiet when they'd gone. Simpkins listened to the hum of the machines. It was a sound he normally didn't notice till it stopped. He picked up a pen then threw it down again. It was all wrong. He should have kept a closer eye on Bedford himself. Instead, he'd brought him into the place and left him to it. Perhaps his warnings would have served no better than Batchelor's. The lad was idle and stupid and his stupidity would cripple him all his life.

Horace came back for the time sheets.

'He's in the wages office now, getting his money.' He snorted. 'A bloody good hiding 'ud happen help to sort him out.'

'I don't think he'll ever have gone short of them,' Simpkins said.

'What d'you mean?'

'Albert Bedford had a mean, violent streak in him. You know that as well as I do.'

'Anyway, we're shut of him now.'

'Yes. And I'll tell you something, Horace. Don't you ever put me into a corner like that again. I'd no choice but to sack him when you'd let things go so far.'

'You mean to say you might have given him another chance?'

'I mean I had no choice. Just that.'

'If you ask me, Mr Simpkins, you want your brains washing.'

Simpkins was silent. Then he sighed. 'Aye, probably you're right.'

But it was failure. A little more to add to a day already full of it.

'Put the light on as you go out, will you.'

He lit his pipe and thought about Bedford and Nick Moffat. Then he dredged up a memory of himself at nineteen. He had been sitting there, hardly moving, for ten minutes when the telephone rang. He reached for the receiver.

'There's a Mrs Moffat on the line, Mr Simpkins.'

'Put her through, please.'

Norma said, 'Tom? I'm sorry to bother you at work. I'm up at the infirmary. They sent for me just after you'd gone. It's Sid, Tom, He's . . . he's dead.'

PART TWO

6

'There are people who think I'm a cool bitch,' Andrea Warner had once said to the man she loved. 'Some are men who've made a pass at me and been turned down. I suppose I must be a special temptation to them, almost like a divorced woman. "She must have to have it from somebody," they think. "Why shouldn't it be me?" Others are women who are discontented in some way; they envy my freedom and what they see as my self-possession. Because I don't share my secrets with them they assume I have none and I'm in calm command of my own life. Very few of them admit it openly. They play a kind of conversational double game, one minute confiding in me about the failings of their husbands or boy friends and the next commiserating with me over my unattached state. Then they tell me that when "the right man" comes along I'll learn what real life is all about. It would interest them all, and surprise quite a few, to know about you, darling.'

'And I can't climb on a rooftop and tell the world I claim you,' he said.

'It doesn't matter.'

'Oh, but it does. When a man loves a woman he should defend her with his honour and protect her with all he has and everything he is.'

It was questions of honour and loyalty, deceit and betrayal which constantly tore Philip apart. Yet Andrea knew without doubt the extent of his need for her. If the day came when he didn't need her, a time when the yearning went out of his eyes, then she would lose her right to love him; she would by taking from him then detract from the sum of his life instead of adding to it as she was so very, very sure she did now. Oh, they should have known from the beginning. They had waded out willingly into the shallows and splashed the invigoration of their personalities over each other. Harmless, hurting no one, the nudgings of tenderness welcomed as giving quality to the experience, and not seen till too late as warning signals of the depths of pain beyond. They should have known. But then, how much they would have missed!

Philip Hart was 32 when Andrea met him. He was a teacher in the English department at Valley Bridge Grammar School, a stocky man of a little over middle height with a dark purposeful look. He helped to run a film society in the town, which gave its shows on alternate Tuesdays in the Co-operative Hall in Market Street. Andrea went out one night with George Bishop, an old friend of hers and her elder brother. George worked in a local bank and had been doggedly wooing Andrea for years. He had proposed to her twice. She was fond of him and thought sometimes that she would eventually marry him. There was nothing desperate in his pressing of his suit. He was kind and steady and he never tried to maul her. She found this lack of passion in his approach to her a convenient thing. She wasn't a puritanical girl and she knew she was physically attractive, but she needed love to spark off her own bodily response and this she hadn't yet found. At twenty-seven she sometimes wondered if she wasn't just a little abnormal. Her mother got impatient with her. She approved of George, wanted to see her elder daughter married and couldn't understand why Andrea rejected such a reasonable match. 'Reasonable' was the word she actually used, and 'unreasonable' was her description of Andrea's attitude. 'I don't understand you, Andrea,' she said. 'You're of an age when you should be thinking about the future. You can't go on like this all your life.'

'Why not?'

'Because it's not natural to waste yourself.'

'Don't you think getting married for the sake of it would be wasting myself?'

'George won't wait around for ever, you know. You'll wake up one day and find yourself alone, with all the eligible men married off elsewhere.'

'Well then, I shan't get married. I'll become somebody's mistress instead.'

'Andrea!'

'I'm sure I'd much rather be the mistress of a man I loved than be married to somebody I didn't love.' She said these things to shake her mother's lower middle-class notions of right living. She meant what she said, in an academic way, but didn't realise the prophetic quality of her words.

'Love,' her mother said. 'You talk about it as if it were some sort of desirable disease. It's something that grows inside the security of a good marriage.'

'Nevertheless, you'd be delighted if I were head over heels in love with George, wouldn't you?'

'Yes, I should.'

'Yes,' Andrea said, 'it would be convenient.'

But instead, she met Philip Hart.

The film was Eisenstein's *October*. Philip spoke about it for a few minutes before the show. He was talking about it again when they saw him in the pub on the corner. George had suggested a drink afterwards and they were sitting at a table when Philip walked in with another man. They ordered pints of bitter and stood at the bar. In the intervals of her own desultory conversation with George, Andrea could overhear snatches of what Philip was saying. He was discussing the film now from the standpoint of political history, with references to the position of any artist in a climate like that of the Soviet Union.

'Man, you don't have to use historical subjects or even work in any representational idiom. You've got to watch it in something as abstract as music. Look at Shostakovitch and Prokofiev. They had to toe the line and admit the error of their ways.'

He turned and saw them, nodded to George and gave Andrea a vague smile, then came over.

'George Bishop, isn't it?'

'Yes. Philip Hart, Andrea Warner.'

'Did you enjoy the film?'

'H'mm,' Andrea said doubtfully. 'In parts. As a story I found it confusing.'

'I suppose it is. I gather the situation was.' He grinned.

'I've seen the bit with the raising of the bridge and the dead horse before.'

'Yes, it's a well-known study extract.'

'Though I must say, I'm always a bit uneasy about the animals concerned in sequences like that.'

'You mean had they to kill a horse specially? Yes, I know what you mean. There's an anti-war film—French, I think—with a shot of a horse with its mane on fire running mad with fear through a blazing village. They must have had to set that up. They depict the horror of the situation by perpetrating it themselves. It seems to me to leave them without much moral standing room.' He drained his glass. 'Can I get you another drink?'

George looked at his watch. 'Oh, I'—but Andrea butted in with—'We've got plenty of time, George.' It was just like him to want to end the evening at the point where it was beginning to get most interesting. 'I'd like a half-pint of bitter, please.'

'Sure you wouldn't prefer a short?'

'Quite sure, thanks.'

He took their glasses away and got them refilled.

'Why don't you and your friend sit down?' Andrea said when he came back.

'May as well.' He introduced the other man without Andrea catching his name and they pulled up stools and joined them at the table.

'Perhaps the next show will be more in your line,' Philip said. 'Gerard Phillipe.'

'Oh, yes,' Andrea said. 'He was a lovely man.'

'Yes, wasn't he? We're reviving *Fan Fan la Tulipe.*

Have you seen that, George?'

'I don't remember it.'

'It's a send-up of the swashbuckling Fairbanks rôles. There's that glorious sequence where Fan Fan and his mates are being led out to be hanged. The soldiers are drawn up in lines and there are umpteen drummers tapping out every step as they march along to the tree. Three ropes on the tree. They stand on the cart with the nooses round their necks. The proclamation is read, the drums roll like thunder. The horses are whipped up. They pull the cart away, and the bough breaks.'

Philip threw back his head and roared with laughter. It was infectious. Andrea found herself joining in with the others.

'What happens then?'

'Oh, they escape in the confusion. It's a beauty. You shouldn't miss it.'

'It'll perhaps bring us a decent audience for a change,' Philip's friend said.

'Yes, we haven't done too well lately.'

'Do you find it hard to make ends meet?'

'We do rather. We used to have a healthy little society a few years ago, but I'm afraid the writing's on the wall now. We've always had a middle-brow policy—they won't take a steady diet of the kind of stuff we've seen tonight—and with all the films they're putting out on television we're losing both our programmes and our audience. We might as well call it a day and sit at home in comfort with our feet up.'

'It's a shame, though.'

'Yes, it is. We've had some fun in times past.'

The landlord called time as Philip emptied his glass again. 'It looks as if we've had it here. What about a finisher-off at the Nitelite?'

'I'm game,' his friend said, 'as long as it doesn't stretch till two o'clock.'

'No, no, no. What about you two?'

'I'm not a member and I don't think George is.'

'I am. I can sign you in.'

'Perhaps another time,' George said. 'I'd better take Andrea home.'

She could have hit him for his stuffiness. She'd never noticed it as much before. But she wouldn't argue tonight.

'Yes,' she said, 'I think perhaps another time.'

They stood up to leave.

'Don't forget a fortnight today,' Philip said. 'And if you'd like to join the Society it's still early enough in the season to make it economical.' He winked at her. 'I've got to boost the takings somehow or other.'

'I'll see,' Andrea said.

In the event, she went alone. Philip spotted her before the lights were put out.

'Hello, no George tonight?'

'He couldn't make it.'

'Oh, a pity. It's a bit more encouraging, though, isn't it?' He waved his hand at the audience.

'Yes.' Andrea opened her handbag and took out her new membership card. 'See.'

'Ah! One more lamb into the fold.'

'Let's just say I've got a weakness for lost causes.'

'I'm only too afraid you'll be proved right.'

She was pleased when, some minutes after the feature film had started, he felt his way into the aisle seat next to hers. He didn't talk but he laughed. You sometimes found a man like that who laughed in a theatre and, in building up a wave of audience laughter behind his own, was, Andrea always thought, worth a fee from the management.

Afterwards he asked her if she had to rush away.

'If you'd like to hang on while we dismantle our gear, some of us will be going for a drink.'

She waited, mildly intrigued by his interest in her. She knew little about him beyond what George had volunteered after their last meeting, but she already felt that he made most of the men she knew seem either staid and dull or immature in their studied raffishness.

'Doesn't your wife ever come to the shows?' she asked as they walked along to the pub.

'No. Kate doesn't think it's worth while wasting a baby-sitter. They're not all that readily available and she prefers to save them for special occasions.'

'How many children have you?'

'Two. A couple of boys.'

They were walking behind Philip's friend, whose name Andrea now knew was Harry, and a girl with long dark hair, heavy-framed spectacles and open mesh stockings, called Ruth. A few other people whose faces she recognised from the Society were already in the pub but they were not disturbed at their corner table. Ruth, a rather frowningly intense girl given to humourless analysis of any topic raised, and with a habit of prefacing her remarks with 'Don't you think, though...?' drank cider. Andrea drank beer along with the men, half-pints to their pints. It was after her second glass that she felt a moment of acute awareness of being buoyed up on the crest of an absurd happiness. Absurd because it had no foundation in any lasting reality, but so intense in its instant of experience that it must be grasped and savoured for as long as possible.

But they had come in late and closing time was soon on them. Philip looked at Harry. 'Nitelite?'

Harry said yes and looked in turn at his companion. 'Ruth?'

'All right. Not for long, though.'

'No, we've all got to be up in the morning,' Philip said. 'What about you, Andrea?'

'It's a question of getting home afterwards.'

'I'll give you a lift.'

'I don't want to be too late and I'd hate to drag you away when you were enjoying yourself.'

'When you want to go, we'll go.' He lifted one eyebrow, looking at her. 'Fair enough?'

'All right,' Andrea said. 'Fair enough.' She found herself smiling at him. She could trust him. There was inside the mild exuberance a gentleness and a core of stability which was not at all like the stability he was already bringing her

91

to impatience with in other men.

The Nitelite was in an old house a couple of streets away. They walked to it. Most of the activity seemed to be concentrated on the ground floor, as Andrea found when she went upstairs to the ladies' cloakroom and, losing her way, wandered through a succession of lighted but sparsely furnished rooms before coming upon a small gaming room where a dozen absorbed people were sitting round a chemin de fer table. Downstairs was a small bar and on the other side of the entrance hall two rooms knocked into one with some dining-tables, a small dance-floor and a bored trio who played soft music that was nevertheless deafening in the confined space. It was all a little shabby and run-down and Philip intimated as much as he signed them in and spoke to a man in a dinner jacket in the hall.

'You know, it really is time you spent a bit more money on this place, Bert. Won't the profits stand it?'

'What profits would they be, Philip?'

'Oh God, he breaks my heart.'

Andrea wrote her name in the visitors' book half a dozen lines below someone who had signed in as 'Cleopatra, Queen of the Nile', and Philip led the way into the big room. Only three or four of the tables were occupied and the band played to an empty floor.

'It must be Christmas.'

'Give it another half-hour,' Harry said. 'When the pubs get properly turned out.'

'Then we'll get those who don't want to go home and those with no homes to go to. You know, the more I see of this place the less I think people *are* at their best at this time of night.'

Andrea couldn't tell whether his apparent moroseness was a genuine shift of mood or affectation.

'Do you come often?'

'This is the second time in about six months. It's a handy bolt-hole for an after-hours drink if the talk's going well and the company's interesting.'

'Don't sit too far back,' Harry said. 'We'll get the smell of the kitchen.'

'Succulent dawn-caught Irish prawns fried in crisp golden batter. Prime Angus steak garnished with dew-drenched mushrooms and tender green peas.'

'Is that the language of the menu?'

Philip laughed. 'There ain't no menu. Bert doesn't waste money on unnecessary trimmings like that. Scampi and chips. Steak and chips. You don't need it written down.'

A waitress came and took their order for drinks. A few more people drifted in. The band stepped up its tempo as two or three couples began to dance. Ruth was engaging Harry in a long intense conversation, her words lost under the throb of the music. Philip drummed lightly with his fingers on the table, his gaze flitting here and there, taking all in. They sat this way for some minutes. Philip had either lost interest in conversation for the time being or found it irksome to try to talk against that background of noise. Andrea didn't feel ignored. She watched him, feeling curiously sorry about the air of purposelessness with which the circumstances had momentarily invested him. She didn't think he was a restless, rootless man of the type who would end up at places like the Nitelite evening after evening, searching for something that wasn't to be found; though she felt there would be in him discontent and concern. He had a conscience. How strong it was she was to find out later. At the moment she found herself wanting to see him in a context of meaningful activity, doing the things he did well. He was probably a good teacher, questioning and analytical, rather than simply instructive. She wondered about his wife, if she was just the mother of his children and custodian of his domestic comfort or all that and the sharer of his hopes, ambitions and ideas as well.

He caught her looking at him and was for a second taken aback by the realisation that she had been watching him for some time. Then he smiled.

'I was going to say "a penny for them" but since they're about me I'll make it threepence.'

'Conceited man.'

'No, unsure enough of myself to be interested in what other people think of me.'

'I don't believe you.'

He shifted in his chair, twisting his shoulders so that he looked her full in the face. 'Don't you, really?'

She didn't know what to say so she shook her head and returned his gaze over the rim of her glass in what she hoped was a sardonic fashion.

'Do you think I'm one of these fellows with all the answers?'

'I think you know what you're about.'

'I find it very important that you shouldn't think that,' he said. 'Though I must impress upon you the high quality of my confusion.' The self-mockery in his smile was underlaid by a gravity Andrea found disturbingly touching.

The trio began to play a slow foxtrot. Philip pushed his chair back. 'Come on. I can just about manage this.'

The tune was one Andrea knew but couldn't put a name to. She hummed it as they began to move round the floor. The tweed of his jacket was soft under her hands. He was dressed like a million other schoolmasters, casually, in sports coat and dark grey slacks, but his clothes were well pressed and his shirt was clean. He kept his distance, holding her without familiarity and just firmly enough to direct her movements.

'Anyway,' he said all at once, 'who are you?'

'Me?' She was surprised.

'Yes, you.'

'Andrea Warner,' she said lightly. 'Spinster of this parish. Secretary to Mr Simpkins of J. S. Simpkins and Son, Engineers.'

'Why aren't you married?'

'I was never asked by the right man at the right time in the right place.'

'With the right man it's always the right time and place, isn't it?'

'Perhaps.'

'H'mm. Do you want to get married?'

'I don't think it's something one should do for the sake of it, do you?'

'There's many a woman done it for just that reason.'

'I'm not many a woman.'

'No. I expect wives hate you.'

'Why should they?'

'Because you're a menace.'

'It had never occurred to me. Would your wife hate me?'

'There might be the tiniest twinge of something not altogether pleasant if she could see us now.'

'Only that?'

'She's not a jealous woman.'

'Perhaps she has no reason to be.'

'Jealousy's not usually founded on reason.'

'I wouldn't know.'

'Aren't you the jealous type, either?'

'I can't remember having occasion to be.'

'What about George?'

'What about him?'

'Where does he fit into the picture?'

'He's a friend of the family.'

'Does he want to marry you?'

'You want to know too much.'

'Sorry.'

'That's all right.'

As they got back to their table the drum rolled and the saxophonist spoke into the microphone.

'Good evening, ladies and gentlemen. Welcome to the Nitelite, Cressley's premier wining, dining and dancing centre. For those who feel lucky there's gaming in the upstairs casino. For those who want to stay put and enjoy a drink and good food, it's cabaret time.'

'Oh, my God,' Philip said. Harry and Ruth had disappeared. 'Come on.'

'Where?'

'Across into the bar. You don't want to hear this, do you?'

'Yes. Why not?'

He subsided into his chair. 'Be it on your own head.'

A girl with platinum-coloured hair and heavy make-up, wearing a yellow and orange frock, appeared through a curtained entrance on the far side of the dance floor. She began to belt out an up-tempo Lena Horne speciality through a hand microphone as she jigged along the perimeter of tables.

'She's not bad,' Andrea said at the end of the first number.

'I always feel sorry for the poor bitches, performing night in, night out in front of half-drunken yobs.'

'They choose the life, don't they? And everybody's got to start somewhere on the long climb to the top.'

'And at the top the yobs wear diamonds and dinner jackets.'

'Sssh!' Andrea said.

The girl finished her act and went off to applause enthusiastically led by two burly red-faced youths sitting behind Andrea and Philip.

'Make their night if they can get an introduction to her,' Philip said.

'And why not? Don't be a killjoy.'

'You should hear the comedians Bert hires. They're the bitter end. Anyway, come on, now, let's find the others.'

They met Bert in the doorway.

'How did you like the cabaret, Philip?'

'Amazing, Bert. I don't know where you find them. But don't you think that bandleader could do with a new script?'

'What d'you mean?'

' "Cressley's premier wining, dining and dancing centre" indeed!'

'It's what the customers go for, Philip. You've got to sell the product to them.'

'You'd sell it better with a piece of soap in the men's bog and a new carpet down here.'

'Oh, you,' Bert said. 'You'd have me bankrupt in a week.'

'I'll give you another six months at this rate.'

'We're establishing a regular clientele.'

'I hope you don't mean me. My three or four beers won't keep you afloat, even on the outrageous prices you charge.'

'No, we've got people who come here two or three times a week, have a meal and a few drinks and play cards upstairs.'

'God help them. Have they nothing else to do?'

'They're people who like a bit of fun, Philip. Not dreary Dannies like you.' He prodded Philip lightly between the ribs with his forefinger and went away, chuckling.

'Dreary Danny, indeed,' Philip said. 'You can't insult him, you know. And I believe he actually likes me. I can't imagine why.'

In the bar Harry was solemnly handing sixpences to Ruth, who fed them into a fruit machine. Every time she got two coins in return she clapped her hands and squealed with pleasure. Andrea, who had wondered what it took to make her smile, watched as she went on feeding the money back till it was all gone.

'Oh! I haven't any more sixpences.'

'Neither have I,' Harry said. 'That's ten bob it's swallowed, not including the winnings.'

'It hasn't paid a jackpot since Adam was a lad,' Philip said. 'How do you think Bert keeps his head above water?'

He felt in his pocket and handed Andrea sixpence. 'Here, try your luck.'

Andrea dropped the coin into the slot and pulled the handle. The tumblers rolled and stopped. Ruth gave a startled 'Oh!' punctuating the pause before the clatter of coins into the basin.

Heads turned at the bar. Ruth said, 'Oh! Oh! And with just one sixpence. Oh! It's not fair.'

Philip laughed. 'Scoop it out and count it. You've got the jackpot.'

There was three pounds fifteen, in tokens which were supposed to be exchanged for goods; but Philip persuaded the barmaid to give them money for them. Ruth went on making exclamations of disappointment. 'After all that,

Harry, and she gets it with her first go.'

Andrea hoped she wasn't going to be tiresome about it. She pushed the money to Philip. 'Here you are.'

'No, no. It's yours.'

'It was your coin.'

Philip poked a sixpence out of the loose change. 'I'll take back my original investment.'

'Look, you must take——'

'No, I've told you, it's yours.'

'Then I must give Ruth some of it.'

'No, why should you?' Ruth said.

Yes, why should I? Andrea thought. But she insisted. 'After all, you did more or less set it up with your money.'

'My money,' Harry said.

'Oh, don't be so stuffy,' Ruth snapped crossly. Her evening was quite spoiled.

Andrea handed her a pound note. 'Here, you take this.'

'I couldn't.'

'Go on. It's only fair.'

'Well, if you really want to.'

'Yes, I really do.'

Philip gave Andrea an amused look as Ruth pocketed the note. 'And now, children, if everybody's happy, I think it's time I took Andrea home.'

Harry looked at his watch. 'I'm ready as well.'

They walked to the car-park, two by two. It was a dry night, with a high clear sky, but cold. Philip stopped by a Mini parked near the entrance and exchanged a few last words with Harry before opening the door for Andrea.

'Now, where do you live?'

She gave him directions and said, 'I hope it's not out of your way.'

'It is, actually, but it doesn't matter.'

He started to reverse then held the car on the clutch as a white Rover 2000 passed behind them and turned on to the street.

'Is that Harry and Ruth?'

'Yes. Nice car, isn't it?'

'What does Harry do?'

'Do you know Mallabys, the carpet people on the market? Harry's the son of the house. Wherever there's a market in this part of the West Riding you'll find one of Harry's family flogging top-grade carpets at give-away prices.'

'Now you mention it, I think I've seen him before.'

'More than likely. He's a nice lad. A good business man, no doubt, but he's developed an awareness of enormous cultural inadequacies. Get him talking after a few drinks and he'll tell you that money isn't everything and what he misses is not having had a real education and read the right books.'

'Not married?'

'No.' He turned his head and grinned at her. 'Not a bad catch. Amiable disposition, bags of loot.'

'I'll let that pass.'

'Yes. Actually, he doesn't seem to have much interest in sex.'

'Is that why he goes for the intense arty types like Ruth?'

'Probably. I don't quite know where he met her. She's turned up with him a couple of times.'

'An odd girl.'

'Oh yes, very. She's a trainee teacher at the Art College. Full of all the current left-wing attitudes but every inch a little bourgeois at heart. All she needs is to catch somebody like Harry and then just watch her change her style.'

'Is that likely?'

'Her and Harry? I don't know. Sillier things have happened. I expect she has a certain fascination for him in the things she says. Politically, for instance, he's always worked from the very simple standpoint of the defence of his own immediate interests, which, of course, is how he's been brought up.'

'I sometimes think most people are like that.'

'Oh, no doubt. The "have nots" demand more and the "haves" defend what they've got. It's economics that creates this strange mixture of bedfellows, because the average

Labour voter, for instance, is as reactionary as most Tories. He's a hanger, a flogger, a keeper down of homosexuals and an advocate of sending the black man back where he came from. The only thing is, there's a bloody sight more excuse for his thinking that way than there is for the others.'

'Why?'

'Why? Because even now he's still a victim himself. Whenever the crunch comes and it's backs to the wall he's the one with his shoulder-blades jammed up hard against the brickwork. He's got no room for manoeuvre.'

'You must admit they haven't done badly over the past few years. It's people like my father—the clerks—who've lost their status and quite a bit of their standard of living.'

'Yes, yes, yes,' Philip said. 'You're like a great many more people who argue these matters in the light of the last twenty years. You must see the situation in the context of a hundred years, a century of industrial exploitation.'

'But why? Times change and politics must change with them.'

'What made them change? The Tory of fifty years ago wouldn't recognise the Tory of today. He'd think he was bolshy. But it's only happened because of constant pressure from the other side. They're retreating all the time, because they have to. History just isn't on their side.'

'Well, we certainly know whose side you're on.'

'I told you earlier that I wasn't sure about as many things as you seemed to think. I'm sure about what I've just said, though. It's not politics in that sense—and you can fire shots at it as soon as you bring personalities and policies into it—but it's an inevitable transformation in the way men live, and as far as the greater good's concerned, it's progress.'

Though much of what she had always thought reacted against his arguments Andrea was impressed by his fervour.

'You should go in for politics,' she said.

'Because I believe in something as basic as that? Does a

100

religious man necessarily have to become a priest? Anyway, I'm not a political animal, just a human being. I'm prepared to see all sides of an immediate question. That's where the confusion comes in.' He grinned at her again.

'You'd probably be good on the town council, though.'

'I wonder.'

'Mr Simpkins, my boss, is a councillor. An alderman, actually.'

'Oh, *that* Simpkins. He stands as Independent, doesn't he?'

'Yes.'

'That means Conservative, of course.'

'Why should it necessarily?'

'He'd be on the other side otherwise, wouldn't he?'

'Perhaps he really is independent.'

'Oh, all right, then,' Philip said, 'I'll allow him a bit of radical liberal feeling.'

'I rather think Mr Simpkins wouldn't need *you* to allow him anything.'

It came out much more tartly than she'd intended and Philip said, 'Oh, dear!'

'I'm sorry,' Andrea said. 'I didn't mean it quite like that.'

'Nice man, is he?'

'I think so.'

'H'mm. But it won't do, you know.'

'What?'

'What you just said. It echoes the assumptions of a great many people in a town like this. The man who owns the mill or the factory has controlled their welfare for so long that there's an instinctive revulsion against questioning his judgement on anything.'

'I don't quite follow you.'

'It's the old master and man complex. They still look up to the boss. Haven't you heard them say that a man who can look after his own money is the best man to look after the public's?'

'Oh, yes.'

'And, my God, we should have disproved that one before

101

now. But as far as the cat looking at the king goes, I'd say that your Mr Simpkins probably came into a business that his father or grandfather had built up before him.'

'So I believe.'

'Whereas I, though nobody, pulled myself up out of a workman's cottage, into grammar school, through university and into my profession. And though, as you intimated before, it's one of those callings that don't command the respect they did before the war, it still means that I can stand on my right to challenge Mr Simpkins on any issue I think fit and proper.'

It was lightly delivered but she took it as the rebuke it was, and which she probably deserved.

'Don't let me overshoot, will you?'

'No, you turn right at the junction, then it's not far. I'm sorry I'm taking you so far out of your way. Will your wife be wondering where you've got to?'

'She'll be in bed if she's got any sense. She knows that Tuesday evenings are apt to drag out a bit.'

'She must be an understanding woman.'

'Oh, come now. I don't go out on the razzle every night in the week.'

'I didn't mean to imply that you did.'

'And I don't usually end up driving strange young women home, either.'

'Why the change of habit?' Andrea asked, and could have slapped herself the instant the words were out. But she was interested in the answer.

'I suppose I find you interesting,' Philip said. 'I think somebody ought to take you in hand.'

'I beg your pardon.'

'There's good material in you but you work from too many inbuilt assumptions.'

'And don't you?'

'Yes, but I've examined mine and they belong to the twentieth century. Yours don't.'

She gasped at his arrogance and said coldly, 'Just here, on the left.'

102

'Shall I take you to the door or drop you on the corner?'

'It doesn't matter. There's nobody watching me. But it'll be easier for you if you stop at the end.'

He pulled in to the kerb and let the engine run.

'Well.'

'Thank you very much.'

'Thank you for coming with us. It made a very nice evening.'

'I'm glad you think so.' Her hand was trying to open the door. Philip said,

'You're not going away mad, are you?'

'Why should you think that?'

'I've hurt your feelings. I didn't mean to. I'm used to people who speak plainly, without striking attitudes ... There I go again. Every time I open my mouth to you I put my boot in it.'

Her anger couldn't last. She said, 'It's all right. I think I was the one who got the conversation on to the wrong track.'

'We'll perhaps try again sometime, eh?'

'Yes, all right.'

He took her right hand, squeezed it briefly and said,

'Goodnight, love. Take care.'

He drove quietly away as she walked along the avenue. Everyone was in bed. As she slid her key into the lock she thought that it was foolish of her, because it was all of no consequence; yet that 'goodnight, love' sang gently in her mind and like a tune that persists in lingering, it would not go away.

And there, she was to think on one of many desolate future days, was the first moment of danger, the time when she could have backed away and gone unscathed. But from how far off did you see liking turning to loving? At what stage did tender fondness become something insupportable?

She could defend against an accusation of their being

103

sinister her reasons for wishing that George would not want to take her to the next film show. He didn't stand up well beside Philip, or even, in another way, the taciturn Harry; and the kind of conversation she'd had with Philip wasn't likely to recur with him present. She had a right to choose her company, had she not?

But George came and when she suggested afterwards that they go for a drink he hum'd and ha'd in a way that made her want to stamp her foot. He was a man who circumscribed his life with regular habits; they were his shield against the chaos outside. He would prefer now to take her home and drink coffee and talk civilised clichés with her parents, then leave early for bed, having forged one more link in the chain of custom which bound them together in the eyes of her mother particularly. Not that it was a conscious plan of campaign, she thought, but more an instinctive turning towards an environment in which he was approved of and away from a less predictable world where, in her eyes, anyway, he somehow fell short.

A fine drizzle was falling. Andrea had nothing to cover her hair and she was standing there in a mounting irritation as Philip came out of the hall with Harry.

'Hello, you two. You're getting wet. Are you coming round for a quick one?'

George gave in. 'All right, then. But I don't want to be too late.'

'You can't possibly be all that late, George,' Andrea said. 'The licensing laws will take care of that.'

They followed the two men striding through the rain. Philip turned from the bar as they went into the lounge of the pub.

'What'll you have?'

'No, no, let me,' Harry said.

Philip grinned. 'By all means.'

Andrea glanced at George's expressionless face. It was another thing about him that annoyed her, his backwardness at coming forward when it came to buying drinks. He wasn't much of a drinking man and he just didn't seem to grasp the principle of paying in his turn. It *was* his turn, too. Andrea distinctly remembered Philip's buying drinks for both of them the last time they were all together. She opened her bag.

'Why not let me? I had a windfall. Remember?'

Philip shook his head. 'I don't remember a thing about it.'

'A windfall?' George said.

'I got the jackpot from a one-armed bandit at the Nitelite.'

'When was that?'

'A fortnight ago. I went after the show with Philip and Harry and another girl.'

'You never mentioned it.'

'No, I couldn't have if you didn't know.'

'No Nitelite tonight,' Harry said, turning and handing round the glasses. 'I've to be up bright and early in the morning.'

'Are you off journeying?' Philip asked.

'Hull. We've opened a new place there.'

'Can you really sell carpets all that cheaper than anybody else?' George said.

'You compare the prices.'

'How do you do it?'

'Buy and sell direct, don't waste money on posh premises and rely on a bigger turnover.'

'Do you skimp on the quality, though?'

Harry took it blandly. 'Compare that as well. What we sell new is as good as you'll get anywhere. When it's damaged goods we tell you, and that goes cheaper still. In a way, that's the best line we handle; stuff that's been in a flood or a fire. Hardly touched, but it can't be put out as new.'

'I like to pay a good price and get the real thing,' George said. Andrea wondered if he could know how offensive his line of conversation sounded.

'A Wilton or an Axminster, at a big discount, with maybe no more of a mark than you can hide under the sideboard or hearthrug?' Harry said. 'Look at the money you save, and who's to know the difference?'

'I'd know,' George said. 'No, I don't like damaged goods.'

For some reason Andrea's heart seemed to miss a beat. She glanced quickly at George but his face was impassive.

'I'm a bit like that meself,' Harry said, 'but I think it's daft unless you've got plenty of money to chuck around.'

'I can't help it,' George said. 'It's the way I am.'

Andrea excused herself and went to the ladies' cloak-room. She stood in the middle of the floor, her pulse racing. Her cheeks felt hot to the backs of her hands and when she turned to the glass over the washbasins she could see the dull spot of colour on each cheekbone. George's remark had surely contained no deep underlying significance; and even if it had, how did it apply to her? She was acting like someone with a guilty conscience. Did she think it could apply in the future. Even that it *might*?

'Come on now, young woman' she said. 'What's the matter with you?'

The face in the glass gave no answer.

7

The dominant features of Andrea's home were neatness and calm. In a family of a boy and two girls, raised voices were not a thing she remembered. Reason—which was a way of describing right behaviour—had always seemed to enter an issue before passions could get out of hand. Her parents were quiet, careful people, in their fifties now. She supposed their marriage to be as successful as one could wish for. They had never had a lot of money—Andrea's mother had none of her own, though her brother had built up a small chain of prosperous grocery shops in and about the town, and her husband, after thirty years with Dawson Whittaker's, had risen no higher than second-in-command of the accounts department under the Company Secretary —though there had always been enough for their modest plans and pleasures, and during the last ten years they had owned a series of small motor cars, each bought new and carefully changed at the age and mileage calculated to yield the best trade-in price. Mr and Mrs Warner lived inter-linked lives which allowed each to follow his innocuous pleasures. Mrs Warner was interested in church activities and Mr Warner read a lot. He devoured books—novels, light biographies and travel stories—at the rate of six or seven a week. He hardly ever bought a book, but borrowed them from the public library and the local branch of Boots'. Every evening, when high tea was over and he had finished his thorough scrutiny of the *Yorkshire Post*, he would read for three or four hours. When he and Andrea's mother did talk it was to discuss immediate affairs. On all wider issues they were in agreement. They voted Conservative, were members of the Church of England, admired the Royal Family and thought Winston Churchill and Field Marshal Lord Montgomery the two greatest Englishmen of the past fifty years. They were alike in thinking that hanging was the only deterrent to murder, and that if a man took a life he deserved to forfeit his own anyway. All this they believed without fuss, as well as agreeing that too many television programmes (from the BBC especially) were unnecessarily disrespectful to established institutions and the traditional British way of life and when they weren't being this they dwelt on sex in a thoroughly unwholesome, if not immoral, way. There was too much sex about altogether. It was described in blatant detail in too many of the novels Mr Warner brought home nowadays, and it was thrown at you from the pages of magazines and newspapers, in the orientation of the advertisements as well as in the articles and reports. The Warners lived in an increasingly immodest world. They gently turned their faces from it and were thankful that they had brought their children up well.

Andrea's brother, Geoffrey, was an industrial chemist, who worked for a steel firm in Sheffield and lived there with his wife and small daughter. A thin, highly strung man, he had had rheumatic fever as a boy and surprised many people who knew him by the tenacity and application he showed in overcoming this setback and going on to excel in his final years at school. Julie, Andrea's younger sister, most closely resembled their mother in the doll-like prettiness of her features. She had wanted to be a model but was now working as a first sales in the women's coat and dress shop of Granger's, the department store, and displaying their clothes on her slim, long-legged body only during their annual spring exhibition. Julie had a boy friend to whom, unlike Andrea and George, she had every intention of becoming engaged and marrying. Bob Harvey's family owned a yarn-spinning mill in Cressley; they were people of substance and the Warners approved of the match. It seemed settled and the formalities were something to be looked forward to with pleasurable anticipation. What anxiety Mrs Warner felt about her children's futures could be concentrated now on Andrea, who seemed irritatingly content to carry on as she was doing for ever.

She had, she knew, always been the one they could worry about least. Geoffrey's illness and, later, Julie's sudden obsession with becoming a model were the kind of causes for concern she had never given them. On this latter issue they had come nearer to open acrimony than at any time Andrea could remember. Julie wanted to tackle the matter seriously by going to live in London and taking a course at a school of modelling.

'I've tried to convince Mummy that it's all perfectly respectable,' she said. 'I told her there's always a chance I'd end up married to an Italian count, but either she doesn't approve of Italian counts or she doubts my ability to make a real success of the job.'

'I think it's partly London,' Andrea said. 'It's two places to Mummy. One is the seat of government and all that's worthy and respectable; the other is an underworld that lures young girls from the provinces and condemns them to lives of unspeakable degradation.'

'I believe she thinks I'd very likely find myself modelling underclothes or even posing naked.'

She was undressing in her room and Andrea, called in for a good night chat, lay back on the bed and looked at her sister as she stood in bra and pants before the mirror.

'You'd do either very well.'

Julie giggled. 'I bet I could charm an Italian count, too, given the chance.'

'Yes.' They laughed together.

'I have got a good figure, haven't I, Andy?'

'Lovely.'

'It's not as good as yours, though.'

'Oh, come on.'

'Well, it might be now; but what I mean is you're the type to stay slim and willowy. I shall get all plump and

109

fleshy as soon as I have a couple of babies. I just know it.'

'I thought models were like ballet dancers; they put their careers before anything else.'

'That's what bothers me. I think underneath it all I'm a maternal type. Sooner or later I'll fall in love with somebody and want some kids.' She undressed fully, slipping her nightgown over her head, and picked up her hairbrush. 'I'd prefer whoever it is to be well-off, though. I don't fancy motherhood in squalor.'

Andrea laughed. 'Do you really mean all this?'

'Of course I do.' Julie looked at her through the dressing-table glass, her eyes wide and serious. 'I'd like three children at least, preferably more.'

'So much for your career.'

'Yes, I'm afraid you're right.' She spun round on the stool. 'Don't you want to get married and have a family?'

'Eventually, I suppose.'

'Will you marry George?'

'I shouldn't think so.'

'Why not?'

'I don't love him and I wouldn't get married for the sake of it.'

Julie pondered. 'I think I might. I mean for the sake of having children.'

'Well, you are full of surprises. Why all the tension and strain about a modelling career if you're planning maternity in a few years?'

'Well, there was a matter of principle involved, and it would have been fascinating for a time.' She paused, pulled some fine hairs out of her brush, then said with her eyes down, 'Andy, are you a virgin?'

Andrea would have liked to say no. She was sure a confession like that would have impressed Julie. But she had to tell the truth.

'Yes.'

'That is the truth, isn't it?' Julie asked. 'I mean, I am, but I wondered if you, being a bit older, might not have——'

110

'No,' Andrea said. 'I haven't.'

'Is there any particular reason?'

'It's just never arisen. I mean, in the circumstances where I might have I didn't want to.'

'You don't think it's wrong outside marriage, then?'

'Not in principle. I think you'd have to take each case on its merits. I wouldn't do it for the sake of it any more than I'd get married that way. And I'd want to know the motives of the man—even if he were an Italian count.' She smiled, but Julie was still looking serious.

'All the people in the magazines—you know, the advice columns—they say no, don't do it.'

'Well, they must, mustn't they?'

'I suppose so.'

On a sudden thought, Andrea said, 'You haven't got somebody at the moment who wants you——?'

'Oh, no, no ... No, it's just that you don't find out about these things unless you talk about them sometimes.'

Andrea sat up. 'Well, for God's sake, Julie, if ever you do, just take care, that's all.'

'The trouble is, what exactly do people mean by taking care? How do you know what's safe and what isn't? I mean, young people these days are supposed to be so sophisticated and knowledgeable but girls go on having babies when they shouldn't, don't they?'

'Well, I haven't made a study of it myself,' Andrea said. 'I expect it's not supposed to bother us because we're such well brought-up young women.'

Innocent conversations like that became something belonging to the period she privately thought of as 'BP'—Before Philip—when she had nothing to hide and the future was a time in which anything could happen.

That last year of her freedom drew towards its close. The months passed quickly enough though Andrea was counting the days between film shows and disliking the long empty week in the middle. George seemed to lose interest and was absent more often than not. One night there was neither him, Harry nor Ruth and Andrea found herself alone with Philip.

'I'd ask you to come for a drink but I'm wondering if it would be wise.'

'Why?'

'In a group we're more or less covered; with just the two of us it looks less innocent.'

'Oh, I see. Do you mind?'

'No, not particularly, if you don't.'

'Well, why not let's risk it?'

He smiled. He had, for her, a smile of rare charm. 'Okay. Only, we'll go to another pub, eh?'

'Just as you like.'

They drove out of town and stopped at a small pub with a warm glow of red-shaded lights coming from its windows.

'You realise, of course,' Andrea said, 'that if we're seen here it'll look a lot less innocent than in the other place.'

'I suppose so. It's stupid, isn't it, the pressures convention puts on your freedom.'

'But we are innocent, anyway.'

'Oh, we can defend ourselves against the accusation. It's when you're convicted by gossip without a charge being brought that's the trouble. A person like that who saw us in the King's Arms would say we were being brazen about it; the same person seeing us here would take our coming out of the way as proof that we'd something to hide.'

'Well, if we can't win,' Andrea said, 'we may as well press on regardless.'

The lounge bar was quiet, with a couple sitting in one corner and two men standing at the bar counter. Across the serving area Andrea could see darts thudding into a board on the wall of the other room. Philip came to her with the drinks and sat down on a stool across the table from her, his back to the room.

'It's funny,' he said, 'once you get on to a subject ... I was thinking up at the bar about a publican friend of mine who told me how he could pick out the illicit couples from

112

the genuine ones.'

'Go on.'

'Well, I expect it presupposes that the illicit ones either haven't been out together before or they don't meet very often. But they, according to my watchful friend, come into a pub, pick out a table, go to it together, and then the man asks the woman what she wants before he goes to the bar. With a genuine couple the man points out a place to sit in, lets the woman go and comes to the bar without asking. If he's drinking beer and she's on shorts, he'll order his own drink first and take a sip while he's waiting for the other glass.'

'All it suggests to me is that illicit lovers are more courteous and considerate than husbands.'

Philip laughed, but there was something not quite free and unembarrassed in its tone.

'Are you feeling sensitive about it?'

'I must admit that the conversation has set up a certain self-consciousness.'

'I'm sorry. It was my fault for accepting so eagerly. You can take me home, if you want to, as soon as I've finished this.'

He shook his head. 'No, no, this is silly. Let's talk about something else.'

'Right, then, what shall it be?'

But he was looking at her directly, dark eyes level under dark eyebrows. She met his gaze, looked away then back and smiled in what she hoped was a bright inconsequential way.

'Well?'

'It won't do, will it?'

'I'm afraid I don't know what you mean.'

'I mean that in the majority of cases there's good reason for people thinking as they do when they see a man and woman together as we are.'

'Do you always over-analyse situations and give the answers in riddles?'

He frowned as though disappointed that she was forcing

113

him to be unwillingly explicit. He toyed with a beer mat and said, his eyes now watching the movements of his fingers,

'Men and women have more to offer one another than sexual attraction. Right?'

'Some have.'

'But the difference in sex is still there—a permanent thing —and unless there is a sexual attraction, however latent, or some specialised interest to offer, it's much less complicated to seek the friendship of other men (for a man) where the basic consideration between men and women doesn't exist to cloud the issues.'

'In other words, you don't believe in platonic friendships between men and women?'

'Oh yes, of course. With the wife of a friend, for instance, or with a colleague. But it's something that comes about through contributory circumstances, not a thing one looks for.'

'And you don't believe,' Andrea said, 'that I could be sitting here just now except on a basis of sexual attraction?'

His eyes flickered up to her face for a second. He hesitated before speaking.

'I couldn't presume to speak for you, of course.'

'I'm sorry. I gathered you were outlining a general rule.'

'I was more trying to analyse my own position.'

'Which exists in a context of my sexual attractiveness. Is that what you mean?'

'Let me put it this way ... Oh, hell! How the devil did I get started on all this?' He threw down the beer mat then immediately picked it up again. Andrea's pulse had started to race, as it had, inexplicably, on that night in the King's Arms. He must notice her excitement, she thought, though the way she was behaving he would probably mistake it for anger at his presumptuousness. 'Look,' he finally said, 'if you were an ugly girl of equal intelligence you wouldn't be sitting there now. Nor would you be were you any one of hundreds of pretty girls, but not you.'

'Thank you.'

He grunted and drank some of his beer.

'Why do I have to talk?' he said. 'There are any number of men who would have chatted you up brightly then proved the point by trying to kiss you in the car.'

'But I'm not here with them, am I?'

And it's not too late for you to try, her mind was saying. He probably wouldn't now because he thought he'd talked too much and embarrassed her as well as himself. But all she wanted was that he should. She ought not to, but she did. She ought to feel ashamed or at least fearful. She ought to know that this yearning had the making of a pain that would hurt like hell; but all she did know was the terrible joy that was in her. How could she stop it from showing so that he wouldn't take fright and run away?

She stood up, said 'Excuse me, please,' and walked across the room on tipsy legs.

He was buying cigarettes when she came back.

'Ready?'

'Are they closing now?'

'I'm afraid so. I'd forgotten it was half an hour earlier outside the town.'

They went out. He unlocked the car and opened the passenger's door for her. She shivered and pulled her coat more closely about her.

'Cold?'

'A bit.'

'The heat will come through in a minute or two.'

He drove in silence back the way they had come till they reached the junction with the main road.

'Do you know the way?'

'Yes. If you go straight across here you needn't go back through the town.'

She could feel tension in him as he drove. He was like a man in a temper and he swore almost savagely as a car on a bend blinded him momentarily with its undipped head-lights. They began to climb and the town opened out below them on the left as strings of lights in the valley and along the far hillsides. A stretch of unlighted upland road lay before them. Philip flicked on his own headlamps, picking out rough grass banks and stone walls.

'Are you sure we're going the right way?'

'Yes, quite sure.'

'It seems a long way round.'

'It isn't really. I won't get you lost. Don't worry.'

He made a noise in his throat then relapsed into silence, driving fast along the straight road. When they saw streetlights ahead of them he said suddenly, 'Oh, hell, I shall have to stop the car.'

She braced herself with her legs as he braked and pulled in to the verge. He switched off the engine and turned in his seat.

'Would you like a cigarette?'

'Not just now, thank you.'

'We hardly know each other...' She said nothing. 'And I'm married ... I'm happily married. I have a good wife and two fine children...'

Still there was nothing she could find to say. He gave an impatient exclamation, more a violent release of breath than any recognisable word, and twisted himself round to look forward through the windscreen. A car came over the far rise and down the hill towards them, travelling very fast. Its headlamps lit them up then flashed by, leaving them once more in darkness. As the angry buzz of the engine died Philip touched the dashboard. Andrea thought he was about to start the car.

'Philip...'

He turned his head to look at her again. She put her hand on his arm. He lifted it, kissed the palm, then held it against his cheek. Andrea was overwhelmed. It was, beyond any other he could have chosen, an action which in its reticence and simplicity took her straight to the edge of tears.

'It's funny,' he said in a moment. 'The warnings are all about lust; but it's tenderness that's the real enemy.'

She looked away from him and across at the lights of the town.

'But I'm not sorry,' he said, releasing her hand. 'You

116

hear me, Andrea? I said I'm not sorry.'

She nodded. 'Yes, I hear you.'

He switched on the ignition and started the car. Then, driving fast again in silence, he took her quickly home.

'Easy does it,' she warned herself. 'Nice and easy.' She must hang on and not let it show; watch for those seductive moments when he swam in between her and what she was doing: the gaps in Mr Simpkins' dictation which were suddenly full of his voice; the middle distances against which her unfocused eyes saw his face, earnest, puzzled, painfully sincere, as his mind struggled with the same ethical considerations that in the still rational centre of her consciousness dismayed her.

'You'd think,' he said to her in those early days, 'that with all the greed and hatred and malice, the violence and death, there is in the world, a little more genuine love wouldn't come amiss. And the most bitter irony is that if we were both free what we feel for each other would be regarded with benign approval.'

'My mother's been waiting for it to happen to me for years,' Andrea said.

'It's how to stop it being destructive.'

'Look, darling: I love you but you're married to someone else. That's my bad luck. I'm no home-wrecker and I don't want to take you away from your family. There can't be much future in it but I'll take what you can give me for as long as you can give it. It seems to me that we should be able to have a little happiness together without hurting anyone else.'

'You're a remarkable girl,' Philip said.

'Because I'm not putting pressure on you to run away with me? I don't see what's remarkable about that.' Her voice became lightly chiding. 'I know I'm the one who's supposed to be free but running off with married men isn't a habit with the women in my family.'

'They'd hardly approve of this relationship, either.'

'No, but it's something I'm stuck with, and they don't know about it.'

'Which seems to be the obvious answer. What people don't know about won't hurt them.'

It wasn't really good enough; but, like the time they could spend together, it would have to do.

They were managing to see each other once during the week between shows; not for a whole evening but for a couple of hours after a night-school class which Philip taught. He finished at nine and picked her up in a quiet sidestreet in town. Sometimes, if he was a few minutes late, she would walk round the block, trying not to feel conspicuous and wondering if the headlights of the occasional passing cars belonged to people who knew her.

The numbers of people they both knew seemed legion when it came to choosing pubs where they could sit and talk for an hour without being seen. The roadhouses, and those newly altered places which attracted car trade, they avoided. They seemed to explore the environs of every town between ten and twenty miles from Cressley, looking for less pretentious houses which were nevertheless clean and decent. It was hard to judge them from outside and with the opening of each new door they faced the comparatively unknown. Sometimes they felt conspicuous as the sole occupants of chilly, cavernous best rooms ignored by the midweek regulars; on other occasions they found themselves trapped in tiny lounges, sitting opposite the appraising stares of middle-aged stout-drinking women, where almost every word they uttered could be overheard and any free conversation was impossible. The friendly landlord of one pub they'd liked and gone back to had greeted them as though he remembered them.

'I'm afraid that's the end of that place for a while,' Philip said. 'The next time we'll be drawn into conversation and that would be altogether too dangerous.'

'But they don't know us.'

'They soon would do, and they cotton quick to people like you and me.'

'You make it sound as though the landscape is full of them.'

'You can be damn' sure we're not the only ones. Though we are the only ones we've got to bother about.'

'It's a good thing we have the car.'

'Yes, without it we'd be sunk. "And to what do you attribute the present high rate of immorality. Professor Hackenthwacker?" "To the invention and increasing use of the internal combustion engine, sir!" ... Actual, real, no-holds-barred adultery,' he added, 'is a different thing. In fact, in this heap it's next to impossible for anybody but a pair of three-foot-six dwarfs.'

Andrea giggled.

'Seriously, though, do you realise that in all these weeks I've hardly laid an improper finger on you?'

'Yes, darling.'

'And has it not crossed your mind as a matter to be pondered upon?'

'It's really up to you, darling. You're making the running.'

'Am I?'

'Oh, yes. I'm responsive, but it's entirely up to you to set the pace. You're the only one who knows what's possible for us.'

'I wonder if it's possible that you can love me as much as I love you.'

'More than possible,' she said. 'It's a fact.' His hand was soft on her cheek. She was continually astonished by the intensity of her response to him. Her skin from head to toe was alive with her awareness of him and when they sat apart the air between them seemed to quiver with their longing to touch each other.

'Philip,' she said. 'All those other people we were talking about ... We're different from them, aren't we?'

'I suppose a few of them think they're exceptional.'

'You see, I've never known what it was to feel about anybody as I do about you. I can't imagine that it could happen to me again, so I suppose there must be people it

119

never happens to at all.'

'Poor people.'

'Yes, poor, poor people.'

He sighed. 'Ah, if only we had a place to go. A flat. Or we could get away somewhere for a couple of days.'

'Perhaps we will.'

'Yes. We must be patient. There's time.'

'Is there, though, Philip?'

'I hope so.'

She nestled her head more closely against his shoulder. 'I'm not a religious person and it's not the sort of thing you could ask God for anyway, but every night when I go to bed I want to pray. I want to say, "Oh, please, please, please, just give us a little more time." '

8

With the approach of spring it was not a shortage of time but a lack of opportunity which formed the immediate threat. The film society's season was drawing to a close and not long after that Philip's night-school term would end. He spoke seriously of the difficulties that lay ahead.

'There'll be some summer courses I could tutor, I suppose. And you could put up for the film society committee. That meets in the out-of-season months to get next year's programme set up.'

'But I know so little about it all.'

'You and most other people involved. Women are always welcome because there's work they're best fitted to do; and there's always a couple of vacancies each year. I'm sure you'd get on.'

'Well, if you think I'd be any use.'

'Oh, the hell with that. I don't care how much or how little use you are to them. It's just necessary that we should find any possible legitimate excuse for seeing each other.'

'There's a little time to go, anyway. We shall just have to make the most of it.'

On the evening of the last show but one George came for her. Andrea was washing her face in the bathroom when her mother called upstairs and announced his arrival. She leaned with her hands in the warm soapy water and said, 'Oh, blast! Blast, blast, blast!' When she went down into the sitting-room George was standing in the bay window while her mother, at his side, pointed out some feature of the houses opposite. Her father, apparently feeling that good manners had been served, lifted the book from his lap and was immediately absorbed.

'I didn't know you were coming, George,' she said with forced brightness. 'I'm going out, I'm afraid.'

'Oh?' Her mother turned with him.

'There's a film society show.'

'Oh,' he said again. 'That's what I thought. I thought I'd take you down.'

Andrea found her handbag and opened it to check its contents.

'It's Rene Clair: *Summer Manoeuvres*. I shouldn't have thought it was in your line.'

'I'd no idea what was on,' George said. 'It struck me I hadn't seen you for a while, so I thought I'd call round and take you.'

She couldn't get rid of him. Any more conversation like that and it would be obvious that she wanted to. Her mother was already watching her with the concentration of a mind uncluttered by anything but the preoccupations of everyday life.

'Surely you'd prefer George's company to going alone on the bus, Andrea,' she said. 'We haven't seen much of you lately, George, now you mention it. You know you're always welcome here.' She looked at Andrea with mild rebuke.

'Well then,' Andrea said. 'I'm ready.'

'Will you be bringing George back for coffee?'

Andrea was surprised her mother hadn't invited him directly, over her head.

'It depends on whether we go for a drink instead.'

'Well, do take your key in case your father and I have gone to bed.'

George drove a Ford Cortina, a newer and more expensive car than Philip's. But then, he hadn't a wife and children to keep. She sat silently beside him on the journey into town. Her thoughts were thrashing about, vainly trying to find some plausible excuse for her to be left alone with Philip later. He might think of something when he saw the

122

situation. If he suggested the Nitelite it was unlikely that George would want to go. But she would say yes. So long as Harry was there too. She could hardly go off with Philip alone; nor was he likely to ask her in those circumstances.

'Are you all right?' George said.

'Perfectly. Why?'

'I just thought you were in a funny mood.'

Desperate was more the word for it. She hadn't seen Philip for a week. There were so few opportunities left and here she was, being forced to waste one by this stupid dolt beside her. She felt quite vicious towards him and seethed with frustration and anger as he drove in an infuriating calm.

Philip passed by their seats once before the film and that was all she saw of him. He acknowledged them with a lift of his eyebrows and a quick smile that, to Andrea's eyes, had some quality of oddness in it. Probably because of George's unwelcome presence, she thought. He was nowhere in sight at the end of the show and they left the hall on their own.

'Do you want to go for a drink, then?' George asked.

That at least was accommodating of him. They walked along to the King's Arms. It was just like the first time she'd gone there with George, all those months ago. Except that then Philip was someone unknown who was about to walk into and change her life. Now she waited for him, urged him through the ether, to come to her as ten minutes passed by, then fifteen.

'It looks as if your friends aren't coming tonight,' George said.

'*My* friends? You knew them before me. Or Philip Hart, at least.' She tried to say his name casually. It wasn't easy.

'You've seen a lot more of them than I have recently, though. I've never known Philip all that well.'

'There's still time for them.'

George glanced at his watch and grunted. 'Anyway, let's have another drink.'

As he turned to the bar the door opened and half a dozen

people came in. They seemed at first sight to be all together. Harry and Ruth were there. Harry held the door for the others and Philip entered last of all. The first couple came ahead and walked by. Suddenly afraid of her eyes betraying her, Andrea looked away. She heard Philip say, 'Well, well, the gang's all here,' then, as she turned her head again, 'Do you know everybody, Kate? George Bishop, manfully doing his duty at the bar, and Andrea Warner...' she realised with a sickening lurch of the heart that she was being introduced to Philip's wife.

George, cornered for once, was asking what everybody was drinking. Andrea managed one quick wild glance into Philip's eyes as his wife, hesitating for a moment, asked for a lager and lime.

'I don't get out to pubs much these days,' she said to Andrea, 'and I never quite know what to drink.'

'I usually drink beer,' Andrea said. 'I like it, and it makes it easier on the men.' She actually managed to laugh but she was horrified at the uncertain pitch of her voice. It came from her breathing, over which she seemed to have no control. Philip moved round and stood with them.

'And how's the ravishing Miss Warner tonight?'

'Fine, thank you.'

'Enjoy the film?'

'Very much.'

Oh, you fool, she thought. You're going to make me blush.

'Kate liked it, didn't you, love?'

Philip's wife gave a deprecatory little laugh. 'It was nice to see a bit of colour and style after all that black-and-white television.'

'Don't mind her,' Philip said. 'She likes to play up her moronic side. Actually, she's got quite remarkable taste in cinema. She instinctively likes all the best things.'

'The trouble is,' Kate Hart said, 'I don't notice names, so I can never tell you who did what and when.'

'Don't you think there are so many people about who know the names and nothing else?' Andrea said, forcing herself to look directly at the other as she spoke. She'd had no idea what Philip's wife was like but had carried a vague image of someone physically similar to herself. That was now erased by the reality of a very fair woman, a couple of years older than she was, not beautiful but with a good bone structure and quite fine grey eyes. She made few attempts at glamour or dressing-up: her hair, though shining clean, was simply combed back off her forehead and she wore no make-up apart from a touch of lipstick. Her stockings were thick wool in a diamond pattern and her shoes had low heels.

'The world's full of people who can carry on an apparently knowledgeable conversation from just reading the reviews,' Philip said. 'In fact, we all do it at times.' He took the glass that George handed across. 'May peace be on your house, my good sir.'

He drank quickly, leaving everyone else behind. Andrea counted three pints in the short time left before closing, and when the barmaid rang the bell for last orders he was ready with his empty glass. She had never seen him so animated, either. There was a strange elation in him and his eyes glittered as he dominated the conversation with a flow of vivid but at times oddly elliptical talk. Ill at ease herself, and angry with him for submitting her to this ordeal, she wondered at his high spirits until suddenly, in a flash of understanding, it came to her. He was fond of his wife—had never tried to hide it—and in love with her, Andrea. Here, now, he had both his women together. For a time he could indulge in an illusion of embracing an abundant and generous world. It was false, and he was sure to know it; but though the ground could open beneath his feet tomorrow, for the moment a fullness of life was his.

'Are you all right, Philip?' Kate Hart asked as they prepared to leave.

'What do you mean, am I all right?'

'Would you like me to drive?'

'Do I appear to be drunk, or something?' The question was addressed to his wife but he made it general by looking round the rest of them. 'Just because a man satisfies a reasonable thirst does he have to suffer innuendo from his nearest and dearest? The answer to that is "yes". So be warned, you two bachelors.'

His wife gave him a gentle push towards the door in a manner born of long familiarity. 'Come on. We've got a baby-sitter waiting for us.' She spoke to Andrea, smiling with affectionate tolerance. 'In this mood he's likely to stand talking till he's thrown out.'

George drove Andrea home. She sat in silence again. 'Nearest and dearest,' Philip had said. Oh, she knew it as a popular euphemism for 'wife', but for him to use it tonight had been a bit tactless. Not, though, as much as his not warning her that Kate Hart would be there. The male ego, wallowing in the affections of two women ... No, that was a little harsh. But he had once said to her, semi-facetiously, that were they Moslems their problems wouldn't exist: he could take her as his junior wife. She had wondered then how women tolerated the conditions in such a society and realised wryly that as Philip's mistress, and apparently prepared to carry on in that rôle indefinitely, she was worse off in that she had no official standing or security, emotional or otherwise. As for jealousy, a number two wife had, if anything, less reason for it than a mistress who was faced with thoughts of her man making love to his wife inside their approved relationship while she stood on the sidelines waiting for any illicit crumbs that might fall her way. It was odd that mistresses could apparently tolerate the physical infidelity that wives were supposed to abominate. But did they so easily? Wasn't there surely in every mistress the hope, however hopeless, that someday, somehow, she would have her man for her own? In the meantime, what you could accept or tolerate was measured by your need. And the big question that this evening had presented to her was how did her need for Philip measure against the knowledge of his wife, not as someone spoken of yet unseen, but as a real live person of flesh and blood?

Andrea had never been a cheat. The occasional under-

hand things she had done as a child had, even then, rein-
forced her instinctive belief that what you couldn't get
fairly wasn't worth having. She loved Philip but hated the
conditions in which that love existed. More so now she had
met his wife. She had found herself liking Kate Hart and had
looked with admiration at a photograph of their two young
sons. They were in danger too. Oh yes, she couldn't leave
them out of the reckoning. It was more than one person
versus another and may the best—or the luckiest—win. All
that Philip and his wife had built together was in danger,
because be as undemanding as she could she was by her
acquiescence in this relationship breeding a discontent in
Philip which hadn't existed before.

'Philip seemed in a funny mood tonight, didn't he?'
George said.

'Is everybody in a funny mood tonight except you?'
Andrea said snappily.

'Well, you are for one,' George said with rare critical
candour. 'You have been ever since we set off.'

'Why do you think Philip was funny?'

'The way he got all kind of lit-up.'

'He'd had a few drinks and he was with his wife and
friends. I don't see anything funny about it. Some men like
to let themselves go a bit.'

George ignored the implied jibe. 'I've never seen his wife
before. She seemed a nice woman.'

Yes, she seemed a nice woman. Easier, perhaps, if she
were an obvious bitch, or even an unintelligent slut. Apparently nice woman or not, though, there could be areas of
discontent inside a marriage that outsiders didn't know
about. Even so, it was no function of hers to provide a
whetstone for the sharpening of barbs whose edges should
be blunted by the give and take of a durable relationship.
After all the evasions and the supposed analysis, the basic
question was: how would she like it if someone did the
same thing to her? The answer was that she would feel like
scratching eyes out. And that a woman like Kate Hart
could come to feel like that about her was not the least

distressing aspect of the whole affair.

There was a light behind the curtains of her parents' bed-room when they reached home. The downstairs rooms were in darkness. She said thank you to George and opened the door.

'I thought I might come in for a minute,' he said.

'There doesn't seem to be anyone up.'

'That doesn't matter. It's not late, and I won't stay long.'

She wondered what was in his mind. Couldn't he see she was tired and depressed? She wanted to be rid of him and on her own so that she could think. But then, she thought, there'd be time enough for that.

'All right,' she said, 'just for a few minutes.'

He followed her along the path and stood by as she found her latchkey. Her mother came to the top of the stairs and called down as Andrea switched on the sitting-room light and shut the front door behind them.

'Is that you, Andrea?'

'Yes, it's me.'

'Is George with you?'

'Yes, he's called in for a few minutes.'

'I won't come down again. If there's anything you want you can get it.'

'Righto. Is Julie in?'

'Yes, she's in bed.'

A good fire still burned in the sitting-room grate. She moved the wire-mesh guard and poked the coals into a blaze, saying to George, who was standing about as though he didn't know what to do with himself, 'Well, sit down. You don't have to ask, do you?'

He sank down on to the sofa. 'I like this room.'

'Oh?'

'Yes, it's always cosy and welcoming.'

Even if not all the people who use it are, she thought. He was right, though. She liked the room herself. It was com-pletely conventional, with flower-patterned covers on the deep-cushioned three-piece suite, polished brasses on the oak frame of the fireplace and a bowl of daffodils on the oval table in the window bay; but a place where you could feel warm and relaxed. She thought of all the hours she had spent here, reading, watching television or just chatting about this and that, as her life moved steadily on into its unknown future.

'Would you like some coffee?'

'If you're making some for yourself.'

'I don't know. I think it might keep me awake.'

'Take more than that to spoil my night's sleep.'

Yes, good old George, steady old George, sleeping the sleep of the solid and righteous.

'I've got a better idea.' She opened the bureau cupboard and took out her father's bottle of whisky. 'What about a drop of this?'

'Scotch?' George said. 'D'you think we should?'

'Why not? It won't poison us and it oughtn't to make us drunk on top of what we've already had.' She held up the bottle to the light. 'Half full. He won't miss a couple of tots, and even if he did he wouldn't mind. I bought it for him at Christmas, and after all, I'm a big girl now.' She looked at him. 'Well?'

'All right, then.'

She took two glasses out of the cupboard and fetched water from the kitchen. George protested as she poured. 'Steady on. I've got to drive home and get up in the morning.'

'Oh, hush your mouth and take your liquor like a man.'

'Like Philip Hart, you mean?'

'Why should I mean?'

'I didn't think he held it very well tonight.'

'Now you can't say he was anywhere near drunk. The trouble with you is you can't tell the difference between that and high spirits.'

'I suppose you'll defend him.'

Wariness came to her. 'Why me, particularly?'

'You like him. Anybody can see that.'

'There's no law against that, is there? I like lots of people. Amiable Andrea, that's me.' The alcohol seemed to go instantly to her knees. She slid over the arm of the chair and into the cushion. George had taken one token sip and was now sitting forward, rolling the glass between his hands.

'Well,' she said after a silence, 'what have you got to say? How can I be of service to you? Can I sew a button on your shirt, mend a tear in your jacket or lend you a fiver?'

George took a drink of his whisky. 'You really know what I want to say.'

'Oh, that again.'

'Yes, that again.'

'I thought we'd had it all out before.'

'I told you I'd ask you again ... Look, Andrea, it's silly carrying on like this. Neither of us is getting any younger and all this is wasting time.'

'Oh, God!' Andrea said. 'Neither of us is getting any younger so we'd better marry each other before we find there's nobody left to marry.'

'You're twisting my words.'

'Am I?'

'I didn't mean it like that. You know I love you.'

Did she? What did it mean to him, how was it measured? Did he feel as Philip felt about her, as she felt about Philip? He'd never seriously tried to make love to her. She knew, slumped in the chair as she was now, that she was showing more of her legs than was decent; yet George didn't seem to notice. Perhaps he would come to it if they were married; perhaps she in her turn would find pleasure in his embraces. The last time she saw him, Philip had brought her to a convulsion of love so fierce she had cried out 'God, oh God!' and wept against his shoulder. Perhaps she was to some extent confusing that kind of physical pleasure with love for him. But could George do anything like that to her, and could she bear it if he tried? She drank some more whisky. It was making her head swim now. She'd had what before—a couple of glasses of beer? No, three, because they'd already drunk one when Philip arrived. It wasn't enough to affect her like this. She

130

must be emotionally drunk: intoxicated with despair at the impossibility of her situation. If she said now that she would marry George she could let circumstances take over that would keep her away from Philip and him away from her. Why not? Why not say yes and commit herself?

'I don't love you, George,' she said. 'I suppose I'm fond of you in a way, but I don't love you.'

'It's not strictly necessary,' George said. 'We get on well enough together. I think we could make a good marriage, and I'd always look after you.'

'Is that all? We're a bit young for a marriage of convenience, aren't we?'

'It wouldn't be that for me.'

She looked at him. 'George, tell me something. If you love me why have you never tried to make love to me?'

He shrugged, ill at ease in another way now. 'I suppose I've got too much respect for you to try to paw you around before we know where we stand.'

'Is it pawing around before and something with a different name after? Do you want to? I mean, do you find me physically desirable?'

'Yes, I do.' Now his eyes moved, but sideways, in an uneasy, almost furtive glance that travelled from her ankles to her neck, then away before it reached her face. She thought of the way Philip looked at her, as though directly into her soul, his heart there naked in his eyes. She scrambled out of the chair.

'I want another drink. What about you?'

'No, no, not for me. Do you think you should?'

'Of course I should, if I want to.'

She slopped Scotch into her glass and added some water. When she sat down again it was on the sofa next to George. He remained as he was, leaning forward, until she said, 'Well, are you giving me the cold shoulder now?' Then he turned his head and looked at her where she lay half sideways, her head resting against the back of the sofa. 'Suppose somebody comes down?' he said after a moment.

'They won't.'

My mother wouldn't interrupt this little tête-à-tête for the world, she thought. She closed her eyes and waited. After what seemed a long time he stirred beside her. She felt his breath on her face before his mouth touched hers and his arms fumbled their way round her. There was no response to give him; her lips were dead against his. His hand moved and touched her breast. She lay still, holding herself in, until a few moments later when his fingertips worked their way inside her blouse and touched her naked flesh. Then, stricken by something like panic, she twisted free and stood up.

'No,' she said. 'No.'

'What's wrong?'

She shook her head. 'I'm sorry. It's no good.'

He sighed. 'Well, you asked me why I'd never tried, and now you know.'

'Do you think it would be any different if we came to an understanding? Or do you think I'm cold, frigid?' He didn't answer and she couldn't see his face because she was standing with her back to him. She didn't care. All she wanted immediately was that he should go. 'I just don't want to, George. I can't.' Oh, how could she ever show him or anybody else the difference between this and what she had with Philip? How she couldn't eat when she was going to see him, wondering—the joy and the anxiety all churning inside her in one feeling of enormous drunken elation—if something neither of them had foreseen would prevent him from being there. It wasn't just hearts and flowers, moon and une. She wasn't a girl any more. He more than anyone else had awakened her out of her long adolescent dream and if she believed in love at all she must believe in this. Didn't the world she knew believe in love? Ah, yes, but in the right place at the right time with the right person. And Philip belonged to someone else.

'Is there. . .' George hesitated. 'Is there somebody else?'

'Does there have to be?'

'I don't know.'

'Wouldn't you very likely know if there were?'

'I don't know,' he said again.

She turned round, her fingers doing up the one button his fingers had unfastened. She let him see and watched his eyes flinch from the sight.

'I'm very tired, George. I'd like to go to bed.'

He got up at once. 'I don't suppose there's anything else to say.'

'No. I'm sorry.'

'Are you?'

'Oh, for God's sake, what does that mean? That I can't be sorry enough or I'd marry you? What do you want?'

'I want you.'

They were the most nakedly appealing words she had ever heard him say. It was all wrong. She should be saying yes—yes, yes, yes—delighting her mother at breakfast with the news and planning with contented heart for an autumn wedding.

'I'm sorry,' she said again. 'I really am.'

He moved towards the door, his hand feeling for his car keys. On the step outside he looked at her once more.

'Be careful,' he said. 'Don't break your heart.'

9

The office, next morning, was quiet. Andrea brought some records up to date and tidied her filing cabinet while she waited for Mr Simpkins to call her in. She was glad of this period of routine work which allowed her time to think. The whisky had put her quickly to sleep last night, her thoughts fuddled and racing. Now her mind still turned over again and again the few basic facts of her problem. The honourable as well as the sensible course of action was to break with Philip now. It would involve pain she could hardly bear to contemplate, yet pain would be their lot in the end and it could only be worse as time brought habit and familiarity into their relationship.

She moved through the first two hours of the day in this trance of distress, a state that remained untouched by the work she did, the people who popped in and out of her office, the occasional buzz of the Dictaphone. She was expecting Philip to telephone her. He would have to get in touch because, unable to speak to each other alone last night, they had made no arrangement for next week. When he did it, she supposed, would depend on his timetable. He'd never had occasion to phone her before and he would perhaps be diffident about it. She didn't know what she would say to him. There was so little one felt like saying on the telephone. She would have to see him again. Oh, yes, yes, again; if only that once.

Mr Simpkins called her in a little after eleven. An acrid fug of pipe smoke hit her as she opened the door and made her cough. 'Do you mind if I open a window for a minute?'

He looked at her in vague surprise. 'Is it that smoky? I hadn't noticed. Go on, then.' He put a match to his pipe and added a few more clouds to the reek.

'Not a great deal,' he said as she sat down beside his desk, 'but one or two are a bit tricky. That one, for instance...' He passed over a letter on the notepaper of one of their customers and waited while she quickly read it. 'I want to say yes to what he suggests but hedge it round with enough qualifications to put the ball back in his court. He's a good customer, but a troublesome monkey. Perhaps you could knock something together and let me see it.'

'I'll try,' Andrea said.

'If you look in his file you'll see what I mean.'

'I remember.'

'Good.' He twinkled at her. 'I can dictate for a while now.'

His telephone rang in the middle of it. He picked up the receiver, said, 'Hello ... Oh, hello, Arthur ...' then listened to what his caller was saying, punctuating with little grunts and exclamations from time to time. He was a well-set-up man with a younger face than his grey hair seen from the back might suggest. He dressed to please himself, ignoring the conventions of different clothes for business and week ends, and his suit of brown thornproof tweed, one which Andrea particularly liked, hung well on his big-shouldered but hardly overweight body. He was a type of man Andrea had been brought up to admire: men who if not the builders of their own fortunes, had consolidated what their fathers founded; men who though variously wealthy lived without flash or ostentation and, though often betraying their origins in the cadences of their speech, had none of the brittle vulgarity of a younger breed of self-made men who belonged to a television age of advertising, meteoric careers in show business and the temporary fashions of sixties' life. Men like Mr Simpkins, Andrea's father would say, were the mainstay of a town like Cressley and the backbone of the country. People infected by the something-for-nothing philosophy of the post-war years didn't, he had said,

135

look up to them as they once had, but that was their loss. A little more imaginative outside business, and rather less ruthless inside it, than some of his kind, he was a person Andrea had no difficulty in liking, even in finding attractive. She wondered why he had never married again after the early death of his wife, and had heard whispers of some not quite regular liaison, whispers she had neither enquired into further nor passed on. He was considerate to work for and treated her in a manner which never overstepped into undue familiarity, but which was easier than was suggested by his formal way of addressing her. What, she thought, would he think of her relationship with Philip?

He finished his conversation and put the receiver down, his hand hovering above it for a moment before he sat back.

'I wonder why that girl can't grasp the principle of not putting calls straight through to me without telling me who's on the line. That could have been somebody I didn't want to speak to. I wish you'd have a word with her, Miss Warner. If I speak to her myself she'll probably pass out on the spot. She looks the type.'

Andrea smiled. 'She is a bit awe-struck.'

'Yes, well. I shall blow her up if she does it again, so you'd better warn her.' He took up his papers. 'Right, then, where were we...?'

The telephone in Andrea's office rang a few minutes later. Mr Simpkins went on dictating without apparently hearing it. It could be Philip, she thought, yet she didn't immediately ask to be excused. Perhaps it was a subconscious wish to put off speaking to him that held her there. The ringing stopped.

Just before lunch she went along the corridor and into the ante-room off the general office where the switchboard was located. It was a small board with four outside lines, and the succession of girls who operated it also did copy-typing. No one performed the duty for long: they either left for better jobs or moved on to full-time typing as a vacancy occurred inside the firm. The present operator was an ingenuous and rather helpless girl of eighteen, an untidy person whom Andrea thought of as never being quite pulled together. Her walk was part of this, as well as her habit of always seeming to wear stockings a size too big, so that they wrinkled loosely at her knees. She sat at the table beside the switchboard tapping, in a manner less than proficient, at the old 'spare' typewriter that nobody else wanted to use.

'Winifred...'

'H'mm?' She glanced away from the keys then back again. 'Oh, damn!'

'I'm sorry,' Andrea said. 'Have I put you off?'

'Oh, it's not you, it's me.' She ripped the sheets out of the machine.

'Couldn't you have rubbed out?'

'If I rub out everybody can see how many mistakes I make,' Winifred said. 'If I do it again they might have to wait a bit longer for it but at least it looks decent.' It had a logic which served her purpose while it didn't cover the wastage of paper. Andrea decided to let it pass.

'You put a call through to Mr Simpkins this morning.'

'Which one was that?'

'Just after eleven. You put it straight through without telling him who was on. He was annoyed about it.'

'Oh, that one. Yes, I knew he would be afterwards. I don't know why I did it. There was another call coming through at the same time and I must have panicked.'

'He asked me to see you about it. He says he doesn't want to have to speak to you himself.'

'Oh, I'd just die if he did.'

'But why? He's not a frightening man, is he?'

'Oh, not to you. I can't imagine you being frightened of anything.'

'Can't you?'

'Well, no. I mean, you're so attractive and efficient and all that you can get on with anybody. Some of the others might think you're a bit toffee-nosed but I don't. I stick up for you because I wish I was like you.'

'The others?'

'Oh, you know. P'raps I shouldn't have said anything, but you must know what a catty lot they are. They talk about you not being married as if it's something to be ashamed of. But I think that's your business. I mean, look at all the fun you can have, going places and seeing things, with different people, without having kids and things to tie you down.'

She was too naïve to be a deliberate bother-breeder, Andrea thought. She said, 'And do you have to stick up for me a lot, then?'

'Oh, no! I wouldn't have said anything if I'd thought it would upset you. You must know who I mean, and they're really not worth bothering about, are they? I mean, you're big enough to rise above all that, aren't you? It's all jealousy in the end, isn't it?'

It was twelve-thirty. People were moving about in the corridor.

'You won't forget about the telephone calls, will you?'

'No. It's just when everything happens at once that I do silly things.'

'All right.'

'Ooh!' Winifred said. 'I nearly forgot. There was an outside call for you earlier on.'

'Who was it?'

'I don't know. A man. He wouldn't give his name. Just said it was personal and he'd ring back.' She smiled at Andrea from under lowered eyelids, as though savouring this hint of the mystery and richness of her enviable life. 'He had a nice voice.'

Andrea had brought sandwiches and a flask of coffee for her lunch today. She washed her hands in the cloakroom before going back to her office. Mr Simpkins came through as she opened her packet of food.

'Do you enjoy lunch that way?'

'Now and again, for a change.'

'H'mm. Did you speak to the little girl?'

'Yes, I did.'

'Righto, then. I'll see you later.'

He went out. The sounds of moving people subsided and all was quiet. The sandwiches were ox-tongue and she didn't want them. She pushed them aside and poured herself some coffee. She was stupidly upset by what Winifred had said. They were silly people who had talked about her, ignorant people ready to condemn as snobbish anyone who didn't subscribe to their commonplace ideas or share their often squalid confidences and gossip. She had never cared what anyone whom she didn't respect thought of her. It must be this business of Philip that was making her thin-skinned. Now she had something to hide, and what a meal the cloakroom bitches would make of that!

It was five o'clock when Philip rang again. Thinking he might take advantage of the dinner hour Andrea, who would have liked a walk in the fresh air, had stayed in her office trying to read *Dr Zhivago*, but in her present mood the dissipation of interest as Pasternak switched from one set of characters to another was too much for her power of concentration. She went and got the clean unopened copy of that morning's *Daily Telegraph* from Mr Simpkins' desk and occupied the rest of the lunch break with that.

'It's that man again,' Winifred said.

'Oh, put him through.' She hoped the girl didn't take it into her head to listen in.

'Hello, Andrea?'

'Hello.'

'I tried to get you this morning but you weren't in your office.'

'Yes, I was told.'

'How are you?'

'How do you expect? A bit annoyed with you.'

'Oh?'

'You must know why.'

'I suppose I do. I couldn't help it, you know. It was all a last minute arrangement and there was no time to warn you.'

'Did you have to come to the pub, though?'

'Harry suggested it and it would have looked odd if I'd refused. In any case, I hardly expected to see you there. I thought you'd have cottoned on to the situation and gone elsewhere.'

'Well, I didn't.'

'I'm sorry. Look, what about next week?'

'I don't know.'

'You mean you've got something else on?'

'No, but——'

'It doesn't make any difference, does it? I mean, the situation hasn't changed.'

'You must see it's bound to have for me.'

'But, Andrea, you don't mean you want to——'

'Look, I can't talk now. I've got some work to finish and somebody's going to walk in at any second.'

'You'll be there, then?'

'Yes, I'll be there.'

'Good girl.' She heard his long exhalation of breath. 'You had me scared for a minute.'

'Look, I've got to see you because we can't talk like this, but I'm upset about it all so don't expect too much.'

The pips sounded on the line. Philip said quickly, 'I'll see you. I haven't any more change.'

They had driven, with little notion of direction, for nearly an hour; talking, partly in sustained conversation and latterly in intermittent outbursts of rhetorical statement which needed only the barest acknowledgement from the other. When they found themselves on the lonely upland road where Philip had made his first tentative declaration of feeling they had both been silent for several minutes. Andrea looked out as he stopped the car.

'Here we are again.'

'Yes.'

A thin light rain was falling.

'I can't help wondering what would have happened—I mean, how different it might have been—if you'd gone straight past here that night and said nothing.'

140

'You may as well think how different it would have been if we'd never met. Think of all the wrong men you've avoided falling in love with because you've never seen them.'

'It's not the same thing, is it?'

'It was already too late that night and you know it. Oh, I know we made it worse by admitting it to each other, but we also made it better, didn't we? Experience is a living, growing, changing thing. You can't shut yourself off from parts of it like stepping into a germ-free cabinet where the infections of life can't get at you. If only one of us were in love this would never have happened; but with each of us loving isn't it far, far better to know we're loved back? What's that line of Faulkner's the girl quotes in *Breathless*? "Between grief and nothing I'll choose grief." Unless you believe that falling in love is the passport to eternal bliss you've got to be ready for the pain that comes with the joy.'

'Sitting here, just the two of us, alone, it doesn't seem wrong,' Andrea said.

'There is nothing wrong in falling in love. That's nobody's business but ours. It's what we do about it that makes the difference.'

'We've got willpower, haven't we? We can say here and now that we won't see each other again.'

'Cut our losses and run?'

'I mean stop now before we do any damage.'

'All this because you've seen Kate.'

'All of it before, Philip. Seeing her just brought it home more acutely. I actually *liked* her. Don't you see?'

'The morality of it's got nothing to do with liking or disliking.'

'All right, then, put yourself in my place. Would you be here now if I were the married one?'

'I don't know ... Probably not. Oh, hell!' he burst out a moment later. 'Everybody wants to compartmentalise things. It's as though they think you've only so much love in you, to be given to one person for ever or transferred wholesale to someone else. I don't feel any less for Kate since I met you. I feel more tender towards her in many ways. Does that mean I can't really love you? Do I have to prove that by deserting her? I know this sort of thing can't be what you want to hear, but it's none of it any good unless I'm as honest as I can be. I've no right to ask you for anything. I doubt if I could leave Kate and the kids if I wanted to, so that means our time is limited in any case because the crunch is bound to come. So what am I doing here asking you to waste perhaps a couple of vital years of your life when I can't give you anything in return? They used to call it "wanting the bun and the ha'penny as well" when I was a kid.'

'I don't think that's being quite fair to yourself.'

'It can't be fair to you when I do all the taking and none of the giving.'

'I love you,' Andrea said. 'It's in my own selfish interest to want to see you because I'm happy when I'm with you and miserable when I'm not. It's not a question of drawing up a balance sheet which shows who's giving most. If it comes to that, look what you're risking by seeing me.'

'I don't even know about that,' Philip said. 'The risk, I mean. It's not as if I'm womanising all over the place. I never have. I've never been unfaithful to Kate before. I'm not pretending I've never wanted to, but I've just never thought the game was worth the candle. Surely she'd respect the genuineness of *this*.'

Andrea said nothing. Rain drummed on the roof over their heads in a sudden downpour. It blotted out all sight of the lights in the valley and streamed in torrents across the windscreen. Philip wound up the window on his side and took out cigarettes. They smoked in silence. The closed windows steamed up on the inside until they could see nothing but their own occasional movements in the dim glow from the instrument dials. This small, secret world was theirs. but only so long as it remained unknown to anyone else.

'Do you know something?' Philip said. 'I've never seen

you in daylight.'

'Is it vital that you should?'

'I don't suppose you change colour, or anything like that; but it's just another example of the restrictions we have to put up with.'

The freedom they craved was that of enjoying their bondage; of creating the sweet habit of being together. A room, perhaps, where they could share their evening meal; concerts, plays, films, books that would become common memories; a bed where she could wake beside him; a time when she would carry his child. Every girl's romantic dream. But Andrea thought she was like a man in that she wanted these things not for their own sake but because they were a part of having him. She could make do with so little, really. Enough, in a way, if she could just be with him where he went, as someone of whom he could say openly, without fear or favour, 'This is Andrea. She's with me.'

Philip leaned forward and turned the face of his watch to the light.

'It's time I was taking you home.'

'It doesn't matter so much about me, but you mustn't be late.'

'No ... What are we going to do?'

'I came all prepared to say I wasn't going to see you again.'

'What do you say now?'

'Do you want me to make it easy for you by saying that? It would settle it, wouldn't it?'

'Can you say it?'

He waited. She said, finally, 'No ... I'm not brave enough. One day soon, perhaps, I shall have to face it. But not yet. Not just yet.'

Summer, with long hours of daylight and fewer legitimate activities behind which to hide their meetings, intensified their difficulties. Andrea refused to put herself forward for the film society committee, saying that the less her name was associated with Philip's the better. They had to find other ways and sometimes they went for three or four weeks without seeing each other. All this increased the sense of desperation which underlay the short hours they managed to spend together. They were keyed up and apprehensive and unable in this atmosphere to forget their problems, they talked incessantly round them. But the very strain under which they pursued their relationship deepened the intimacy between them in a way some other couples might have taken years to find. There was no ambiguity between them: they were naked before each other and the complexity of their innermost fears was something apart from their commitment of feeling. On a still July evening—one of the rare occasions when they had more than an hour or two to themselves—they walked into a wood, far from home, and lay down. There, in the middle of a silence which seemed to contain the whole world, Philip held her with the frenzied tenderness of an imminent parting and they made love. It was still novel enough for her to be nervous, not of the act itself, but that she might fail to please him. His gentleness moved her to tears and he, misunderstanding, was contrite.

'Darling, what is it? What is it, darling? Don't cry.'

She held him to her in an access of joy. 'Oh, Philip, you are a fool. You tell me I could be spending all this valuable time looking for someone else. How could I accept anyone else when I love you so much and you make me so happy?'

'Do I make you happy? Really and truly?'

'Yes, love. Yes, in spite of everything I'm so glad I didn't miss all this. It frightens me sometimes to think that I might never have known about it.'

They wandered back towards the road, their arms round each other, and were startled by the sudden appearance of a man in gaiters, carrying a stick.

'Do you know these are private woods?'

Andrea held on to Philip's hand. She had thought they were completely alone and now her heart was beating quickly. The man's gaze passed over their joined hands, his expression combining disapproval of their trespassing and a knowing leer at their probable recent behaviour.

'We've just been for a stroll,' Philip said. 'I'm sorry but we didn't see any notice.'

'Set the lot afire with your cig ends, then what?'

'I'm a bit more responsible than that.'

'Oh aye. Well I'm responsible if owt happens an' you've no right wanderin' round here where you don't belong.'

'We'll get along out of your way, then.'

'Aye, you do. Saw your motor car down yonder. Knew you were in here somewhere. I could report you, y'know.'

'What good would that do?'

'Be a lesson to other folks.'

'You get a lot of people in?'

'Too many. Allus somebody ready to go where he's no business.'

'I don't expect you'll have to bother about us again.'

'I hope not. I wouldn't let you off another time.'

'You don't know us,' Philip said. 'How could you get our names?'

'Don't need 'em. I've got the number of your car.' He bared his teeth in a humourless grin and tapped his forehead. 'In here.'

Andrea felt Philip's fingers twitch in hers and knew he was losing his temper. She pulled at his hand.

'Come on, Philip. After all, we are in the wrong.'

Philip glanced at her without speaking and then, after another glance at the man, he let her lead him away.

'Pompous little bastard.'

'I'm sorry if I robbed you of your dignity,' Andrea said, 'but that's just the sort of silly way we could be found out. You couldn't explain what you were doing here, could you?'

'No, you're right.'

'You don't think he could have seen us earlier, do you?'

'No, I shouldn't think so.'

Andrea shuddered. 'The thought of somebody watching us...'

He squeezed her hand. 'Don't worry. I'm sure he'd have taken pleasure in walking in on us in the middle of it.'

For a while they had been alone and safe; now everything they had seemed open to the leering appraisal and the strictures of others. It was always what they came back to. How long, she wondered, did people in their situation bear it before they either turned on the world in open defiance or crept back under the comfortable cloak of conformity?

10

'Her name's Moffat—Norma Moffat. My brother's wife lives up at Edgehill and she knows all the family.' Agnes Sutton looked at Andrea in the glass over the cloakroom washbasins. 'I should have thought you'd know all about it, you being his private secretary.'

'If I did pry into his personal affairs I shouldn't gossip about what I knew in the cloakroom,' Andrea said coldly.

Agnes Sutton was a plump woman in her early thirties with dark hair and a white skin. She'd been with the firm for three weeks, having come out to work again now that both her children were at school. She prided herself on straight talking and speaking her mind. What she did say was rarely complimentary, and grudging when it was. It was her unabashed way of staring at people that had made Andrea dislike her at once, and she'd found no subsequent reason for changing her mind.

'Oh, well, it's in your interest to keep your mouth shut, isn't it?'

'I should think it might be in yours, seeing that you're working for him. He wouldn't like it if it got back to him.'

'Don't you think it's true, then?'

'I don't know and I don't care. It's none of my business.'

'Ugh! Aren't you a frosty madam!'

Andrea held her tongue. She splashed her face with water and felt for her towel.

'Fancy Mr Simpkins, though,' Jenny Crossley said. It was she to whom Agnes had been talking originally. She leaned on the third basin, next to Agnes as the latter fussed with her hair. A scrupulously neat and tiresomely unimaginative girl from accounts, Jenny was aflame with interest in Anges's revelations about their boss.

'It's been going on for years,' Agnes said. 'I tell you, my sister-in-law knows them all, the kids as well.'

'How many children are there?'

'Two, Nicholas and Shirley. He's away at university somewhere and she's at grammar school. In fact,' Agnes lowered her voice, 'they do say the girl is *his*.'

'What?' Jenny said. 'You mean——?'

Agnes nodded, pursing her lips. ' 'Course, nobody knows for sure, so I'm not saying one way or the other.'

'Fancy Mr Simpkins, though,' Jenny said again. 'I never thought he was like that.'

'Like what?' Andrea put in.

'Well, I mean ... Well, it's not what you'd call right, is it?'

It was more a failure of vocabulary than an indictment, but Andrea could not let it go.

'You mean you're going to sit in judgement on him now? I can't decide whether you're mealy-mouthed or just plain stupid.'

'There's no need to——'

'What do you know about him or his life that you should start getting all sanctimonious? Who the hell are you to judge him?'

'Well, well!' Agnes said. 'We know where you stand, don't we? Have you got a fancy for him yourself, then?'

'Be your age, woman,' Andrea snapped, 'and stop talking like a child. I just think that he—or anybody else for that matter—deserves more than being pulled apart by a couple of bitches in ten minutes' gossip.'

'Who're you calling a bitch?' Agnes's eyes flashed, and Andrea gave her look for look.

'People judge you by what you say and do. You've only been in the place three weeks and you've done nothing but give the impression that it's your personal mission to sort everybody out.'

'What's up—are you scared somebody might take your place as Queen of the Walk?'

Andrea threw up her hands. 'You're just impossible to talk to. I hope you know, though, that what you've just said will be all over the factory in twenty-four hours.'

'If you mean me . . .' Jenny began.

'If the cap fits, put it on,' Andrea said. 'I only hope for your sake you prove me wrong.'

She walked out, nearly bumping into Winifred in the doorway. The bell rang for afternoon work as she went along the corridor. Someone spoke to her but she didn't answer. Her cheeks felt flushed. She could imagine the tone of the conversation now she had left them. And there was Winifred on the spot to defend her and incur the hostility of Agnes Sutton. You couldn't reason with them: they were ignorant; small-minded at best and maliciously harmful at worst. You could only steel yourself to your duty of standing up to them when they went too far.

In her office, she sat down and tried to collect herself. Mr Simpkins had not been in that morning. He'd telephoned her saying he had some business to attend to elsewhere and asked her to ring his sister and say he wouldn't be home for lunch. He was passing the buck there, putting on to her the placating of the formidable Mrs Hargreaves, who was not a woman to inconvenience lightly. Years and years, though, Agnes Sutton had said. She'd no reason to doubt the basic facts of the story: they fitted in with the snippets of gossip she'd heard before. But years and years . . . How had he managed to establish such a permanent relationship? It had surely long ago lost the frantic uncertainty of her affair with Philip. But she had known him for only a little more than a year. Was it that, with the passing of time, habit and custom gave even an irregular relationship a permanence in the eyes of others, that in this way it established its own identity, its credentials, even eventually assuming its own kind of respectability? Then the longer she and Philip could survive together the harder it would become for anyone to separate them. She was heartened by this thought, no less for the knowledge that it was Agnes Sutton who had led her to it with her gossip.

Her Dictaphone buzzed. Mr Simpkins had arrived. She took her shorthand notebook and pencil and went in to him. He was a man of consistent temperament, not given, like some more erratic people, to moods of excessive geniality alternating with bad temper, and she sensed at once that a part of him was withdrawn and preoccupied. He put down the pipe he was fiddling with and his hands fussed in an abstracted way with the papers on the desk in front of him.

'You did ring Mrs Hargreaves and give her my message about lunch?'

'Yes, I did.'

'What did she say?'

'She thanked me for letting her know.'

'Is that all?'

It wasn't. Andrea could hear Mrs Hargreaves' clear, incisive voice now: 'Really, Miss Warner, men can be as unpredictable as children. He was as grumpy as a bear over something I said to him last night, and now he's staying out for lunch...'

'She sounded just a little testy.'

'Ah.' He sat up to his desk. 'Well, let's see if we can get rid of some of this mail.'

His mind drifted away from concentration a number of times. He would pause in his dictation as though searching for a word or phrase and remain silent for several seconds before asking her to read back what he had already said. After half an hour he gave up.

'I think that's all for now.'

'Oh, by the way, Mr Batchelor tried twice to get you this morning.'

'Righto. He'll try again if it's anything important.'

Andrea had crossed the carpet and opened the door to her own office before she decided to speak about what was uppermost in her mind.

'There was something else.'

150

'Yes?'

'I wasn't going to mention it because you've been out this morning and you might want to do some extra work to catch up. But if I could possibly get away on time I'd be grateful. I've got a rather special engagement this evening.'

She could say that much. He was much too polite to ask where she was going.

'I shouldn't think it's beyond the bounds of possibility.'

She gave him a smile. He really was a very nice man. 'Thank you.'

The date was with Philip. Miraculously, an opportunity had arisen for them to spend a long, long evening together. His wife was going away for a few days with the children and he would be alone, free to come and go as he pleased. They planned to drive out to some remote pub and have a meal. Hours and hours they would have with each other and Andrea was curbing her desire to wallow in anticipation of it in case anything should go wrong. She had no easy way of contacting Philip before then. She wasn't going home before meeting him, a precaution she had taken against having to answer awkward last-minute questions from her mother as well as some catastrophic accident such as George's blundering in. They had talked of the possibility of spending the night somewhere—a wonderful, longed-for event they were both aching to bring off—but Andrea had no excuse except that of staying with a friend, and no friend she cared to confide in enough to provide her with an alibi. She put a letterhead into her typewriter. 'Oh, my love,' her heart sang. 'Soon now, soon, soon, soon.'

Some time later Horace Batchelor came in with a boy in overalls. There was an air of dignity and self-importance about Horace which always amused Andrea.

'Mr Simpkins wants to see this feller, Miss Warner. D'you mind if I leave him here a minute while I go in?'

'No, of course not.'

With an abrupt gesture that was almost like bringing a dog to heel, Horace motioned the boy to a position by the window, then tapped on Mr Simpkins' door and went in.

Andrea got up to switch on the light and indicated the chair by the wall. 'Why don't you sit down?' The boy's only answer was to twist his mouth in an expression that was half embarrassed grin and half knowing leer. She was reminded of the man in the woods and felt the boy's sidelong gaze on her as she sat down again and resumed her typing. It was a relief to her when Horace opened the door and called him through into the other office. He was in trouble; she knew that from the unusual sound of Mr Simpkins' raised voice before she saw Horace's face, taut with anger, when they came out. They went away down the corridor, but only a few minutes later Horace was back. She had almost finished the typing she'd got and hoped that if he wanted to do any more dictating Mr Simpkins would call her in soon. That meant as few interruptions as possible.

Horace left once more. Andrea went on with her work. She had just taken the last letter from her machine and was about to check it when the connecting door opened and Mr Simpkins came through, pulling on his overcoat.

'I've just had an urgent telephone call. I shall have to go now.'

'Will you be back later?'

'No. You might just——' He stopped. It crossed Andrea's mind that he'd been about to ask her to phone Mrs Hargreaves again. 'Never mind. You can sign what letters you've done, in my absence, and we'll do the rest another time.'

The door closed behind him. She heard his footsteps, heavy and hurrying, along the corridor. Whatever the news the phone call had brought it had shaken him. Someone ill? Perhaps connected with Mrs Moffat. Or even the woman herself. A new part of Mr Simpkins' life had appeared in hazy outline to her and because it was irregular she was interested in it, had, indeed, wanted to know more about it at the very time she was castigating the cloakroom gossips. Relationships of this kind fascinated her now and she was drawn by any mention of them, particularly in records of the lives of famous people whom she could respect. That these unions had been only one part of these celebrities' lives—in many cases rarely mentioned—and their achievements were securely based despite them, reassured her rational knowledge that, despite what she sometimes guiltily felt, her affair with Philip neither rendered her morally bankrupt nor detracted from whatever other qualities she might bring to bear on life. How long and how dangerously ill would she have to be, though, before she could rightfully call for Philip?

Her telephone rang.

'Personal call for you, Miss Warner.'

'Thank you.' Oh, he wasn't going to tell her it was off after all, was he? Oh, please, no; not at this late stage.

'Andrea?'

'Hello.'

'Andrea, you are all fixed for tonight, aren't you?'

'Yes, everything's all right. It's worked out very conveniently actually.'

'I just wanted to make sure. I'll see you, then.'

'Is everything all right?'

'Why?'

'You sound a bit odd.'

It seemed a long time before he answered her.

'I wasn't going to say anything now. The balloon's gone up. I'm afraid Kate's found out.'

11

'But how, Philip? And who?'

He shrugged his shoulders, hunched over the table, his hands turning the pint glass.

'I don't know. She wouldn't tell me. Whoever it was, though, had said enough to let her throw me so that I coughed up the rest. It was like something preordained, a moment I'd been waiting for and dreading from the beginning. Then, as I've told you, I simply came out with it and said I loved you. I don't know what I expected to achieve by telling the truth. I must have known it couldn't go on once I'd confessed. But I just couldn't lie about it. It was as if lying would have debased the feeling I have for you. I also had some instinctive idea that she'd respect me more for this than if I'd just been having a casual bit on the side.'

'A casual fling doesn't threaten her. I suppose she'd think this does?'

'Yes, I expect you're right. Oh, I handled it all wrong, but I just expected all the wrong things. What *did* I expect, though? I don't know. But not a reaction so utterly bloody conventional that we were at each other's throats from almost the first word. I could hardly recognise her. I couldn't talk to her any more. I had an appalling feeling of being trapped in an emotional nightmare. She was going on at me, telling me what to do, as though I were a piece of her personal property. I almost hated her, the way she wept and shouted and laid down the law. If it hadn't been for the boys I think I'd have walked out there and then. Maybe not

... I'd have been scared she might harm herself.' He shrugged again, hopelessly, and drank from his glass, making a face at the flatness of the beer which had been standing for a long time while he talked.

'I can't blame her,' Andrea said. 'I can't blame her for hating me, either. From where she's sitting I'm a scheming, immoral bitch. I've only to put myself in her position to see it.'

'Oh, I could have handled it so much better,' Philip said, his voice full of irritation at himself. 'But I *want* to be open and honest and uncalculating. To me, it's the way life should be lived. I hate craftiness and manipulation. Instead, I find it's my way that makes things break down. You've got to be either free of temptation or a saint to make it work. Perhaps it's because the truth can't be communicated in all its complexity. It becomes damaging. People need their fantasies to live by and without them they're lost. All I can think of is how sheerly ludicrous it is that I should be prevented from ever seeing you again.'

It was ludicrous to Andrea that they were sitting here like this, talking about it. There was a part of her that still could not grasp what was happening. The naked, defenceless core of her feeling that would take the full pain of it all was still partly numbed by shock. Stretch this moment into infinity and they would be together always. As it was, the clock was ticking away all the time that was theirs. Now they were together. In a couple of hours it would be over. It ought not to happen this way. If she couldn't stop the clock and secure him for ever there should be some cataclysmic severance, something immediate and final, not this inexorable ebbing away of the minutes, minutes they couldn't even enjoy because they foreshadowed the long, long deprivation that was to come.

'Has she stayed at home?'

'No, no. She went off as planned, to see her parents in Lancaster. "Get it all cleared up before I come back," she said. "Tell her you won't see her again. Promise me that you'll tell her." God, it was awful. It drove itself into a

155

vicious circle. The more she railed and wept and savaged me, the less I was either able or inclined to reassure her. I just fought back, tooth and nail.' He pushed his beer away. 'I'm sick of this stuff. It wasn't really worth drinking even before it went flat.'

It seemed good enough to Andrea. She said nothing, but watched him as he got up and went to the bar counter. The pub was in the foothills of the Pennines, in a village that was no more than a straggle of dour stone cottages along the steep road. Here, in the high places, there was snow and a bitterly cold wind had cut at them as they crossed the yard from the car. The room had a floor of flagstones and they were alone in it except for two old men sitting in spasmodic conversation by the fire. Her gaze lingered on Philip at the bar counter. She could have wept for love of him. Why, she asked herself, was love so arbitrary, so casually disinterested in where it struck? Why him and not any one of dozens of others with whom she would have been free to fulfil herself? All this talk of hers about being glad despite everything that she'd met him, that whatever happened she would not be sorry to have loved him.... Yes, she had meant it. She meant it just now. But what about tomorrow? Would she then find herself wishing that she'd never known him, that she could find some way of cutting all knowledge of him out of her heart?

He brought back two large whiskies, with a bottle of dry ginger for her. He had added water to his own Scotch.

'That's better ... The concentrated essence.' He looked at her. 'If I left Kate and went away, would you go with me?'

'Yes.'

He shook his head. 'I'm sorry. It's the nearest you've ever come to saying what you want, and I shouldn't have asked you. You see, it's as though I'm bound by certain inexorable moral laws. There are some things I can't do if the world is to carry on. One of them is to leave Kate. What would happen to her if I did? She's built her life round me for so long. She doesn't deserve to be kicked in the teeth like that. What would happen to all I stand for, all I believe in, if I did that to her? I could only do it if I were so desperate there were no other choice. I love you. I don't know what I'm going to do without you. But I haven't reached that state of desperation yet.' He smiled at her with rueful sadness. 'Does my honesty upset you too?'

'Is it absolutely as clear as that? I mean, you don't know if you could live without her, either?'

'No ... No, I suppose I don't. The ironic thing is that not only can I not leave her, I can't put her in a position where she feels she has to leave me. I don't know whether she sees this just now. She's full of injured pride as well as fear, and I've got to protect her from both ... It's a situation as old as the hills outside and here we are, bashing our heads against it like thousands before us.' The skin drew taut over his cheekbones and his eyes blazed as he let the frustration possess him. 'What the hell's wrong with life that people can't be happy and give each other a little joy? Why does all this pain have to be built-in, an inevitable part of it all?'

The sound was small and neither of them seemed for a second to realise what had happened. Then she followed his gaze as he looked down at his right hand. The glass had shattered in the fierceness of his grip and as Andrea looked blood began to ooze between his fingers.

'What a damn' silly...' he said.

She started to get up. 'I'll see if the landlord has a first-aid box.'

'No, no. I'll go.' He held his handkerchief balled against his lacerated palm as he went over to the bar. There was a spot of blood colouring the whisky in the bottom of the broken glass. It held Andrea and she watched it in a kind of fascination.

'You must have put a rare old grip on it,' she heard the publican say.

'I mustn't know my own strength.'

He invited Philip behind the bar counter where he held his hand under the cold-water tap. Then he produced a box of Elastoplast and put a dressing over the cuts.

'Be all right for driving, will you?'

'Oh yes, I should think so.'

'It's snowing again, out. If you've a way to go I wouldn't leave it too late. That road in the bottom soon gets drifted up.'

'Thanks for the warning. We'd better be on our way. I'm sorry about the glass. I'll gladly pay for it.'

'Oh, that's all right. It all comes under wear and tear.'

'Well, thanks again.'

He came back to her. 'Nice old chap.'

'Is there any glass left in the cuts, do you think?'

'If there is it'll work itself out. Neat job, eh?'

He held out his hand, palm upwards, across the table. She took the fingertips and looked at it. Then, suddenly, the tears came. She bowed her head.

'Hey,' Philip said. 'That won't do.'

'I'm sorry. I remain obstinately dry-eyed all evening and then a silly thing like that starts me off.'

'You'll have them thinking I ill-treat you.'

'Oh, where's my blasted hankie . . . It doesn't really matter what they think now.'

'Finish your Scotch. You'll feel better.'

'You have it; it'll make me sick.'

'I expect that's because you haven't eaten. I'm sorry; I should have looked after you better.'

'You know I couldn't have eaten anything tonight. I told you.'

'The man says there's a lot of snow about.'

'Yes, I heard him. We can go when you're ready.'

'Sure you're all right now?'

'Yes, I'm fine.'

Outside, the snow drove at them over the rim of the yard, carried on the wind down the open valley. There were no lights to be seen. The car was cocooned in a thick white coat and Philip made Andrea get in while he cleared the windows. Their way lay across the valley bottom and up the other side. Philip was silent at first as he eased the car on to the road, his feet delicate on clutch and throttle. No one had driven this way since the new snow began to fall

158

but here progress was easy enough. It was down there, where the snow would drift and pile up in the trough of the valley, that they might find themselves in difficulties.

'I just hope,' Philip said, 'that the wind is sweeping that far road clear so that the tyres can bite through to the tarmac.'

So it proved. Andrea sat in a curious detachment as Philip now urged the car on with little grunted coaxings and exhortations. She developed a fantasy in which the storm was their ally, intent on keeping them together here, far from their world and all who knew them. It was impossible for them to go on. They abandoned the car and trudged back to the inn where, soaked and exhausted, they threw themselves on the mercy of the landlord. He, ignoring her lack of a wedding ring, gave them a room where they lay together in a huge feather-mattressed bed while the flames of an open fire threw flickering shadows over walls and ceiling.

Philip was saying something to her as they topped the rise. She said, 'I'm sorry. I was in bed with you.'

'Oh, God. And I was just going to say how lucky we were to get out.'

'We are, I suppose. I hadn't got as far as thinking about tomorrow. Or even the little matter of what I could have said to my mother on the phone tonight.'

'Tomorrow. It always comes. It was a thought I reassured myself with when it seemed so long before I'd see you again.'

'Tomorrow is Day One,' Andrea said. 'AP.'

'What's that?'

'After Philip.'

He reached for her hand in a sudden rush of feeling. 'Oh, my dear love, what have I done to you?'

'You've given me a wonderful, painful, miraculous year,' Andrea said deliberately; 'and a love that, even though I might not see you again, no one, no matter what, can take away from me until you yourself don't feel it any more.'

'I can't imagine a time when I shan't love you. Just as I

can hardly remember what it was like before I did.'

'Oh, please,' she said. 'Please don't forget me.'

Soon they passed through a small town where yellow sodium lights lined the main road and occasional figures hurried out of the snow which was turning here to sleety rain. Philip asked her to light cigarettes and when she reached down for her handbag her fingers touched another object by her feet. It was a toy pistol. She held its hard positive shape in her hands for a moment before slipping it between their two seats where it would be safe.

He took her straight home and stopped the car with its engine running at the corner of the street.

'How shall I know you're all right?' he said.

'I don't know. But if you need me any time—I mean, if you want to talk to me, if only for a few minutes—you know where to find me.'

'Yes . . . Goodbye, then.'

'Goodbye.'

He waited as she walked away along the avenue. She was conscious that if she turned round now he would still be there. She could still run back to him, cry out and touch him, hold the moment a little longer. But once he had gone . . . She walked on, not looking back, till she reached the gate. As she turned her head there the car moved away. A cloud of exhaust smoke hung for a moment in the air, all that was left of him, and evaporating fast. Then, before the sound of his engine had finally died away, there was nothing left to see.

PART THREE

12

'If I may begin,' Nick Moffat said, 'by expressing sincere regret that the talented gentleman who has just spoken to you should, so early in his career, have chosen to espouse a creed which is in decline and expend such dazzling erudition and wit on the propagation of ideas (if we may dignify his thoughts with such a name) which have at best only a limited future. It is sad that in the long lifetime which we all surely hope lies before him he will be inevitably consigned to a rôle in opposition to the great insistent tide carrying forward the future of our people.'

The words called for an urbanity of utterance which, locked in nervousness as he was, Nick couldn't give them. His voice was too low, and jerky in its delivery. He was also slightly worried about his accent. It wasn't, in this formal manner, the 'Ah' for 'I' which his more casual private speech revealed, but the occasional dropped aitch which bothered him, and the tendency to emphasise even more than usual that giveaway Northern 'u'. He stopped, took a deep breath and forced himself to glance sweepingly across his audience. It was all right. The laughter was good natured and ready. He had scored with his opening and now, out of it, came a happy, if not original, image to take him on.

'As an organisation of professional Canutes my esteemed opponent's allies are no more successful in turning back the tide than that king of ancient lore. Where they differ from that modest monarch is in their insistence on their power, and the right to demonstrate the failure of that power again and again, to the point of nausea. Luckily for them, the British electorate is a phlegmatic body whose bilious attacks are minor and quickly forgotten. So far, though, ladies and gentlemen. So far. For even the strongest of stomachs will eventually revolt against a diet which is basically inimical to its well being.'

Another pause. Give them time to take and appreciate his points. Look at them ... The motion before the union debating society was 'That this house would welcome the Socialist way of life'. It was the first time Nick had spoken in a debate and the challenge of it, accepted some weeks ago, was one of his reasons for coming back when his father was lying dangerously ill in hospital. He had regretted it all the way down in the train. How could he leave his mother at a time like this? But she had insisted. 'You must go back,' she had said. 'There's nothing you can do here and you can't miss your classes. Education like that is a once-in-a-lifetime thing. You must make the most of it. I've got Shirley here,' she said when he protested. 'I'm not on my own and it'll only make it seem worse if everybody hangs about as though it's a funeral.' He'd caught the look in her eyes as she let go the unwitting words. 'Like a funeral...'

The debating chamber of the union building was packed, the sea of faces filling the tiered seats back to the rear wall with its huge window and undrawn lime-green curtains. It was a new building in a new university which, after five years' intake of students, was still partly dependent on temporary accommodation in scattered areas of the town. Faces blurred into faces. Roger's white trousers seen in the corner of this vision were the only familiar feature Nick could make out. His palms were sweating and he resisted the desire to take out his handkerchief and wipe them. He lifted his hands and let them rest lightly on the lectern beside his notes. 'Take it easy,' he told himself. 'Raise your voice, and don't rush.'

'We hear much from my opponent and his friends about "the freedom of the individual", of their efforts to prevent bureaucracy from strangling the ordinary man with red tape, from ringing him round with legislation which will cripple him and stunt his development. My senses grow alert, ladies and gentlemen, when I hear this phrase "the freedom of the individual". To the core of my being I distrust it as a battle cry. I can hear it ringing down the ages as the excuse for every kind of chicanery and exploitation. When the first caveman shared his kill with his neighbour rather than fight over it with him, when they built a communal fire against the dark outside, when they formulated laws which protected both the weak and the strong alike, they were taking necessary steps for their survival; they were sacrificing "the freedom of the individual" to the common good. A man who has no wish to exploit his fellows will not oppose legislation which forbids him to do so. It was not the nineteenth-century manufacturers and industrialists using child labour for the amassing of their profits who saw that this exploitation of young children was cruel and wrong. It was men like Richard Oastler who, cursed, abused and execrated, laid the foundations for their relief. There is no freedom for the underprivileged and oppressed. The word is a sophistication. All it has meant in many instances down the years is the freedom to starve.

'My opponents may accuse me of raking over dead ashes. What is all this talk of child labour? We don't do that kind of thing nowadays. I would ask them, were those who exploited children in this way monsters of depravity and corruption? They were not. They were men and women thought of in their own time as being as decent, civilised and humane as circumstances permitted. (So, incidentally, were the judges who sentenced children to be hanged for stealing.) We have their like among us today; people concerned not with the broad stream of human affairs but with the day-to-day protection of their own interests. They share with their forerunners the characteristics of being always with us and everlastingly vocal. They look back rather than forward but their backward glances teach them nothing about the tides and movements of today. One may cite the

165

example of those fierce American ladies who write letters to English newspapers which have been critical of right-wing extremist movements in the United States. "You English," they say, "with your Royal Family, your Beefeaters, all your outworn mumbo-jumbo. Who are you to criticise us? Have you forgotten that we threw you out two hundred years ago?" What these reactionary ladies, borrowing the credentials of long canonised revolutionary fervour, never recognise is the equivalent of that fervour today, nor do they realise that had they been alive in England at the time they would have been the most fiercely loyal subjects of George III. The Oastlers of today are still cranks; at their least harmful do-gooders and softies, at their most militant dangerous trouble-makers and Reds.

'It is a pattern so persistent down the centuries that one can only stand amazed at anyone's failure to grasp its essentials. "The Conservatives," Mr Evelyn Waugh once said, "have failed to put the clock back one minute." You may think that remark typical of a man who, during a general election, could also say that he did not presume to advise his Sovereign on her choice of her servants. But it is true and unless we are all to be as eccentric towards these matters as Mr Waugh we should draw from it the only possible lesson. We cannot put the clock back and we should not wish to do so. That the Tory of today would be unrecognisable, except as a raving bolshevik, to the Tory of fifty years ago is indicative of the way the tide is moving. Virtually every reform they introduce is a concession to an irresistible state of affairs born out of the constant efforts of radicalism and the left. You might say I've forgotten to mention natural progress. Not at all, ladies and gentlemen. It is, indeed, my clinching argument. I ask you, on whose side has progress of this kind shown itself to be? With which set of beliefs is it most closely allied? Would not a man who declines to advise his monarch on her choice of servants admit that our present sovereign is a very different one from the first Elizabeth or Henry VIII? For better or for worse, ladies and gentlemen? The answer is yours. But

Donne's requiem for James I rings oddly in our ears today.

'The tide is irresistible. You may—indeed all of us can at times—regret some of the incidental flotsam it deposits on the shores of human affairs. But if we belong to the human race we share responsibility for its future. We cannot turn our backs, nor can we turn back the clock.

'Finally, let us remember when we come to accept or reject the motion before the chamber, that we are not holding a general election. Our purpose here is not to choose those persons, right, left or centre, who will represent us at Westminster, and I offer you no champions in shining armour. We are casting our votes for or against a way of life.

'Despite all that has been said before me, and all that is no doubt bursting to be said when I've finished, there is no question in my mind of the proper, the fitting and in the end the most noble, way to choose.'

Nick turned and walked off the dais and sat down in the empty seat on the front row of the audience. The applause was warm and generous. He felt that he'd been successful even though he'd said only a fraction of what he wanted to say and arranged what he had said in less than the most effective manner. Why, even after preparations, did the most telling phrases come to mind too late? And telling phrases and memorable images were necessary when one's case was based not on statistics or concrete evidence of success or failure, but on an emotional and instinctive conviction of what was right. Not only tomorrow, but later tonight, he would think of so many more forceful points he could have made.

'Great, man, great,' Roger was saying. He squeezed Nick's knee, letting his hand stay there longer than was necessary. Roger embarrassed Nick at times, both with the fulsomeness of his praise and his liking of physical contact. A paper on Fielding and Richardson given to the English Society had seemingly convinced Roger that Nick had it in him to become a great critic. Nick, in his more realistic moods, inclined to the truth of his tutor's comment, that the

167

chief merit displayed by the paper was his persistence in having persevered through the multi-volumed *Clarissa* and *Pamela*. (But then, Mr Ledbury was a Fielding man and Nick had come down decisively in Richardson's defence.) It was good to be liked and praised but what made Nick uneasy was a suspicion that Roger's attentions were based on something more than a normal affection between man and man. He supposed he was queer. Caroline Chambers said so and women were supposed to have an instinct for divining such things. On the other hand, it could be sour grapes. Caroline's interpretation of people and circumstances was slanted to conceal her own inadequacies. She wás not above saying that Roger was queer on the two inconclusive counts that he had not made a pass at her or any other girl she knew of, and he was obviously coming between her and Nick.

'I now call upon Mr Terence Spencer to speak against the motion.'

Nick's mistake with Caroline had been in making a pass at her himself. It had happened when he'd had more than enough to drink, at a party in the town. Always with the vague idea of breaking his duck, but lacking the taste for setting about that task persistently and systematically, Nick had gone for Caroline because there seemed to be little competition for her and she was, therefore, potentially available. The bottled beer he'd drunk gave her an attractiveness he was later unable to discern sober. He took her into the garden where she let him kiss her and fondle her through her clothes, but stopped him when he tried to go further. It was surprising with how much importance she invested those few minutes of drunken fumbling in the dark and Nick was too kind to tell her to her face that he was tired of meeting her in place after place where he went. Roger offered to do it for him. 'The dreary bitch,' he said. 'Doesn't she know what a smelly drag she is?'

'Smelly?'

'Don't you think she is?'

'I can't remember noticing.'

168

'Perhaps I've got an extra-keen nose.'

Nick.had to admit that Caroline wasn't too fastidious in her appearance and he couldn't blame Roger with his slim neat body, his shining Hamlet-like cap of blond hair and the impression he always gave of having recently got out of the bath, for disliking her with no more reason than this. But listening to each of them criticise the other was sometimes like being caught between two competing and jealous women. He could understand Caroline, lonely and unwanted, making as much capital as possible out of his once having shown some interest in her but not why Roger should have singled him out. If he was actively queer and not just passively inclined that way why didn't he seek out the others of his kind who were likely to exist among the hundreds of students in the university? Didn't like recognise like, as he'd always heard? But no activity of this kind on Roger's part was known to him.

Nick's knowledge of homosexuality, or any kind of deviation, was confined to what he'd read and the very occasional manifestations of the darker side of the working-class life he'd known as a young boy. A man who lived alone in the next street had once, after Nick had run an errand for him, taken him into the house and exposed himself to him. It was just a pathetic half-hearted attempt at some kind of satisfaction and Nick was more embarrassed than shocked. He said nothing about it to anyone but thought afterwards that the man must have lived in fear that he would. Some organised homosexual activity was discovered among the night-shift workers at a local mill. The town buzzed with the news and gossip, as though anxious that a good scandal should not suffer through the insignificance of its real participants, added the names of several prominent local men who could not possibly have been involved. Even the press reports of the preliminary hearings in the magistrates' court and, later, the trial at quarter sessions, though rich in detail, did not totally cleanse the reputations of these innocent men. 'There's no smoke without fire' was what those ready to give credence

169

to any hint of both vice and influence in high places muttered knowingly. The point was, all activities of that kind which Nick had known about were marked by their real furtiveness and the smell of degeneracy they gave off. When brought to light they disturbed in the same way, if not to the same degree, as instances of sexual interference with little girls and were treated with the same kind of disapproval by both courts and public.

To classify someone like Roger with those people was like comparing his mother, because of her relationship with Uncle Tom Simpkins, with the slatternly woman in Edgehill who had entertained a succession of men in her cottage and was eventually fined for keeping a disorderly house. Not everyone was as discriminative in opinion. Nick was not yet in his 'teens on that hot day during the summer holiday when, lying in the long grass on 'the piece' behind the houses, he heard very clearly two women talking over the wall.

'I see't landlord were visiting again last night.'

'What a pity I didn't see him. I want him to do something about that leaking fall pipe. Every time it rains it——'

'Oh, he's got more on his mind when he comes up here than your fall pipe.'

'What d'you mean?'

'He comes to call at yon' end house.'

'Mrs Moffat's, you mean?'

'Aye. Been coming for years.'

'Well, I mean, I don't know about these things because I'm new here, but he seems a nice enough feller to me. I've nothing against Mrs Moffat, either. She's always very pleasant.'

'Got room to be, hasn't she, with her rent paid and company for when her husband's away?'

'Well, I know nothing about it, Mrs Crutchley. Live and let——'

'Ask me, she's not much better than yon' woman behind t'church, wi' her door—and her legs—open all hours o' day an' night.'

170

'Oh, I've heard about *her*. But I mean, *she's* a ... well, she's——'

'A whore? So's a married woman 'at carries on with other men. One or a dozen makes no difference.'

Nick looked up the word. It didn't seem to apply technically to his mother but he wondered what behaviour on her part could have encouraged its use even in malice. Uncle Tom had been a feature of his life for as long as he could remember. He had always accepted him without question. Now he began to probe.

'Mother, is Uncle Tom my real uncle?'

'Well, no, but he's been a friend of ours for a long time and he let you call him that when you were a baby.' Was there just a hint of wariness in the calm reply?

'How did we get to be friends with him?'

'I once went to him for some advice because he was on the council.'

'Did me dad get to know him then as well?'

'Yes. It was me that went to see him because your dad was poorly at the time and he couldn't go himself.'

'He's been poorly a lot, me dad, hasn't he?'

'Well, it was the war that did that. You should always be proud of your father for what he did and went through in the war.'

She hardly ever missed a chance of praising his father to him. And there, he felt instinctively, was the crux of the matter. He could be shocked by the association of his mother and Uncle Tom with the sexual images which were becoming more and more a part of his questioning mind— and the presence of this other man implied an appetite in his mother that was surprising and less than decent to him, brought up conditioned by her natural reticence about sex—but he saw through intuitively to an answer in the difference between the two men. There was on the one hand a sense of inadequacy and failure, on the other an air of steady purpose and a grasp of the essentials. Whether his mother's relationship with Tom was the result of his father's failings or their partial cause was a question he had

171

never satisfactorily answered to himself and it had kept the issue open in his mind as something he had yet finally to resolve.

He learned to accept Uncle Tom in another way. His father was attentive to him but the time came early in his 'teens when Nick could feel his intellect outgrowing his environment. His mind, opened at first by teachers like Philip Hart and then taken forward into the questioning and analytical world of the university, soon outstripped in its considerations the preoccupations of his father and mother. Tom Simpkins could ask many of the right questions and always listen perceptively to the answers. Nick became grateful to him as a buffer between the new life and the old. He was, in a way, an insurance against the feeling of alienation which oppressed so many of Nick's fellows from similar backgrounds.

A porter appeared. He stood just inside the door and waited till the speaker had finished before walking across to the dais and saying something to the president. Nick had a quick breath-snatching premonition of what was coming in the moment before the president's gaze fell on him. The porter's head turned as the president spoke to him. He stepped off the platform and approached Nick, bending with his face close so that Nick caught a whiff of onion breath.

'Mr Moffat? There's just been an urgent telephone call for you. They'd like you to ring back straight away.'

'Mrs Lomas, was it?'

'Yes, that's the name.'

This was it. Nick got up and followed the porter out. They crossed the big lobby, Nick walking a couple of steps behind the man's uniformed back. There were a few people in the bar. A gust of laughter was released from the auditorium as someone else opened the door. The porter indicated the telephone on the desk in the office. 'Help yourself.' He closed the door on Nick and strolled away to stand looking out at the darkness beyond the glass of the entrance doors. Nick dialled his landlady's number.

'Mrs Lomas?'

'Oh, is that you, Mr Moffat? Oh, I'm so glad I've found you. There's a telegram arrived for you just a little while ago.'

'Would you open it, please.'

'Just a minute, then.' The receiver was laid down. He clearly heard the tearing open of the envelope and the rustle of the telegram form, stiffened by its pasted-on words.

'I'm afraid it's bad news.'

'Read it to me, please.'

'It says ... it says "Father died this afternoon. Please come soonest. Deepest sympathy. Tom." Oh, I am sorry Mr Moffat. Is there anything I can do?'

'I don't think so, thank you, Mrs Lomas. I shall probably be along soon.'

'Well, if there is anything at all.'

'Thank you very much, Mrs Lomas. I'll tell you if there is.'

He put the telephone down. He'd known the telegram wasn't from his mother before Mrs Lomas got to the expression of sympathy and the signature. His mother would never have used 'soonest' in that context, nor in a transmitted message would her usual plain speaking have carried her beyond the euphemism 'passed away' to Tom's simple and accurate 'died'. He stepped out of the office. Roger was standing there.

'Is it bad, Nick?'

Nick nodded. 'Yes.' He flinched from the word himself. 'He's gone.'

Light from the big window of the auditorium fell across the vehicles in the car-park. They were still debating their stupid motion in there. As if it mattered which way the voting went; as if it would make one jot of difference to anything. And he, standing up there being clever and showing off before them all when he should have been at home where his duty lay. Never mind what his mother had said;

173

he was man enough now to make his own decisions and handle some of the family responsibilities. His father had let his mother shoulder too many burdens and she had passed some of them on to Tom. Was he, Nick, no better? He was going to regret for a long time his not being at home.

Roger's Sunbeam Alpine stood with its nose close to the wall of the building. Roger had money; his parents had divorced and married again and he got allowances from both sides. 'Conscience money,' he'd been heard to call it. His father, a Birmingham business man, had given him the car on his nineteenth birthday and his heavy sheepskin car-coat was a present from his mother with whom he lived out-of-term. He described his step-father as a man with no visible means of support: 'I think he must be a master criminal.' About his parents he was hardly less facetious and his airy, nonchalant references to them seemed to Nick a deliberate disguise for his real feelings. He had come here from a minor public school after failing Oxford entrance. 'You stand to benefit from it,' he said to Nick. 'I'm just batting my time out and hoping to get a second or at worst a third, which won't be too disgraceful; then I'll either go in with the old man or get one of step-daddy's cronies to teach me to blow safes.'

He was quiet now as he backed the car out of its place and turned it towards the gates.

'This is very good of you, Roger.'

'Don't talk silly. Why don't you let me take you all the way?'

'What, up to Yorkshire?'

'Yes. You'll never get a train tonight and we could be there in three and a half hours. Less, if I get my foot right down.'

'It's good of you, but I couldn't take you all that way.'

'What are you going to do, then?'

'I don't know. I must make a phone call first.'

Mrs Lomas met them in the hall. She was a widow in reduced circumstances, a woman like many others to whom the coming of the university and the increasing influx of young people needing accommodation had been a blessing. It allowed her to keep on her fine early Victorian house, one of a row overlooking the river with lime trees along its walk. Nick thought himself lucky to have found a place there: it was one of the pleasantest parts of the town and Mrs Lomas was a good-natured woman who looked after her boarders well. Too good-hearted for Nick in his present situation, for the compassionate look with which she faced him was the kind of thing he was already beginning to dread. It made him acutely self-conscious. He was shaken by his father's death but did not honestly know at present the depth of his sorrow. Before other people, particularly someone as sympathetically concerned as Mrs Lomas, he felt almost as though he were acting the part of a bereaved son and wondered, absurdly, how much grief it was fitting that he should show.

He took the telegram which she handed to him and glanced at it. He didn't know what to do for the best. They had no telephone at home. Tom would more than likely be with his mother, and if he tried to phone him he would get Mrs Hargreaves. She existed in that part of Tom's life that he—and, so far as he knew, his mother—had hardly any contact with. He didn't know how much she knew or what attitude she took towards what she did know. He didn't know how *any*one else saw the situation, how open a secret it was. Within his own home it existed without being talked about. He had never spoken of it with his mother and while they must realise that he was aware of something more between them than the apparent surface friendship they had never flaunted indications of it, in the way of intimate gestures, before him.

'I doubt if you'll get a train tonight,' Mrs Lomas said.

'That's what I've told him,' Roger said. 'I've offered to run him up myself.'

'I could send a telegram saying I'll be there as quickly as I can tomorrow,' Nick said indecisively. He went on, with a touch of irritation, 'I wonder why they didn't send word

175

earlier.'

'They may have tried to telephone in the late afternoon or early evening while I was out.'

'I should never have come back. I should have stayed at home where I was needed.'

'There's no use rebuking yourself like that, Mr Moffat. I'm sure no one else wants to reproach you on that score.'

Nick made up his mind. 'I'll try a phone call.'

Roger said he'd stick around till they saw what happened, and Mrs Lomas took him along to the kitchen for a cup of coffee, leaving Nick alone in the hall. The telephone was mounted on the wall and had a coin box. He took all the loose change he had out of his pocket and piled it beside him on the table, not knowing how much he would need. The night operator was a talkative man with an almost Northern turn of dry humour.

'Cressley, Yorkshire? I once spent a fortnight's holiday there. It rained every day.' Nick could hear him humming as he manipulated the plugs. 'Not as bonny a spot as Wigan but not bad when the weather's fine.'

He was through surprisingly soon. 'The number's ringing now.' A woman answered.

'I wonder if Mr Simpkins is there.'

'Who is that?'

'My name is Nicholas Moffat.' As though they were complete strangers. He had met Mrs Hargreaves a couple of times and she must know who he was.

'Oh yes. I'll get him.'

There were voices beyond the clear range of the receiver then Tom came on the line.

'Nick. I wondered if you might think to ring here. I should have put it in the telegram. I'm sorry, Nick. It's a rotten business.'

'How's my mother?'

'Oh, you know what she's like. She's taking it very well on the surface but she's very upset underneath.'

'I thought you'd be with her. Is there nobody looking after her?'

176

'She's here, Nick. Shirley as well. I brought them both here after Shirley left school and got Bess to give them a meal so's your mother wouldn't have to bother. Not that either of them's eaten much.'

That was something he hadn't expected. So Tom had brought it out into the open to that extent. And his mother had let him, which was even more surprising.

'I suppose Shirley's taken it badly.'

'I'm afraid so. She's uneasy here as well. She wants to be at home, in familiar surroundings. I was just going to run them back. Perhaps it wasn't a good idea but I thought I was acting for the best. I'd get here as soon as you can, Nick. Your mother's not saying much but I think they both need you.'

'There's no train till morning.'

'Can't you hire a car or something? Don't worry about the expense. I'll see to that.'

'As a matter of fact, a friend has offered to drive me up.'

'Let him do it. Do you want to speak to your mother?'

'I think I'd rather wait. Give her my love and tell her I'll be home about one o'clock. I think we should make it by that time.'

'Well watch what you're doing. Your mother's got enough on her plate without you getting into any mishaps.'

They rang off. Nick walked along the hall and into the kitchen.

'There's a cup of coffee here for you, Mr Moffat,' Mrs Lomas said. 'Did you get through all right?'

'Yes. They want me to go as soon as possible. I'd like to take you up on that offer, Roger.'

'Now you're making sense.'

'You ought to have something to eat before you start on that long journey.'

'No, thanks, Mrs Lomas. I couldn't eat a thing.'

'Me neither,' Roger said. He stood up. 'I'll just make a phone call myself and then we can be on our way.'

177

Nick missed most of the journey. An unaccountable tiredness was already fumbling at his brain soon after they left the town, passing under the pinnacles of St Saviour's Church as the clock in its tower struck ten. He gave Roger general directions: 'Make for the A1 then head north till you come to the turn-off for Wakefield.' The radio was playing a programme of jazz records. Roger was mad about jazz. He was an accomplished pianist, much in demand for parties, and his conversation often sounded to Nick like dialogue written for a film about jazz musicians. They spoke little now and once they had reached the featureless middle section of the drive, up the dual carriageway of the A1, Nick let the tiredness take him, and slept.

He was mildly sorry afterwards; even a silent passenger was better company than an unconscious one. Then he thought that Roger might have been glad of the chance to drive at his own speed, which was a little too persistently fast for Nick's real peace of mind. As it was, they made remarkably good time. Nick woke of his own accord after the swift unimpeded dash up the trunk road changed to an erratic fast and slow progress into the West Riding conurbation. It was after midnight but there was commercial traffic coming off the A1 and here on the winding link roads you could be held up behind a heavy lorry for minutes on end.

'Where are we?'

'Somewhere near Wakefield. I was just thinking I should have to wake you for a spot of pathfinding.'

'We've made good time, haven't we?'

'We'll lose a bit here.'

Nick pushed himself up in his seat, stretching his legs as best he could and rubbed his eyes. A little while later they topped the rise and the lights of Wakefield lay spread out before them. Nick was sometimes haunted by a vision of the fabulous city, a place where the good life abounded, a place born out of his memories of the great mysterious metropolises of Leeds and Bradford seen in childhood, when visits there, taken in the unassailable context of his

178

mother and father, were expeditions which tapped deep into reservoirs of seemingly inexhaustible magic. But he had watched those towns shrink, their mystery fade, as he came to know them too well, and not London, nor Paris, nor Rome could beckon him with the same smile of promise. His parents were not the touchstone of his experience, but frail like everyone else. His father now was dead. The magic city, if it existed at all, must lie hidden somewhere in his own heart.

In half an hour now they were home. Tom's car stood on the piece. Roger switched off the engine and stretched himself. 'There we are then.'

'I really can't thank you enough, Roger.'

'Oh, hell, man, play the flip side, will you.'

The front door opened and Tom was silhouetted in the light. He turned his head and said something over his shoulder.

'Look,' Roger said, 'you go in first and call me when you like.'

Nick saw the point. 'Righto.' He dragged his case up from behind the seats and got out. It was much colder here and there had been some snow. Tom waited in the doorway for him.

'Nick.' He took Nick's hand in a firm grasp. 'Well done, Nick . . . Is your friend coming in?'

'Later.'

'Yes. I see.'

Nick dropped his case at the foot of the stairs and made for the kitchen. His mother came through the door before he reached it. 'Oh, Nick.' He saw the tears start in her eyes. The sight of her broke him. His throat was suddenly choked and his lips trembled. He put his arms round her and buried his face in her shoulder to hide his own tears.

'Oh, Nick . . . Monday he was all right, on his way home. Now he's gone.'

'Come on,' he said. 'Come on and sit down.'

He led her into the kitchen and gently pushed her down into a chair. Her fingers pulled ceaselessly at the small

179

square of her handkerchief. Nick had never seen her in such an extremity of emotion. It made him feel older than his years, as though he was thrust into maturity by her grief. At the same time he wondered at the equivocal nature of her sorrow. She had not lost everything; her love had not reposed entirely in the person of one man. Did the sharing of it diminish its quantity? Had she loved his father less because of Tom? Would she mourn him less also, or were both sorrow and love so infinitely variable they could not be measured in such terms?

'Your Uncle Tom's been ever so good, Nick. I rang him from the hospital and he's never left me since.'

'There'll be arrangements to be made . . .'

'Don't you worry about that,' Tom said. 'It's all taken care of.'

'Is Shirley in bed?'

'Yes. She was tired out with it, poor lamb. I gave her one of my sleeping pills to make sure she gets a good night's rest.'

'Since when have you been taking sleeping pills?'

'Oh, I don't use them all the time. But sometimes when your father's been away I've found it hard to drop off.' She put the handkerchief to her face and spoke through the threat of fresh tears. 'He was a good man, Nick. I don't want you ever to forget that.'

Nick could never afterwards tell just what triggered off the spasm of bitterness which made him say what he did then. Perhaps his viewpoint slipped its context so that for a second he saw the scene as someone less sympathetic, in possession not of understanding but merely the bare facts, might have observed and judged it, shot through with insincerity, or at best covered by a veneer of the most atrocious sentimentality which disguised uneasy consciences but came nowhere near genuine mourning for the man who had died.

'He must have been, mustn't he?' he said. 'Either that or spineless beyond belief.'

His mother gave him a startled glance, then looked at

Tom who was frowning and staring at his feet. Tom lifted his eyes and met her gaze, then cleared his throat.

'There are a lot of things, Nick——' he began.

Nick stood up. 'Roger's outside. Roger Coyne. You've heard me mention him. He drove me up. I ought not to keep him out in the car for too long.'

'You should have said before. I never thought.'

Nick went out. Roger was curled up with his eyes closed, behind the steering wheel. He woke at Nick's tap on the window.

'Man, another few minutes and I'd've been hard on.'

'Come inside. It's not a mansion but it's home.'

Roger was at his most graciously polite. He held Nick's mother's hand for a moment and said, 'I'm awfully sorry to intrude at a time like this, Mrs Moffat. I know how everybody must be feeling.'

'Thank you very much for bringing Nicholas home so quickly,' Nick's mother said.

'This is my——' Nick began, but the words 'Uncle Tom' stuck in his throat. 'Mr Simpkins.'

Tom held out his hand. 'Roger...'

'I ought to get something ready for you two boys,' Nick's mother said. 'You can't have eaten for hours.'

'Just a cup of something for me, Mrs Moffat,' Roger said. 'If it's not too much trouble.' He looked at his wrist watch. 'I mustn't be too long in starting back.'

'But you're never going to drive back all that long way tonight!'

'Perhaps I can get Bess to fix him up with a bed, Norma,' Tom said.

'Bess'll be in bed and asleep herself by now. There's no problem. I can go in Nick's room and they can have the big bed. They won't mind that just for this once, two young men together.'

'I couldn't possibly——'

'Now you're staying here,' Nick's mother said, 'and that's an end of it. I wouldn't dream of letting you drive back tonight. I've seen enough of what can happen to a tired man behind a steering wheel.'

'I'm sorry,' Roger said. 'I didn't think.'

Nick turned away as he felt himself beginning to blush.
He couldn't get out of the situation. How would everyone
react if he said. 'I can't sleep with Roger because I think
he's a queer and I suspect he fancies me.'?

'If Nick doesn't mind . . .' Roger was saying.

'You certainly can't do the return journey without sleep,
Roger.'

Tom left, saying he would be over in the morning. Nick's
mother saw him out. For a few moments the murmur of
their voices could be heard in the hall, then the front door
opened and closed and Nick's mother came back. She stood
just inside the door looking vague and distracted. The long
day was drawing to its close. Soon she would be alone with
her thoughts.

'If you could show me where I go, Nick, I'll clear out of
your way,' Roger said.

'I haven't made you that drink,' Nick's mother said. She
passed a fretful hand across her forehead.

'There's no need to trouble now that I'm staying.'

'It's no trouble. In fact, you find yourself glad of things to
do.'

'Perhaps Nick will bring it up for me, then.'

Nick took Roger upstairs. He showed him the bathroom
and the main bedroom and got him clean pyjamas from the
chest of drawers in his own room. Shirley's door stood a
little ajar. Nick pushed it open and stepped quietly in. Light
from the bulb on the landing fell across his sister's face. She
was sleeping but not altogether peacefully. As he watched
her she turned over in a restless movement. The pressure of
her head against the pillow pushed out the flesh of her
cheek. He was arrested by something in the look of her,
some aspect of her features that was at once familiar yet
strange, like an object or a view one has known all one's life
seen suddenly from a new angle. It tugged at some uniden-
tifiable association in his mind. Then Shirley moved her
head, settling it more comfortably, and what he had seen

182

was gone.

There were three mugs of cocoa on the kitchen table. Nick, wondering foolishly if Roger would know what it was, and what beverage they drank as a nightcap in his world, took one of them back upstairs and left it on the bedside cabinet. Then he returned to his mother.

'Has your friend got everything he wants?'

'I think so. He's still in the bathroom.'

'He's a nice-mannered boy. Does he come from a well-to-do family?'

'Yes. There's money on both sides. His parents are divorced.'

'It makes a lot of wheels run smoother, money.'

'I shouldn't have thought it had there.'

'Because his parents parted, you mean? You'll learn. Money helps you to look your feelings straight in the face without other problems coming into it.'

'Perhaps it makes it too easy not to face the real problems.'

His mother's mind was not given to tussling with abstract ideas; she preferred the surer guide of particular example from which the rules of life could be formulated. The rules were related to the facts of one's existence. Fifteen pounds a week were a different fact from fifteen thousand a year and produced different rules. Decency and right living were not constant elements but varied according to the means of survival. Estrangement, for instance, could be comfortable enough in a mansion but a constant murderous strain in the enforced confinement of a shared bed and breakfast-table in a one-up-and-one-down. But while pain was much closer so, Nick thought, was the possibility of reconciliation.

'Are you picking this time to judge *me*?' she asked him, persisting.

'Why should I do that?'

'Because of what you came out with earlier, while Tom was here, and because young people are sometimes apt to see things in black and white.'

183

'No,' Nick said, 'I'm not judging you.'

'I can't tear out of myself what I'm feeling for your father and hold it up for you to measure. It's not a simple feeling, anyway. I've done things in my life to make sure I got through. You never know how much things like that cost other people.'

'Doesn't everybody feel remorse when someone close dies?'

'It's not remorse, either. I'm not sorry for the life I've lived and I'd do it again the same way. I'm just sorry that things are never as simple as they ought to be, and the way some people think they are. I could have left your father a long time ago, Nick, but I didn't. There's some who'd've thought better of me if I had.'

'They don't matter, though, do they, those people?'

'No, but you do.'

'He was my father, the only father I'll ever have.'

'And I'm your mother, Nick, and I'm still here.'

He couldn't keep still. He sprung up and strode to the back of the room.

'Mother, I know my father was a poor man in many ways. There was something missing right in the middle of him. But I don't know how much saving yourself was responsible for making him like that. I just don't know and I think it's bloody unfair of you to ask me ... to ask me for absolution over his open coffin.'

Oh, what an image to throw to his debating-society friends; what a phrase to savour and roll off one's tongue. It cut like a knife straight to his mother's heart. The moan that tore out of her throat froze him for a second in horror. He had faced her spirit with his, conscious of her strength but testing his own through his need for identity and survival, and not realising his terrible power to wound. He threw himself on his knees beside her, gripping her arms and pressing his face into her breast.

'Mother, Mother. Oh God, Mother. Please.'

He was a long time in calming her. He held her, speaking soft and gentle words. He had not uttered words of love to

184

her since his childhood, yet there was no person in the world he loved more, no one he less wanted to hurt and no one he could hurt with such ease. He was shaken by the responsibility of this power. The child with his harmless tantrums and rebellions was gone; what his mother faced now was the judgement of the almost-grown man.

The sobbing exhausted her. Finally she lay back still. Nick moved to the arm of the chair, perching awkwardly on the wooden rail, and held one of her hands. She was quiet for a time and he wondered if she was falling asleep. Then she stirred and spoke.

'Oh, Nick, I have had a day! Such a day!'

'You're worn out. Shall I get you one of your pills before you go to bed?'

She told him where they were and he brought the little white box to her. He had drunk his cocoa but hers stood cold in its mug. He reheated it then watched her swallow a tablet between sips.

'Right,' he said. 'Off you go now.'

She swayed a little as she stood up.

'What time will your friend want to get away?'

'He'll be in no hurry. You lie in as long as you like.'

'I shall have to be up to get Shirley's breakfast.'

'She can have a day off tomorrow. I expect she'd prefer it.'

'Your Uncle Tom will be round in the morning and there'll be things to see to.'

'We'll manage, don't worry. Now off you go.'

'I'll say goodnight then.'

'Yes, goodnight, love.'

He kissed her on the lips and turned her gently towards the door.

When she had gone he washed the mugs at the sink and put them away. He placed the guard in front of the fire and got out sticks and a firelighter and put them on top of the coal in the bucket ready for the morning. He checked that both front and back doors were locked then, groggy with tiredness, went upstairs.

Roger seemed to be asleep. Nick undressed by the light from the landing and got into bed beside him. He turned over as Nick settled down.

'Have you been rowing with your mother?'

'Not exactly. She's very upset, for all kinds of reasons. It's not easy.'

'Show me a situation that is.'

'Yes, quite.'

'Nick,' Roger said after a moment. 'I didn't plan it this way, you know.'

'No.'

'But I'm still glad it happened.'

Nick didn't know what to say. He turned on his side and felt Roger move up closer. His arm came over Nick's hip and lightly embraced him. It was oddly comforting. He fell asleep.

13

There was a temporary arrangement of steel tubing lashed across the gap Nick's father's lorry had made in the fence on top of the bank. The vehicle had torn up two of the concrete posts and bent the three-inch lateral tubes as a man might twist a length of wire in his hands. The scars of skidding wheels were burned deep into the road. Those, Nick thought, marked the moment when he would know what was happening. How long had they seemed to him, those seconds of life-and-death struggle before all was lost?

With Tom beside him Nick looked down the steep fall of rough grass. Twenty-five feet.

'They'd have a job lifting it out.'

'Yes. They had a winch up here, so I understand, with the road blocked and all traffic diverted.'

'Have you talked to the police?'

'Yes. They don't seem to know what happened.'

'If there was any negligence on the owners' side there could be a case for compensation, couldn't there?'

'They'll examine the wreckage carefully,' Tom said, 'but I shouldn't bank on anything like that. I wouldn't get your mother set off on that track, either.'

'No.'

Nick turned away and strolled back to the car. It was very cold up here and there was no shelter from the wind. He opened the front passenger door and got in. Tom followed him and settled himself behind the wheel.

'Home now?'

'I suppose so. But look, you drop me in town and I'll get

a bus up.'

'It's no trouble to run you round.'

'All this is keeping you from your work.'

'The job won't stop because of it. Anyway, I keep looking in to see that things are all right.'

He was formidably big in his overcoat. Nick had seen people turn their heads as he walked by. He looked like a man of consequence, someone to be reckoned with. It was easy to see the attraction he'd had for Nick's mother, but what were the qualities in her which had kept him constant all these years? Nick didn't betray his mother when he admitted that she lacked culture. Not that Tom was an intellectual but he did read and he liked music. The only books in Nick's house, apart from a home doctor and a one-volume encyclopedia of household decoration and maintenance, were what he'd brought in himself. (Tom had bought them a piano when Shirley showed interest in learning. She rarely played now. Nick's mother kept the book of Chopin waltzes proudly displayed on the unopened instrument as proof of the experiment's success, but Tom must be disappointed that this commonplace taste was as far as Shirley's aptitude had taken her.) Perhaps for Tom the purely womanly qualities in a woman were enough. To Nick intellectual communication and understanding were vital. He had neither fully made love to a woman nor been in love, and he understood the grip that long familiarity exerts on people only through filial relationships. He saw that love might be arbitrary in the way it struck; he couldn't see how it could survive without some satisfaction of mind as well as heart.

'Your mother tells me you're talking about leaving university, Nick.' The remark appeared to come casually, out of that part of Tom's mind which was not concentrated on driving.

'It's a possibility I've got to think about.'

'It'd be a shame to miss it, wouldn't it, all that opportunity?'

'Things aren't the same now. You know what my father

188

left. That's all my mother will have apart from her pension. Shirley won't be earning anything for another two years; longer if she stays on and takes 'A' levels, as she ought to do. I've a couple of years to do, and more if I tried to go as far as I think I could.'

'Isn't that the point? You think you could go so far, and wouldn't it be a pity to waste that talent?'

'I suppose I should let her go out and scrub floors for me?'

'That's silly talk, Nick. You know she'll never scrub floors while I'm around. In fact, she'll never want for anything while I can help it.'

'She my responsibility, not yours.' It came out with the stiffness, the awkwardness of his youth. He regretted the curtness of the comment but not the content.

'Let me tell you something, Nick,' Tom said mildly. 'My responsibility to your mother began a long time before you knew anything about it, and it still exists today.'

'I'm not my father,' Nick said.

'No, you're not. But if you do this thing for the wrong kind of pride you'll be doing something you'll regret for the rest of your life. I'm asking you to carry on as you were doing; to go as far as your ability will take you, and to forget about money.'

'It's very kind of you.'

'Kindness has nothing to do with it. It's a matter of waste. You'll not only waste yourself, you'll waste it for your mother, and me—yes, and your father as well. You might not see what I'm driving at just now but you will if you think about it. After all,' he finished dryly, 'you're an intelligent lad.'

'My mother never became ... never became friends with you because of your money.'

'No, she didn't. But it would be a pity after all this time if it stood idle while people ruined their lives.' Tom turned his head and looked at Nick. 'You've no need to be scared of it, you know. You've had some before, in times past, and it comes without strings.'

Nick was silent. He looked out at the people moving through the cold morning streets. This town was his town, all he had really known before he went up to university. There were times when he loved it for its associations, times when he hated it for its stuffy provincialism. He could love it the more with the knowledge that his life was not circumscribed by its life and customs, when he could contain its qualities within an awareness of a world outside, a world which awaited the growing sureness of grasp that education would give him. To give up now, to take a job in some office, would be to let it trap him as it had thousands of others. Unlike those thousands, he had choice; but it was a choice that came now not solely by virtue of his ability, but through Tom's money. He could take that and carry on as though nothing had changed. What memories had he of his father which weren't overshadowed by his mother's stronger personality and Tom's more perceptive encouragement? They could put his father into the furnace, then scatter his ashes and behave as though he had never existed.

Shirley was helping her mother to prepare lunch. Rising fifteen, she was rapidly losing her long-legged gawkiness and blossoming into young womanhood. She seemed to Nick to add a couple of years of maturity as soon as she got out of her school uniform of blouse, tie and skirt.

'Oh, you're back,' Nick's mother said. The whine of the vacuum-cleaner died, leaving the scrape-scrape of Shirley's knife on the potatoes. Nick's mother was calmer now. It was idleness which left her raw and vulnerable and now her emotions seemed protected by the carapace of practical activity. He could imagine her uttering the formula 'As long as you keep going. It's when you stop that you've got time to think, and it gets you.'

Tom relit his pipe and pulled at it with quiet enjoyment. He cut the standard figure of the knowledgeable friend of the family. There must be comfort for her in him, Nick thought; a reassurance in his solid presence even had she loved her husband more and him less.

'What did you make of the insurance people?'

Nick let Tom speak. 'They'll be sending somebody to see you. They'll want to see the policy, the death certificate, your marriage certificate and proof of probate.'

'How long will all that take?'

'Only a day or two.'

'All that messing about.'

'You can't expect them to hand five hundred pounds to anyone who walks in and claims it, Norma.'

'They're quick enough to see you pay your dues.'

'Be fair, Mother,' Nick said. 'They're only doing their job.'

'And what do they think widows are supposed to live on while they mess about with their bits of paper?'

Nick clicked his tongue in impatience. This was the side of his mother which irritated him most, the side which indulged in highly coloured visions of 'Them' and 'Us'. 'They' were anybody in authority who hindered the lives of ordinary folks by their perverse indulgence in obstructive procedures and rigmarole which no one but They could understand and which were expressly designed for Their benefit. It was a view of life bred into Nick's people through long generations of struggle and deprivation, and as such understandable; but there were some blind and unthinkable aspects of the attitude of which Nick would have expected his mother's relationship with Tom to have cured her. The irony was that, to many of those it was concerned to help, Socialism itself brought a hopeless feeling that 'They' were even farther away and less accessible than before. Which must be one of the reasons for the existence of the working-class Tories whom Philip Hart sometimes talked about; those deferential people who looked to men like Tom for guidance in local affairs and beyond him to his counterparts in national politics. Philip sometimes argued that a couple of generations of real education would eradicate these anomalies, but as Nick saw it, too much of Socialism's rise had been founded in the realities of material deprivation, and too many people once they acquired a measure of material prosperity began to lean towards the party which gave them more of what they called 'personal freedom'. It wasn't easy. Nothing stood still, and the conditions in which these elements existed were changing all the time.

His mother and Tom had been talking as he let these thoughts occupy him. Now he realised that Tom was going.

'So, I'll see you tomorrow.'

'Aye, get that over with and...' His mother let the sentence go unfinished. 'I've never been to a cremation before.'

'It's all very quiet and dignified,' Tom said.

'It's the way he wanted it, anyway. He once told me so. He had a fear of being buried alive.'

The scrape of Shirley's knife had stopped. She stood motionless, her head bent over the bowl of potatoes. The swing of her shoulder-length hair hid her face from Nick until she suddenly moved and, brushing between the standing form of his mother and his knees where he sat in the chair, hurried out of the room. Tom turned his head as she went, a little frown between his eyebrows.

'You ought to be careful what you say, Norma. You know how hard she's taken it.'

'Oh, I know...' Nick's mother made a helpless movement with her hands. 'I'll go to her in a minute.'

Nick stood up. 'It's all right. I'll go.' He paused in the doorway. 'I'll see you later, Uncle Tom. And thanks for ... for helping to sort things out.'

He went out and up the stairs before Tom could answer. There was no one in Shirley's room and the bathroom door was closed. These upstairs rooms were not places to linger in at this time of year unless you were in bed. Nick thrust his hands into his trousers pockets and stood at the window. The best view in the house was from this side; its extent open or confined only by the weather. Nick had seen it every way, vast as well as limited. He had seen fog stand like a still wall of smoke along the edge of the piece; watched rain move in vertical columns down the valley with sunlight nudging it from behind; seen rainbows arch the near hills and known the far heights in every blue from grey to ice. Today it was all closed in by mist and nothing was visible beyond the looming bulk of the middle spur.

He heard the back door close and saw Tom walk round and get into his car. Nick leaned closer, his breath steaming the glass. Once, as a small boy, sent to bed on a hot night for some misdemeanour, he had leaned out of this window and looked down on his father making a flower border in the stony soil. He had eased himself far out, seeing but not seen, and moved by a long forgotten intensity of resentment, brought a gob of saliva to his lips and let it fall. Yes, there was a memory: he had spat on his father's head.

Shirley's 'Oh' from the doorway brought him round.

'Shirl,' he said, 'are you all right?'

'Yes.'

'You've been crying again.'

'It was the way my mother was talking. It brings it back all the time.'

'She's feeling it as well, you know, Shirl. You won't have to be too hard on her.'

'I don't think any of you loved him like I did. He was just somebody about the place. My mother prefers Uncle Tom, anyway.'

'Come on, Shirl. It's not as——'

'I'm not a little kid any more, Nick. I know about marriage and the way other people can come in and spoil things.'

'I was only going to say it's not as simple as that. Or, at least, I'm ready to give my mother the benefit of the doubt and say that it isn't. Uncle Tom's not a bad man, Shirl. He and Mother aren't wicked people. He's done a lot for all of us.'

'We could have done without it.'

'I don't know.' Nick gave a dry little laugh. 'It'll be through him if I stay on at university.'

'You've got your scholarship grant.'

'A fortune that is! The point is, who's going to keep you

193

and Mother?' He didn't think she'd thought of it before.

'I can always leave school and get a job.'

'But that's just as bad. You can't leave like——'

'No, it isn't as bad, Nick. I shan't go on to university anyway. I don't want to. I was going to leave after 'O' levels even if this hadn't happened.'

Nick wanted to argue with her, to urge her to go as far as she could, but he'd seen signs of her inclination before. He shrugged.

'You won't get any farther than grammar school if you don't want to, that's for sure. But you're to stop talking about leaving now. There's no question of it. I could pack up university and prove that we can't manage without Dad by going into some lousy office. What good would that do him or us? Do you think he'd be happy about it if he knew?'

'Oh, it's so awful. I keep wanting him to walk into the house and I know he never will again. If he'd gone away somewhere for a long time it wouldn't be so bad. But it's for ever and there's nothing you can do about it.' She put her hands up to cover the puckering of her face as she began to cry once more.

'I loved him. I know how sad and hopeless he was but I loved him just the same.'

Nick embraced her. 'Come on, Shirl. Cry it out if you like, but accept things as they are. Mother won't let herself be dependent on us and you know it; so there's no use in our making sacrifices for nothing.'

He gave her his handkerchief as her sobbing turned to a series of little sniffs.

'I was thinking,' he said; 'that the part Tom has played in this family is typical of his attitude to life and politics. He's kind and benevolent while he looks after his own interests, but he does nothing to eradicate root causes. My going back to university on his money will mean I'm no longer a product of state education but of private patronage.'

'I don't understand you.'

'It doesn't matter. I've been thinking about politics quite

194

a bit lately. I took part in a debate in the union the other day.'

'Did you do well?'

'I don't know. Not bad, I suppose. They were all half-digested ideas of Philip Hart's anyway. Do you see much of him at school?'

'He doesn't take us. He once stopped me in the corridor and asked about you.'

'I must go and see him.' He took the damp handkerchief she held out to him. 'All right now?'

'I suppose so. I don't know how I'll get through tomorrow, though.'

'I'm dreading it myself. Still, it'll soon be over.'

'Then we can all get back to normal,' Shirley said.

'Shirl, don't get bitter on top of everything else. You're the one who's at home, and Mother's going to need you.'

'She's got him.'

'We've ... we've never talked about this before, but how did you come to realise what was between them?'

'They were upstairs together one day when I came home. I don't think they were doing anything then because they came down straight away. But my mother had a funny look on her face and it came to me all at once what was going on. I always thought Uncle Tom was just a nice friend of us all. I didn't know he and my mother went to bed together when we were all out. I think it's filthy and disgusting.'

'You're exaggerating a bit, aren't you?'

'No, I'm not.' Shirley's shoulders twitched in a shudder. 'I could be sick just thinking about it.'

'Is that just this situation or sex in general?'

Her eyes were vague. She wasn't unintelligent but she thought in almost entirely intuitive terms. She must rarely have thrashed out an issue by rational argument. He had gone much farther than she in acquiring this ability yet he knew that what he saw in her were his own limitations magnified.

'I mean,' he said, 'does the idea of sex upset you?'

'I don't let lads mess about with me like some of the

195

other girls do,' she said.

He didn't think she was being deliberately evasive. It struck him, though, that the man who did eventually get her would have two ghosts to exorcise.

Their mother called from the foot of the stairs. 'Are you two up there?'

Nick shouted back. 'Yes. Coming.'

Shirley stirred by the window. 'I suppose I'd better go down and help finish the dinner.'

'Take it easy for a bit, eh, Shirl?' Nick said.

She sighed. 'Yes. All right.'

As she turned the pale winter light fell across her face and Nick was once more acutely conscious of that indefinable something he had seen in her as she lay asleep. Now he felt he almost knew the secret and he said quickly,

'Just stay like that a second, will you?'

'What's the matter?'

'Nothing. Turn your face away a bit as you were before.'

It had gone. No, as her head moved another fraction he saw it again. It was in her jaw and the set of her mouth seen like this. He wondered why he had never seen it before. Perhaps because the idea of it had never occurred to him. Even now he found it hard to take it in, yet it was, when you faced it, so very possible.

'What's wrong?' Shirley said. 'What are you looking at?'

Nick's pulse was racing. He tried to keep his voice level.

'It's just occurred to me,' he said, 'that you're going to be beautiful.'

14

Nick had to take two buses to get to Philip Hart's house. The Harts lived in a three-bedroomed semi on an estate up a hill from the bus stop on the main road. Nick, who had lived in the house in Edgehill for as long as he could remember, always felt that a lack of permanence hung over estates like this one, as though the families living there were people in transit, settled for a short time before moving on somewhere else. Nor could the feeling be put down simply to the comparative newness of this particular scheme, which on one side was being developed further, the extended ribbon of road running between the shells of houses and stacks of bricks. It was perhaps the bricks which gave the clue. The older parts of the town, dreary and inadequate though they might be, were like something thrust up out of the earth itself, a landscape which had torn out of its own vitals the materials to meet the demands the nineteenth century had made upon it. These bricks estates were the same in which ever town you found yourself. They seemed to belong everywhere and nowhere; and it was this impression which Nick felt was, from the outside at least, carried over into the people who occupied them.

The front of Philip's house was dark but his Mini stood in the open garage and as Nick walked up the drive to the kitchen door light thrown on to the back lawn through the dining-room window became visible to him. He rang the bell. He had come unannounced and he was suddenly diffident about intruding. Not that Philip stood much on ceremony: he was one of a younger generation of teachers who with the simultaneous dropping out of a number of older men had come into their own at Nick's school. Men like Philip relied for their authority not on an undue insistence on the dignity of their position but on the establishment of a *rapport* between themselves and their pupils. They were not remote academics but human beings, who tried to make what they were teaching as directly relevant to life as possible, so turning school from an obligatory chore into a fascinating voyage of exploration. Which wasn't to say that Philip, for one, couldn't be tough. Nick had seen him settle the game of one persistent troublemaker with an accurate and lightning-quick swipe of his hand, a measure not, strictly speaking, within his rights, but one which was held afterwards in the minds of all of them as something the more to be avoided because of its rarity. The real displeasure which provoked it was something Nick could still remember being acutely conscious of and anxious not to incur.

Philip himself answered the door. 'Nick!'

'Hello. I hope I haven't come at a bad time.'

'No, no. Come in.'

Nick stepped into the kitchen. It was tidy, with pots that had been washed but not put away, in the wire rack by the sink.

'Kate's just putting the little one to bed. Come through here.'

In the dining-room Philip's elder boy was kneeling on a chair at the table, writing figures on a sheet of paper.

'Here's Nick, Christopher,' Philip said. 'You remember Nick, don't you?'

The boy smiled at Nick, who went and looked over his shoulder. 'What are you doing, then, Christopher?'

'Sums.'

'Mad about arithmetic,' Philip said. 'It beats me where he gets it from.'

Nick motioned to the exercise books piled on the other side of the table. 'If I'm interrupting your work . . .'

'No, this isn't urgent. And I've marked most of them,

198

anyway. Sit down. What are you doing home?'

'It's my father. He died this week.'

'Oh dear! Was it a long illness, or——?'

'An accident. He had a smash in his lorry.'

There was a pause, then Philip said, 'Not that big artic that went over the top up Greenbank?'

'Yes, that was it.'

'I came round there. Couldn't get through. The police had stopped the road. What a lousy thing to happen.'

Philip appeared to be genuinely upset for Nick. He frowned and bit his bottom lip, standing there for so long that he seemed after some time to have slipped into a preoccupation of his own. The tread of feet in the hall brought him out of it. Kate Hart came in.

'Look who's here, Kate.'

Kate Hart gave Nick just the hint of a smile. 'Hello, Nick. How are you?' She looked drawn and tired, as though the day had driven her to her physical limit. Philip butted in with Nick's news.

'How dreadful!' Kate Hart said. 'I am sorry. How's your mother?'

'Oh, she's coping with it. She's ... she's pretty tough.'

They had cremated Nick's father that morning. There were no relatives and the funeral party consisted only of themselves, Tom and two representatives from the firm Moffat had worked for. Nick held his mother's hand and felt its convulsive grip as the coffin slid through the velvet curtains to its destination. It was all very clean and efficient. A plaque commemorating Moffat would be fixed to the kerb bordering the path through the crematorium grounds and the page on which his name was recorded in the book of remembrance would be open to view on the anniversary of his death. It was a fair journey to the crematorium but they left nothing behind them which would need their attention.

'Yes ...' Kate Hart said vaguely. She sat down with obvious relief. 'I'll have five minutes before I start Christopher on his way.'

'You should have stayed another day or two and let me fetch you home in the car,' Philip said.

'I'd had long enough.'

'There was no need to waste all that time and knock yourself out struggling with the two of them on trains.'

'I thought home was the best place for me.'

Philip didn't answer. Nick had sat quietly through this exchange, conscious that there was something in the air—or rather a lack, as though the oxygen had been sucked out of the atmosphere. He had not seen them like this before. But then, he had dropped in without warning and caught them at a tired time. They seemed dull with each other, jaded; and neither bothered to look at the other when speaking. It must often be so in marriage, Nick thought, as familiarity took its toll, blurring the memory of the days before they knew each other and of the occasion when they looked at each other for the first time. He hoped his presence wasn't unwelcome. He was too diffident to feel at ease immediately with Philip. The pupil–teacher relationship died hard, and it seemed only yesterday that he was just one in a class of twenty with Philip presiding over all of them. But on each of the occasions they'd met since then Philip had urged him to keep in touch and visit them any time he liked.

'I'm sorry, Nick,' Philip said. 'Kate's been visiting her mother in Lancaster and she just got back today.' He sat down at the table and tidied the exercise books into a neat pile. 'A teacher's work is like the poor—always with him. How's yours going?'

'All right, thanks.'

'You're coping okay, are you?'

'I think so. I spoke in a debate in the union the other day.'

'Oh yes? What was the motion?'

'That this house would welcome the Socialist way of life.'

'Oh, my God!' Philip said. He laughed. 'Again?'

'We're only a new university,' Nick said. 'We've got to

200

have time to catch up.' He slipped the folded sheets of paper out of his inside pocket and said shyly, 'I've got my notes. I thought you might like to read them.'

'Please.' Philip reached over and took them from him. He read quickly and smiled at one point. 'I like the references to Waugh, though you perhaps made a mistake in bringing him into it.'

'Oh?'

'There might be those in the audience who confuse what you say with an attack on his work. You could alienate them.' He was reading as he spoke. 'Yes, I like it. A bit short on facts and figures but rhetoric does no harm in a speech like that.'

'I'm not really interested in figures,' Nick said. 'You can twist them to suit any argument.'

'That's why they're so useful in political propaganda.'

'I didn't think of it as being propaganda. I was saying what I believe.'

'You mean it's the truth when you believe it and propaganda when you don't? Come on, Nick, you know better than that. If you plead a cause or a way of life you use every bit of evidence that will support your case and either ignore, or interpret to suit your own ends, the bits that don't. Your purpose isn't a dispassionate examination of all sides of the question but to convince people that your way is best. You're persuading them to give you power.'

'The end justifies the means?'

Philip smiled. 'No. I said "ignore" or "interpret" not "suppress" or "twist". I'm not saying you should corrupt either yourself or your case by telling lies, but everything is open to interpretation or presentation in the best or worst possible light according to what you initially believe. The world is full of facts, Nick, but the search for truth involves an interpretation of those facts. One man's meat is another man's poison and everybody, *everybody*, has an axe to grind.'

'Look, Daddy,' Christopher said. He held out his sheet of paper.

'That's very good,' Philip said, glancing at what his son had done. 'You keep that up and we'll have a Transport House statistician in the family. Somebody to sober up the emotional arguments of all these arts types,' he added to Nick. He leaned forward and looked at his wife's face.

'I think it's time you were getting into your pyjamas, Christopher. Your mummy's flaked right out.'

'I'm not asleep,' Kate Hart said; 'just resting my eyes.'

'I'm sorry.' Nick half rose from his seat. 'I've come at a bad time.'

'You stay just where you are,' Philip told him. 'We don't see much of you these days. When are you going back?'

'In the morning.'

'You can't dash away now, then. Come on, Christopher, do as you're told.'

The boy got down off his chair and took pyjamas out of a drawer. He went behind Nick to undress.

'The modesty bug's bitten him,' Philip said. 'Six months ago he'd have taken his clothes off and stood dreaming, naked, in front of the fire no matter who was here. Now he hides behind the chair.'

'It's just a natural growth of good manners,' Kate Hart said without opening her eyes. 'There's nothing deeply significant about it.'

'I expect not. I did write and say I'd enjoyed the paper on Fielding and Richardson you sent me, didn't I, Nick? It sent me back to *Clarissa*. They had to dig it out of the cellar at the public library. It hadn't been on the shelves for years. Come to think of it, I was probably the one who had it out last time. It's a damn' fascinating piece of work. Nothing quite like it before. All that introspection and analysis of motives. If it weren't so unmanageably long I'd try it on some of my senior girls. They might think Clarissa herself a bit wet but I'm sure they'd get a lot out of it.'

'You always get the two of them compared because they were contemporaries and so different,' Nick said. 'And Fielding usually gets the vote because he's extrovert and supposedly healthy and outdoor, and Richardson works in a hot-house. But Fielding's people bash on according to their characters, or humours, and I suppose I'm more interested in Richardson just now because I'm at a stage where I find issues complex and I try to analyse my own motives and find out which pressures one should accept and which resist.'

'The closed inactive world of one's own dilemmas,' Philip murmured. It sounded like a quotation but Nick didn't recognise it.

Kate Hart suddenly opened her eyes and sat up.

'Are you ready, then, Christopher?'

'Yes, Mummy.' The boy walked out from behind Nick's chair.

'Off you go, then. Brush your teeth properly. You can look at a book for ten minutes providing you don't blunder about like an elephant and wake your brother up.'

'You'll come and tuck me up, won't you?'

'In a little while. Say goodnight to your daddy and Nick.'

The boy kissed his father on the cheek and cast a shy backward glance at Nick. 'Goodnight.'

'Goodnight, Christopher.'

Christopher went out. He was a sturdy lad, with Kate Hart's colouring and Philip's features. There was no mistaking his parentage. He'd grown a lot since Nick saw him last. You noticed these things more when you saw people at intervals, particularly young people still in a fairly rapid stage of development. Perhaps he would not have noticed what he'd seen in Shirley had he been at home all the time. On the other hand, it could be something which was going to become more markedly obvious as she moved through her teens to adulthood. Then other people would see it. Unless he was wrong and what he'd seen was an illusion.

He had gone and searched his own face in the bathroom mirror and said casually to his mother, when they were alone, 'How old was I when you got to know Uncle Tom?'

'Oh, no more than a baby.'

'You'd never known him before that?'

'I'd seen him but I'd never spoken to him.'

'It was before Shirley was born, though, wasn't it?'

'Oh yes, quite a while before then.'

Did she realise what he was after? She made no sign of it and he, suddenly fearful of what he might disturb, did not probe further.

'Would you like a cup of coffee, Nick?' Kate Hart asked him.

'Not unless you're making one for yourself.'

'I was thinking I might take Nick out for a drink,' Philip said. 'That's if you do drink, Nick. I suppose you'll have got a bit of practice in at university.'

Nick smiled. 'A bit.'

'Righto, then.' Philip got up, his indolent lolling with one arm resting on the table transformed into purposeful action as he moved about the room, putting on tie and jacket and checking his pockets for money and car keys.

'I shall have a bath and go to bed,' Kate Hart said, 'so make sure you've got your latchkey.'

'Okay.'

'Do, please, tell your mother how sorry I am,' she said to Nick.

'Yes. Thank you.'

They went out. Nick walked to the gate as Philip backed the car down.

'You must be feeling pretty low, Nick,' Philip said as they started along the road. 'If you don't feel like a drink I'll take you straight home.'

'It's a bit of relief, really, to get out of the house.'

'Yes, perhaps so. Is there any particular place you'd like to go?'

'I don't really know the pubs at home.'

'I seem to know so many nowadays,' Philip said. 'Let me think . . .'

They went to the Waterman's Arms, by the river, a former beer-house which had recently been altered and decorated in a ridiculously inappropriate scheme designed

204

to attract the car trade. It must be nearly a hundred years since anyone had fished the black greasy waters which slid by outside, and then not with oars and nets and lobster pots.

'Never mind,' Philip said. 'It's handy and the beer's good.'

They took their pints of bitter to a table by the wall. Philip drank deeply from his and exhaled his breath, looking round the room. 'That's better.' He seemed more at ease now, relieved, like Nick, to be away for a while from home and family.

'You were ready for that,' Nick said.

'Yes, I was. The man who invented it ought to have a medal . . .' He paused for a second then began to recite:

'Why is there no monument to bitter in our land?

The hops and malt and barley brew

Reviled by temperance band . . .'

He closed his eyes, smiling. 'Wait a minute . . .

'The man who made it, all should see

Upon a plinth in London Town

Marked "Wallop, RIP".'

Philip laughed. 'A bit missing in the middle. Acknowledgements to Spike Milligan.' He drank from his glass, becoming serious again.

'How is this upset going to affect you at university?'

Nick shrugged. 'It could. It ought to be up to me to go out and earn the family's living now. I suppose I'm lucky, though. We've got a friend, a kind of honorary uncle, who has plenty of money and he wants me to keep on.'

'You don't seem too happy about it.'

'It's a bit . . . complicated.'

'Has he made any conditions?'

'Oh, no, nothing like that.'

'Well, if it's just a matter of pride I'd think hard before chucking my future away.'

'What do you think my future's likely to be?'

'That's a big question, Nick; and not one I can really answer. You'll do all right because you're a bright lad. I

205

used to be a bright lad. My mother was both proud of me and puzzled by my cast of mind. She never said much because all education was a good thing to her. I mean as a means to an end, a way of getting on in the world. But sometimes I got hints of what she was thinking. Why did I fill my mind with all these abstract ideas and questions? Why not something practical like designing bridges or buildings, finding a cure for cancer or learning how to graft human limbs? Even inventing a better can-opener. Facts are what a man can seize on and stay happy with. Why bother your head looking for truth when there's a world full of useful facts to be had for the taking? When this happens the litmus paper turns blue, when the other thing happens it turns red. Reproduce the conditions precisely and the same thing happens again. Facts give birth to new facts, and you discard the worn-out ones as you go along.'

'It's not quite as simple as all that, is it?' Nick said.

'No ... And I'm afraid I'm assuming that all these "facts" will protect you from moral dilemmas, from having to choose between one course of action and another. Which is ridiculous.'

'Surely the man who's read about and been educated in the moral dilemmas of others will have a broader perspective to test his own against.'

'It's one of the aims of an education in the arts. Wisdom, as against ingenuity, comes from reading the thoughts of other and greater men. When I'm pessimistic, I think it all comes down to education bringing perception and perception bringing vulnerability. If you don't know, you can't care, can you?' Philip shrugged. 'Oh, you'll make out, Nick. You'll get a good degree. You might become a teacher, a bit more aware and concerned than the average, and write occasional fillers for *The Guardian* on what kids should be reading in schools and why the educational system isn't as good as it could be.' He was looking at Nick now with a small sardonic smile in his eyes. 'Or you could go into advertising, television or journalism; review books, maybe write a couple yourself, or a Wednesday Play full of some fierce intent message. Some of these things you could perhaps do without finishing at university; but you'll stand more chance of doing them, and have more choice, than if you go selling insurance or pushing a pen in some office or bank. It's only this once, Nick. Chuck it now and you'll never have the same chance again.'

Nick nodded. 'I know.'

There was no one Nick admired more than Philip. It had begun with an instant liking, developing quickly into hero-worship at school and found a firm foundation in the passionate humanity and logic of Philip's views of life and literature. He had copied the casual neatness of his clothes, even the way he had his hair cut, and found himself, away at university, aping his mannerisms, his delivery of a sentence, the movements of his hands—in particular the habit he had of holding both hands up a little, palms down, when he was momentarily lost for the right word. He was proud of Philip's liking for him and that they had established a relationship outside the classroom. He wanted now to confide the secret of his mother's relationship with Tom, to use Philip's years and wisdom to invest the situation with some rationality, to get bearings on it impossible through his own inexperience and closeness to it. But he hesitated to betray his mother to the judgement of someone who did not know her, someone moreover who had a fierce moral conviction about the way people should be treated, and who was himself in his marriage to an admirable woman so far removed from that kind of situation. He would see how the evening went, whether a good moment would arrive . . .

He noticed a stocky middle-aged man in neat dark suit and white shirt, who kept turning his head to look at Philip from his place at the bar.

'There's a chap over there seems very interested in you.'

'Where?'

'The man with sandy hair.'

'Oh yes . . . Hold it, I believe he's coming over.'

'Excuse me butting in . . .' The man stood over them with a pint glass in his hand. He had a ruddy complexion and

207

blue eyes under sandy eyebrows. 'It is Mr Philip Hart, isn't it?'

'Yes, that's right.'

'I'm Walter Whitehead. Councillor Walter Whitehead.'

'Oh, how d'you do? I was just thinking I ought to know you.' Philip started to rise but Whitehead said, 'No, don't get up.'

Philip indicated the bench seat. 'Would you like to ...?'

'Just for a minute, thank you.'

Whitehead put his glass on the table and sat down. He produced a twenty packet of Players and offered them round. Nick, who didn't smoke, refused. Philip took one and Whitehead lit that and his own with a gas lighter which he carefully returned to a soft red pouch before slipping it back into a pocket of his waistcoat.

'Oh, by the way ... Nicholas Moffat,' Philip said and Whitehead nodded, giving Nick a brief intent look from his blue eyes. Tom's eyes were as blue and piercing, but they had a wider play of expression, reflecting a lively, ranging mind; unlike Whitehead's which, Nick guessed, was given to humourless absorption with the subject in hand.

'My son told me what a good talk you gave to the Young Socialists,' Whitehead said.

'Oh yes. They got on to me through one of the sixth-formers at school.'

'George Orwell, wasn't it?'

'That's right. It seemed to go down pretty well.'

'Yes, Martin said they'd all enjoyed it.'

'Frankly, I didn't know what to expect. They turned out to be a lively lot. If you'd dropped me down among them without prior knowledge I'd have guessed by looking that they were Young Conservatives.'

'I beg your pardon,' Whitehead said.

'I mean I was pleasantly surprised to find so many lively and well-set-up young people in something as actively political, rather than negatively so, as a Young Socialists group in a town of this size in this area.'

'I don't see why young people shouldn't join a group like

that, do you?' Whitehead said.

'No, indeed. Don't misunderstand me. But as I see it, the political tradition in this valley is one of a kind of independent radical liberalism. But it's anti-Socialist rather than anti-Conservative; so it's gradually become pro-Conservative as active Liberalism went into a decline and Conservatism moved towards the centre. It's something that comes from the top, from the mill- and factory-owners who've influenced people for generations. The influence isn't as strong as it once was but there's still a strong and instinctive feeling that anybody who gets on is one of *them*, in the way he thinks at least. "Them 'at has summat is summat; them 'at has nowt is nowt".' Whitehead nodded; he knew that old maxim. 'What it means is that when a person starts to get on there's no need for him to vote Labour; in fact to do so will be to his own detriment because Labour policy is to take from those who have. I was glad to see bright young kids who see things the other way.'

Whitehead's gaze had not left Philip's face while he was speaking. He said now. 'Well, I'm just a practical politician, Mr Hart. Have you ever taken part in active politics?'

Philip shook his head. 'No. I've been a member of the Labour Party since university, but that's all.'

'You are a member in good standing?' Whitehead asked.

'As far as I know, I am.'

'H'mm.' Whitehead picked up his glass. 'Can I get you a drink?'

'I'd like a pint of bitter, please.'

'What about you, young man?'

'Just a half, please.'

'Do you know who he is?' Philip said as Whitehead went away to get the drinks.

'I've heard of him.'

'He's the leader of the Labour group on the town council. One of our practical politicians.' He grinned at Nick.

'I thought all you were saying was going straight over his head.'

'Maybe,' Philip said. 'Maybe ... But it never pays to

underestimate people like Whitehead. They're the boys who get things done—rightly or wrongly—while the rest of us sit around talking and wringing our hands.'

When Whitehead came back he said without preamble, 'Have you ever thought of putting up for the council?'

'Not seriously.'

'But I expect you think you could do better than some of them that's on, eh?'

'There's surely hardly a man in Cressley who doesn't think that,' Philip said, and Nick, to his surprise, saw that Whitehead could smile.

'Aye, you're right there ... You know we haven't got a majority at present?'

'A couple down, aren't you?'

'That's right. We'd like to take control, get things done that they can't. They're a raggle-taggle-bobtail lot when you really weigh 'em up, with no policy except to oppose what we try to do. Some of 'em hate organised measures like poison and when we come into the chamber with a definite policy in mind they sniff at it as though they were being asked to support something criminal. Sometimes we can persuade a couple of them to vote with us—fellers like Tom Simpkins, who really do think for themselves—but it's damned hard work fighting every inch of the way, and knowing you're going to have to before you ever get in there. If we could get some new blood into the field for the next election, young men with some standing, who've obviously thought it out for themselves—not just old party workhorses—then we might swing a ward or two where we've never had any luck before.' Whitehead looked at Philip. 'It's fellers like you we want.'

Philip took out his cigarettes before answering and Whitehead went through the small ritual with the lighter again.

'It's very flattering,' Philip said, 'but it needs some thinking about.'

'I wouldn't be too flattered if I were you,' Whitehead said bluntly. 'We've no safe ward to offer you—not that there is

210

anything that safe in this game—and all you might likely end up with is a bit of experience for another time.'

'You're honest about it, anyway.'

'You wouldn't think I'd much respect for you if I tried to shoot you a big line, would you?'

'No ... As I say, it needs some thinking about. How much time is there?'

'Before the election? Six months. Look, why not come along to headquarters one night and meet a few people? I'll let you know the best time. Are you on the phone?'

'Not at home. But I'll give you my address and you can drop me a note. Or you could ring me at school, in the lunch break. I can't make any promises, of course.'

'Neither can I,' Whitehead said, pocketing his diary. 'This is just an informal preliminary approach. There are various procedures to be gone through before you could be officially adopted. But,' he said, the knowing man of influence, 'I shouldn't worry too much about that side of it.'

Whitehead glanced at his watch then drained his glass.

'Well, gentlemen, I shall have to leave you. I'll hope to see you again, Mr Hart.' He got up abruptly and walked away from them, leaving his glass on the end of the bar counter as he passed.

'Just like that,' Philip said. 'Just like that ... Are you all right, Nick? How are you feeling?'

'I'm okay,' Nick said.

'You just say the minute you feel like going and we'll go.'

'I'm probably better off here than brooding at home,' Nick said. He looked round the room. It had filled up considerably since they came in and people who couldn't find a seat were standing in ones and twos and small groups in the middle of the floor.

'What do you think you'll do?' he asked.

'I don't know. Just at this moment I don't feel either mentally or morally equipped to fight an election.' He leaned his head back and closed his eyes. Nick noticed for the first time the shadows under them, as though he had lost sleep or gone through a time of strain.

'This might be a chance to get in on some of that practical, useful work you were talking about.'

'I suppose it could be. Except you're never sure whether you're right or wrong. And even if you're right and everything goes your way you can only reduce the sum total of human hardship; try to see that people are well housed and well fed and not subjected to unjust laws. After that they're on their own and there's no legislation which will ensure their happiness. Or our own.'

'You know the man Whitehead mentioned—Tom Simpkins?'

'By name.'

'He's the, er, uncle I was telling you about earlier.'

Philip was silent for a moment, looking at Nick. 'It's a small world,' he said at last. 'I ... I knew someone who works for him—a young woman—Andrea Warner. Do you know her?'

'I don't think so.'

'So Simpkins is the man who wants to see you through university?'

Nick nodded.

'And what's the problem?'

Nick moved his hands in embarrassment. He had never put it all into words for anybody before and he didn't know how to begin. It was none of Philip's business and he had no right to deliver up his mother for his judgement.

'I suppose,' he said, 'it's a matter of loyalties and principles and self-respect.'

'Is that all?' Philip said. 'And I thought it was something serious, like money.'

Nick looked sharply at Philip but his face was straight. He was being ironic but at whose expense Nick didn't know.

'You don't have to tell me if you don't want to,' Philip said when Nick became silent again. 'But I'd like to help if I can.'

'My mother and Uncle Tom ... Simpkins ... are a bit

212

more than friends,' Nick said. 'It's something that's been going on for years and years, ever since I was a kid.'

He waited for Philip to take his meaning, then glanced up to see the other's frown.

'All that time?' Philip said. 'But how on earth did they manage to——'

'My father knew,' Nick said. 'As far as I can gather, he knew.' He looked at Philip again but he had nothing to say. He was watching the smoke curl up from a newly lighted cigarette and still frowning, as though Nick's revelation had set off thoughts of his own.

'I should explain about my father,' Nick said, 'though I don't really know enough to ... He was a shadow of a man in many ways. He had a lot of poor health. The Japs had him during the war. He was kind of withdrawn a lot of the time. He couldn't have been all my mother needed. She took up with Uncle Tom when he'd helped her with something. She turned to him but stayed with my father and kept the home and family together. If my father was ever bitter about it he never showed it, though he was sometimes bitter about himself. The trouble is, I've never been able to sort out cause and effect. Did my mother let him down or did he, in a way, betray her by marrying her in the first place? Now he's dead, and it looks as though it's my turn.'

'You mean you could be betraying him by letting Mr Simpkins keep the family while you go through university?'

'Yes. I'm his son. I could work to keep us all going. If I let Tom do that he's got us all and my father has nothing.'

'And if you throw away your future he's sacrificed you too. He's not only wasted his own life but yours as well.'

'I've had a similar argument put to me,' Nick said.

'It's the only proper and sensible way to look at it. The other way would be damn' near criminal, Nick.'

Nick swallowed. 'It's just that he's dead, and nobody had a chance to ask him. Nobody really asked him about anything.' His lips trembled. God, he was going to cry; break down and make a fool of himself in the middle of all these people. He shaded his eyes with his hand and shredded the edge of a beer-mat with his thumbnail.

Philip waited a while before speaking. Then he said, 'You've come to a lousy man for advice on principles and loyalty, Nick. What I think, though, is that you should honour the dead but look after the living. And I can't see any loyalty that would be served by your wasting your future.'

He touched Nick's arm. 'Let's have another drink, shall we?'

Nick dropped his hand and blinked his eyes. 'It's my turn.'

'Save it for your education,' Philip said as he got up.

'No, honest, I've got some money.'

'You can get the next round, then.'

Philip had been gone only a moment when a man in his late twenties with a pale pink girl in a pale pink coat came round from behind Nick and made as if to take the space on the upholstered bench along the wall.

'That's someone's seat,' Nick said.

The man gave him a cold stare. 'How many?'

'One.'

'There's room for all of us, then.'

He motioned the girl before him and they sat down, the man turning his head and speaking into the girl's ear in a low mutter, as though continuing something he'd been saying before. Nick felt his ears burn with anger at the man's rudeness in not bothering to ask and then taking the seats when it was obvious that the person who had left would have to inconvenience the people on the other side by jamming himself into the tiny space still available. He was surprised by the intensity of his hatred for the man. Everything about him—the shape of his head, the small cold eyes, the line of his mouth—spoke to Nick of what he was: a pusher. A man who would never lack knowledge for diffidence in asking; who would never be left out of anything going and who would make sure he was well up in the running even if it meant trampling someone else underfoot to achieve the position. He belonged, Nick reflected, indul-

214

ging his hatred in an analysis of some of its many manifestations, to a type of person who could be relied on to make uncomfortable and blunt the pleasure of all around. He seemed to have seen it most often in women, where it came out in a quarrelsome insistence that they and their children were not to be taken advantage of, an insistence which usually ensured their taking advantage of everyone else. In the well-to-do it could be seen in a constant loud-mouthed quibbling about service, and the humiliation of those in inferior positions. A narrow-eyed unselfconsciousness was the mark of them all, and 'ignorant' the word which, for Nick, best described them.

Philip's return interrupted his thoughts. He looked across Nick's shoulder at the man sitting there and said amiably, 'Hello, Jack.'

'Philip,' the man said. 'How are you?'

'Pretty fair.'

'Have I got your seat?'

'It looks like it.'

'I think we can make room for a little 'un.'

Damn' civil of you, old man, Nick thought as the two of them moved closer and Philip squeezed into the space they made. How they came to be acquainted Nick didn't know but they spent the next few minutes exchanging news of their own doings and those of people they both knew while Nick, still in a mood of sullen anger, drank his beer and wondered why the comparatively little he'd had was already taking effect on him. He was not yet a practised drinker, consistent in his resistance to alcohol. Sometimes he could drink what seemed like enormous amounts with little ill-effect; at other times a single pint of beer, as tonight, made his head swim and threatened to blur his speech. Perhaps it was his empty stomach: he'd eaten very little lunch after the funeral, and nothing since then. More likely, it was a reflection of his mood. You didn't mind slurring your words and staggering a little when you were happy-drunk, only when you were depressed and the drink sank you deeper into melancholy. He thought he could have worked it out of himself with Philip's help, but there was, for all his interest and apparent attentiveness, something self-absorbed about Philip; and the intrusion of this obnoxious man—with Philip knowing and seemingly liking him—was enough to pitch Nick over the edge.

He got up and went out to the lavatory, noting with some relief that his walk was steady. Still, the evening was spoiled. He had got sensible advice from Philip but the kind of reassurance he'd received before—that whatever was wrong with life and the world, and it was plenty, there were always ideas, goodwill, compassion and plain common sense in action trying to improve things (that, in fact, Philip himself was solid and reassuring)—was simply not coming through. It might mark the end of hero-worship and the beginning of real friendship, but it left him more reliant on himself and, at the moment, despondent and lonely.

Philip and his friend were still talking when he got back to the table. The pale pink girl clutched a gin and orange and looked vacantly round the room. Her gaze touched on Nick impersonally as he sat down. Just then something the man said came clearly to Nick out of the conversation he was not listening to '... and of course, the twits who put this government in...'

'Everybody's a right to his opinion, Jack,' Philip said mildly. Too mildly so far as Nick was concerned.

'They ought to be locked in a nuthouse,' the man said. 'I heard a good one about him the other day. They asked him to appoint a successor in case he died suddenly, in office. "Oh, that's not important," he said. "I'd be back in three days anyway." ' The man bellowed with laughter and Philip smiled.

'Yes, not bad. Except it was originally about de Gaulle.'

'Isn't it funny,' Nick broke in, flushing angrily, 'how any bloke who sounds off about politics without being asked is always a reactionary, peddling the same old stuff that's never solved a thing in a thousand years? And anybody who doesn't agree with him is a candidate for a mental home.'

'You mean to say you voted for them?'

'I haven't got a vote,' Nick said, 'only opinions, which I don't go about shoving down people's throats.'

'You're just one of these young pinkoes.'

Nick made a gesture of disgust and Philip said quietly, 'I voted for them.'

The man called Jack turned his head to look at him. 'My mistake,' he said. 'I hadn't realised the company I was keeping.'

'You weren't asked to keep it,' Nick flashed. 'You took somebody else's seat, if you remember.'

The man moved his shoulders away from the wall. 'You know, you're bloody rude.'

'Coming from you, that's the quote of the week.'

Philip put his hand on the man's forearm. 'Steady on. There's no need to get steamed up. I should explain that Nick's upset today. He's had a serious——'

'Oh, for God's sake, Philip.' Nick got up. 'I'm going. I'll see you outside when you're ready.'

He turned and walked away from them and out through the door. The cold damp air enveloped him and he took deep slow breaths of it, feeling his heart racing. Across the road, through a gap in the low wall, he could see the water of the river, apparently motionless, with the still reflections of street-lights on the far bank. He walked across and leaned with his arms resting on the wall. The water was high but you could watch for some moments before discerning its smooth flow. Once it had been clear crystal to its bed, running to the sea between wooded hills and across empty plains. The sea had brought the fierce men from the north countries, raiding up the valley, taking their plunder, leaving the maimed and the dead. Later they had come to stay, exacting their tribute, ruling all this land and founding the settlements which were the towns of today. There was no peace: they were defeated, their conquerors defeated in their turn and the land ravaged once more. Five hundred years passed, with wars of bitter division when York fought Lancaster and Parliament, the King. Then the peaceful pursuits: the hills sustained the sheep, the swift-flowing streams washed the wool. Practical men made machines to speed the work and other practical men came in the night to break them. Peace had another kind of conflict smouldering beneath it: that between master and men, Them and Us; though each depended on the other and the land was the inheritance of all. 'What we want,' thought Nick passionately, as though the fabled city were as near as the lights across the water, 'is men's rights, not privileges; a system which can embrace us all, undivided, in which men still have choice—indeed, more real choice for more people than ever before—and can work with skill and ingenuity, with enthusiasm, courage and compassion, without fear; pledged not to private gain or personal power, but secure in the knowledge that what they do is for the good of everyone. And if we have to change a lot of people to make it work, then by God, that's what we must do.' It had all been said many times before. What was necessary was to go on saying it, and working for it, until it came to pass; not in bloody strife but in the final inevitable realisation of the age-old yearning in men's hearts.

The door of the pub opened behind him and he looked round as a group of people came out. They were laughing and talking together. Nick turned away and resumed his contemplation of the river. He didn't know that Philip had come out also until he came soft-footed across the road and leaned on the wall next to him.

'Well . . .'

Nick grunted.

'Feeling okay?'

'Yes, I'm all right. I'm sorry I upset your conversation.'

'That's okay. I admired your spirit. He's a bit of a pillock and it does his type good to be stood up to now and again. Argument, as such, is impossible.'

'I didn't care much for Whitehead, either, if it comes to that.'

'Neither did I.' Philip turned his head and Nick could sense rather than see the faint sadly ironic smile. 'Isn't it a

218

pity we can't ship all the bastards to some vast colony and leave us nice people at home? Except, what makes you and me think we're so nice?' Philip twisted round and leaned with his back to the wall, looking across at the pub.

'All that brass flowing across the counter to pay for the décor.'

'People enjoy it.'

'*I* enjoy it,' Philip said. 'It can let you off the hook for a while, but it's no cure for anything.' They were quiet for a time. 'What do you want to do now?'

'I suppose my mother will be waiting for me.'

'Yes ... I'll take you home.'

They walked across the road and into the car-park.

'Why don't you go a bit further into that matter with Whitehead?' Nick said as they got into Philip's car.

'Do you really think it would do any good?'

'In what way?'

'If I went into local government. If I got in, that is.'

'You mean you don't think there's any room for people like you?'

'What influence can one man exert on it? It's like so many institutions nowadays. We're living in a world where our actual influence diminishes as our commitment spreads itself.'

'I'm surprised to hear you talk like that.'

'Are you? Why?'

'You don't just wring your hands about the general state of education, do you? You're in there, teaching. And if you want an example of what that kind of particular influence can do, there's me. For what it's worth.'

'I'm touched, Nick,' Philip said. 'I really am.'

'I'm not trying to flatter you. Just reminding you that somebody's got to care in the right way. You know that well enough because it was you more than anybody else who showed me.'

'Now I stand rebuked.'

'Look, all I'm saying is that you can give me a number of perfectly good reasons for not having to go, but the one I

219

can't accept is that you'll do no good if you do.'

Philip's inconsistency disturbed Nick. He could describe Whitehead as a practical man who got things done while others stood around talking, yet later doubt his own ability to do as much. More than that, there had been behind all his talk a kind of world-weariness that Nick had never seen in him before. For some reason his purpose had been sapped and Nick wondered if he could be ill.

'You'd better give me some directions,' Philip said.

Nick told him the way to go then fell silent again. He was recalling the atmosphere in Philip's house and investing it with new significance. It was somewhere there that the trouble lay. The thought saddened him. Everything he looked at now revealed aspects of itself that he hadn't seen before. Nothing was sure any more, nothing real all through. It was like coming back to a familiar town to find that what had seemed like solid buildings were no more than the false façades of a film set and the people in the streets just actors in fancy dress.

At the inquest on Nick's father's death the police said
there was no evidence of negligence on the owners' part in
not maintaining the vehicle properly; nor had Moffat been
exceeding the law in the number and length of his periods
behind the wheel. There was no ice on the road at the time
and no one would ever know why Moffat, who knew the
bend, had on this occasion failed to negotiate it safely. It
was an accident. Just one of those things.

The report came to Nick in a letter from Tom; a sad and
bitter complaint against the loss of any hope of compensation came in another one from his mother. It was uncharac-
teristically querulous from one in whom common sense and
level-headedness had always been prime virtues, and as a
continuation of an attitude he had seen in her while at
home it both irritated and upset him. She wrote of Shirley,
too: 'I know she is taking it hard and I can understand, but
I thought she would spend more time with me instead of
staying out more than she's ever done. She makes excuses
about societies at school and there's a youth club she's
taken to going to. She was never interested in that sort of
thing before. It's alright but...'

Close the ranks, Nick thought. It'll be all right as long as
you act as though it is and rally round me ... But he and
Shirley were no longer children to be fobbed off with excuses and evasions of the facts of life. They were people,
with opinions and judgements, and however inadequate
and immature those opinions and judgements might be in
arriving at truth, loyalty was one thing, a blanket approval

another. They had their own selves to come to terms with. He himself was finding it difficult to establish a rationale which would allow him to settle back peacefully into his studies and his restlessness in the first weeks after his return steadily focused itself into an awareness of women the intensity of which he'd never experienced before. He was surrounded and overwhelmed by them; they moved in an unending and tantalising procession across his vision. He was hardly concerned to communicate with them any more: they were objects of a desire in him which, more than the localised nag of unsatisfied flesh, became a yearning to make love to them all at once. Yet he had no more heart for systematic pursuit and conquest than before when his desire had been spasmodic and associated with an occasional feeling of inadequacy for his lack of experience. He quailed at the thought of talk, or involvement that would lead to more talk and further analysis. He craved something primitive, spontaneous and as life-enhancing as the breast a mother gave her child; a coming together in which he could lose self yet feel the pulse of the universe. 'Wanted,' he thought, 'one attractive golden-hearted whore as immortalised in literature; required to excite, instruct and comfort young undergraduate who has recently lost his mother. May herself be enshrined for a limited posterity in a future novel about university life ...' There must be someone among all the girls surrounding him. He watched for the wayward glance, the arched-back flaunting of breasts, the casually deliberate display of thighs which might constitute invitation. He saw all these things yet could not relate them to himself. It was because the display was so casual, even the talk so free, that the opportunities for error seemed to him so great. He was inexperienced in the game and his fundamental seriousness set him at a disadvantage.

A letter came from Philip: 'Thinking about that night I felt afterwards that I might have let you down a little. The truth is, I was preoccupied with a problem of my own and couldn't enter fully into your mood or make enough effort to change it. That idiot man didn't help matters. I hope you've settled down again, though.

'Whitehead phoned me and I went along to meet his merry band. They gather in a rather austere room over the Trades and Labour Club in town. They got their own business out of the way before I went in. By that time I'd had a couple of pints and got nicely warmed through. It was all very informal. The thing that struck me was their general untalkativeness, or perhaps it just seemed that way in contrast to my sounding-off. I really wanted one or two of them to come out with statements of belief, whereas they might have been craftier than I think in realising that reticence on their part was the best way of encouraging me to come out with mine. One crusty old sod called Williams, a miner man and boy for forty years, seemed highly suspicious of my feelings and motives. Why should a young man like me, with a university education and a secure career, want to become a Labour councillor or, indeed, a Socialist at all? He didn't put it quite like that but it was his meaning. So I asked him if Socialism was a system for all the people or just an instrument whereby the traditionally underprivileged could get their own back on everybody else. If he wanted to keep it to himself he was working on a law of diminishing returns because he and his generation would die off and people who weren't particularly underprivileged (and was he now, for that matter?) and who'd never known the 'thirties would have no way of picking up the reins and carrying on. And, I added, if he thought Socialism simply a matter of economics then his idea of it was narrower than mine.

'Had I any ambition to get into Parliament? one of them asked me. I told him I'd had no particular thought of standing for the borough council, even, until Whitehead approached me. And as far as that went, I hadn't made my decision yet, so I hoped this wasn't an adoption meeting as I'd simply been invited to come along and meet them informally.

'Afterwards a few of us went down into the bar and as I stood there chatting it struck me that we were no bunch of leftish intellectuals changing the world over a couple of drinks. These men, who might become my cronies, were the workers in the field, the boys in the front line, instituting the policies and making the decisions. It was, perhaps, the strangest moment of the evening.'

Nick dreamed of Caroline Chambers. It was a completely unexpected and very erotic dream, and she was a different Caroline from the one he knew. She appeared before him in the black wool stockings she habitually wore and which he'd always rather disliked until now, when they were the only item of clothing between her and nudity and he saw how they set off the plump whiteness of her body. 'You are a silly boy,' she murmured. 'Why did you never realise...?' She sank down beside him, her hands feeling for him. He woke at the height of a spasm of pleasure and switched on the light and examined the sheets in anxious anticipation of Mrs Lomas's disapproval.

When he met Caroline what his eyes saw alternated with the image of how she had appeared in the dream. Her sidelong glances told him she was aware of this new interest in her. How ludicrous, he thought, if she had been dreaming at the same time of him. How more ludicrous he then thought if she had not. He had made love to her without her knowledge or approval and for the space of the dream it had been as vivid and exciting as the reality must be. He mused on a dream theory he had read in some novel that you could train yourself to remember all your dreams and, on waking each morning, write an accurate account of them. The next step, once you had mastered the recall, was to will yourself to dream what you liked. Nick smiled at the notion of possessing all the desirable women he met, in unending succession, without their consent and with neither involvement nor consequences.

He got up to get another cup of coffee at the cafeteria counter and found Caroline beside him.

'People start talking about you if you sit around smiling to yourself.'

'Oh! Do they?' He was startled. He hadn't realised she was watching him so closely. 'Can't you smile, at your own thoughts, then?'

'As long as you don't start laughing out loud.'

'I've often wanted to. Don't we set odd limits to what we call normal behaviour?'

He paid for her coffee but she pressed the money into his hand, her insistence on independence in such a trivial matter irritating him. It was one of her ways of asserting herself and making a man feel somehow less than he was. There was an empty table behind them. Nick motioned to it. 'Shall we...?' Caroline looked across the room at the group she had left.

'All right.'

They sat opposite each other. The pleasure she felt in the attention he was paying her showed in the faint flush of colour in her cheeks and the way she kept her eyes down most of the time. He wondered why his own feeling was more like vague dismay than gratification.

'How's your mother?'

'Fine,' he said automatically, then corrected himself before her quick direct glance. 'Well, you know what I mean...' He wished she would leave the subject alone. She had been embarrassingly effusive in her sympathy on his return and disdainful when she learned that Roger had driven him up and stayed the night.

'It must have been very upsetting for all of you.'

'Yes...' She wasn't *bad* looking. If only she would make a bit more effort. He had an idea that her figure might be better than average under those casual, concealing clothes she wore. Her dark eyes were quite fine too and she drew attention to them by her shortsighted way of looking closely at you when you spoke to her. Not wearing glasses on all the occasions she should was her only touch of physical vanity. Otherwise she didn't bother. But Roger was surely wrong in going so far as to suggest she wasn't clean. 'Have you seen *Zhivago*?'

'No, not yet.'

'You intend to see it?'

'Yes, I'd like to. I think the book's marvellous.'

'What about going to see it together?'

'When?'

'Tonight, if you like.'

She thought for a moment then said, 'Yes, all right.'

'I'll meet you in the pub next to the pictures—The Golden Ball—at six. Okay?'

She nodded. 'All right.' Her eyes narrowed at something she could see past his shoulder. 'Enter Iago.'

Roger came up, took them both in, said 'Hi' and passed on to the counter.

'It's putting it a bit strong, isn't it?' Nick said.

'You can't deny he influences you.'

'No, but still, I influence him, if it comes to that.'

'You don't disapprove in public in such a childish way, do you?'

Nick saw that Roger, having bought a glass of milk, was making his way to a far table. He shrugged to hide his irritation with both of them.

'Doesn't want to butt in.'

'I hope that applies to the pictures.'

'What?'

'You won't turn up with him, will you?'

'No, there'll be just the two of us. Anybody'd think you thought he owned me.'

'He does his best.'

'Oh, don't talk such rubbish, Caroline.'

But Nick felt awkward, later, in telling Roger about the date. He had known he would and he was angry both with the absurdity of the situation and himself for feeling it.

'I thought you'd said something about us going bowling.'

'We didn't set any special time. We can go another night.'

'I don't know what you see in her.'

226

You wouldn't, Nick wanted to say. 'Do you have to?'

'Of all the birds in the university you have to pick that one.'

'It wouldn't really matter which one I picked, would it?' Nick said.

'What do you mean by that?'

'Whatever you think I mean. I'm taking her out, and,' he added viciously, 'if I get the chance I shall poke her.'

'I could be sick at the thought of touching her.'

'Well, that's you, not me. I wish you'd mind your own sodding business and stop trying to run my life.'

'I never thought you saw it that way. I thought we were friends.'

'We are. But that's as far as it goes.'

A deep blush coloured Roger's fair skin. 'If that's the way you want it.'

'What other way is there?'

'It's surprising how it comes out,' Roger muttered.

'Look, Roger, get me right, will you? I'm just a ... an ordinary bloke who likes birds. Caroline's not the sex-pot of the bloody place but she happens to like me, so if I want to take her out I shall. And I don't think it necessary to ask your permission.'

'Oh boy!' Roger said. 'Who brought the subject up in the first place?'

'I knew you'd seen us talking. If I'd gone off without telling you you'd have sulked for a week.'

'You know your trouble, man?' Roger said. 'You think everybody's hanging on every move you make. You've an inflated sense of your own importance.'

'Oh God,' Nick said.

'And nobody really cares. You can do what you like. You don't have to come running to report to me.'

'Now who thinks he's important?'

The trouble was, Nick thought, that any disagreement between them, like this, was made worse because both of them evaded the real issue. He would be tempted to come right out with it and release himself once and for all from the false position he found himself in; but he always stopped just at the edge of the direct statement which might wound Roger and destroy their friendship. Despite what Caroline said, and his own suspicions, he couldn't be sure.

16

Caroline insisted on paying her own way that evening. 'It's the only sensible thing,' she said, 'when everybody's hard up together.'

Well, at least, he couldn't be accused of having tried to buy her with a couple of halves, a ham sandwich and a seat at the flicks. He wondered if she accepted sex on the same basis of mutual convenience and satisfaction rather than something to be conceded reluctantly, as a favour.

They walked afterwards, talking about the film. Caroline filled in, in lengthy and confusing detail, the parts which the novel had but the film had not. He was attentive at first and then abstracted as he tried to think of a place where they could go. His digs were no good; nor were hers. It would have to be outside. He unobtrusively guided their steps towards the river until Caroline paused at the mouth of an alley with a single light mounted on an iron bracket and said, 'Where are we going?'

'I was just walking,' Nick said.

'I mustn't be too late.'

'No ... If we go down here and turn right we can complete the circuit.'

'All right.'

The alley gave on to a paved terrace built up several feet above the water meadows which the bed of the river turned into a low island trapped between it and the town, and flooded over at certain seasons of the year. Some way along the terrace they came to a flight of stone steps leading down to a path. Nick took Caroline's hand. She resisted a little.

'Where are we going now?'

'Down here.'

'But whatever for?'

'I want to look at something.'

'Won't it be wet?'

'I don't think so.'

She went with him. At the bottom he guided her round into deep shadow.

'What do you want to look at?'

'You,' he said.

To his surprise she giggled out loud. 'You could have seen me up there.'

'Not like this,' Nick said. 'Desdemona.'

'What?'

'You set up the images.'

'Oh, I see. As long as you're not thinking of strangling me.'

'There's quite a lot of action to get through before then.'

'Oh, is there?'

'Yes.' He kissed her tentatively. 'I was dreaming about you the other night.'

'What was I doing?'

'I hardly like to tell you.'

'I see. You can't hold me responsible, though.'

'No, but still . . .'

He kissed her again, holding her this time. She kissed him back in a curiously inexpert way, with tight lips, and wriggled against him in an excess of movement that suggested someone acting a part, doing what she thought was expected of her rather than responding naturally. She was still, as though switched off, as soon as he drew away from her.

'We've been in this situation before,' he said.

'You'd had too much to drink then. You just picked me at random.'

'Do you think I'm doing that now?'

'I don't know.'

'Why you, rather than dozens of others?'

'It has to be somebody, I suppose.'

'I don't see that it follows. Anyway, you're the one who's here.'

He slipped his hands inside her open coat and under the bottom of her jumper. She drew in her breath as his palms touched her skin.

'Cold?'

'No.'

He moved his hands upwards, excitement rising in him as she stood quite still, making no effort to restrain him. The feel, a moment later, of her totally unencumbered breasts under the jumper was a trigger as powerful and immediate as the vision of her in his dream. He trembled violently, electrified by the charge of feeling, and clutching at her flesh as though trying to mould it into even more perfect shapes.

'Oh God,' he said.

'They're my best feature,' Caroline said. 'Though it's not everybody you can prove it to.'

'They're beautiful,' he said. 'Beautiful, beautiful . . .'

'I never wear a bra during the day. I don't need one and I can't stand being restricted. I sometimes wear one in——'

He cut short her prosaic explanation by pressing his mouth to hers. With reluctant necessity he dropped one hand to fumble at the waist of her skirt. She put her hand over his and held it.

'No.'

'Oh God, Caroline, don't you want to?'

'I can't . . . not now.'

Someone walked by above them with clear staccato heel-taps. They stood silent as though afraid of discovery, Nick leaning against Caroline and holding her, his breath coming in short agitated gasps.

'I'm sorry if you're all worked up,' Caroline said. 'But I couldn't mention it before.'

'I don't suppose it'll kill me.'

He felt her hand on him. 'Poor you . . .' She brought her mouth up close to his ear. 'There's no need to go away like that.'

'No, it's not...' Nick began. This wasn't as he'd imagined it at all. But her touch was more than he could bear. He stood away for a moment then reached for her again. 'There...'

When she asked, just before they mounted the steps, 'Do you feel better now?' he could have slapped her face.

It had all gone wrong. He should have known that she wasn't a person to him but a temporary projection of his appetites. And that after all he had failed to take her and had given himself over into her hands filled him with self-disgust. She had possessed him for a brief time there. She, of all people, had shown him that reversal of rôles and he was angry and sickened with his own weakness. She had given hardly anything of herself while robbing him of his male prerogative and pride. He didn't even know if she had been speaking the truth. He flushed in the darkness as they walked, asking himself was there any greater degradation than to abandon yourself to someone whom you not only did not love but who did not even offer an equivalent surrender in return.

She felt his silence and said with that exasperating directness of hers, 'You're sorry now, aren't you?'

'For what?'

'I don't know. Perhaps asking me out at all.'

'I don't see why.'

'All because of a dream.'

'Don't be silly, Caroline.'

'Anyway, I'm not sorry.' They had reached the gates of the women's hall of residence. Lighted windows broke the dark bulk of its four floors. She turned to face him.

'I am sorry there won't be another time, though.'

'What makes you think that?'

'You can tell when something doesn't click. Your pride's hurt now.'

'Do you always have to beat everything to death by

232

analysing it?'

'I was afraid you'd do that and turn it into some silly reason for avoiding me.'

'Oh, come on——'

'Well, you needn't, you know. Because if it had been another time it might have been different. Another couple of days, in fact.' She looked at him, then away. 'Now you've got a bit of *my* pride.'

He didn't know what to say. He moved his feet, looking down at them in silence.

'I shall have to go.'

'Yes, so shall I.'

'Oh, heavens,' Caroline said, 'I can't just turn and walk away like this. Nothing's changed with me. I still want to be ... to be friends.'

'It's all right,' Nick said.

'Are you sure?'

'Yes. You must go now. I'll see you.'

'I hope so.' She stood up on her toes, kissed him quickly then turned and ran through the gate.

He watched her shape move through the pools of light and shadow along the drive, then walked away himself. It was late and he strode out, fretting as he went at the responsibility the evening had thrust upon him. He didn't love her and there was no disguising the fact to himself. But a part of him already knew that he would be tempted again by the remembered excitement of her breasts and the promise she had half held out to him. Rejection by him now would be harder for her to take than before and she would be ready to accept him for a time however he went to her. There lay the danger, that in the mixed emotions of temptation and the desire not to hurt he would hurt her all the more and himself as well. Others might carry it off, exploiting the situation to the full and regarding the taking as its own payment to her. But he was too serious minded, too ready with self-disgust to play the flippant lover. He knew this well. What he had yet to find out was the extent of his own weakness.

233

The sight of a car parked at the end of his road stopped him dead. Roger. Anger welled in him. If this concern about his movements was pathetic it was also monstrous. He'd had enough. He toyed with the idea of walking round the block and entering the street from the other end. But he would still be seen. He crossed over briskly and walked towards the car. He passed it without stopping and had gone several yards beyond before he heard Roger call out to him. He went on. Roger called again, then the car engine started.

'Nick,' Roger said as the car drew alongside. 'Nick, I've got to talk to you.'

Nick stopped and turned. 'What's the matter?'

'Get in.'

'Look, I'm not messing about——'

'Please, Nick,' Roger said. 'Please get in.'

Something in Roger's voice made Nick do as he was asked.

'Look, what the hell are you doing hanging about here?'

'I'm in a bit of a jam, Nick.'

'I don't get you.'

Roger moved his face so that light from a streetlamp fell on it. Nick drew in his breath.

'Jesus! What have you been doing?'

Roger's left eye was a slit in a mound of swollen flesh. Trails of dried blood led from his nostrils across his upper lip. The corner of his mouth oozed blood even as Nick stared, horrified, and Roger dabbed gingerly at it with the blood-stiffened pad of a handkerchief. Nick took out his own handkerchief and handed it to him.

'Here, that one's no use now ... For God's sake, Roger, who did it? Where?'

'Two fellers, back of a pub called The Horseshoe.'

'But why?'

'Don't you know about The Horseshoe? It's got a reputation of ... of a certain kind. People go there, certain kinds of people, so I'd heard.'

'And what the hell were you ...?' Nick stopped and let

234

Roger go on.

'I may as well tell you ... I was mad with you, thinking about you with that bird. I went there, met these two men. Only one at first. He picked me up. I let him. Then his friend came. I've never done anything like that before. I changed my mind, tried to back out. They chivvied me along, all very light and friendly at first, then it all started turning nasty. They got me round the back, in the car-pack, wanted me to go with them, take them somewhere. I said no. They said I'd led them on, got them to buy me drinks, like a tart taking a bloke for a ride. One of them hit me, then they both started. Somebody came out or they'd probably have kicked me to death. They went off and I lay still till it was all clear.'

'Why didn't you go straight home and get some attention? You might need a doctor.'

'I couldn't. If anyone finds out what I was doing I'll be in it up to the neck.'

'Oh, surely——'

'Use your brains, Nick. I was practically bloody soliciting, man. How clear do you want me to put it?'

'But couldn't you say——?'

'I want you to alibi me. Say we were together. It happened when you left me for a while. Somewhere else altogether.'

'But I've been with Caroline.'

'You can fix her.'

'I don't see what good it will do, Roger.'

'I'm scared, Nick. And I want to lie down. If I don't I shall be sick.'

'Drive the car along to the house,' Nick said.

'What about your landlady?'

'I'll think of something. You just keep your mouth shut and let me do the talking.'

Roger felt for the starter. 'You can think what you like about me, Nick. Just let me get past this and I'll leave you alone.'

'Shut up,' Nick said. 'I'm trying to think.'

Roger swayed and almost fell when he got out of the car and Nick supported him up the steps, fumbling for his latchkey with his free hand. He sat Roger on the stairs and went to find Mrs Lomas.

'First-aid box? Why, yes. What exactly is it you want?'

'It's Roger Coyne, actually. He got into a bit of trouble and——'

She bustled past him into the hall. She gasped as Roger lifted his head and said politely, 'I'm awfully sorry to put you about like this, Mrs Lomas, but you were nearest and Nick suggested——'

'Saints in heaven! Whatever have you done to yourself?'

'It wasn't self-inflicted, I assure you.'

'Well, never mind that. Get him along to the kitchen, Mr Moffat, where I can see to him ... Heavens above, I've never seen anything like him.'

When Roger had taken off his outer clothes and Mrs Lomas was dabbing at his face with antiseptic-soaked pads of cotton wool, Nick went through his story, conscious that he could have improved on it with time.

'Well, when we came out of the pictures we decided to have a stroll, it was such a pleasant evening. We walked down by the river. There was a party of lads hanging about down there. They could have been just locals, killing time, but it turned out they were yobs. I left Roger for a minute. To tell the truth, I wanted to, er, to answer a call of nature. So I went down into the field and Roger must have strolled on some way. One of the lads said something to him and he answered back. So he told me, that is, because I didn't actually see it. By the time I got to him they'd set about him and he was down on the ground. They ran off when they saw me coming...'

It would be up to Roger to fill in the gaps and make it sound fully convincing. There was no reason why they shouldn't be believed. The touch about going for a pee was one he rather liked. It was just the sort of detail to give credence.

'It isn't safe to walk the streets at night any more,' Mrs

236

Lomas said. 'It really isn't ... Hold still, Mr Coyne, it may hurt a little but I shall have to clean you properly or all these places will go the wrong way. You ought to have a doctor as well.'

'I'm all right, Mrs Lomas, really. No broken bones or anything. What I really want is to lie down and sleep.'

'I thought perhaps he could have my bed, Mrs Lomas. Just for tonight. He's really not fit to drive home.'

'Well ... I shall have to telephone your landlady. And what's more I think I ought to report this. I have my own position with the university to consider. You do understand that?'

'Yes, of course. Why don't I pop up and run a hot bath? Then he can see if there is anything else wrong with him.'

A little while later Nick walked upstairs behind Roger and into the bathroom.

'So far, so good.'

'Yes. You'd better test the water, see if it's right. I'll go and find you some pyjamas.'

'Don't go, Nick. I'm still a bit groggy. I wouldn't want to pass out in the tub on my own.' Roger cleared a patch on the steam-clouded glass and peered at himself. 'That'll be a beaut in the morning. Now showing—The Public Eye of Roger Coyne, in glorious Fisticolour.'

'The vicious bastards,' Nick said. 'We ought to get a bunch of the lads together and go look for them.'

'What a touchingly loyal thought,' Roger said. 'And all the time you're thinking I was bloody stupid for setting myself up.'

'Come on,' Nick said. 'Get in and have a soak.'

He helped Roger off with his clothes.

'Are you sure you've nothing broken?'

'I don't think so. My ribs are sore . . .'

He touched gently with his fingertips at an area over the left side of his rib-cage where the skin was marked by an angry flush of blood. The movement of the fingers as they touched and probed drew Nick's gaze over Roger's body. He conceded its beauty. In its slim, lithe lines it was like the

237

figure of a classical statue, a young god winging a message across some legend of antiquity. There was a bloom on the skin like that of a young girl. The pubic hair, darker than the hair on Roger's head, was darker again than the golden bloom of skin and feminine in its close neatness. The penis, small and flaccid, was like that of a child in a renaissance painting.

All this in the few seconds before it occurred to Nick that there might be pleasure for Roger in his scrutiny; then he averted his eyes, suddenly embarrassed by the other's nakedness. 'Get in then, before the water goes cold.'

Roger lowered himself into the bath.

'How do you feel now?'

'A bit dizzy.'

He doesn't want me to go, Nick thought. He's keeping me here.

'Christ! What a night!'

'You ought to have your head seen to.'

'I have heard it offered as a possible treatment,' Roger said wryly. 'A bit less drastic than castration.'

'I'm sorry. I keep saying the wrong thing.'

'It's so easy, isn't it? Like saying "I see" when you're talking to a blind man ... Did you hear about the queer who took the pill because he didn't want any backward children?'

'Lay off, will you?' Nick said. 'For Pete's sake, Roger, there must be something ...'

'I can do about it? Man, I don't mind the condition. It's the circumstances surrounding it. Suppose ninety-five per cent of women were lesbian, how would you make out?'

'About as well as I'm doing now.'

Roger cocked a look at him from his one open eye. The glance was, in that battered face, almost comic. Almost.

'What will you say to Caroline?'

'As little as I have to. Unless she turns stupid about it.'

'And can she be stupid!'

'Oh, I don't know,' Nick said. 'No more than anybody else. It's usually some obsession that makes us all seem

238

stupid sometime.'

'What's her obsession? As if I didn't know.'

'Obsession's perhaps a bit strong. I think she wants me and she's jealous of you.'

'What do you want?'

Roger had his head down. He filled the sponge and squeezed it, watching water pour out. Nick said deliberately,

'Woman. With a capital letter. No particular person but some symbol of the whole sex. In my mind's eye I can see a pair of long silken legs that I can lie between and both lose and find myself.'

Roger pressed the sponge between both hands till it was dry. Then he released it to spring back to its normal shape and let it float on the water.

'It plays hell with what I want,' he said after a silence.

'I don't understand what you want,' Nick said. 'I just can't feel it.'

17

Nick looked for Caroline the next day. She was maddeningly elusive. Before, he had seemed to see her almost everywhere he went; now he had to seek her out. When, late in the afternoon, he had decided he would have to telephone her at the hall of residence he caught sight of her walking across the lawn towards the Union Building. He ran after her. She turned with pleased surprise at his shout. Then an instinctive reserve masked the momentary honesty of her reaction.

'Caroline, last night . . . Roger got into a bit of trouble.'

'Trouble?'

'He had a run-in with a couple of men in town and got thumped. The thing is, he wants me to say he and I were together if anybody makes anything of it.'

'I don't follow.'

'You don't have to. All you have to do is not blurt out that you were with me, if it comes up any time.'

'But who's going to ask and why shouldn't he have been on his own? What difference does it make your pretending to have been there?'

That maddeningly clear voice and its careful construction of sentences . . .

'I don't think it matters for a minute, but he's got the wind up.'

Her eyes narrowed. 'You're not telling me all of it, are you? What's he been up to?'

'Oh, God, Caroline, why can't you just——?'

'If I'm supposed to tell lies I have a right to know more.'

'You're not going before a court to perjure yourself. Just don't put your foot in it. There's no danger. He's scared for nothing, but really scared, under all his flip talk.' He waited, then broke before her sardonic silence. 'What you've suspected about him ... It seems it's true.'

There, unmistakable, for a second's duration, was the flicker of triumph. He hated her for it.

'Why do you want to get involved?'

'Because he's my friend.'

'What did they do to him?'

'Punched his face, kicked him about a bit. He's at home in bed now. He's not a pretty sight.'

'Nice company he keeps.'

'It's easy enough to be snide.'

'Yes, he's always found it easy enough with me. I know some of the things he's said about me.'

'Okay, you don't like each other. But I'm in the middle.'

She shifted her load of books from one arm to the other.

'If we weren't together last night you must owe me a night out. You did ask me.'

He stared at her, baffled. 'Well, I ...'

'Shameless, aren't I?' she said. 'I surprise myself sometimes.'

As he groped for something to say a sudden flurry of rain saved him. They began to walk together towards the building. She really was the most unusual girl he had ever met. She could throw you in a moment. It was both flattering and disquieting.

'It's all right,' she said as they reached the steps and shelter. 'I'll do what you ask, and without strings.'

'No, look ...' He took her arm. 'What about tonight?'

They went through the doors, parting to pass a knot of people standing just inside. When they faced each other again she seemed to manage to look at him while just avoiding direct contact with his gaze.

'Tomorrow,' she said. As he watched her a slow wave of delicate colour flooded up out of the neck of her jumper. Then it was as though her courage left her. She said in

241

throaty haste, 'I'm late,' and went hurrying out through the
door, the way they had come.

There was a letter from Philip in the rack in the hall
when Nick got back to his lodgings early in the evening.
Mrs Lomas came out of the dining-room as he tore open
the envelope and moved towards the stairs.

'How is Mr Coyne?'

'He's all right, Mrs Lomas. There's nothing to worry
about.'

'As long as there isn't. I did say something about report-
ing it to the university authorities, but I don't want to make
any unnecessary fuss. Were you thinking of going to the
police?'

'No. Mr Coyne doesn't want to make a fuss, either.'

'I expect he doesn't. You young people at university
nowadays, you seem to have as much freedom as you like.
It's not like it was in my husband's time. He was an Oxford
man, of course, and I suppose that makes a difference.'

Nick, who had heard about the late Mr Lomas before,
waited politely.

'Then you had to be in college by a civilised hour and
there was none of this drinking in the public houses and
mixing with undesirable people.'

'From what I've read, it didn't stop them from finding
trouble, Mrs Lomas.'

'Perhaps not. But it was more high spirits, and all carried
on in a gentlemanly way.'

High spirits in them, hooliganism in the lower orders.
Nick didn't argue.

'They must have been good days—for the fortunate few.'

'Oh, much, much better days than these. Still, I suppose
everything has to change. None of us can stand still, much
as we might want to ... Will you be in for supper this
evening?'

'If I might come down and collect a tray. I have a lot of
work to do.'

He walked slowly up the stairs, his books wedged precariously between his arm and his side, as he fumbled with Philip's letter. He read it very quickly until he got to the part which brought him to a stop on the landing:

'Well, they said they hadn't any easy ride to offer me and they certainly seem set on proving it and finding out what I might be made of. I remember your offer of help and I was grateful at the time. I shan't hold you to it now, of course. The fact is, you see, that the ward they're putting me up for will mean a fight between me and your friend Mr Simpkins...'

PART FOUR

18

Simpkins' six-year term as alderman was nearly over. He felt reluctant to go through all the rigmarole of standing for re-election to the council. His tentative voicing of this feeling shocked Baden Roberts.

'You're never going to give up after all this time?'

'That's the point about it, Baden. Perhaps I've gone on too long. I feel tired, somehow.'

'Tired! Look at me. I'm not tired and I can give you ten years. How long is it you've been on now?'

'Eighteen years.'

Baden snorted. It was nothing beside his thirty-five years of unbroken service during which he'd been three times mayor. Simpkins winked at Baden's wife, Maude, and she, looking up from her embroidery, gave him back a small smile. Baden's parents had managed to commemorate two heroes for the price of one when they christened him in the year of Mafeking. Adding a few months to his age, he himself had seen the end of the First World War in the trenches in Flanders. Simpkins sometimes felt that it was not a mere ten years which separated them, but two world wars. The years of his boyhood before the first war were the golden age that Baden looked back to. 'It all ended after that,' he had said more than once. 'That's when it all fell apart. Do you know how many crowned heads there were at Edward VII's funeral? Well I saw that. My father had taken me on my first visit to London. I was ten years old. We never saw its like again.' It was no use arguing that the quality of life was better for more people now, because Baden wouldn't have it. 'There were men working for my father who had six, seven and eight bairns. They brought 'em up all right. Of course they hadn't much money but they could buy a lot with what they had. Now it's all grab, grab, grab. Summat for nowt, if you can get it. Money and more money, for bingo and booze, motor cars and holidays abroad. And nobody's happy, Tom. That's the trouble. Nobody's happy any more.'

Were they ever? Simpkins wondered. Was an obsession with keeping body and soul together a necessary prerequisite of human happiness?

They were talking in the new bungalow Baden and Maude had moved into out of the big old-fashioned house now occupied by the son who was assuming more and more responsibility for the running of the shoddy mill old John Edward Roberts, in his day, had relinquished to Baden. It was a comfortable, well-appointed place built of expensive dressed stone, with a landscaped garden sloping down to a busy main road. The old house was too big for the two of them, anyway, and the peace and quiet of that backwater, much prized by other people, had begun to oppress Maude, so Baden had built here where she could find amusement by sitting in the window and watching the traffic go by.

'A drink, anyway, Tom.'

'I'd not say no to a drop of Scotch, Baden.'

The floorboards trembled as Baden crossed the room to the sideboard.

'You'll have this place falling round your heads, Baden,' Simpkins said. 'How much do you weigh?'

'Too much,' Maude chipped in.

'Oh, I don't know,' Baden said with a touch of asperity. 'Fifteen and a half, sixteen stone.' And add a bit to that, Simpkins thought.

'You must have cast iron legs. I'm bigger than you and I don't scale that much.'

'You haven't got my belly, though, Tom.' Baden turned and placed his two hands on the expansive swell of his

248

waistcoat. 'It's all good solid stuff, you know, not just a bag of wind.'

Maude tut-tutted—'Really, Baden'—while Simpkins laughed.

'As long as you're happy carrying it around.'

'Oh, there's nothing ails me. In spite of Maude always going on about it.'

'It's no use me saying anything,' Maude said. 'He stopped listening to what I say years ago.'

Simpkins sensed some bitterness behind the mild delivery of the comment. Always headstrong, and domineering where he met resistance, Baden instinctively treated women as people to be kept in their place: to be acquiesced to in small matters which pleased them, charmed if young and attractive, pushed brusquely aside if interfering, used or resented (depending on loyalties) if militant, but always patronised as a sex which could not possibly understand the full facts of life. The two women councillors on his side of the chamber he tolerated as passengers, useful mostly when it came to a show of hands; with Councillor Mrs Pauline McIver on the opposition bench he clashed often. Baden disliked Socialists of any kind; one in a skirt who opposed him with a will as strong as his own was anathema.

'We can't let 'em have the seat,' Baden said, handing Simpkins his whisky and settling back again into his chair, 'that's for sure. A couple of upsets like that and they'd have control. Then where would we be?'

'I'm surprised they've not managed it more often,' Simpkins said. 'After all, we are a constituency that's returned a Labour MP ever since the Liberals cooked their goose.'

'It's because people don't like party politics in their local government, Tom. They'll vote for the man they know, especially if he's independent and can speak his mind without finding out what the boss thinks first. But all that apart, they've got the tide running their way just now and we can't afford to take any chances putting new chaps up even in safe wards. It's up to everybody to rally round, and when fellers with your experience and standing start talking

249

about packing up, well ... Maude, get that box of cigars out of the sideboard drawer and give Tom one.'

'Good heavens,' Simpkins said when he saw the size of the Havanas in the cedarwood box which Maude held out to him. 'I'll still be smoking this at bedtime.'

'Take a couple for later,' Baden said. 'They'll go dry if they're not smoked. A supplier of mine sent 'em over and I never use 'em.'

Simpkins carefully lit the cigar and Maude sniffed appreciatively at the smoke.

'That smells lovely.'

'Oh, I don't mind the smell of a good cigar meself,' Baden said.

'Have you never smoked, Baden?'

'No, never. Well, I'm saying never; I did have a go with a pipe once as a young man but all I did was fill it full of slaver.'

'What do you know about this young feller they're wanting to put against me?' Simpkins asked.

'Not a lot. His name's Hart, isn't it? He's a school-teacher.'

'Where?'

'Valley Bridge. He's paid by the County but he lives here in Cressley, so he seems to be eligible.'

Shirley would know him, so probably would Nick. Simpkins could sound them out for information on this dark horse no one seemed to know much about.

'I've heard he's a bright young feller,' Baden said. 'Very well thought of. All I can say is, he's getting in with a right lot.'

'If it's his conviction, Baden.'

'Conviction? What conviction can make a young feller like him want to join them? Half of 'em haven't two ha'pennies to rub together, yet they want to tell other people how to live their lives. What do they want interfering in everything that's going on?'

Simpkins smiled, but to himself this time. For all he knew Maude shared Baden's view about this.

'You're a thundering old reactionary, Baden. Trying to keep everything as it is.'

'Nay, I'll not have that. I'm not against change as long as it's good and necessary change. But we're the fellers who know what this town needs, Tom, men like you and me and Bobby Carter, men who've lived here all our lives, running businesses and giving people work. Why should we have to listen to outsiders who come in and think they can take over? Do you want to be ruled from Transport House?'

'No.' Simpkins admitted. 'But I'm not right sure about Conservative Central Office, either.'

'They are a bit of a wishy-washy lot,' Baden said, taking Simpkins' point only obliquely. 'They don't seem to have anybody to match this crafty beggar Wilson. We get a Yorkshireman for Prime Minister and he has to be one of them!'

'The greatest living Yorkshireman after Freddie Trueman,' Simpkins said.

'Aye, that's as maybe. They wanted a change and they've got one. And I'll tell you something, Tom: people are looking at these new Labour MPs with their college educations and they know they're different from the old guard, the colliers and railwaymen and trades union politicians. If these fellers think it's right there might be something in it—that's how a lot of people look at it. It could happen here, in our local government, as well. If there's one thing folk round here respect nearly as much as brass it's education, and one or two chaps like this Peter Hart could upset the apple cart for all of us. That they're wrong, and time'll prove it, doesn't matter beside the years it might take to shift 'em again and the damage they'll do meanwhile.'

'There's a limit to what they can do even if they get a majority, Baden.'

'They can make a mess of all sorts of things,' Baden said. 'Education—rushing at this comprehensive business like a bull at a gate—housing, town planning. All sorts of things, I just can't believe you're serious, Tom, when you say you might not put up again.'

'Oh, it's all the palaver and messing about,' Simpkins said.

'You know you'll enjoy it once it starts. You always have before.'

'Aye, maybe.' Simpkins sighed. 'I don't seem to want to think about it. I've had one or two things on my mind lately.'

Baden cocked a glance at Maude whose head was bent over her embroidery again. She was making a firescreen for her daughter-in-law and the bird of paradise grew in its brilliant plumage of coloured silks under her deft fingers.

'I wonder,' Baden said, patting his pockets, 'if you can put your hand on my glasses, Maude.'

'You had them earlier, didn't you?'

'I might have put 'em down in the bedroom.'

Maude got up and went out.

'For a feller who doesn't care about his weight you've got your fetching and carrying nicely organised,' Simpkins said.

'Why don't you marry her?' Baden said.

'You what?' Simpkins was taken aback.

'You know what I'm talking about.'

'Well, apart from anything else, it's a bit——'

'Oh, I know he hasn't been dead all that long. But why not let a decent time pass by then wed her? You've known her long enough to know your own mind, haven't you?'

'Aye, perhaps I have,' Simpkins said.

'Might you have trouble with Bess?'

'There's all sorts of things to think about.'

'Well, you can tell me to mind my own business if you like——'

'I can.'

'—but it strikes me that if she's good enough for one thing she's good enough for t'other.'

'You sanctimonious old bugger,' Simpkins said, more in surprise than anger.

Baden liftened his hand to silence him as the door opened and Maude came back.

'I can't find them anywhere.'

252

Baden dipped his hand into the capacious side pocket of his jacket. 'I'm sorry, love,' he said blandly. 'I had 'em here all the time.'

Maude's glance took them both in. She might be mild, Simpkins thought, but she doesn't miss much.

'I hope you're not going to let Baden bullyrag you into doing anything you don't want to, Tom.'

'I don't think I shall let him do that, Maude.'

'You've known him long enough to know he likes his own way.'

'He's known me long enough to know I talk sense,' Baden said. 'Now come on, Tom, stop acting like a coy young lass and say you'll stand again. Then we can get the wheels in motion.'

'Oh, I suppose I shall, Baden.'

'That's more like it.' Baden held out his glass to Maude. 'Just give us another drop apiece while you're on your feet, love, and we'll drink to Tom's success.' He rubbed his hands together in satisfaction as Maude took their glasses to the sideboard.

'Don't count your chickens too soon, Baden. If this young feller's as bright as you hear there could be some surprises.'

Baden brushed Simpkins' remark aside. 'You've never lost an election in that ward yet, Tom. Or anywhere else, for that matter. Get you back in your place and we can settle down to a nice time.'

19

She saw him, astoundingly. After three months without sight or word of him, there he was, crossing the street ahead of her. In her first astonished glance she could not tell whether he was alone in that huddle of people or with someone else. Her panicky instinct was to hide. How could they face one another here? She turned blindly, stepping into the road, and in the next uncomprehending second was thrown violently across the pavement into a shop front by the wing of a passing car.

Her mind would not will her to move. Voices bobbed on the edge of her consciousness: 'Are you all right, love?' 'Can't you get up?' 'Damned motorists.' 'Nay, she stepped right into him.' Did someone say 'Andrea'? Was he there? 'She went with a rare bang.' 'Can you sit her up?' 'Better not move her.' The heavier voice of authority. 'How do you feel, miss?' A navy-blue uniform, silver-gilt buttons. 'Andrea.' 'Do you know her?' 'Slightly.' Philip. Nothing.

Movement. Riding. Warm under blankets. No pain. Slow, quick, stop, start, quick, slow, stop. Carried. Painted walls, echoes, smell. Hospital.

'Philip.'

'It's all right, dear.'

Her mother's voice. Two anxious faces by the bed.

'How do you feel?'

'All right.'

Her left arm wouldn't move. 'Steady,' her father said. It was held up, bent, in a grotesque apparatus of sling, wires and pulleys. 'Good God! Is that me?'

'You were saying "Philip",' her mother said.

'Was I? How odd. How long have I been here?'

'Since this morning. Whatever were you doing to——?'

'I don't know. Is it just my arm?'

'You were lucky it wasn't——'

'Are they going to keep me in?'

'For a little while, until they see how you are.'

A nurse pushed aside the flap of the curtain drawn round the area of Andrea's bed and stepped inside.

'Oh, you're awake and taking notice. How are you feeling?'

'Not so bad.'

'Well, then, we'll have these away so you can see what's going on.'

The curtains were whisked aside and Andrea saw that she was at the very end, nearest the door, of a long public ward. There were visitors at most of the beds and the nearest heads turned at the swish of the curtain-rings. The stout woman in the next bed smiled across.

'Feeling better now, love?'

'Yes, thank you.'

'You look a bit better colour than when they brought you in, anyway. Accident in the street, wasn't it?'

'I couldn't have been looking what I was doing.'

'Me neither. Funny how things happen. You go out like on any other day to do your bit of shopping and next thing they're pulling you out from under a bus. You fared better na me, though, by the looks of it. I lost a leg.' She nodded towards the middle of her bed and Andrea noticed now that the sheets were resting over a cage.

'Oh dear!' Andrea's mother said. 'What a dreadful thing to——'

'Oh, aye. T'idea took some getting used to, but there's things in this life you mun learn to abide. An' there's worse things happen at sea, I allus say.'

'And are you on your own?' Andrea's mother asked.

'Oh, no, no. I have a husband, love, only he's on late turn this week so he can't get up at nights. Me lads are grown up

255

and married and living away. They've both been to see me since it happened but they can't come so often owing to the time and expense. They're both good lads, though. We brought 'em up well and they've never turned away from us. It's nice when you can say that.'

'Yes,' Andrea's mother said. 'Yes, indeed.' She leaned closer to Andrea. 'Your father and I were wondering ... If you'd like to be moved to a private room we'll make enquiries and see what can be done.'

'No, I'm all right here.'

'You don't have to worry about the expense, Andrea,' her father said.

'I'll be better off among people.'

'Well, if you change your mind ... People can get on top of you in such confined circumstances.' Andrea's mother rolled her eyes meaningfully in the direction of the stout woman. 'You know, when they won't let you be quiet.'

'I really prefer it here,' Andrea said. 'It won't be for long.'

'Andrea, how did it happen? They seem to think the motorist wasn't to blame, that you stepped straight in front of him.'

'It couldn't have been his fault. I wasn't looking where I was going.'

'Were you on your own?'

'Yes, why?'

'Did you tell them your name and address?'

'I don't think so. I expect they got it from something in my bag.'

'The policeman was saying something about a man who knew you. He told them who you were.'

'I suppose there could have been somebody passing. It must have been when I was only half conscious. I don't remember.'

'You've no idea who he could be?'

'No. Is it important?'

'No, but it's the kind of thing that bothers you when you——'

'All I know is I stepped off the pavement and something

256

knocked me off my feet. I didn't even see the car. I don't know how big it was or even what colour.'

'The police will probably want to come and talk to you.'

'I can't tell them any more than I've told you. I just hope they don't decide to have a go at that poor driver, because it wasn't his fault.'

She was impatient for them to go and leave her with her thoughts. They chattered about what she would need, and the things they would bring tomorrow. Then a bell rang and she realised they had spent the greater part of the visiting period waiting for her to wake up. Each of them kissed her on the cheek, pressed her hand and murmured words of reassurance. Then they left.

As the last of the visitors passed the foot of Andrea's bed the ward fell quiet. Then the voices of two women talking to each other across the space between the two rows of beds set off a series of conversations. The thoughts Andrea had wished to surrender to now invaded her in a tide of hopeless melancholy. She wanted to cry and knew that to give herself up to tears might help; but trussed as she was there was no way she could hide her face and she dreaded anyone's mistaken sympathy.

A police constable was brought to her by the ward sister, his appearance provoking cries from several beds : 'Hey up, here'st t'bobby come to see us. Who's been doin' summat she shouldn't?' A blonde half-way along the ward called up, 'Send him down to see me when you've done with him, love.'

The constable apologised for the intrusion and took down Andrea's statement about the accident. She asked as he was about to leave,

'How did you get my name and address?'

'There was a man on the spot who said he knew you. I was going to ask him if he wanted to notify your family but when I turned round again he'd gone. I didn't get his name but I don't think he was an actual witness.'

She watched him go through the door and closed her eyes in a spasm of impotent fury at the idiocy of it all. What was

257

Philip thinking, wondering, now? He was probably at home, perhaps marking exercise books while his wife saw the children to bed. She could not visualise him with any sureness in his surroundings, but she could summon up his face and will him to think of her thinking of him at this very moment; try, try, try for some kind of contact across the space that separated them.

She heard the soft brurp-brurp of a telephone bell somewhere beyond the curtained double doors of the ward. A little while later the sister, a red-cheeked young woman of about Andrea's own age, appeared and spoke to her, her hands occupied in automatic tucking and tidying movements with the sheets as she did so.

'There's just been somebody enquiring about you on the telephone.'

'Oh?'

'A man. He said he was a friend of yours.'

'Did he sound young or old?'

'Well, it's hard to say. Young rather than old.'

It must be him. And just as she was willing his thoughts to come to her.

'Are you comfortable?'

'Yes . . . But I wish I wasn't quite so flat on my back.'

'We'll lift you up a bit, then perhaps you can drink your nightcap without a feeding-mug.'

'I hope so.'

The sister cranked a handle on the bed and Andrea felt her back and shoulders lifted.

'How long do you think I shall have to be here?'

'Oh, we shan't keep you any longer than we have to. You've fractured your collarbone as well as your arm. That's why you're held up like that.'

'Damn' silly thing to do,' Andrea muttered, feeling the remark somehow called for.

'Accidents will happen. Thank your lucky stars you came out of it as well as you did. There's always somebody worse off than you.'

Clichés. You lived your life by them and there were

258

several for every situation. You should have thought about it before you went into it. You've only yourself to blame. You made your own bed ... Three into two won't go. But why wouldn't it go, when she wanted him, needed him so desperately, yet was prepared to make do with so little of him? Why, why, why?

She slept badly, dozing through short restless periods and waking again and again to the strangeness of the ward, the tall windows, the shadows under the high Victorian ceiling, the shaded light on the desk.

'Can't you sleep?' the stout woman, whose name was Mrs Moore, asked softly.

'Only on and off.'

'Me neither. It's that foot. There's times in the night, when I've nowt else to think about, I could limb it. Only, it's not there.'

With a rustle of petticoats the night nurse was between them.

'Is anything wrong?'

Andrea told her.

'You slept most of the day, that'll be why. Try to settle down now. It'll soon be morning. And no talking. You'll disturb the others.'

She rearranged Andrea's pillows and left them.

The daytime routine of the ward got under way before dawn. Andrea suffered herself to be washed by two young nurses who chattered across her as they sponged then dried her. Her embarrassment at being handled in such an intimate manner seemed foolish in the face of their unemotional performance of their routine. Afterwards, cranked up again into a semi-sitting position, she managed to comb her hair and put on some lipstick.

Mr Simpkins visited her in the afternoon. He arrived when her mother was there, bringing chocolates, a parcel of paperback novels and a huge bunch of mixed flowers. Her mother flushed with pleasure at his appearance and the esteem the presents testified to. He stayed for twenty minutes, gravely polite at first, then relaxing into a vein of

259

banter that usually revealed itself only at office parties or other social events connected with the firm.

Andrea asked who was doing her work.

'I used Mrs Sutton yesterday,' he said. 'I might carry on with her. She seems efficient and she's more mature than some of the others.'

Her displeasure did not escape him.

'Don't you approve?'

'She's ...' Andrea began reluctantly. 'She's a bit of a gossip.'

'Oh, is she? Well then, I shall have to confine her to work she can gossip about if she feels like it.'

'You never know. She might choose to keep her own counsel now she's next to the seat of power, as it were.'

'There's no chance of her taking your place permanently, you know.'

'I wasn't worried about that.'

Mr Simpkins twinkled at her honesty and spoke to her mother. 'It's nice to have people around you who know their own worth, Mrs Warner.'

'I'm sure Andrea always tries to give every satisfaction, Mr Simpkins.'

'Oh yes, and she succeeds. I shall miss her, and I want her back as soon as she's able to come. But not a moment before. You concentrate on getting well and don't worry about us.'

Andrea asked her mother to give him some keys from her handbag which Agnes Sutton would need. She didn't like the idea of that woman's poking about in her files, but they weren't her private property; nor was Mr Simpkins, though she had the proprietary regard for him of all secretaries who work for some years for a boss they like.

Mrs Moore, who had overheard most of the conversation while her husband, a big grey-faced man in a baggy raincoat and steel-rimmed glasses, sat morosely silent beside her bed, was very impressed.

'Was that your boss, then, love? He must think well of you.'

He did, and it pleased her.

She longed in the routine of the days that followed for some activity which would relieve her mind of its most constant thoughts. She read everything that came her way, tried the crossword puzzles in several different newspapers and listened to the radio through her headphones. Her inability to do much for herself irked her and she envied those patients who could walk about and chat and visit the bathroom when they liked. A bath of hot water into which she could slide and soak herself became a luxury to be dreamed of. In the meantime she put up with the ministrations of whichever nurse was assigned to the morning toilets. Apart from occasional dull pangs as her bones knitted she felt little pain, though her skin inside the plaster itched abominably at times. She watched the dressings trolley with its jars of bandages and gauze and trays of instruments come into the ward towards mid-morning and was thankful she wasn't Mrs Moore whose stump the sister dressed personally behind drawn curtains. She had her temperature taken and was given pills of various colours. The doctor on his rounds would stop by her bed, ask how she felt, glance at her record card and the apparatus holding her arm and pass on with a smile. There were too many 'get well' cards for the top of her locker so she displayed just two or three and kept the others in the drawer. Letters came too, some from people she hadn't seen for a long time. Her mother had been busy spreading the news. She was never without a visitor either afternoon or evening. Everyone came except the one person she longed to see.

With some of her visitors conversation became tedious. They felt compelled to sit there for the full hour and she exchanged the umpteenth recital of the ward's routine and snippets of information about the other patients for items of news from outside. George turned up with her mother and his long silences convinced her once and for all that marriage to him would be a hell of boredom. Julie, the first time she came, exclaimed with horror at the sight of her sister. 'You poor thing! You'll look a pippin if you've still got it stuck out like that at the wedding.' She was marrying Bob Harvey in two months' time and Andrea was to be chief bridesmaid.

On an afternoon in the second week her mother sat alone beside the bed. The regular visiting seemed to have exhausted their small talk and there were long periods of silence in which there grew in Andrea a strong feeling of her mother's unease. There seemed, behind their spasmodic talk, to be a subject her mother wanted to broach but dared not, and there was a lack of frankness in the meeting of their eyes.

Andrea, with so much time to wonder about it afterwards, could not let the impression go unchallenged. She said, finally, with only a few minutes of visiting time left,

'Mother, is something wrong?'

'Why should you think that?'

'I don't know. You just don't seem at ease with me today.'

Her mother glanced almost furtively over her shoulder at Mrs Moore who was lying with her face turned away and talking to her husband on the other side of her bed; then she pulled her chair in closer and opened her handbag. 'This came...' She produced an envelope. 'I opened it by mistake. Your initial is the same as mine and I thought it said *Mrs* A Warner. I don't know why. When I looked again it was plain enough. It wasn't deliberate, though. I wasn't prying. But once I'd started to read it I couldn't stop.'

'There's no harm done, is there?' Andrea said. Even now, seeing her mother's obvious embarrassment, it didn't dawn on her. That prim and proper woman would be ashamed of any such unwitting breach of her daughter's privacy. It was a moment later, when she took the envelope out of her mother's hand, that it suddenly came to her what it must be. She fumbled the letter out, her mother's hand reaching to help her then drawing back. She took in the first few lines, could read no more with her mother there and rested her head back, her eyes closed, her face flaming with colour.

'He's the man who was there, isn't he?'

'Yes.'

'Who is he?'

'Someone I used to know.'

'I don't have to ask why we never got to know about him, do I?'

'You've read the letter.'

A silence. Then: 'Oh, Andrea. How could——?'

'How could a well brought up girl like your daughter ever get involved with a married man? I know. Well, it just happened. I suppose it happens all the time.'

'Perhaps to other people, without principles or a knowledge of proper behaviour.'

'You find yourself thinking that. That it's something that happens to other people, not to you. And when it does you think it must be special, almost unique. It can't possibly be like it is with anybody else, because it's not the sort of thing you do, not the sort of thing that happens to you. You invent a special category for yourself.'

'I gather it's . . . it's not going on now.'

'No. It finished when his wife found out.'

'That poor woman. Didn't you ever think about her when you were getting into it? Didn't it ever occur to you the harm you were doing?'

'Oh yes, we both thought about all those things. We were neither of us flippant about it. There was pain and loss built into it from the start but we thought the joy was worth it. I suppose because we gave each other joy we felt that gave us some kind of right to take it. I know you must be shocked,' she said, after a silence during which her mother seemed at a loss for something else to say, 'but there's no point in chastising me now. Don't talk to me about what I should or shouldn't have done. That morning, just before the accident, was the first time I'd seen him in three months. Three months without a glimpse of him or even the

263

sound of his voice. And it hurts. It hurts, it hurts, it hurts. If you think I should be punished in some way for getting mixed up with a married man, well I can tell you that it's happening. It's happening now, this minute, and it goes on happening every minute of the day, except when I'm asleep.'

She should, she thought, be declaiming in a ringing, room-filling voice, but she spoke in a low passionate undertone which would carry no farther then the dismayed figure of her mother sitting up close beside her.

'If he were dead,' she said, 'I'd have to accept that. But he isn't dead. He's walking and talking, and breathing the same air I breathe. If he didn't want me I'd have to accept that too. But he does want me. And I can't go to him. We can't see each other, or talk, or touch. Not ever again.'

'I don't know what to say,' her mother said eventually.

'There really isn't anything to say.'

'If only you'd settled down, made a good marriage with some steady young man——'

'Oh, Mother, Mother, Mother.' She rolled her head on the pillow in an agony of frustration, and the tears came. 'Doesn't anything I've said mean anything to you? Don't you understand? I don't mean approve, I mean understand.'

'But what do you expect me to say, Andrea?'

'Nothing.' She rolled her head away, consumed with a violent longing to wrest herself free of that ridiculous apparatus and express something of her pain in physical action. 'Oh God,' she said. 'Oh God, Mother, please go away.' She began to choke on her speech. 'Please, please go away.'

The bell rang for the end of the session. Andrea's mother said,

'I can't leave you, all upset like this.'

'I'm all right,' Andrea said. 'I'll be better when I'm on my own.'

Her mother hovered by the bed till she was the last visitor left in the ward. The sister came to the door and

264

looked all round.

'All visitors should be gone by now.'

'Yes, yes,' Mrs Warner said. 'I'm just . . .' She bent and pressed her lips to Andrea's cheek. 'I'll see you again to-night. This is just between us. I shan't say anything to your father.'

Andrea managed a word of goodbye and watched her mother go. She didn't really care, in her present mood, whether her father knew or not. Except that she couldn't bear the idea of two dismayed parents at her bedside.

The tea trolleys appeared, bearing big pots of tea, plates of brown and white bread and preserves. In that diversion she opened and read properly Philip's letter.

'My love, How are you? I was there. Ten seconds after it happened, *I was there*. And what could I do? I gave the policeman your name and address and I told him I knew you slightly. Slightly! Oh, my God! What could I do then except watch them carry you away? I rang up afterwards to see how hurt you were. Since then I've been walking about on a razor's edge of anxiety and indecision, wanting to see you, to come to you, yet not knowing how. I'm full, sometimes, of great bold gestures which by their very lack of inhibition would sweep all opposition aside. Yet if I walked in to see you how would you explain it to your parents, your friends, even the other patients? What good is the big brave gesture if it can't be carried right through, if it only leads to a host of further complications and embarrassments?

'I love you, I love you. I can't stop loving you. I don't miss you, I mourn for you. Things have been pretty hellish all round, with my refusing to be ashamed of loving you, or ingratiating myself again by pretending that all we had together was a misguided fling, a mere scratching of the perpetual male itch. It's too late now to make that kind of pretence. At the beginning, yes, when the first storm blew up. If I'd admitted then to just a casual lust I should perhaps have got away without all this terrible, terrible bitterness and acrimony. Better still if I'd denied it all, said

265

you were just a friend I was fond of. We might even then have been able to carry on, using care. But when I was challenged all that bottled-up disgust at the furtiveness and deceit just exploded into the truth. I can still be forgiven just as soon as I'm ready for it. But I refuse to be forgiven for loving you. It's as simple and as complicated as that . . .'

20

'Calm yourself down a bit, Norma,' Simpkins said. 'It won't do any good you getting all worked up.'

'Of course I'm worked up. Where can she be till this time of night? She's barely fifteen years old, Tom, not eighteen, and it's not old enough to be gallivanting about and stopping out till all hours.'

She lowered her handsewing and looked at the clock on the mantelshelf for what must be the twentieth time in the last fifteen minutes, light from the overhead bulb flashing across the lenses of the glasses she had lately admitted to needing for close work. She had, with unexpected vanity, been reluctant at first to let him see her wearing them and he had not tried to express the curious protective tenderness for her that they aroused in him.

'Young people nowadays, Norma; they demand more freedom than you and I ever had.'

'There's freedom and freedom. I don't know what's come over her. She was never like this before Sid got killed. She used to be happy enough to stay at home, or spend the odd evening at a friend's house. Now she's here, there and everywhere. I don't know who she's with or what she gets up to while she's out. Short of locking her up I don't know what I can do about it, either. I can't talk to her any more. God knows I've rowed enough with her but it does no good. It's a dangerous time of life for a lass and a mother's bound to worry. They grow up so fast nowadays they're like women when they're still only bairns. And they can get into the same sort of trouble women get into. Suppose she walked in here one day and said she was pregnant? Oh, it can happen. It happens all the time. Where would she be then? What would people think of me for letting her go where she likes when she likes? And you're not much help.'

'I don't like it either, Norma, but I can't come the heavy father.'

'Who's got more right, may I——?'

'Not in her eyes, Norma,' Simpkins said.

'You . . . you don't think she knows, do you?'

'Not *that*, anyway.'

'She knows enough, though,' Norma said. 'I'm not daft altogether. I can see enough to know she's trying to take it out on me.'

'She thought the world of Sid,' Simpkins said. 'It cut her up.'

'Aye, him going so sudden like that brought things home to all of us. It's coming home to roost, Tom.'

'All this——' Simpkins began irritably. He was cut short by Norma holding up her hand and saying 'Listen!' He heard the front door open and shut.

'She's here.' Norma stood up and smoothed down the front of her frock. Simpkins said, 'Now take it easy.' But it was unheeded. Norma's mouth was set and as soon as the inner door opened she let fly.

'Now then, madam. And what have you got to say for yourself?'

'What about?'

'What about? About stopping out till this time when no-body knows where you are . . .'

Concern grew in Simpkins as he looked at Shirley standing sullen-eyed just inside the door. She had changed a lot in the last few months. It was as though she had passed from child to woman in just that short period. For she was a woman and the total impression of the burnished wings of golden hair, the lipstick on her sulky mouth, the long legs in dark nylons and the filling out of hips and breasts was just that. Men would already desire her and a pretence of two or three years on top of her real age would be no

268

obvious lie. And she was his daughter, something he and Norma had made in the act of love, this beautiful, insolently silent young creature who mourned for a father in name only and out of her loyalty to him rebelled against circumstances she saw in a fierce glare of youthful incomprehension. There had been a time when she clambered on to his knee as readily as on to Sid's, and except for the latters' more frequent presence hardly distinguished between them. These spontaneous demonstrations of affection had dwindled to occasional dutiful kisses, then nothing. Now, when he often longed to embrace her, he held back for fear of misinterpretation. In her wholehearted disapproval of him and his relationship with her mother she was capable of investing any such move of his with sexual overtones. Was he being too fanciful? He dared not risk it, nor dared he imagine her reaction in her present state of mind to the whole truth. She had a right to know. He desperately wanted her to know. But the time for telling her was nowhere in sight.

He said, as Norma paused in her tirade, 'You know, Shirley, you really do worry your mother when you go off like this.'

She was barely civil in the look with which she acknowledged this and she spoke not to him but to her mother.

'We've been to a new discotheque in Leeds, that's all.'

'A what?'

'A discotheque. It's a kind of club where they play all the latest records and you can dance.'

'And drink, I suppose?'

'Soft drinks and coffee.'

'And who's "we"? Who've you been with?'

'Just a gang.'

'Did you have to stop out till this time?'

Shirley blew softly between her lips and rolled her eyes.

'Look, I left them and got on a bus. I felt a big enough drag leaving when I did.'

'I don't care, Shirley. It's just not good enough, all this gadding about every night. You're just not old enough. You

269

might think you are, but you're not. Apart from all the funny company you must get mixed up with you've got your schoolwork to think about.'

'Oh, that . . .'

'Yes, that. Time enough to go gay when you're earning your own living.'

'That can't come too soon for me.'

'You'll think it's a damn sight too soon if you make a mess of your exams and have to look for a job without any qualifications to back you.'

A shrug. 'Oh, something'll turn up.'

'That's you young 'uns today all over, isn't it?' Norma cried. 'Something'll turn up. There'll always be somebody to provide. Anyway, this is the final warning. You pull yourself together and start behaving in a manner more fitting your age.'

'I'm not stopping in every night.'

'You'll do as you're told or I'll know the reason why.'

Shirley swung her bag by its strap as her mother smoothed her dress once more, as though marking the end of the discussion, before turning away.

'I don't know what your Uncle Tom thinks of you these days, I'm sure.'

'I should have thought he'd be glad to have me out of the way for a bit.'

Norma swung round. 'What do you mean by that?'

Simpkins was suddenly sickened by the unmistakable leer in the sideways shift of Shirley's eyes. 'So's you can have some privacy. You can't put me to bed now like you used to, can you?'

For a moment Norma was struck dumb. 'Why you . . . you nasty-minded young madam! Get out of my sight before I clatter your impudent young face. Go on, get up to your room. I'll sort you out later. You just see if I don't!'

She moved towards the fireplace as Shirley went out. She kept her face from him but Simpkins knew she was close to tears.

'When my own daughter tells me,' she said after a mo-

270

ment. 'And her still only a bairn.'

'Now, Norma, she's only——'

'What else have I shown her, if it comes to that? Who's to blame, if we're all telling the truth? It's coming home to roost, all of it. I knew it would some day.'

'All this talk about retribution and days of reckoning, Norma.' Simpkins knocked his pipe out into the fire and spoke with some impatience. 'It's all daft.'

'You think so, do you? It's not just her, you know. It's both of 'em. Nick as well. He might not be breaking out like she is, but it doesn't mean to say he likes it. If it comes to that, I don't know what he mightn't be getting up to while he's away. It's a right mess we've got into, all round.'

'Shirley's judging,' Simpkins said. 'Nick won't. He's old enough to know that things are rarely as simple as that. We shall just have to hang on and wait till she comes round.'

'Aye, and in the meantime she could muck up her future and get into God knows what kind of trouble.'

'Don't you think you're exaggerating a bit?'

'Good God, Tom, you've seen her. You're a man, you know what men are like. In her body she's ready for some-body's bed now; in her mind and feelings she's still only a bairn. And who am I to tell her how to behave, to preach right and wrong to her? She's capable of getting into trouble to spite me and then turning round and telling me I never showed her any different.'

He couldn't argue with her. It was, in the quiet times of the night, a fear which haunted him. He saw no way out of it at present, except to hang on and hope for the best. His own hands were tied; any influence he could exert was in-direct. He sometimes thought his very presence exacerbated the situation, whereas the function he had seen himself best fitted to perform was in giving the future of all of them a new stability. Not that that would necessarily mark the end of it. He had long since ceased believing in and looking for ends in life, working towards ideal states when everything would be placid and everyone happy. There was no end except the grave and until then you went on through life's endless ramifications, watching not so much things coming home to roost (a phrase for him too laden with guilt and remorse, and finally, as a philosophy, life-destroying) but the limitless unprophesiable patterns of cause and effect, actions and consequences.

'You can always let me make you an honest woman.'

'Oh aye, that'd change everything, wouldn't it?'

'The offer's there.'

' "Offer." Yes, that's what I thought.'

'Don't pick my words up so quick. I'm asking. Will you?'

'And Sid only three months gone? She'd likely spit straight in my face if I so much as suggested it.'

'I don't mean tomorrow, or next week. We'd let some time pass by and get people ready for it, nice and steady.'

'Including your sister?'

'Bess doesn't run my life.'

'She runs your house. How d'you think she'd like me walking in and taking over? Or am I supposed to let her go on doing it while I sit about all day like Lady Muck? She doesn't approve of me, either. As far as she's concerned, I'm your fancy woman; not too bad as long as I'm kept quiet and in my place.'

'Bess is perhaps more broadminded than you think, Norma.'

'Well, good for her! Broadminded enough to share the same house, is she? Or were you thinking of turning her out?'

'It's always been convenient for us to live together, but she's quite well off enough to set up on her own. I could build her a little bungalow, or find her a nice small house.'

'At her time of life. After all those years.'

'For all I know she might fancy retiring to blasted Bournemouth. How do I know I'm not tying *her* down?' The exasperation in his voice at the way Norma was emphasising obstacles he was already aware of brought her round to regard him steadily. He rarely lost his temper and she invariably stopped to reconsider when he did.

She shook her head after a silence and said, 'What about

your friends and the people you mix with? How would I measure up as your wife among them?'

'Cressley high society?' Simpkins gave a derisive snort. 'Their handbags are better lined than yours. That's the only difference.'

'You know there'd be talk, though, when you took me among them.'

'Some of 'em have no room to talk.'

'But they will, just the same.'

'Damnation, Norma! Are you going to let them rule our lives? Look, love, I can give you all a new, settled background. I could do things for you I can't do now. Nick's more or less made his break and he might never come back for long; but there's still Shirley. Her resentment won't last for ever. Give her the novelty of a new home and she might stand a chance of coming out of it all right. She's been fond enough of me in times past and I could at least assume the responsibilities of a father to her even if I couldn't tell her the truth.'

'Do you think you owe us all that?'

'I don't come here to pay my debts,' Simpkins said.

'It's funny to think that if we hadn't made that one mistake fifteen years ago we might be talking now in a different way altogether. On the other hand, we might not be talking at all.'

'Shirley's not the only reason I've kept coming back, Norma. And it's no use you seeing her now as some form of retribution or ... or a kind of walking embodiment of our consciences. She's a person in her own right, another generation, life going on. There never is a point in life where you can say "let's stop now, everything's all right". It's like people trying to get to the moon when the money they're spending could cure most of the problems here on the earth. You can no more stop people reaching out for something new than you can prevent life going on and changing. I first got involved with you seventeen years ago. I've never tried to break that involvement and I've never wanted to. It's grown into something more than just you

273

and me finding pleasure in each other. It's taken in other people. All I'm trying to do now is carry it on to its logical next step.'

Norma looked into the fire and her face softened as a memory of the pleasure he had spoken of came to her.

'They were good times, weren't they, right at first?'

'They were, that.'

'It's not like that now, though, is it?'

'Passions cool down,' Simpkins said. 'People get older. I used to get in a fever for you. You can't live like that for ever.'

'Perhaps . . .' a shy smile passed across her lips, 'perhaps if we shared the same bed regular we might get a bit of it back.'

Simpkins laughed. 'You're a shameless piece.'

'I sometimes think I must be. But I'm still a young enough woman and I still sometimes want——'

'Come on, then,' Simpkins broke in. 'What say we try it? We'll start off with a right good honeymoon, somewhere in the sun: Spain or Italy or Portugal. You name it and we'll go there. What do you say, Norma? Shall we give it a try?'

But the softness in her expression had given way again to doubt. 'I don't know, Tom.' Simpkins sighed.

'Nick's coming home this week-end. Perhaps he can help to sort Shirley out a bit.' She turned her head and looked directly at him. 'It's got to be all right with them, Tom. It's no good at all unless it's right with them.'

21

Nick travelled up on Friday afternoon. It was a journey
which involved changing trains twice and a bus ride from
Leeds. He was tired at the end of it and depressed by the
necessity of coming to a decision about Caroline. He found
it impossible to take things as they came with her, to let the
relationship run on free of all that self-questioning and
analysis. There were times when, wanting her and knowing
she was there for him, he felt his hold over her like a swag-
ger in the mind, or something to be worn like a badge
marking him as a fully fledged member of the male sex.
But, always, the unsatisfactory circumstances in which they
culminated their assignations—never in the privacy of a
room but in field or wood or on the river bank—brought
back the guilt which was an inescapable part of the knowledge that while she was in love with him, he was only
using her.

As he waited in the bus station for his last connection to
Edgehill he saw Shirley swing off a bus which drew in
across the way. His arm half-lifted involuntarily and he
opened his mouth to call out to her. Then he held back,
realising she was too far away, and watched her walk
quickly round the corner into the street.

The house was warm and welcoming after the two hundred yards walk from the bus stop through a cold drizzle
and it was more and more a luxury for him nowadays to
stretch his legs in front of an open fire. And yet, something
had gone from it when his father died. It was odd how that
quiet ineffectual man, often absent himself, had provided a

still centre for the household, and how peripheral their lives seemed to have become since his death. Nick could not believe this was the pattern for the future. They were like people waiting for a new and meaningful way of life to be imposed upon them.

'You'll be hungry,' his mother said. 'What can I get you?'

'Oh, anything will do.'

'Well, you've missed tea. What about egg and bacon?'

'Fine.'

'Shirley's out,' his mother said as she busied herself over the gas-cooker in the corner.

'I saw her in the bus station.'

'Did you speak to her?'

'No, she was over the other side.'

'She's supposed to have gone to see a friend in town.'

'Supposed?'

'I mean that's the excuse she gave me. I can hardly believe a word she says these days.'

'Is it as bad as that?'

'Oh, aye. She's got till she comes and goes as she pleases and tells me what she wants me to know.'

'But surely you can keep her in order. She's only a kid.'

'I could have done at first. But I saw her wanting to get out more as her way of finding relief after your dad died. By the time I realised what was really wrong it was too late for anything but my will against hers and somehow I just haven't the strength for a continuous stand-up battle. Oh, I could do it, even now. In fact, I do curb her a bit. But when she stops in there's an atmosphere you could cut with a knife.'

'What kind of atmosphere?'

She turned her head and looked at him briefly. 'She hates me.'

'Oh, now, Mother. That can't be——'

'You don't live with it all the time. You haven't seen it, day after day.'

'She might ... she might disapprove of some things,'

276

Nick said awkwardly, 'but she can't just suddenly conceive a hatred for her own mother.'

'You sound as though you've talked to her.'

'I know she was upset about the time of the funeral. She was saying a few ... well, a few wild things then; but I thought she'd get over it in time.'

'Like you, you mean?'

'I don't follow you.'

'You disapproved as well, didn't you? Have you changed your mind now?'

Nick shrugged. 'I try not to judge people.'

'That's what your Uncle Tom said.' She lifted the fried bacon on to a plate then broke an egg into the pan, splashing hot fat over it for a moment before letting her hands fall to rest on the rim of the stove. 'It's not what your father would have wanted, you know. None of it. He'd be hurt if he could see all this.' She wasn't pleading; just quietly and sadly stating what she saw as fact.

'I never had a chance to talk to him about it,' Nick said.

Her head turned again to give him a long silent look. Then she went on with her cooking. Nick felt mean, hating in himself the silences and ambiguities with which he punished her. Yet something stood between them, a barrier of caution and reserve he could not break through to give her the loving reassurance she craved without letting go some essential part of himself.

She set a place for him at the table and put there the plate of eggs and bacon, buttered bread and a pot of tea.

'Will that be all right for you?'

'Yes, fine, thanks.'

'I'll cut you some more bread, if you want it.'

She poured herself a cup of tea and sat down opposite him.

'There's something I want to say to you.'

'Oh?'

'Your Uncle Tom's asked me to marry him.' His quick glance saw faint colour flushing her cheeks and neck. He was suddenly conscious of the power that was his. His mother was in the palm of his hand. He could close his fingers and squeeze her heart in a relentless grip. He knew that if he said no, she would never marry Tom.

'Well, I'm not surprised.'

'Aren't you?'

'I suppose it's the least he can do.'

'Is that how you see it, as his duty?'

He wavered but could not altogether let go. 'How can I say what he thinks or feels? Surely you're best qualified to judge that.'

'I want to know what you think of the idea.'

'I think it's a bit soon.'

'I know, but apart from that, what——?'

'It's not me he wants to marry. You'll have to decide what you want.'

'There's more to it than that. There's you and Shirley to think about.'

'Shirley won't have it in her present mood.'

'Oh, for God's sake, Nick, stop playing with me. We can sort out what Shirley thinks afterwards. I want to know what you think. I don't want to go ahead with this and have you hate me for it ever after.'

'I don't hate you, Mother,' Nick said in a low voice. 'I never have and I never shall.' He watched her fingers nervously gather and knead together breadcrumbs off the tablecloth. 'What about Uncle Tom? He must be pretty settled in his ways by now. And there's his sister, Mrs Hargreaves.'

'He says he can manage all that side of it.' She went on earnestly, 'Nick, will you talk to Shirley?'

'What, about this?'

'No, no. I don't want you to mention this yet. Just try and find out her general frame of mind and whether there's any chance of bringing her round. You can get closer to her than I can just now, Nick. She'll say things to you she wouldn't say to me.'

'You think I can make her see sense?'

'I don't know. But she can't go on like this. It'll lead

278

nowhere but to trouble. She can't ruin her life, Nick. She can't.'

'I don't suppose it's a good time to tell her the whole truth.'

He was surprised by his own words: it was knowledge he had thought of holding back until some future set of circumstances he couldn't foresee and it had come out almost involuntarily. He had never seen his mother so visibly startled before. The delicate colour still touching her cheeks deepened to a vivid scarlet and her hand went to her throat. Her voice, when she finally spoke, seemed to fight its way past her indrawn breath.

'What ... what do you mean?'

'It's beginning to show,' Nick said. 'Twice, while I was at home for the funeral, I caught her at just the right angle. Then I guessed. I'm still guessing. You can tell me I'm wrong.'

'I wondered when somebody else would notice ... She couldn't have seen it herself, could she?'

'She'd probably be the last person to——'

'Nick,' she said urgently, 'she mustn't get to know. God knows what it would do to her the way she is now. You mustn't say anything. You understand?'

He nodded. 'I know.'

'Sometime, Nick. But not now.'

He picked up the plates and his cup and took them to the sink. He put them in the bowl and ran hot water till they were covered, then went and sat in the easy chair by the fire. He rested his head back and stretched out his legs. He closed his eyes to escape the pathetic uncertainty of his mother's glances and was lying like that when they heard the car draw up outside.

'That sounds like Tom now.'

'Does he come up every day?'

'As often as he can manage it.'

There was a perfunctory single rap and the back door opened.

'Hello, Nick. How are you?'

279

'Oh, pretty well.'

Tom plunged his hand into the deep pocket of his grey overcoat and took out a crumpled white handkerchief with which he wiped his face.

'Is it still raining?' Nick's mother asked.

'It's turned into a downpour. It drove straight into my face as I came round the end of the house. And I thought a week ago we were going to be blessed with a fine early spring.'

He took off his coat and Nick's mother got up to feel at it.

'If that's wet it wants hanging in here where it'll dry.'

'No, no. It's only caught a drop. It'll be all right.' He went through into the hall to hang the coat on the pegs there. Pipe and tobacco pouch were already in his hands when he came back.

'How much tobacco do you get through?' Nick asked as Tom pressed the rubbed flake into the pipe bowl.

'Oh, seven or eight ounces a week, I suppose.'

'That must be keeping it going pretty well all the time.'

'I smoke a lot of matches as well,' Tom said, twinkling. 'And I waste quite a bit of tobacco scraping dottles out . . .' He turned his head. 'Is Shirley . . .?'

'Out,' Nick's mother said. 'Gone to a friend's house in town.'

'Did she know Nick was coming?'

'Yes. But you know she won't stop in for anything these days if she can see a chance of getting out.'

Tom sighed. 'Have you said anything to Nick about it?'

'Yes, we've talked about it.'

'I've said I'll talk to her,' Nick said. 'I don't know what good it will do and, to be quite honest, I can't blame her for what she thinks. If that's her opinion, she's a right to it. But this is no way to go about registering her disapproval.'

'You really think that's what it's all about?' Tom said.

'Oh, yes,' Nick said. 'You can be pretty sure of that. She'd got it into her head some months ago that she was the only one who'd ever really loved my father and she's out to

280

carry the banner of loyalty single-handed.'

'The daft, headstrong little chit,' Nick's mother muttered.

'Not daft, Norma,' Tom said. 'Just young and emotional and grieving.' For a moment he looked older as he contemplated his hands.

'I lose all patience with her.'

'Aye.' Tom looked steadily at Nick's mother. 'But you can't and you mustn't.' He put a match to his pipe and expelled fragrant smoke.

'I was going to ask you, Nick, if you knew a teacher called Hart, down at Valley Bridge. Peter, is it, or Philip?'

'Philip,' Nick said. 'Yes, I know him.'

'I thought he'd be Nick's Mr Hart,' his mother said.

'He's Head of the English Department. He used to teach me.'

'You see him now, occasionally, don't you, Nick?'

'Did you know he was interested in politics?' Tom asked.

'I've heard him talk about Socialism in a general sort of way.'

'Yes ... The Labour Party are putting him up against me in the next council elections.'

'I know,' Nick said. 'I was with him the night Walter Whitehead first approached him.'

'Were you, now?' Tom looked surprised.

'In fact. I encouraged him to accept. I ... I told him if they gave him a ward I'd help him to get in.'

'You did what?' His mother looked at him, astounded.

'I said I'd do what I could to help. I'm a Socialist, Mother, and Philip's a friend of mine. It's as simple as that.'

'Do you call turning on your Uncle Tom—stabbing him in the back like this—a simple thing? What's this Philip Hart ever done for you compared with Tom?'

'He got me to university. Him as much as anybody.'

'Aye, and Tom's the one who's keeping you there.'

Nick's mouth tightened. 'I don't need reminding of that.'

'Hold on, Norma,' Tom butted in. 'What he does for either of us can't make that much difference. Let's not get

281

carried away.'

'He's doing it for the wrong man, though.'

'He's got a right to his choice, Norma,' Tom said, each word slow and deliberate. He was hurt, as Nick had known he must be. It was all very well being tolerant of others' views, leaving politics inside the chamber and having amiable drinks with people who thought differently from yourself; but this must seem like going to a friend for a reference and finding, after all the jokes and laughter and good fellowship, that there were things about you which prevented him from giving it.

'You think he's the best man for the job, do you. Nick?'

'I wish it hadn't happened this way,' Nick said. 'I'd have liked you both to get on. But you picked your allies, and they're not mine.'

'They're not all mine, you know, lad.'

'No, more's the pity. But if you choose to hide your real views behind a flag of independence you can't blame people for misinterpreting you. Not that it won't have stood you in good stead with a lot of voters.'

'I've never found it that simple,' Tom said.

'I don't see how you can back every horse in the race. There comes a time when you've got to decide, and make it simple ... I'm sorry; I'm not presuming to advise you; just explaining my own position. When it's all boiled down I know which side I've got to be on. And that's the time to stand up and be counted.'

'I don't know what this is all about,' his mother said. 'Your Uncle Tom's been on that council for donkey's years. He's always been a good man and he's tried to do his best for everybody.'

'I know that, and I've said I'm sorry.'

'But you'll go your own headstrong way, won't you? It doesn't matter what you owe people and that your loyalty starts at home, with the people nearest you.'

'No, Mother.' Nick jabbed a finger at his own chest. 'Loyalty starts here.'

'Aye, with Number One.' It was a foolish remark, but the

282

bitter lack of reason in it stung him to an equally bitter reply.

'Don't *you* start preaching to me about loyalty and looking after Number One.'

It went straight home. His mother stood as if paralysed, the angry colour draining from her face. Tom had started forward in his chair. 'Now look, this is going too far.' But Nick's mother found her voice and spoke through thin drawn lips.

'This is your way. This is how you get your own back.'

His temper snapped. 'For God's sake! The world doesn't revolve round your guilty conscience.'

Tom stood up. 'Nick. Norma. That's enough. You'll both be sorry for it tomorrow.'

'I'd better clear out of the way for a bit,' Nick said.

'Aye,' his mother said, 'go and look for your sister. You're two of a kind.'

'If this is the sort of thing she has to put up with week after week,' Nick said, 'I don't wonder she goes out every night.'

He walked into the hall, unhooking his coat from the pegs as he passed, then opened the front door and left the house.

He went down to the main road and stood in fretful indecision at the bus stop. He supposed he would go down into town because there was really no other direction in which he could go, and he might have walked, working the edge off his feelings in that way, but for the rain. As it was, he could get just as wet waiting here, for the service was not very frequent at this time in the evening. Even this small choice seemed too much for him as he walked to and fro on the pavement and when, after a few minutes, he actually did start out down the hill at a brisk pace he had left it too late, for in less than a hundred yards he heard a bus top the rise behind him and he was forced to turn round and run back the way he had come.

He paid his fare as far as the bus station and sat on the lower deck turning over in his mind ways of spending the next couple of hours until he felt like going back home. He could probably catch the last show at a cinema, if there was anything he wanted to see. Or he could visit Philip, as he had intended to this week-end anyway. He decided to do the latter and, the choice made, he felt his thoughts cooling as the bus neared the town. By the time he had crossed the station and boarded the second bus he was regretting his impulsive action in leaving the house in anger. Gestures like that settled nothing and his tonight could only have made matters worse, confirming to his mother that his every decision and act were a reflection on her. It couldn't go on like this. They each had their own lives to live. He promised himself he would talk to her tomorrow, calmly and reasonably, declare himself wholeheartedly on her side, persuade her to accept Tom's offer of marriage. He would renew her faith in the courage of her own convictions but make her see that she must leave him with his. He felt confident in his power to do this. Only Shirley stood in the way. All he could do with her was exert some influence and hope that time would do the rest.

The rain had stopped by the time he walked through the estate to Philip's house. He was going to confirm his support, and looking forward to Philip's account of his experiences in this new world of practical politics. As before, the front of the house was dark but the car stood in the garage. There was a light in the kitchen and his hand was already reaching for the bell by the back door when he heard the voices from inside. They were raised, vengeful, full of spleen and a desire to hurt.

'... talking any more. Why should I when you either twist everything I say to ... even understand what I'm talking about?'

'Other people do, of course.'

'For Christ's sake, woman, get off my bloody back.'

'Philip, it's not like that.'

'Look, look ...' Nick had never heard such venom in

284

Philip's voice ... 'You might as well have nailed my head to the bloody gatepost the day we got married and put up a sign— "no one else shall love this man: *he is mine*".'

'But it's the kids. Look at Christopher tonight. He'd never have——'

'Kids, kids. Let's get me straightened out, shall we? Kids are all right if they're fed and get their spending money regularly.'

'You know you don't mean that. You're foul. Foul and selfish and cruel. I don't know you any more. I——' Kate Hart's voice broke and Nick thought she was crying.

'That's why I'm here, isn't it, because I'm selfish?'

They moved farther into the house, away from him. The kitchen light snapped off and an isolated roar from Philip of 'Oh, for Christ's sake...' was the last Nick heard before an inner door slammed and the voices were lost.

Nick, standing there in dismay, thought that three or four minutes later he would have arrived to this apparent calm and cut the quarrel in mid-flow with his ringing of the bell. Now, though one or both of them might welcome the interruption, he could not bring himself to walk in there and watch them rearrange their faces for his benefit while wondering what he had overheard.

He went away, telling himself that he had no more right to judge or take it too seriously than someone who might have been standing on *his* back step forty minutes ago. It was hard to assess the real rancour and depths of other people's quarrels, or their ability to assimilate such incidents into the stream of their daily lives together. What depressed him was the knowledge that Philip and Kate could quarrel at all like that. He chided himself for his naïveté but the depression persisted as he rode back into town.

The Plaza was the nearest cinema to the bus station and they were showing a western he had seen before. He was tempted for a moment to take the easy course of going in and seeing it again, then he decided against it, turning aimlessly away and wandering to the edge of the pavement, unable to summon enough interest to do the rounds of the other cinemas. He was left with nothing to do but go home; unless he went for a drink.

The lighted windows and doorway of a pub some way along the street caught his eye. It looked a quiet place until he got near to it when he could hear the grinding thump of a juke-box inside. But he went in, thinking that the music would create a diversion for his thoughts. There was a long bar counter in the room he entered, extending beyond a part wall which separated this place from the back room where the juke-box was. He ordered a pint of bitter and stood drinking it opposite a calendar on which February's girl was lifting her scarlet sweater to reveal the lower half of her breasts. Like Caroline, she wore no bra.

Pubs were still a comparative novelty to Nick; each one he went into added to his experience of their variety, and he found this one unwelcoming with its lino-covered floor and the Formica-topped counter. 'Cheap twentieth-century hygienic,' he dubbed the style, and disliked it. But the landlord was amiable enough. He commented on the dreadful weather as he served Nick and then changed half-a-crown into sixpences for the fruit machine. Nick, alone in this room, said, 'You get all the action in the back, do you?'

'It draws the younger ones,' the landlord said.

'And puts the older ones off?' Nick suggested.

The landlord shrugged. 'You've got to tempt somebody in, with trade like it is.'

'Oh?'

'Oh, aye. There's too many houses chasing too little money.'

'I didn't know that. I thought most pubs did well.'

'You'd learn better if you were in the trade for a bit.'

He went to serve a customer in the other room and Nick turned to the one armed bandit. He played it, winning a little and losing it, till his original stake was gone. Then he went into the passage to look for the lavatory. The walls of the gents' seemed recently decorated but the graffiti were

286

already beginning to reappear, including the inevitable 'A Merry Christmas to all our readers' and the message of the man who had presumably been the first to strike a blow for freedom of expression, with 'The painter's art is all in vain, the pisshole poet has struck again'.

He was coming out when the door to the back room swung open to let through a tough-looking youth of about his own age with a thick mop of black hair and long sideburns. Nick glanced at him then past him as the door shut on its spring. He stood stock still then, thinking that he must be mistaken but at the same time convinced that the girl whom the partly open door had momentarily revealed was Shirley. He pushed open the door and held it, looking across at her for several seconds before she, feeling his presence, lifted her eyes and saw him. He walked across and leaned over the table, speaking to her in a low voice under the throb of the juke-box.

'What are you doing here?'

There was guilt in the uneasy shift of her eyes and it undermined the apparent defiance of her answer.

'What does it look like?'

The eye-shadow, mascara and lipstick she must have put on since leaving the house. The effect was ridiculous in Nick's eyes, yet it also confirmed in a startling way the impression she sometimes gave of being older than she really was. He reached for the glass of orange-coloured liquid standing before her and smelled it.

'Is this gin?'

'What if it is?'

He was filled with an appalling sense of her vulnerability. The situation of her being here like this seemed like a forecast of her possible future, the grotesque falsehood of the make-up and the gin beckoning her along a path of misery and degradation. The prospect before her was so horrifyingly vivid to him that when he spoke out of this fear that she herself could not perceive it was with a harshness which only intensified the instinctive defiance in her.

'You silly devil; what are you up to?'

'I'm trying to have a good time. And I was till you came in.'

He embodied as he stood there the authority against which she was in rebellion. He felt that himself and knew there was no other rôle he could play.

'Don't you know you can get into trouble for——?'

'Did *she* send you after me?'

'Who?'

'My mother.'

'I just came in by accident. Look, Shirley, haven't we got enough trouble without——?'

'I didn't start it.'

'Maybe not. But this kind of thing will get you nowhere. Come on home with me.'

She shook her head, the wings of silky hair shimmering in the light. 'I'm staying.'

He glanced round. 'You're not on your own, are you?'

'No, I'm with a friend. A boy.'

'He ought to know better.'

He felt a hand on his shoulder then, and as a voice behind him said, 'What's going on?' he straightened up and turned to face the youth he had passed in the corridor.

'Is she with you?'

'That's right? What's on your mind?'

'Don't you know she's under age? What the hell do you——?'

'Who are you to be sticking your nose in?'

'I'm her brother.'

'Oh, I see. I thought you were some joker trying to cut in.'

'I am cutting in, and taking her out of here before there's any trouble.'

'There was no trouble before you came, mate. You're not going to make any, are you?'

'Don't you know how old she is?'

'So she's under age. Where's the harm in it 'less nosey

parkers start sticking their noses in?'

'The harm is that she's too young to be sitting in this place drinking gin when her mother's at home worried out of her mind about her.'

'Worried about herself, you mean,' Shirley said.

'You're not a spoilsport, mate, are you?' the youth said.

'I'm spoiling your little game, anyway,' Nick said. 'I can see you looking after her if she gets too much.'

'Now just a minute——'

'Look, she's coming home with me.'

'What do you say, love?' the youth said to Shirley. 'He's not being very nice about it, is he?'

Shirley's mouth was set in a sullen line that made Nick want to swing across the table and slap her face. The jukebox thundered in the corner, hiding what they were saying but not that the three of them were quarrelling. People were looking at them. He had to get her out before real trouble started.

'What do you want to come in here for? Why can't you leave people alone?'

'Come on,' Nick said. 'We'll talk about it on the way home.'

'I'm not going.'

'You heard her, mate,' the youth said.

'Right,' Nick said, turning on him. 'You hear me. Unless she goes out of here with me now I'll tell the landlord how old she is. He'll soon shift her out, and you as well for bringing her in.'

'Go on, you wouldn't——'

'On your feet, Shirley. I'm telling you, I'll call him over if you don't. He won't risk losing his licence.'

Shirley looked at the youth. He gave her a little nod. She reached for her glass, staring defiantly at Nick as she gulped down its contents, then stood up. He followed her to the back door, the youth behind him. As the door opened the landlord called to him, holding up the half-full glass which he had brought through from the other room. 'Hey, you didn't drink up.' Nick waved his hand at him. 'Another time.'

They stood in the damp darkness of the yard as the door closed behind them. For a moment no one spoke.

'Come on, then,' Nick said finally. 'We'll go and catch a bus.'

'I'm not going with you,' Shirley said.

'Look, don't start that again. I won't tell them where I——'

'I'm not going. You've got me out of there but you can't force me to go with you now.'

'What will you do? Find another place where he can pump gin into you?'

'Look, what do you want?' the youth said.

'It's what you want that bothers me. Do you think she'll be easy game after a few drinks?'

The youth took hold of Nick's coat front in the darkness. 'I don't like that kind of talk, mate.'

'I don't like you, if it comes to that.'

'Okay, so why don't you bugger off and leave us alone?'

'She comes with me.'

'I've told you, Nick, I'm not going. I'm not going till I'm ready.'

It exploded out of Nick then: the fear for Shirley and now anger at her stupidity which was forcing him into a corner where he would have to fight the youth for her.

'You daft bitch. Do you want to find yourself up some alley, stoned on gin and with your knickers off?'

The grip on his coat tightened. He lifted both hands and pushed hard at the youth's shoulders. The hold on him relaxed for a second, then the boy came back at him, his fist driving at Nick's stomach. He doubled, winded, as the blow took him just below the ribs. Shirley cried, 'No, no; stop it!' as the second blow slammed into Nick's face. He went down, feeling the tide of blood pumping out of his nostrils.

'Leave him alone!' Shirley cried. 'Stop it, stop it!'

He was conscious of the boy standing above him with

raised fists as Shirley crouched beside him and he began to pull himself up on to his knees.

'Nick. Oh, Nick, why didn't you leave me alone?'

'Get away from me,' he said. He could taste the blood in his throat. He coughed, then spat.

'Oh, are you all right, Nick?'

'I'm fine. No thanks to you.'

'You shouldn't have tried to make me go home to them. I thought you were on my side.'

'Go where you like,' Nick said. 'I don't care. I'm sick of hearing about your bloody sulks and tantrums every time I come home.'

'I hate them. Him especially. Always there, always trying to get round me mam. Why doesn't he go away and leave us alone?'

She was crying and her tears drove him to further anger.

'He loves you. He can't go away and leave you because he loves you. He's your father.'

There was silence. 'I . . . I don't believe you. You're making it up.'

'All right, I'm making it up.' He wanted to retreat now but she came back at him, insistent.

'You're lying, aren't you, Nick? You're making it up.'

It was too late. He had said it. Here was where the truth came out, not in calm and measured conversation but in the darkness of a pub yard with him on his hands and knees, gushing blood.

'Tom's your father, Shirley. He's your father.'

He felt her move beside him. He lifted himself up, reaching for her, wanting now to explain and comfort and reassure. But she was gone. He heard her feet move quickly across the yard and then he was alone, the thump of the juke-box coming to him through the closed door. He supported himself against the wall, terrified now at the enormity of what he had done. He coughed and retched, clearing his throat of blood and mucus. He sensed someone pause at the end of the yard and look towards him through

291

the darkness. When whoever it was had passed on he moved too. Holding his handkerchief to his face he went out of the yard the way Shirley and the youth had gone, swaying a little as he walked.

22

The uniformed inspector's name was Lightfoot and Tom had known him since he came to the town from another force, several years ago. There was, Nick thought, some small comfort to be drawn from Tom's standing, which had allowed him to go as far as the Chief Constable in his efforts to ensure that no possible action was neglected in the search for Shirley. But it was five days now, and they seemed no nearer to finding her than at the beginning. Lightfoot's uniform dominated his small office in the police station. He was a big, assured man, in his fifties, who looked as though he had seen it all; but he was plainly baffled now.

'How's the mother, Tom?'

'She doesn't know where to put herself with worry.'

'You know, it's on the strength of what you say that we're not treating this as suspected foul play.'

Tom shook his head. 'It's a bit far-fetched.'

'It happens.'

'It's logical, on the basis of what she felt, to assume she's just run away.'

'But where to, Tom? She has no relatives or friends outside the immediate area. We've questioned everyone we know about, including her chums at school, and no one's seen her since that day.'

They had also dragged the canal and a stretch of river below the weir. Nick shut the images out of his mind and said,

'She hadn't enough money to make a long journey.'

'A young girl like that, they can usually beg a lift. No, I'm afraid that if she really had wanted to put some distance between herself and here she'd have no undue trouble in doing it.'

'She could be anywhere, in that case,' Tom said.

'She could.'

'I still think she's not far away.'

Lightfoot sighed and shook his head. 'I don't know. Her picture's appeared in the press. The county police know about her as well. We've done all we can in that direction. The one real lead seems to be the feller young Mr Moffat saw her with.' He looked at Nick. 'I take it you've had no blinding revelation about him?'

'No.' Lightfoot's bland stare lingered on him, taking all in. He seemed to reserve judgement on everything, taking nothing for granted.

'No. And none of her friends can give us any information about that association.'

'It seems to be something she was keeping to herself,' Nick said. 'I mean, from the number of nights she was out of the house but not with her friends we can assume she'd seen him more than once before.'

'But not in that pub. You know yourself the landlord only remembered them at all because you reminded him of the circumstances.'

'Can we believe him?'

'Why should he lie? He's already scared of being charged with serving minors; he's got nothing to lose by admitting they'd been in before. No, the lead is that boy, and somehow we've got to find him. I'd hoped he might come forward and get in touch with us, but now I wonder whether we oughtn't to ask the West Riding CID to set up an Identikit picture for us. You know what one of those is, do you?'

Nick nodded. He'd seen them on television. 'But I can't even bring his face clearly to mind now. I only saw him for a few minutes.'

'Oh, you'd find the process reminding you,' Lightfoot

said. 'You'd start off with the broad outlines and fill in the details as they came back to you.'

'Look,' Tom said, 'if all the town knows she's missing, why *hasn't* he come forward to tell us what he knows?'

'You'd be surprised how easy it is for a thing like this to pass right over you. He might never read a newspaper—lots of people don't—or he could live somewhere else. He could also be scared of getting involved.'

'Why?'

'Oh, some people just are. They could have run away together as far as we know.' Lightfoot paused. 'It could be that he's been in trouble before.' He got up. 'Excuse me a minute.'

When he had gone out Nick said, 'Do you think he knows what he's at?'

'I expect he's doing his best.'

'I can't say he fills me with confidence.'

'This is real life, Nick, not television. Would you feel better with Charlie Barlow in charge?'

'Just for once I'd go for Lockhart's record.'

'Aye ... me too.'

The thin smiles they managed to exchange relieved for a moment the strain they were living under. For a moment—then Nick burst out,

'Oh God, I could kill myself every time I think of it. If only I'd kept my temper and held my tongue none of this would have happened.'

'Ease up, Nick,' Tom said. 'You've had enough stones thrown at you for it. It was there and it had to come out sometime. There may be a pattern—who knows?—a kind of logic in these things, and it might be all for the best in the end.'

'With my mother half out of her mind for the past five days? I wish I could see that.'

'Your mother's emotions have been raw ever since your father died. I've tried my best with her but I always seem to come up against a blank wall.'

'The blank wall being me and Shirley.'

Tom shrugged. 'You're people. You've a right to your opinions and feelings.'

'We've got the rest of our lives to come to terms with our feelings,' Nick said with intensity. 'My mother hasn't ... Look, Tom, if we come out of this all right I want you to make my mother marry you. I want you to take her out of that house to a new life.'

'Is that what you really want?'

'Yes, it is. It's the best thing for all of us, and certainly her. If she doesn't find some sort of emotional security before long she'll go round the bend. And if Shirley can't see it she'll have to put up with it till she can.'

The door opened and Lightfoot came in with a thick photograph album which he placed on the desk, motioning Nick round into his chair.

'It's a long shot,' he said, 'but one we haven't tried yet.'

'What is this?' Nick asked. 'The rogues' gallery?'

'Yes, that's just what it is. Photographs of all men who've been convicted of criminal offences inside the area of our jurisdiction. I want you to look at them carefully, taking your time, and see if our man is there.'

'He was only a young man,' Nick said, 'about my age.'

'People can get into a lot of trouble by the time they're your age, Mr Moffat.'

'It seems a bit ...' Tom began.

'If he won't, or can't, come to us, Tom, we've got to use every available means of finding him. This is just a start, one stage we can't overlook. In a really efficient totalitarian state they'd probably have pictures of everybody; we can only start with what we've got.' He picked up some papers from the desk. 'I'll just attend to another matter while you're doing that.'

Nick turned the pages of the album. It gave him an odd feeling to see all the faces in there. 'You can't escape altogether, can you?' he said. 'They say you discharge your debt to society and that's that. But here you are, docketed and filed, branded for life.'

'You wouldn't think the police were very efficient if they

didn't keep records like that, would you?'

'No. And if you're innocent you've nothing to fear, have you? Except the coppers leaning on you and asking questions every time there's a bit of trouble.'

'They have a job to do, Nick. It's in the interests of the public—you and me—that they should do it as well as possible.'

'And what does Lightfoot want me to do now? Pick out somebody who vaguely resembles that kid so they can kick up some dust and justify their existence?'

'Why shouldn't they question five hundred people with records if it will help to bring Shirley back?'

'But how can a kid like Shirley disappear without somebody knowing something? Even if she hitched a lift and got far away she's still got no money to live on. She's bound to be lonely and hungry and who can she turn to for help without their becoming suspicious?'

'You said yourself she could pass for seventeen.'

'I know, but——'

'I've got a growing conviction that if we find the boy we'll find her.'

'What kind of trouble does that mean for him?'

'It depends. She's only fifteen.'

'He's either barmy, or she's——'

'Or she's been very persuasive. It's obvious she's not coming back under her own choice.'

Nick let a moment pass, then he said, 'Tom ... You don't honestly think she could have...?'

'Done away with herself?' He looked directly at Nick. 'It's something that's haunted me ever since we waited up for her that first night; and the fear's greater the closer you are to a person and the more you love her. But rationally I'm convinced she's just hiding somewhere. Either intending to stay away for good—which I don't see either—or feeling now that she's stuck with the consequences of running off and staying away that first night.'

Nick had been turning pages without really looking. He now went dutifully back as Tom said. 'The way I feel now,

I think there's more chance of finding her than there is of making her happy when we have. And I hope to God that...'

'What?' Nick said.

'Nothing... There's another thing we haven't cleared up. Perhaps now isn't the time, but since it's between us...' He met Nick's questioning gaze. 'The election. I don't suppose you've thought about it much since Friday night.'

'No, I haven't.'

'No... I've got to ask you, Nick, and I want an honest answer. Is there anything personal in it, any spirit of revenge?'

'No.'

'Your mother thinks otherwise.'

'She doesn't understand. She's so self-centred now that she sees everything in relation to her own problems.'

'You just feel that you must help this Philip Hart?'

'Yes. I didn't know it would be you he was fighting when I offered. But I believe in what he stands for so I'm going through with it. I'm just sorry it's on a personal level now.'

'I couldn't blame you for resenting me.'

'This has got nothing to do with it.'

'Well, you've said you approve of my marrying your mother. I suppose I can accept that as enough for now... I've always cared, you know, Nick, in my own way. I've prided myself on not being too stuffy, of asking questions, and not living my life thinking that we in this day and age are the chosen inheritors of God's law and there's nothing wrong that a big stick or a couple of well-placed bombs couldn't put right. I'm conscious that men in a couple of hundred years will look back as we look back on our predecessors and see a few good things but a hell of a lot of mistakes and ignorance. There are good things we can pass on to you young ones but they've to be set alongside a heritage of mistakes and a load of doubtful dogma that's done little but create potential disasters all ready for touching off. Perhaps if we leave you alone a bit and don't try to impose our faulty likeness on you we can free you to do a

298

bit better than we have. All this is really saying that you should do what you feel you have to do. The only thing I do hope—that I wish for on a personal level—is that somewhere among it all you might find a little respect for me.'

'I don't think you need worry about that,' Nick said.

Tom blinked and looked away before getting up and taking a few steps about the room. He occupied his hands with pipe and tobacco. Nick, hearing voices in the passage, wondered where Lightfoot could be. The telephone on the desk before him rang and he glanced at Tom's back, wondering if he should answer it.

A moment later he turned a page in the album and stared for several seconds in disbelief, before speaking to Tom.

'Look at this.'

'What?' Tom spun round and came to his side.

'His hair's shorter here, but . . .'

He heard Tom suck in his breath. 'Are you sure?'

'As sure as I can be.'

Tom's hand came over and shut the book. He walked away again as Nick looked up at him in surprise. 'What's wrong?'

'Nick,' Tom said. 'Keep this between us for the present.'

'But what——?'

'Just don't say anything to Lightfoot when he comes back.'

'I don't understand why we——'

'I'll explain, Nick. I'll explain as soon as I've had time to think.'

'You know him, don't you?' Nick said, as the truth dawned.

'Yes,' Tom said. His fingers stuffed tobacco into the bowl of his pipe with nervous clumsiness, as though working unknown to him. 'Yes, I know him.'

The taproom of the pub was occupied by demolition workers slaking the dust in their throats with pints of bitter and black-and-tans. It was not their number which filled the room but a sense of the physical harshness of their jobs, naked now before baths and changes of clothing softened or disguised it. Simpkins and Nick were the odd men out here, among the donkey jackets and old heavy sweaters, the wool and felt caps and hair streaked with stone and plaster dust. But their entry, as they were guided through from the chilly best room where the fire had only just been lit, though a self-conscious intrusion to themselves, was accepted with no more than a few incurious glances. The men were secure in the context of their own kind and, outnumbered, Simpkins and Nick stood up to the bar counter behind which the shirtsleeved landlord, with the faded blue designs of old tattooing on his forearms, waited to serve them. The house was known for the number of its regular customers who had been in trouble for petty criminal offences and Simpkins, though aware of its reputation, had never been in it before. But if, from height and build, he could be mistaken for a policeman at all it was, he thought, in his expensive overcoat and shoes, one of an unusually high rank for such a place and company.

He ordered a Scotch for himself and a half of bitter for Nick. An exuberant game of dominoes was going on at the table just behind them and three men were playing darts, throwing the width of the room into the board over the fireplace.

'The weather doesn't pick up much,' the landlord said.

'No. It's about time it was showing signs.'

'I allus like to see the back of March, meself. It's a month I don't trust.'

'It can be tricky,' Simpkins agreed. He sipped at his whisky as the landlord turned away to pull more beer. 'Take it easy, Nick.'

The boy was on edge, only vaguely comprehending their reason for being here.

'What're we hanging about for?'

'I want to ask a couple of questions.' Simpkins spoke to the landlord again as he finished serving. 'All this work across the road must be good for your trade.'

300

'It's lost me a lot of me locals.'

'Demolition workers now, builders later and a new set of locals when the flats go up.'

'Aye, if they can afford to pay the rents and drink as well,' the man said pessimistically.

'Does Albert Bedford still live round here?'

'Albert Bedford? You're a bit behind the times. He's dead and buried.'

'Is he now? It must be fairly recently.'

'Two or three months. Let me think. Aye, they buried him just before Christmas. Did you know him?'

'He used to work for me at one time.'

'That couldn't be lately. He hadn't worked for years.'

'No, it is a while ago. What's his lad, Don, doing now, then?'

'Oh, he's still about. Comes in here occasionally. I don't know where he's working but as far as I know he's still living in the house on his own. Up top of the hill.'

'Yes,' Simpkins said, 'I know where it is.'

He nudged Nick a moment later and drank off his whisky. 'Ready? It's time we were on our way.' Nick left an inch of beer in his glass when they went out.

'So he's in the house on his own, is he?' Simpkins said outside.

'What do we do now?'

'Pay him a call.'

'Wouldn't it be better to let the police do it?'

'After your little homily on police victimisation?' Simpkins said. 'You know Bedford's got a record.'

'Yes...' Nick said reluctantly. 'All the same...'

They got into the car and crossed the main road, relieved now of the evening's exodus from the town centre, and drove up through the clearance area where a mechanical shovel and a bulldozer stood monstrous in the darkness gathering across the rubbled foundations of the demolished streets. The summit of the steep cobbled rise marked the beginning of another densely populated district, due for clearance under a future order. The houses in the first street faced the falling ground and had, for the time being, an unaccustomed view across the northern edge of the town to the far side of the valley.

As Simpkins turned up along the row Nick said, 'Don't you think we should park down here?'

'Surprise him, you mean?' Simpkins said. 'We might need the car, and anyway, he'll know we're here soon enough.'

He drove to the very end of the street and stopped before the last house where the road took a sharp turn under a high stone wall which held back a cliff of earth. At every turn in this town you came upon evidence of how the people had cleared living space for themselves, excavating earth and blasting rock as the houses spread out of the narrow valley bottom and the settlement, reached, except along the river's course, by footpath and packhorse trail, grew into an industrial city.

The mournful hooter of a diesel railcar passing along the valley sent up to them the first three out-of-tempo notes of the *Tannhäuser* overture as they stood together before the door and Simpkins knocked. He thought he saw the small movement of a curtain from the corner of his eye but there was no answer. Simpkins knocked again, then pounded at the panel with the side of his clenched fist. A key was turned and the door opened half-way. The light behind Bedford was dim and his face was in shadow but it was enough for Nick. He nodded 'Yes' in answer to Simpkins' 'Well, Nick?'

'What do you want?' Bedford said truculently.

'A few words with you.'

'I've got nowt to say to you.'

'It won't take long, then. What about asking us in?'

'Why should I?'

'Because you're in trouble if you don't.'

'I don't know what you're after, so you can clear off.'

As the door started to swing shut Simpkins took the step in one bound, his shoulder crashing the door back against the wall. Nick followed him. The room was lit by a paraffin lamp with a smoking wick and a couple of candles.

'What a hole,' Simpkins said. 'Have they turned the power off?'

'What's it to you?' Bedford said. 'You've got no right to come barging in here like this. Who do you think you are?'

'Be thankful we're not the police,' Simpkins said. 'Where is she?'

'Who?'

'Oh, come on. Shirley Moffat. We want to know what you've done with her.'

'I don't know what you're talking about.'

For a second the hope faltered in Simpkins.

'The girl you were with in the Prince Albert last Friday night. His sister. Remember knocking him about in the yard, don't you?'

'How should I know where she is?'

'She's been missing for five days. You were the last person to see her.'

'I left her with him.'

Simpkins closed on him, his shadow blotting out Bedford's in an enormous flickering shape on walls and ceiling.

'You're bloody lying, lad. Take the lamp and look upstairs, Nick.'

Bedford started to move round from the other side of Simpkins. 'You're not going anywhere without I say so. This is my house, not yours.'

Simpkins took him in both hands. He was surprised at the strength his anger gave him. 'Go on, Nick.' As Bedford struggled he spoke into his face from a distance of six inches. 'I'll smash you like the little rat you are if you don't stop arsing around.'

'You——!' Bedford said. His arm came over in a hampered swing and Simpkins, taking the weight of both of them on his back foot, pulled him half round then threw him across the room. The edge of the old-fashioned sideboard took Bedford across the middle of his back and he cried out and went down as Nick called from the top of the stairs. 'Tom! Up here!'

Simpkins went up the dim enclosed stairs two at a time. There was a stump of candle burning in the front bedroom and the light from that and the lamp in Nick's hand showed the shape of Shirley under the covers in the bed.

'She's ill, Tom,' Nick said. 'Her forehead feels like an oven.'

Shirley lifted herself on one elbow as Simpkins moved towards her. 'Uncle Tom? Take me home.' She began to cry silently, the tears running down her flushed face. 'Please take me home.'

'Yes, love,' Simpkins said. He sat on the bed and embraced her through the sheets. 'It's all right now. It's all right.' His heart seemed to melt as he held her. He pressed her feverish face to his chest and crooned to her, his nostrils filled with the sour odour of her body rising out of the warm cave of the bed. She could not have washed for days.

They heard a sound from the doorway. Bedford stood there.

'What's wrong with her?' Simpkins asked.

'She's got flu. It started the day after she came.'

'Have you had a doctor to her?'

'How could I with everybody looking for her? I've been giving her stuff from the chemist's.'

Nick drew Simpkins' gaze to the clutter of bottles and packets on the cabinet beside the bed.

'Suppose she'd died?' Simpkins said. 'You bloody fool, suppose she'd died?'

'I did me best,' Bedford muttered. All the fight had gone out of him now. He slouched, shoulders down, in the doorway. 'I didn't ask her to come. She ran after me, begged me to take her in.'

'Do you know how old she is?'

'Seventeen, she told me.'

'Fifteen.'

'She told me seventeen and I believed her. I didn't know otherwise till I saw it in the paper. What could I do then, with her badly in bed?'

'Have you heard of carnal knowledge?' Simpkins said.

304

'Sexual interference with a minor?'

'I've never touched her.'

'And her naked in this bed,' Simpkins said. 'How stupid do you think I am?'

'Look, you've got to believe me,' Bedford shouted. 'I slept in the other room. Ask her if I laid so much as a finger on her. Ask her, see what she says. Do you think I don't care what happens to her?'

'You'd have shown your concern better by sending for us before.'

'She wanted to get away from you all. She said she hated you all. She told me all about it, all about you messing about with her mam. She begged me to let her stop here.'

'She's not begging for that now.'

'Mebbe not now. She's scared. She's badly and she's only a kid, used to summat better than this. It's not much of a place ... But I've looked after her. I've fed her and dosed her and carried her slops out to the back. That's how much I care about her. I've done everything for her and I've never laid a finger on her. She'd have let me, an' all. That first night she was ready to let me.'

'Shut your filthy mouth.'

'Yeh, it's filth with me but summat else with high and mighty Simpkins, isn't it? All that time you were messing about with her mam.'

'I said "shut up"!' Simpkins roared.

'I want to go home,' Shirley moaned, and Simpkins cradled her closer.

'Yes, my love. You're going home now.'

'Do you think we ought to move her with a temperature like that?' Nick asked.

'We can't leave her here. We'll have to wrap her up as warm as possible and risk it. Where are her clothes?' he asked Bedford.

'Under the other side of the bed.'

'She can't dress herself, and I doubt if she's fit to walk.'

'No,' Simpkins said. 'She goes as she is. You take her clothes and go down and open the back door of the car ...

305

Shirley, I'm going to wrap you up in these blankets and carry you down. So hold still while I get you up safe. You——' he said to Bedford as he pulled the bedclothes free and drew them up round Shirley—'you go ahead with the lamp and light my way downstairs.'

Bedford silently obeyed. Simpkins stood up, bringing Shirley's dead weight with him. Her mind seemed sunk in a trance into which broke only the knowledge that he and Nick were here and that she wanted to go home. Of Bedford she seemed oblivious. She gave him no word, nor even the smallest flicker of expression when, at the bottom of the stairs, he looked at her and said, 'It's okay now, Shirley. You'll be okay when you get home.' His gaze lingered on her then fell before he turned away with the lamp.

He said before Simpkins carried her through the door, 'I don't suppose I'll ever see her again.'

'Do you wànt to?' Simpkins asked.

Bedford ignored the question. 'Why didn't you bring the police?'

'You work that one out for yourself.'

'Big favours,' Bedford said. 'You and them together, you'll soon have her saying I kept her here against her will.'

'It's not much good talking to you, is it?' Simpkins said.

'I've heard too much talk,' Bedford said. 'Most of it lies.'

'You've got to learn to tell the difference.'

He carried Shirley out and slid her into the back of the car beside Nick. 'Hold her close, Nick, and keep her warm.' He got into the driving seat and looked up once at the house. The door was already closed, the dim glow of that pathetic light showing only faintly through the curtains. He switched on the engine then bowed his head as he was suddenly overcome. They had found her. They had found her and got her back; and with a bit of luck now they would keep her.

Lightfoot would not be fobbed off. He was at the house

the next day, aware that he had been bypassed, if not deliberately deceived; he knew from Simpkins' evasiveness on the telephone that Shirley had not walked in of her own accord.

'Concealing a felony, Tom,' he said. 'Accessory after the fact. These are serious matters.'

'There is no felony, Ned. Shirley's back and it's all over and done with.'

'Is it, then?' Norma said. 'It wouldn't be if you let me have my way.'

'Norma,' Simpkins said.

'Why should he get away with it? that's what I want to know. Keeping my daughter away from home for nearly a week, and her on the verge of pneumonia.'

Simpkins' mouth drew down in an angry line as Lightfoot said, 'Who are you referring to, Mrs Moffat?'

But Norma had taken warning from the look on Simpkins' face. 'You'd better ask Tom. He knows him, not me.'

Lightfoot looked at Simpkins. 'Come on now, Tom. Where's the sense in concealing this?'

'There's nothing to conceal, except...'

'What?'

'Except his name. He's been in trouble before and there's no need to bring him into contact with the police again.'

'If he's done nothing he's got nothing to fear.'

'How do I know what technical charges you can bring against him?'

'Oh, now Tom. What do you think we are?'

'I know what he is. He's stupid and lazy, and he might commit other criminal acts in the future. But he's also sure nobody's going to do him any favours and he'll be waiting for the knock on the door to confirm it.'

'You saw his picture in the station, didn't you?'

'Yes.'

'And you went out without telling me. How do you think we can operate if the public withhold vital information?'

'All right,' Simpkins said. 'Charge me with obstructing the police in their investigations.'

307

'No, Tom. I want this man's name. And I know you're going to give it to me.'

'Don Bedford,' Simpkins said at length. 'Both he and his father used to work for me. The old man's dead now. Don did a period in reform school for pinching cigarettes and a car. I gave him a job when he came home. He was in the pub with Shirley that night when Nick saw them. He and Nick had a fight outside. Shirley ran after Bedford and asked him to let her stay with him. She fell ill the next day and she was in bed from then until we went for her. Otherwise she might have come back. I don't know. Bedford says she told him she was seventeen and he believed it till he saw her real age in the newspaper.'

'Why didn't he let somebody know then?'

'For the same reason he took her in in the first place. She wanted to hide from us and he let her talk him into it. He was probably a bit scared too when he saw she was only fifteen.'

'A likely story,' Norma muttered.

'Is Shirley saying anything different?' Simpkins said.

'She's not saying anything much at all yet.'

'Was there any suggestion of sexual interference?' Lightfoot said.

'No.'

'Yet you say they'd been living alone in the house for five days and nights?'

'She was ill for most of that time.' He met Lightfoot's steady gaze. 'Bedford said not when I challenged him and Shirley's confirmed it since.'

'It would be natural for her to deny it. A medical examination might prove something.'

'That's what I think,' Norma said. 'Then we'd know.'

Simpkins' temper snapped. 'Then you'd know what? That you'd time to fill her full of hot gin or procure an abortion? What do you want, Norma? Do you need a scapegoat so badly that you're willing to sacrifice your daughter's trust and affection altogether? Do you want her to run away again as soon as she's well? She says what

308

Bedford says and you've got to take her word for it. You must. You put her through the humiliation of an examination and you'll lose her for ever.'

Norma flushed a dull red and kept her eyes down.

'You don't leave us with much, Tom,' Lightfoot said. 'Why don't you charge him with buying alcohol for a minor?'

Lightfoot frowned. 'I can't understand either your obstructiveness or your sarcasm, Tom.'

'I'm sorry, Ned. This is a problem of human relationships and it won't be solved by policemen looking for charges to press and our not believing what people say. There's no harm done. In fact, we're better off than we were before. Shirley's glad to be home. It's the first time we've been able to say that for months and it's enough for me for the present.'

Lightfoot stood up and took his hat from the table. 'Well, naturally I'm glad it's all apparently turned out well. Despite your going behind my back. That's not a course to be recommended, Tom, and you as an ex-magistrate should know it.'

'I stand rebuked,' Simpkins said.

'I shall have a word with Bedford, of course, and see what he has to say.'

Simpkins sighed. 'I wish you wouldn't, Ned. Don't be such a copper all through.'

'But I am, Tom. I've got to answer to my superiors and I've got to be satisfied in my own mind first. I'm sorry.'

'Aye,' Simpkins said. 'So am I.'

PART FIVE

23

It was all right for him, she thought at those extreme times when, after frustration, melancholy and that numbing sense of deprivation, there was only resentment for the hurt to throw up. He'd got something to fall back on: his wife, his children—a fruitful life. She had never yearned for these things for their own sake, feeling husband and family and a home of her own as a logical fulfilment which would come to her in their own good time. But how could she ever get them now that he'd shown her how very good they might have been? How, when he had given her a glimpse of the best, could she settle for anything less? 'I'm spoiling you for other people,' he had said more than once, and she had laughed his concern away. 'I never wanted them before and I want them even less now.' It was as simple as that. In those days there had seemed to be nothing lost which could remotely compare with what was gained. Only now, in those rare moments when despair brought a shaming self-pity with it, did she tell herself that though his hurt was real also he had a life which could console him into resignation, while she had nothing.

Julie was married now, living with her husband in their flat, and Andrea was left at home to be the focus of her mother's concern. They had never discussed her affair with Philip again but Andrea was aware of how much it and its possible effects occupied her mother's thoughts from the dolefully reflective looks she intercepted when they were sitting quietly in the house. Her mother was sorry for her, but whether for the hurt itself or the foolishness which had caused it, Andrea didn't know. She wondered how long it would be before the pity gave way to a more characteristic impatience. In the meantime, George's qualifications as a suitor were not so openly pressed. His appearances, indicating that he still considered himself in the running, were perhaps enough for the present.

Andrea went out with him at least once every week. He was quiet, knowing perhaps more than he ever acknowledged but making no reference either to that or his own hopeful claim on her, and she didn't mind his company. It stopped her for a while from sinking too deeply into her own thoughts, though the end of an evening with him always brought its counter of depression, because she could not prevent herself from playing the game of turning her head away and pretending it was someone else who was sitting beside her.

She examined the possibility of going away and starting a new life on her own. The novelty of a job in London and looking after herself might dull the edge of it all. But she couldn't bring herself to take what she saw as so irrevocable a step. She liked her present job and while she stayed here there was always hope. Just what form her salvation might assume she couldn't think. The recovery of Philip in some way was paramount in it and though she saw this as improbable it was at certain times of irrational optimism enough to sustain her.

She was fully recovered from her accident except for a stiffness in her elbow which brought her the habit of walking with her left arm slightly bent, never swinging completely free, and gave her some trouble in re-adjusting to the typewriter. She suspected that, despite physiotherapy sessions at the hospital, it would always be so and she accepted it as a tiny disability which could be lived with without fuss.

She went back to the office to have the story of a sensation she'd missed recounted with relish by Agnes Sutton.

'And you didn't know about it? It was in the papers.'

'I must have missed it. Or not connected it with him.'

'Missing from home for five days, she was. I told you my sister-in-law knew the family, didn't I? They say the girl's his daughter. Anyway, he was away more than here during that time. Worried out of his wits. Then all of a sudden she was back. Whether she came back of her own accord or was fetched from somewhere nobody seems to know. They don't know where she'd been, either. Everybody kept quiet about it. She was at home, poorly, for three weeks after it, anyway, so you can't tell what had been going on.'

'She's all right now, is she?'

'As far as anybody knows.' Andrea caught the look in Agnes's eyes.

'What d'you mean?'

'Well, there's some things that take a while to show themselves.'

What a mind the woman had! Andrea said, 'Well, if she's at home and they're all happy, that's all right, isn't it?'

'Aye, but the funniest thing was when I got to know she was back. He'd said nothing about it, of course, and his name wasn't mentioned, but I couldn't resist saying something. It just came out one afternoon when I'd finished taking his dictation. I said, "I'm very glad to hear your——" And there it was, on the tip of my tongue. I nearly said "your daughter" but I caught meself and said "girl". "I'm very glad to hear your girl is back home, Mr Simpkins." Even that was near enough. He gave me such a look. He was thunderstruck for a minute. Then he said, "You mean my god-daughter, Mrs Sutton. Thank you very much." Then I went out, wondering what had made me nearly put me foot in it like that. God-daughter, indeed! Nor made in heaven, neither!'

Mr Simpkins brought up the subject himself a couple of days later when she took his morning coffee.

'You know, it's good to have you back if for nothing more than your coffee.'

She laughed. 'It's a bit of a dubious compliment, but thank you all the same.'

'Mrs Sutton's coffee was terrible. I didn't know anybody could make such a mess of a simple operation.'

'Perhaps you're just more used to mine.'

'Hmmm.'

He seemed to want to talk so she lingered by the window, feeling the warmth of the sun on her back through the glass.

'She's been looking after you all right in everything else, I hope.'

'Oh, she's a proficient enough shorthand-typist, but I can't say I care for her personally.'

'Oh?'

'It's difficult to explain. She always gives you the feeling that she thinks she's one up on you, that she knows more than you think she does. I remember you telling me at the hospital that she was a gossip.'

'I didn't want to give her a bad reference but I thought you ought to know.'

'Yes, quite. I suppose you heard about my god-daughter's little escapade?'

'When she was missing from home? Yes, I heard.'

'Mrs Sutton had the cool cheek to congratulate me on her coming back. Shirley's picture was in the paper, but I didn't know anyone here connected her with me.'

'Is there any reason why they shouldn't?' Andrea said.

He darted a look at her. 'You're not starting it as well, are you?'

'I don't understand.'

'This ... this poker-faced manner of assuming knowledge of my affairs.'

'Your private life is none of my business, Mr Simpkins. You assumed that I knew something a moment ago. I heard that your god-daughter had been missing and I heard from somewhere else what connection there was between you. That's really all I know. If it's supposed to be secret, I'm sorry. I've no intention of discussing it with anybody else.'

He took the rebuke with a wry glance at her. 'I'm sorry, Miss Warner. I didn't mean to . . .' She waited as his voice dropped and tailed off. 'Just what are they saying about Shirley?'

'Oh, very little, really. That she disappeared for five days then reappeared rather mysteriously and was ill for a few weeks afterwards.'

'No speculation about where she'd been?'

'No. They don't seem to know whether she came back on her own or if she was brought.'

'I see. Is that all?'

How far could she go? Ought she to tell him about the more serious allegation, and would he be offended or at least embarrassed by her mention of it?

'You perhaps . . . you perhaps ought to know that there's talk that Shirley is your daughter.'

'Ah! I see.' He threw down the pencil he'd been toying with and rubbed his hand across his jaw. 'And how widespread is this talk?'

'I've only had it from one person.'

'Whom I can guess at,' he said. 'Well . . . it's true.' She said nothing. 'Does it shock you?'

'Of course not.'

'Not to think of your worthy, respectable boss with a secret life?'

'People's lives are often other than they seem to be on the surface,' Andrea said. 'And sometimes what's underneath and hidden is the best part of all, the part of real value.'

His head came round so that he looked at her full-face. 'Now how do you know that?'

'Does it matter?'

'No, I suppose not.' His gaze lingered on her. 'I don't know why I should have chosen to confess to you, except that I like and trust you and if there are rumours I'd prefer you to be forearmed with the truth from me. Not, of course, that I expect you to pass on what I've said.'

317

'I wouldn't think of it.'

'Mrs Moffat and I are going to be married. Sometime soon.'

'Congratulations. I hope you'll be very happy.'

'At my age, Miss Warner, you learn to settle for contentment.'

'It's nice if it comes at any age.'

Again the speculative look. 'Perhaps so.'

Back in her own office Andrea plugged in the electric kettle again to make her coffee. There was a curious feeling of excitement in her. That girl, Shirley, was nearly a woman now; in any case, a person in her own right with feelings strong enough to make her run away from home. Who, despite the reasons for that, which were not hard to guess at, could say now that it were better if she'd never been born? Which most severe censor of morals would, given the power, choose to turn back the clock and erase the relationship which had brought her into the world? There was in it all, she felt, some significance for her. It refused to be formulated, lying tantalisingly beyond the clear grasp of her reasoning, but it seemed to stir her blood to new and more affirmative life.

It was in the same week that Mr Simpkins said, 'By the way, you know I'm putting up for re-election to the council in a few weeks' time?'

'I hadn't realised,' Andrea said. 'I thought aldermen were more or less fixtures.'

He laughed. 'God forbid. No, you're voted on to the aldermanic bench by your fellow councillors for a period of six years. That's twice the term of a councillor. When your time's up you have to go back to the electorate for re-election as a councillor; unless, of course, the council value your services so highly they'll re-elect you alderman themselves to save you the bother of going to the polls. I can't remember when anybody round here was considered so indispensable, or was so favoured by all factions that he could accept such treatment without causing trouble and

318

strife.' He twinkled at her. 'We believe in democracy in Cressley. If the people want you they'll vote for you. If they don't want you, then nobody does.'

'It must mean that a number of good people get knocked out through unfortunate circumstances and a number of less capable people get elected.'

'I suppose it does. You can have the case of two first-class men opposing each other in one ward and two mediocrities standing in another. However it turns out, one of the good men has to go and one of the poorer ones will be elected. The way round that though is that you might have another chance to stand the next year, because we don't clear the lot out at once, as they do with Parliament at a general election; we vote each year for a third of the council strength at a time ... What I was wondering, actually, was whether, if I gave you the necessary time off, you'd care to give me a hand.'

'In what way?'

'You could do a bit of canvassing for me, if you liked. Going round the ward, knocking on doors and asking them if they're going to vote for me. You can never be sure if you're getting the truth but sometimes it gives you a rough picture. At the same time you find out if they want a car to call and take them to the polling station. That's important with older people and busy housewives with children and perhaps a husband on shift work, who don't want to leave the house for long.'

'How can you be sure you're not taking your opponent's voters for him?'

'Well, there are some obvious ones you miss out, but by and large, in my ward, the bigger the total vote the better the chance of my winning. The other thing you might be good at is helping in my headquarters on polling day. We've plenty of good ladies who can make tea and cut sandwiches but you could help my sister to check the burgess' list as the numbers come back from the station, and organise the cars to best effect, so that we neither have them standing idle nor chasing each other up the same streets to no purpose.'

'It sounds interesting.'

'You might find it so. It has its own small excitements. You realise, of course, that I can't offer you any financial inducement.' He grinned, suddenly boyish. 'But there'll no doubt be a couple of gin and tonics around when it's over.'

'Beer,' Andrea said, smiling. 'Draught for preference.'

'You're on.' His smile died. 'I'm afraid I've been assuming you have no political objections. If you have you——'

'No, no,' Andrea said. 'I'll be glad to help.'

'Good.' He took an election leaflet with bold red lettering on its front out of his top drawer. 'I've been studying my opponent. I suppose I ought to have his picture on the wall, like Montgomery had pictures of Rommel & Co. in his caravan in the desert.'

'Do I know him?'

'You might. I don't, except from information I've got from other people.'

She went forward and took the leaflet as he slid it across the desk. 'He's a teacher at Valley Bridge.'

How steady her hands and voice were! She surprised herself with her control though she had no power to stop the drain of blood from her face and its rush back in a scalding flood.

'Oh, yes, I have met him.'

'What is he like?'

'Sincere. Likeable. More emotionally committed than politically, I'd have thought.'

'Well, they've got him in harness now. You don't know him well, do you? I mean, if you want to change your mind . . .'

She evaded the question and said, 'Would you mind if I kept this and read it?'

He opened the drawer again. 'Here's one of mine to go with it.'

Why, she wondered later, had she not seen the press report on the adoption of the candidates? It must have appeared while she was in hospital, and a possible answer came readily to her. Her mother, who read the weekly *Argus* from front to back, would not have missed it, and she had exercised her own censorship by omitting to bring her that issue. And so given her a more uncomfortable moment just now. The picture of Philip looked specially posed for the occasion, the picture of a direct, earnest and intelligent young man with nothing on his mind except an eager desire to serve the citizens of the town; the picture of a man who might never have known and loved Andrea Warner.

The main body of the text consisted of a resumé of five points of local Labour Party policy and was probably common to all their leaflets. There was a short biographical note which emphasised Philips rise from humble beginnings, through university to minor academic distinction, and a personal message from him to the electorate: 'Friends, the voters of this country last year returned a Labour government to power at Westminster. We in the Cressley Labour Party earnestly entreat you to show the same faith in giving our representatives a majority on the Borough Council in the forthcoming municipal elections. In this way you will ensure that we have the power to initiate and put into action the vigorous policies needed to make Cressley a town fit for *all* its citizens to live in. I personally come before you as a new and untried candidate for the Council. I have no record of past public service to offer as my credentials; nor, on the other hand, am I burdened by any legacy of outworn ideas which could hamper me in my efforts to see that progress does not pass us by. I ask you to vote for me on Thursday 6th May and I give you my assurance that, if elected, I shall spare no effort to serve you and justify your confidence in me. Yours sincerely, Philip Hart.' 'A VOTE FOR HART IS A VOTE FOR PROGRESS' was the message across the foot of the page.

Andrea turned to the back of Mr Simpkins' leaflet and

read his address: 'Friends, I come before you at the end of my term as alderman to ask you to renew your confidence in me by voting for me in the forthcoming municipal elections. Many of you will know me personally. I was born in Cressley and I have lived here all my life. My business interests are in the town and I have had the honour of representing this ward on the Borough Council continuously for the past eighteen years. I have served on many committees during this time, my main interests being Housing and Finance. I was Mayor of the Borough in 1955/56 and I am also an ex-magistrate and a past governor of the Grammar School. In my rôle as Independent Councillor I have always been free to support those measures which I considered were best for all, regardless of party pressures. I respectfully offer to put this experience at your service again by asking you to vote for me on Thursday 6th May, and take this opportunity of assuring you that your confidence will not be misplaced. Yours sincerely, T. J. Simpkins.' 'VOTE FOR SIMPKINS, THE MAN YOU KNOW.'

Andrea found a wry amusement in visualising a professional letter-writer, in some dingy office, composing master addresses with a common tone of respectful sincerity, which candidates could rearrange according to their interests and experience. Poor Philip, to have his personal commitment distorted into a po-faced begging for votes; with, moreover, a possibility amounting to a likelihood of rejection at the end of it. What had brought him to it; surely not her casual suggestion of long ago? It seemed to her uncharacteristic of him and she wondered how much of this foray into public life was an attempt to divert his thoughts from the dilemma of his private one.

She scrutinised her own loyalties. Philips political views were not hers—not that hers were particularly committed in any direction—but she would, in other circumstances, have supported him without question. However, she had agreed to help Mr Simpkins and she would go through with it. Nothing she could do would vitally influence the outcome. She only hoped that Philip would not see it as a betrayal; that he would be shrewd enough to recognise it for what it had now become: a chance to be active in the same sphere, to come in contact with him, to see him again.

24

A local government election in the 'sixties, Nick soon discovered, was not an event most people considered central to their lives. It hovered, as it were, in the corner of their mind's eye, to be looked at briefly, perhaps, on polling day itself and acted upon if not too inconvenient. You could live through it all without being aware of its happening, and a lot of people did. There were no bands or bunting, no street-corner shouting matches between rival candidates, no public addresses at all before the event; for it was a waste of time and money hiring premises for speech-making when the audience would not turn up to listen. There would be loudspeaker vans in the streets on the day and small signs of activity as private cars bearing their candidate's window-stickers called at the houses of those who had asked to be taken to the polling station; then the counting of votes, which the public could observe from the gallery of the Town Hall, followed by the short addresses of both successful and unsuccessful candidates. In the meantime, the only way of making himself known to the electorate was for the candidate to visit as many houses as possible in his ward and, assessing support, opposition and apathy, try in those brief doorstep interviews to make an impression which would linger favourably in the voter's mind until the moment when, pencil in hand and voting slip before him, he registered his choice. In all this Tom had eighteen years' start on Philip.

'There are people in this ward who'd vote for a pig in a

muffler if it wore a red rosette,' Philip said to Nick, 'but there aren't enough of them. They're outnumbered by those who are naturally Conservative, those who are scared to death of Socialism and the supporters of Simpkins the man, the faithful gathered over the years. It's the others we ought to find and concentrate on: the unconvinced, the apathetic, the ones who think local government's a farcical carve-up of personal interests, and the new people on the developments who don't know Mr Simpkins any better than they know me. Among that lot there's the floating vote that helped to put the Labour government in last year. If we can do a bit of persuasion on them *and* make sure as many as possible of our own faithful actually do turn out to vote we shall have done the best we can.'

The boundary line of the ward cut through a mixture of streets, well-to-do and poor. The town wasn't big enough to have either vast unrelieved areas of slums or districts where only the wealthy lived. Pockets of affluence existed cheek by jowl with others of comparative poverty. In the rapid and haphazard growth of the town in the latter half of the last century masters had often lived close to their men. You could not assess a man's status or background by knowing which district he lived in; you had to know the street. In this sense there was no clearly defined 'wrong side of the tracks'.

'I had a tour round with Whitehead in the car the other day,' Philip was saying. 'He briefed me as well as he could, but as they're in the habit of losing regularly here I don't know how much use it was.'

'Who are the other two councillors for the ward?'

'Crowther and Hawthorn. One Conservative, one Independent. Labour haven't had a seat here since 1951.'

'They're not exactly handing it to you on a plate, are they?'

'No, mate, they're not. It's a tough number and I'd have fancied my chances against either of the other two better than your friend Mr Simpkins. Still, you never know. The game's full of surprises, as I think a score of well-meaning people must have told me.'

They had parked the car and were standing at the lower end of Howard Street, a single row of two dozen stone-fronted semi-detached houses opposite a churchyard, with square bays on the ground-floor front and dusty privet and laurel growing in their narrow front gardens behind the low stone walls from which the railings had been swallowed in the Second World War's greed for scrap metal, and never replaced.

'Now that lot,' Philip said, pointing, 'is, I'd guess, almost solid pro-Simpkins. Lower middle-class; quiet, careful, in-drawn lives. I think we'll start here and test the temperature of the water. You from the top, me from the bottom and meet half-way. Okay?'

Philip was already knocking on the front door of the first house as Nick walked up along the row. The front door of the top house had an old-fashioned mechanical bell which emitted an agonised rasping ring when he twisted the handle shaped like a large wing-nut. An old woman with thick white hair, and a knitted shawl over her bent shoulders, answered.

'Good morning,' Nick said, launching into his patter for the first time. 'I'm canvassing on behalf of the Labour candidate in the municipal elections. I wonder if we can rely on your vote?'

She peered at him doubtfully. 'Are you from Mr Simpkins?'

'No, Madam. I'm here on behalf of the Labour candidate, Mr Hart.'

'Oh, we belong to Mr Simpkins. Mr Simpkins is our man.'

'I see. In that case——'

'We shall be there to vote if he sends the car. But we must have the car. My sister hasn't been too well; she can't possibly make her own way there.'

'I see,' Nick said again. 'I'm sorry to have troubled you.'

'That's all right, young man.'

He turned away. 'Good morning.'

'If you see Mr Simpkins you might remind him about the car.'

Nick smiled. 'I'll see what I can do.'

At the next house a tall elderly man in a maroon cardigan, with a pink clean-shaven face, answered his knock. He listened to Nick with a faint smile on his lips, as though in possession of a secret.

'I think you can rely on us to exercise our franchise,' he said when Nick had finished.

'Could you tell us if we can rely on your vote?'

'I stand on the privilege of secrecy in casting my vote.'

'I see. Thank you very much.'

He met Philip before the last house and shook his head in answer to his look.

'Me neither,' Philip said. He looked at the number on the door of the house facing them and checked the name of the occupants in his notebook, which had sections of the burgess' list pasted into its pages. They went up the path together.

'Mr Jenkins?' The burly man in the doorway nodded. 'I'm Philip Hart, the Labour candidate for this ward in the municipal elections. I wonder if I can rely on your vote?'

'Labour, you say? What would I want to vote Labour for?'

'There are many good reasons why you should.'

'And a lot more why I shouldn't. Once upon a time, maybe, but people are getting too educated for all that nowadays.'

'I've got quite a bit of education myself, Mr Jenkins, and I'm a Socialist.'

'Ah, well, a young man like you, you've got your own way to make, haven't you? Your own axe to grind. That's up to you.'

'You mean I stand to gain personally. As a matter of fact, I agree, but it rather defeats your argument, doesn't it?'

'I don't know anything about that and I don't want to waste time standing here talking about it. You want to try round in Fortune Street. Promise 'em some council houses and a bit more National Assistance and you'll be all right there.'

'The old fallacy in action,' Philip said as the door closed. 'I'm doing nicely now so why should I vote Labour? Immediate personal well-being is the yardstick. And he's got the nerve to suggest that I've got an axe to grind ... Well, he suggested Fortune Street so we might as well do that before we explore the estate.'

They walked through an alley between a mill wall and a scrap-yard into the cobbled stretch of Fortune Street. It was two virtually unbroken parallel terraces of stone-built cottages. Some of the front doors, which gave directly on to the worn, uneven pavements, stood open in the warmth of the morning sunlight and a gang of children played noisily at the far end. There wasn't a lick of fresh paint to be seen and the moulding on the panels of the first door they came to was broken away in several places. Philip knocked and then addressed himself to a gaunt woman in her late fifties. She listened impatiently, her eyes moving restlessly, as though she had heard it all many times before.

'The only time we see any of you in this street is when you're begging for votes,' she said. 'What do any of you ever do for us that we should bother to vote for you?'

'If we can win this seat and a couple more, Mrs Baxter, we shall have a majority that will give us the power to make changes. But we can't do it now.'

'See,' she said abruptly, 'come you in here and see for yourself.'

They followed her across the threshold and into the single downstairs room. The dominant feature of it was the bed against the far wall and the atrociously thin and wasted man lying in it.

'That's me husband, see? He hasn't been up the stairs or out to the back for going on five years. Bronchitis, it is, and him only sixty-three. If he'd been able to get out of this lot ten years ago he wouldn't be finished, like he is now. More little bungalows are what we need. Warm places where we can live quiet without stairs to climb or a cold back yard to walk across to the lavatory. You look at him and ask me to vote.'

'I can assure you that we've got all these problems in mind, Mrs Baxter. More housing of the type you mention and a smoke control scheme that will give us clean air. Our opponents have been stalling on these things for years. They've preferred saving coppers on the rates to people's lives and health.'

'Oh, you've no need to think there's any love here for Mr Simpkins either,' the woman said. 'His father used to own all these houses round about. But he was clever enough to sell up after the war, when he thought they'd all be coming down. But that's twenty years ago and they're still here, still good enough for the likes of us. And we shall be stuck here till they raze the lot to the ground and find us somewhere else.'

'Then they'll be daft enough to give us a flat five floors up,' the man in the bed said. The short utterance took his breath and Nick heard from across the room the painful rasp of air in his chest.

'Mrs Baxter,' Philip said, 'I do beg you to give us a chance. We're hamstrung at present but if we do get into power I promise you I'll do everything I can to see that your case and all others like it have something done about them.'

She regarded him sceptically but not without kindness. 'You're a new chap, aren't you? Is this your first time of trying?'

'Yes, it is, and I——'

'I've no doubt you mean well, but even if you do get on you'll have to listen to all them other fellers who've been doing nothing for years except wear their britches' behinds out and talk hot air.'

'I'm asking for your vote, Mrs Baxter. If I send a car for you will you come and vote for me?'

'Well . . . I'll think about it.'

'What about Mr Baxter?'

329

'I've told you, he hasn't been out for years.'

'But he should be entitled to a postal vote.'

'Nay, lad, we've never gone to all that trouble.'

'I'll see what I can do. I'm not sure if there's still time, but I'll look into it.'

They went out. Philip stood in thought on the edge of the pavement. ' "The good and comely life",' he said. 'Christ!'

In a moment he began, quietly, as though to himself: ' "In peace there's nothing so becomes a man/ As Modest stillness and humility..." ' He cocked a look at Nick, teacher to pupil again.

'*Henry V*,' Nick said.

'Do you remember how it goes on?'

' "But when the blast of war blows in our ears," ' Nick said.

' "Then imitate the action of the tiger;
Stiffen the sinews, summon up the blood;
Disguise fair nature with hard-favoured rage." '

'Yes,' Philip said. 'It's a war we've only just begun. What they want isn't a "modest stillness and humility" or charity. It's their rights. It'll take generations. We've only begun to scratch at the surface in the last twenty years. It'll happen, Nick. That much we shall achieve.' He smiled. 'And when it does happen "gentlemen in England now a-bed/ Shall think themselves accursed they were not here".'

They moved along the street, taking a side each. They met apathy but they also found reassurance in the number of people who pledged themselves to vote for Philip. One man, crouched against the wall by his open front door, looked up as Philip spoke to him. 'Allus vote Labour,' he said laconically. 'Allus have, allus will.'

'As talkative as Clem Attlee,' Philip said. 'Well ... there's support on there, all right. The only thing is, how many of them will actually turn out on the day?'

'If I were you,' Nick said, 'any time I'd a car to spare I'd have it into there and all the streets like it and get them down to the station. Give them no excuse at all to sit at home without voting.'

'Yes, you're right. And if you're here on the day you can organise it.'

'Thanks,' Nick said wryly. 'Where to now?'

'Woodfield estate. We've time to do at least part of that before we go for a beer and a sandwich. It's places like that that the surprises might come from.'

They drove up the hill and on to the estate. It was a private development built during the last three years, larger than that in which Philip lived and with more variety in the design and cost of the houses. The streets all bore the same prefix: Woodfield Avenue, Woodfield Grove, Woodfield Crescent, Woodfield Rise and, at the farther end, cut off by the boundary of the ward, the most expensive property, in Woodfield Court. Nick and Philip met after the first batch of calls and compared notes.

'What do you make of it?'

'A mixed response,' Nick said. 'Quite a few people seemed sympathetic.'

'Yes, same across the road. There are a lot of people new to the town. It's mainly a matter of getting them interested enough to turn out. I did have a stroke of luck at number five—a young Scot called McLauchlan. He not only said he'd vote for me, he offered to bring his car on election night.'

'That's marvellous.'

'Yes, isn't it? Well...' Philip looked at his notebook. 'We can't do all this lot this morning. Would you like to adjourn now or do some more?'

'It's up to you.'

'I don't want to flog you too hard. After all, you're not getting paid for it.'

'Let's just work up to the bend there,' Nick suggested, 'and have our break then.'

'All right.'

Another half hour passed by. Nick had finished his quota but he couldn't at the moment see Philip, who was working more slowly because, he assumed, he found more opportunities for extended conversation. He waited on the pavement and was standing there, enjoying the warmth of the sun, when the Austin nosed out of the next street with Tom at the wheel. He got out and waved to Nick, who raised his hand in reply and walked across to him.

'Our paths are crossing,' Tom said.

'Yes. I didn't know you were coming up here.'

A dark girl in a very pale green suit of some soft rough-textured cloth came out of a gate and walked up towards them.

'You don't know my secretary, Miss Warner, do you? This is Nick Moffat.'

The girl nodded and smiled and Nick said hello.

'Is your friend about, Nick?' Tom asked. 'I might as well meet him if he is.'

'Is that protocol?' Miss Warner said.

'Why not? It won't do us any harm to have a look at each other.'

Nick scanned the street as Philip came down from the side door of one of the houses. 'There he is.' He waited till Philip seemed to be looking their way then waved to him. Philip stood for a moment then turned his back.

'He must be shy,' Tom said.

'I'll go and get him.' Nick trotted along the pavement and caught Philip up. 'Philip, there's Tom up there. He'd like to meet you.'

Philip stopped. 'Who is that with him?'

'His secretary. She seems to be helping him.'

'Do I have to?' Philip said.

'Come on,' Nick said. 'Be civilised. You're not scared, are you?' He was looking intently at Philip's face. There was an odd expression on it that Nick could not understand. 'Come on,' he said again. 'He's a nice chap. He won't bite you.'

They walked together towards Tom and Miss Warner. Nick introduced them and Philip and Tom shook hands.

'I suppose I can't really ask you how you're doing, can I?' Tom said.

'Not really.' He was curt, drawn in and unresponsive.

332

Nick was puzzled. He surely couldn't disapprove of Tom so wholeheartedly.

'Don't you two know each other, by the way?' Tom asked.

Philip nodded gravely. 'How are you, Andrea?'

'Oh, pretty well.'

'How's your arm now?'

'A bit stiff, but nothing worth complaining about.'

'I believe we've worked in from opposite ends,' Tom said. 'If we're both covering the same ground we'd perhaps be advised to leave the rest for another time. People can have too much of a good thing.'

'You're probably right. We were just thinking of going for lunch, anyway.'

Nick, watching Philip as usual, saw that although he was speaking to Tom he could not keep his gaze off the girl's face. She, on the other hand, kept her gaze averted except for two moments when it came round and up, drawn it seemed almost against her will, and locked into Philip's with a naked intensity that blazed across the space between them. On impulse, he took Tom's arm, asking if he could speak to him, and led him several yards away. The domestic inquiry he invented then to account for his action brought a frown between Tom's eyes. He was puzzled by Nick's behaviour but he stayed there as Nick talked and glanced back along the street to where Philip and Miss Warner had moved closer together and were now deep in conversation.

'How is he liking his new experience of canvassing?' Tom asked.

'I don't think he expects too many answers in advance.'

'He won't be too disappointed, then.' Tom's gaze ranged over the houses round them. 'All this is new territory to me.'

'Philip says it's where the surprises might come from.'

'He could be right ... Anyway, we'd better go back or he might think you're giving his secrets away.'

'He knows I shan't do that.'

Nick watched Philip and the girl move slightly apart as they approached them, and Philip shot him a glance as though wondering whether his action in taking Tom away had been deliberate. But he didn't refer to it even when they were alone in the car again.

'Will beer and a wad be enough for you now?'

'Oh yes, fine.'

'We'll drop down into town, then, and see what we can find. We can perhaps get out a plan of campaign for this afternoon as well. Mr Simpkins is right when he says it won't do any good our following each other round the same streets. I'll leave the rest of Woodfield for another time.'

He fumbled with the ignition key as the Austin passed, going off the estate ahead of them, with Tom at the wheel and the girl beside him.

'What did you make of him?'

'Oh, I liked him well enough. I think I could be friends with him in other circumstances.'

'I feel just a bit mean,' Nick said. 'I remembered while I was talking to him that a rather eccentric old dear in Howard Street asked me to tell him to send a car for her, and I deliberately didn't mention it.'

Philip smiled. 'That sense of fairness of yours. It'll kill you one of these days.' He started the car and was quiet for some time before saying seriously and not entirely to the point, but obviously speaking out of something deeply felt, 'I've thought a lot about the nature of the liberal's dilemma and the fatal paralysis it leads to.

'It's finding the strength to take a course of action knowing that although people will suffer they'll live after it. And to be capable of doing this yet balancing it with, and not destroying, his everlasting concern for all the selfishness and casual callousness which makes people suffer for some spurious expediency. If the balance is wrong it can lead to a fatal inaction, or a mental torture that can drive him out of his mind with his sense of his own helplessness. He goes slowly mad, wringing his hands. He reminds me sometimes of those Chekhov characters whom Frank O'Connor once analysed as causing untold unhappiness by their venial sins because they hadn't the strength to commit the mortal sin which would put at least part of the matter right.'

'All that's rather in personal terms, isn't it?'

'What other terms are there in the end?' Philip said. 'Or in the beginning, for that matter?'

'Hmmm.' Now Nick was quiet in his turn. Then he said, 'Philip, what do you honestly think your chances are?'

'I'm not awfully taken with them,' Philip said, and it wasn't until a few moments later that Nick realised he didn't know whether the answer had referred to the election or something else altogether.

25

Simpkins took Norma and Shirley to Scarborough for the week-end before the election. He and Norma had never been away together, nor had Norma slept in a four-star hotel before. They had three adjacent rooms, overlooking the South Cliff and the sea. Norma looked at the bed, the telephone and the radio in her room, peered into the bathroom, then drew in her breath as she caught sight of the tariff on a card on her dressing-table.

'Why, it's a week's wage just for one night for the three of us!'

'Nay, lass,' Simpkins said, straight-faced, 'we haven't had dinner yet.'

'Do we have to pay extra for that?' She snatched up the card and peered at it again. 'Good heavens! It's daylight robbery.'

'You've no need to worry,' Simpkins said. 'It won't damage my next week's wage. If you want a bit more freedom than Mrs Grundy's Bella Vista boarding house, twenty-five bob a day all in, you've got to pay for it.'

'I just feel out of place. That I'm here under false pretences.'

'You're here with me, love, and that's good enough. Now you relax and enjoy yourself, or it *will* be a waste of money.'

'I'm sure they all know, though. That girl downstairs and the feller that carried the cases up. I'm sure they all know I've never been in a place like this before.'

'They don't know, and if they did it wouldn't matter. Just

don't get too chummy with the chambermaid and start telling her about your operation for gallstones and you'll manage beautifully.'

'What operation for gallstones? Oh, Tom, you're kidding. I'm not as bad as that. Anyway, I doubt if I shall say a word to anybody unless I'm forced to. I don't want to let you down, that's all.'

'Don't be daft. I shall get cross with you in a minute. The future Mrs Tom Simpkins is not to be intimidated by receptionists, porters, waiters or flunkeys of any kind. Or I'll know the reason why.'

He took her in his arms and held her fondly.

'It's nice to think things are working out, isn't it?'

'H'mm.'

'Shirley seems all right now, doesn't she?'

'She's a bit too quiet for my liking.'

'She had a scare. I think she's still working out what the consequences of that might have been.'

A tap on the door brought them apart and Norma crossed the room and let Shirley in.

'Oh, I'm sorry.'

'Come in, Shirley,' Simpkins said. 'Is your room all right?'

'Lovely, thanks.'

He couldn't help the twinge of embarrassment at being found alone with her mother which Shirley's apology provoked. Would they never all feel normal and easy with one another? Oh, and she was becoming so beautiful, a girl any man would be proud to have as a daughter. But how long must it be before she would at least think of him as her stepfather and not a friend of the family who had suddenly, shockingly turned into her mother's lover?

'I came in to see if you'd got any tissues,' Shirley said.

Her mother opened a box of Kleenex and passed a handful to her.

'We can go down to dinner any time you're ready, Shirley,' Simpkins said.

'What do you think I ought to wear?' Norma asked.

'Anything you like.'

'I haven't got any evening clothes.'

'Nobody dresses up for dinner, Norma,' Simpkins said gently. 'Except on the pictures or in one or two special places.' He moved to the door. 'I'm going to have a bath and change my shirt and that'll be it. Ready in about half an hour, eh?'

He was happily conscious, later, in the restaurant that the other diners and the waiters would take the handsome woman with the wedding ring to be his wife, and the girl his daughter, and he enjoyed the feeling of proprietorship it gave him to guide them through the menu and help them choose their food. With it came the wine he had ordered and he brushed aside Norma's mild protests as he filled Shirley's glass. 'It won't hurt her at all. Just make her feel rosy all over. That's what it is—rosé.' He laughed alone at the feeble joke and watched with great pleasure as Norma, her diffidence forgotten, ate her duckling with enjoyment.

'How was that?' he asked as she laid down her knife and fork.

'Lovely.' She wiped her mouth with her napkin. ' 'Course, it ought to be, the price they charge for it.'

'Will you get the subject of money off your mind, Norma. I shall begin to think you intend to institute a regime of austerity and economy in our old age.'

'Oh, I know you're too set in your ways to stand for that.'

'And well enough off not to need it.'

'Anyway, speak for yourself about old age. I've still to see fifty, remember.'

'I'm quite sure you're capable of seeing off two like me,' Simpkins said lightly, and was surprised to see Norma blush and throw a quick look at Shirley. He condemned himself for tactlessness. He'd meant nothing by it except that she was a fine healthy woman; but apart from her having been widowed once, she could have taken the remark as a reminder of her sexual appetite and he was sorry if his own recent shortcomings in that respect should, after

338

all the years, have made her self-conscious about it.

The waiter appeared with the menu and Simpkins asked them if they would like something more. Norma shook her head.

'I couldn't eat another thing.'

'You, Shirley?' She had not eaten more than half of her main dish. 'What about some fruit, or an ice cream?'

'No, thanks. I'm not hungry any more.'

Simpkins sent the waiter for the bill and when he had signed it against his room number they went through to the great green and gold lounge for coffee. He ordered a brandy with his and filled and lit his pipe.

'I could fancy some music now,' he said, looking towards the empty dais at the end of the room. 'A bit of light Palm Court stuff.'

'I thought your tastes ran to something heavier.'

'Oh, different music for different moods. If there was a full scale concert handy I'd gladly go, but here, just now, a trio and some Ivor Novello would suit me nicely.'

It was a pity, he thought, that Shirley had never really taken to music. She had attained a reasonable level of technical proficiency on the piano, then virtually abandoned it. As a non-musician who was passionately fond of music, Simpkins often wished he could play for himself. There were, indeed, times when he felt as though all that prevented him from sitting at a piano and playing it was the necessary act of faith. It was curious, that; how he sometimes felt that he could surely play and that the desire itself would be enough to guide his fingers magically over the keyboard. And yet the world was full of people who could read the notes on the page and strike the keys accurately but had no real feeling for music at all.

'Did Nick say he was definitely coming up again next week?' Norma asked.

'I think he plans to come Wednesday and go back Friday. That'll give him the full election day at home.'

'I don't know how he can manage all that time away from his studies.'

339

'It's not like school, Norma. He can plan to suit himself to some extent.'

'He's going to a lot of trouble for this friend of his.'

'It's nice to see friendship working like that.'

'I still think it would have been more fitting if he hadn't taken it outside, to somebody else.'

'Now, Norma, Nick's got his own views and he must act according to them.'

'So you keep saying. You're a sight fairer about it than I should be in your position.'

'So it is my position, and I'm the one who stands to lose by it. It's a pity he couldn't have stopped over, then he could have come with us. It would have been a change for him and company for Shirley.'

'I'm all right,' Shirley said.

'If there's anything you particularly fancy doing, Shirley, just say so,' Simpkins said. 'And don't feel you have to stick with your mother and me all the time.' And now, he thought then, she might feel she's in the way. He found it hard to say anything to her that didn't immediately strike him as double-edged and open to misinterpretation.

'I don't suppose their season's started yet,' Norma said.

'No, the summer shows won't be here yet but there's enough to do for a couple of days. You two can spend an hour or two looking round the shops tomorrow. I'm sure you'll be content enough doing that.'

'I'm content enough just sitting here being looked after for a change.'

Simpkins laughed, pleased. 'Good! That's the idea.'

'I think I'd like to go for a walk by the sea,' Shirley said.

'Why don't we all go?'

'I've told you, I'm happy enough,' Norma said. 'You two get your warm coats on and get off for half an hour. I'll sit here and read a magazine and weigh up the other guests.'

'Do you mind, Shirley?' Simpkins said. 'I'd rather like a blow myself.'

'No,' Shirley said. 'I'll just run up and get my coat.'

Ten minutes later they were walking down the steep zig-zag path from the top of the cliff to the foreshore, Shirley sure-footed, Simpkins treading more warily as he thought of the possibility of his leather soles slipping on the asphalt. The tide was out and the darkness hiding the sea was pricked only by the navigation lights of a single vessel standing out in the bay. Shirley waited for him at the bottom of the path and they walked together on the beach side of the road towards the harbour. They had been silent so far but it was enough for him at the moment that her acceptance of him could embrace their being alone together. He remarked on the row of closed arcades, shops and cafés.

'I suppose they'll be getting into their stride in a week or two.'

'I don't like it when they're like this,' Shirley said. 'They're sad, like empty houses.'

'And I don't like it much in the season, when they're shouting up their bingo games, selling cheap souvenirs and people are wasting their time and money playing the slot machines. But I see what you mean: if a thing exists it ought to fulfil its function.'

'We once came for the day, only we spent it up on the north side. There was a miniature naval battle on the lake in Peasholme Park. Nick liked that but I wasn't bothered. Me dad brought us. He borrowed a car.' There was a silence, then she said, 'It's funny, but I don't know what to call him now.'

The sadness of her unexpected confession went straight to Simpkins' heart. 'You must refer to him as you've always thought of him, Shirley. Uncle Tom's good enough for me. I'm not asking to take his place in your affections.' He felt that talking to her was like stalking a timid animal through the dry, crackling underbrush of a forest. She had let him sight her and he wanted to say nothing which would drive her back into the cover of her silence.

'Anything you might come to give me is something I must win for myself,' he said carefully. 'There's no question of what you owe me, no duty that I can demand. That kind of affection was reserved for your dad, and what you gave to me in the same spirit when you were a little girl is something that's past and gone. I love you very dearly, and nothing you do, no question of giving or withholding, can change that. What I don't want you to feel is that anything you might want to give me would have to be subtracted from the memory of how much you loved him. It doesn't work like that. Human beings are not rationed in their capacity for loving. There's not just so much and when that's gone it's over. We love different people in different ways and I sometimes think that the more you love the more you're capable of loving.'

'You mean like me mam with you and me dad? But when you love somebody it's supposed to stop you from hurting them. The marriage service says "forsaking all others".'

'Yes, it does. And people inside a marriage have a right to ask that. But we're only human beings, none of us perfect, and sometimes people's rights give way to other people's needs. In the eyes of a great deal of the world your mother was wrong. But if she was unfaithful in one way she was loyal in another. In some people's eyes, you see, your dad would have been wrong, because he couldn't sustain her as she needed sustaining; he couldn't give her the support and strength she had to have to go on. He knew that, you know. He was very clear-sighted about himself. Because, after all, there was another way open to her, and that was to leave him. I gave her a chance to do that when we knew you were on the way. But she wouldn't take it. She'd committed herself to looking after your dad and she kept to that commitment.'

'She stayed with him out of pity.'

'No, no, Shirley. You mustn't see everything as either-or. You mustn't dismiss your mother's feelings out of hand because they don't conform to the ideal that's held up to us.' They had reached the fish pier. He said on impulse, 'Look, I'd like to show you something.' He took her elbow and guided her across the empty road, leading her away from the sea front into the narrow streets of the oldest part of the town, where the houses clustered together, clinging to the steep ground between the castle and the harbour. They climbed for several minutes and once Simpkins thought he was lost. Then he got his bearings again and stood with Shirley before the tall house with the dormer window high up in the pitch of its roof. He had been back only once, twenty years ago, when the diversion of war was over and the threads of the old life must be picked up again, but without Nell.

'Thirty years ago,' Simpkins said, holding Shirley's arm and pointing upwards, 'I spent three weeks in that room with the girl I'd just married. They were the most superbly happy weeks of my life. We only had three years of marriage in all, then she died. When that happened I thought my own life might as well have ended too. Now I can remember her without pain. I'm grateful for what we had and I shall always cherish her memory. But it neither changes nor makes any less my affection for your mother. I've never in my life felt for anyone as I felt for Nell. But am I to discount what I feel for your mother because it isn't the same thing?'

'Would you have gone with somebody else while you had her?'

'No, probably never. But it was a rare and complete relationship, and from inside it I could love the whole world.'

'It's the only kind I'm interested in,' Shirley said.

'For yourself? Yes, of course. I'm not making excuses for any of us, love. Just giving reasons. And God forbid that anything I've said should sour the world for you, make you think there's nothing in it that isn't shoddy and shopsoiled, and cause you to sell yourself short. But neither should you ever despair of people's ability to make something worthwhile out of less than the best.'

He turned her away. 'Shall we walk back through the town?'

'If you like.'

343

'You know,' he said as they strolled through the streets of shops, 'when I was at the grammar school, before the war, we had a final examination for what was called School Certificate. There were certain minimum requirements in that exam and you either passed or you failed. Failure in one of the compulsory subjects, for instance, meant you'd failed the lot. Now you have your 'O' level exams and you can pass in two, three, four, five or whatever you're up to. The point is that those who are less than the best have something to show. I failed my School Certificate and I'd got nothing.'

'I've thought about it all,' she said presently, 'and I know that all the trouble I caused was like me saying I wished I'd never been born. But it takes so much getting used to, having everything turned upside down and finding out that you're just an accident, something nobody specially wanted.'

Simpkins smiled. 'Millions of people in this world were "accidents". You were at least conceived in some kind of joy and commitment. You were certainly more God's gift, if you like, than the result of some poor, tired, dutiful Saturday-night coupling that had nothing to commend it but legal recognition.'

'Would I have been any different, though?'

'You could have been less wanted now. Every child, accident or not, has to take its chance on that.'

As they came in sight of the huge Victorian edifice of the hotel Shirley said, 'Did you ever hear anything else about Don Bedford?'

'No, except that the police went to see him. I didn't want them to but they did. Nothing came of it.'

'It was my fault, you know,' she said. 'I ran after him and persuaded him to take me home with him.'

'Were you . . . were you fond of him?'

'He was fond of me. He told me he loved me. That's why I knew he'd do what I wanted if I cried to him and persuaded him hard enough. I liked him. He was older and tough and he'd been about and had some adventures.'

344

'I wouldn't call Borstal an adventure, exactly.'

'No, he once told me some of the things that went on there. It sounded awful.'

'But it's over. He should put it behind him instead of carrying it like a chip on his shoulder.'

'You gave him a job, then sacked him, didn't you?'

'Is that how he tells it? I sacked him because he was lazy and stupid.' And that's how I tell it, he thought. Forgetting that I knew he was stupid before that, but I didn't bother to keep an eye on him, so the responsibility passed into the hands of others, until it was too late and I had to let him go for their sake.

'There's always somebody else to blame,' he said as they reached the steps to the door. He felt that there were other things he ought to say, that they should walk for a little longer while he said them. But he guided Shirley in before him and they crossed the lobby and went into the lounge where Norma took off her glasses as she saw them coming.

'There, have you got the cobwebs blown off you?'

'It's quite a still night,' Simpkins said. 'But I think we've cleared our thoughts a bit.' He glanced at Shirley who had perched on the edge of a chair without taking off her coat.

'I think I'll go straight up.'

'All right, love,' Norma said. 'Have you got everything you want?'

'I think so.'

Shirley got up and kissed her mother. 'Goodnight, Mum.' She moved round as though to pass Simpkins then leaned over from behind and brushed his temple with her lips. 'Goodnight.'

It took him unawares and he half lifted his hand to grasp hers; but she was gone. He glanced at Norma as his eyes misted. He expected her to say something and hoped she wouldn't. But she looked down at the magazine in her lap as though she had noticed nothing out of the ordinary.

'I don't think I shall be long in going up myself,' she said presently.

'No ... If I can find a waiter I'll have another brandy,

345

then that's me for tonight.' He rang the bell and gave his order to the man who came. 'Can I get anything for you, Norma?'

'No, thank you.'

'Why don't you go up, then, if you want to? I shan't be many minutes.'

'Oh.' The look she gave him from under her eyelids as she took his meaning was almost shy in its sudden expression of pleasure. 'All right.'

He drank his brandy slowly, deciding against filling and lighting a fresh pipe and ten minutes later walked up the stairs to the first floor landing. He went into his room and got into pyjamas and dressing-gown then went quietly out and tapped softly with the tip of his forefinger on Norma's door.

She got out of bed to let him in. The cotton of her white nightgown, with ruffles at throat and wrists moved under his hands, slipping over the firm flesh of her back and hips, as he took her in his arms. She offered soft lips to him, asking huskily, 'Have you come back to me, then?'

'Yes, love.' He held her to him in a warm tide of feeling that belonged to now, to here and now and them, and was not just an echo of two other people in another time. 'Yes,' he said. 'I've come back.'

26

Mr Simpkins' election headquarters were in the Sunday-school room under Albert Road Congregational Methodist Church and Andrea was there early on polling day in the company of Mrs Hargreaves. Most of the chairs had been stacked in the corners and there were several trestle tables set out in the middle of the floor. Copies of the burgess' list were pinned out on two of them.

'Now these,' Mrs Hargreaves explained unnecessarily, since Andrea had used them on her rounds with Mr Simpkins, 'are lists of all the people in this ward who are eligible to vote. They're in number order and broken down into streets. The names with the blue pencil mark against them are the people we're sure about. We know them from past experience and from the canvassing you did with Mr Simpkins.' Mrs Hargreaves tapped at the lists with the end of a wooden ruler. With her good grooming, unsmiling mien and manner of delivering explanations that suggested she would do it once and once only, she fitted a popular conception of the middle-aged woman school teacher. Andrea would hardly have been surprised if the ruler had swung suddenly round on her with a demand that she name all the monarchs in the House of Stuart or the date of the Treaty of Utrecht, whatever that was.

'We have people at the polling station who will ask for the voters' numbers as they go in. They're not bound to give them but there's no reason why they shouldn't. Those numbers are brought back here periodically and the names crossed off our lists. In this way we know who's been to vote and who hasn't. It tells us how heavy the poll is and helps us to roust out the lazy ones who think we've forgotten them. The first batches of numbers should be in after nine o'clock, when all those people who call in on their way to work are done with. It will probably slacken off then till the middle of the morning, when the housewives come down and combine voting with their shopping.'

'I suppose the big rush is in the early evening?' Andrea said.

'Yes, any time between six and eight is busy. That's the time when we use the cars to comb out the last-minute voters. There's a big boxing match on television tonight and that won't help us to get the men out of their homes if they haven't done their duty earlier in the day. But we'll cross that bridge when we come to it.'

'It's not a very promising day for it all.'

'No, but as long as it doesn't set to and pour down all day it shouldn't affect things much.'

Two elderly women wearing aprons under their coats came in and presented themselves to Mrs Hargreaves, who addressed them by name.

'Good morning, Mrs Pocock, Mrs Cummings. Thank you for coming. You know where everything is in the kitchen, don't you?'

'Oh, aye, you just leave it to us,' one of them said. 'I know that geyser in the kitchen as well as anybody. It allus was a handful for anybody who didn't know how to humour it.' She glanced round the big austere room. 'I've waited on at some stock of Faith Teas and Bring and Buy Sales in this place.'

'There's not so much of that kind of thing nowadays, Elsie,' the other woman said.

'No, I've heard tell they've got plans to pull the whole chapel down.'

'A shame.'

'Aye, but they're nowt but white elephants nowadays. Who wants religion now, except maybe the Catholics?'

'It's sad to see all these old places go all the same.

348

They're full of happy memories for a lot of folk.'

'They'll all die off in time, then it'll be done with.'

'You just hold your horses. Some of us have a bit to go yet.'

'I should think so,' Mrs Hargreaves said. 'I hope we shall have your help at a few more elections yet.'

'God willing, Mrs Hargreaves,' the woman said. 'Allus glad to give Mr Simpkins a hand up. He's been a good man for Cressley, Mr Simpkins has.'

'Well now,' Mrs Hargreaves said. 'If I can leave all that to you ... There's tea and sugar and butter in the kitchen. The baker's delivering a couple of trays of teacakes about ten o'clock, and Mr Simpkins is calling for some boiled ham and tongue on his way down here.'

'We may as well get a mashing on straight away.'

'I wouldn't mind a cup. But use one of the smaller pots since there's only a few of us. Then you can make some fresh later when the others start arriving.'

The two women went off into the kitchen.

'Willing hands,' Mrs Hargreaves said. 'They're worth any amount of promises at a time like this.'

She reached for a thin sheaf of slips of paper. 'Now these are important so they mustn't get mislaid. They're the names of the people who want cars to call for them and they're arranged under the various times. They'll be added to during the day and some of them will be altered as people change their minds.'

'Is there a lot of that?'

'Oh, what happens is that somebody says half-past six and when the car goes for them they say they can't get out just then. So we persuade them to give us another time. Anyway, you know the ward now you've canvassed it, so if I'm not on hand you'll be able to see how trips can be combined, and make sure nobody gets overlooked.'

Mr Simpkins' election agent arrived shortly after this. He was a dapper, grey haired man in black jacket and striped trousers.

'Tom not about yet, Mrs Hargreaves?'

'Not yet, Mr Learoyd. He's gone up to the Works to look at his post and see that everything's all right. He should be down about half-past nine.'

Mr Learoyd grunted acknowledgement of this information and lit a cigarette which made him cough helplessly for several seconds. As agent it was his function to guide his candidate through the legal requirements of offering himself for election. He checked that his man was in fact eligible, obtained the signatures of proposer, seconder and the necessary number of nominators, registered his candidate's intention to stand, acquired copies of the burgess' list, booked premises for headquarters and kept an eye on the conduct of the election to ensure that none of the regulations governing it was contravened, so rendering his man liable to disqualification or prosecution. With an experienced candidate like Mr Simpkins some of these duties were no more than formalities. In Philip's case, Andrea supposed, the Party would take care of them. She wondered if he was about yet and what he was doing. A similar routine to this one would be under way in Labour Party headquarters but as they had several candidates in the field the activity there would presumably be more intense. There was certainly no sense of urgency or excitement here yet. Now that Mrs Hargreaves had finished her briefing the tone and tempo of the proceedings seemed to reflect the unhurried cosy casualness of the two women in the kitchen, making tea.

At least this feeling of having no importance, that her presence here could not influence the course of the election in any real way, relieved her mind a little of the thought that, politics apart—and what, for God's sake, did they matter?—if she couldn't actually help Philip she ought not to be aiding his opponent. Not that he was resentful. He'd made that clear in those few precious moments of contact on Woodfield Estate.

'So you're helping Mr Simpkins?'

'Yes.'

'And all my attempts at indoctrination into the true faith

350

have gone for nothing?' Gentle humour relieved the yearning in his eyes, a yearning that she knew was reflected in her own.

'It isn't that. But when he asked me it seemed like a way of keeping in touch.'

'Yes. I could hardly set you on canvassing for me.'

'You know I would. You know I'd do anything for——'

'Yes. Yes, I do know ... I wonder how long Nick can hold him down there.'

'You think he did it deliberately? Does he know?'

'No, but I think we might have given ourselves away.'

'I just can't help it, Philip. I haven't spoken to you for nearly six months. Seeing you like this, I can hardly breathe, let alone pretend indifference.'

'I know. How are you really?'

'Oh, I'm well enough now.'

'I hope your mother isn't doing the outraged parent bit.'

'No.' She had written him one letter from hospital, addressed to him at the school, telling him what had happened. 'We never talk about it. It's a relief in a way for someone else to know what's on your mind, even if they don't approve. What about you? How are things at home?'

'They vary from placid to hellish. It's my fault, really. If I settled down, showed that I was reconciled, everything would be okay.'

'Oh, Philip, I'm sorry.'

'I ought to be, but I can't. I still can't be.'

'They're coming back.'

'There's so much I want to say. But you know the main thing.'

'Yes. Me too.'

'It's something.'

'Yes.'

Something ... Better than nothing, even if from day to day it resolved itself into a deprivation that was like rain in the heart.

They had a cup of the powerful tea brewed by Mrs Pocock and Mrs Cummings. A man in an overcoat whose

351

checks were as loud as his voice came in and asked what time of day the services of himself and his car would be most useful. Mrs Hargreaves consulted her lists and asked him to come back after lunch. Two men in raincoats wandered in after him and hung about vaguely for five minutes before wandering out again.

'You wait until later on,' Mrs Hargreaves said to Andrea. 'It'll turn into a right calling shop. There'll be all sorts of people standing about.'

Presently Mr Simpkins arrived, carrying two greaseproof-wrapped bundles from the butcher's. He had also called at the polling station and collected the first batch of voters' numbers. Mrs Hargreaves gave the list to Andrea who picked up ruler and pencil and began to cross the names off the electoral roll. With this positive action the day proper began.

Who cared? The activity in all the ten wards of the town—in Moorend, Common, Greenford, Edgehill, Valley, North, South, East, West and Central—was not enough to create any real sense of occasion. There were neither big issues to whet the imagination nor scandals to add spice. The men who provided housing, schools, roads, parks, libraries, health clinics, swimming baths, a police force and refuse collection did so according to general patterns approved by Whitehall and there was little to choose between them whatever their political colouring. The national swing to Labour resulting in last year's change of government would no doubt be reflected, perhaps strongly enough to give Labour power at local level. But would it make any real difference? many people wondered. Wouldn't the result of it all, in the last resort, be as meaningless to the man in the street as the messages of those loudspeaker vans with their sibilants and consonants lost in an unintelligible exhortation to 'Ho hor Heeho, heha hoo hah hee hoh hah!' which, except for the stickers displaying the candidate's name, could well have been invitations to try a new washing powder or an advertisement for trips to the moon? Nevertheless, the choice was made, and if in the case of about forty-five per cent of the electorate it was made by sitting at home and letting others take the decision, fifty-five per cent—the density of voting varying from ward to ward—would somehow or other, with whatever feelings of interest and concern, or a semi-apathetic adherence to duty, make its way to the polling stations between eight in the morning and nine at night. Perhaps the sight of an election leaflet on the mantelshelf at breakfast would send some men in on their way to work, or a child unaccustomedly underfoot remind a housewife that the day had its own particular significance. For if there was any one section of the community, apart from the candidates themselves, who awoke that morning immediately conscious that the day was special, it was not the electorate but the children who, in all quarters of the town, enjoyed a holiday while their schools were in use as polling stations, and democracy in Cressley on 6 May, 1965 rumbled through its due processes of selection.

People sitting inside the doors of polling stations asking for voters' numbers to send back to their headquarters. Small boys outside on the steps asking also, but for no other reason than that small boys collect numbers, whether belonging to railway engines, motor cars or citizens exercising their franchise.

A couple in the back of a car, bowling along in style, the wife embarrassed and embarrassing her husband by whispering too loudly, 'But we're not going to vote for this lot.' 'Shurrup and ne' mind. It's all t'same as long as we get there.'

Andrea out of headquarters and into the streets with Mr Simpkins, hoping for just a glimpse ... Supporting the elbows of two astonishingly old and frail ladies in Howard

Street who looked as though they might well not survive the short trip.

Mrs Baxter of Fortune Street to her husband: 'Now you're sure you'll be all right while I get back?' 'Aye, get yerself off, for what good it'll do.' 'Well, I did more or less promise.' Nick: 'I'll have you there and back in ten minutes, Mrs Baxter.'

A man confronted by a slip bearing the names of two Smiths turning from the cubicle to enquire across the dignified quiet of the polling station: 'Which of these two buggers is which?'

Andrea thinking of Philip.

Nick watching Philip thinking of Andrea, and thinking himself of Philip's wife, and Caroline, and his mother and Tom, and the whole labyrinthine complexity of human relationships.

Ham sandwiches and strong tea.

A man in greasy overalls at the door of his house, addressing an eager young ferrier in whom the day has generated a spurious tension: 'Nay, t'wife might ha' said half-past six but I've nobbut just walked in. We'll make our own way down later, when I've got out of me muck.' Disappointed youth, wondering if he means it, and if he dare risk annoying the man by coming back later to make sure.

Nick, warned with ponderous jocularity of the Merry Widow of Ladysmith Street, disappointed too to find not a voluptuous blonde in a transparent negligee with a you-know-what look in her eye but a coarsely attractive woman in her forties with a voice like cigarette smoke and a man-

354

ner that suggests she's seen it all and doesn't care tuppence for any of it any more.

A group of stout middle-aged matrons jollied with great charm away from a small whist evening to wedge themselves into a big car which has never seemed smaller and pop out at the other end like corks from a bottle. 'Eee, Ethel, you're showing all you've got.' 'Nay, lass, there's nowt there they haven't seen before.' 'Ooh!' 'Haha!'—the implications of this remark picked up, kicked around, beaten to a small death.

'Councillors? I've shot 'em.' 'So and so's a good man, though.' 'They're all good men, for themselves.'

The number of deleted names growing on the burgess' list, but leaving too many gaps for Mr Simpkins' liking, also for Andrea, who is now suffering from a tidy-minded desire to cross off the very last name of all at a little after nine this evening.

'It looks like a low poll.' 'Not any more than average.' 'Yes, but I usually do better than average. I haven't put up for six years and I'd have thought they'd rally round better than this.' 'Oh, I shouldn't worry.' 'I'm not, but . . .'

'It looks like a low poll.' 'Is that good?' 'Well, generally speaking, the bigger the poll the bigger the vote for him.' 'The harder we work now, then, the more votes we bring in for him?' 'Yes, it's tricky to judge it. But you did the canvassing. I'd make sure you get all your likelies in and leave the rest alone.' 'It's a bit frustrating not being able to really go at it.' 'I know, but you can rest assured that a lot of his people aren't bothering to turn out.' 'Can you tell already? There's still part of the evening rush to come.' 'Aye, but I can see the pattern now. Cross your fingers and hope for the best.' 'I'm good at that. The battered but eternal optimist.' 'Have you remembered to cast your own vote? There's one of our chaps needing that.'

'How many cars are there free at the moment?' 'Two, I think.' 'Right, let's see the list ... Get them both into Raeburn Street. Tell them to go from end to end and get as many people out as possible. Don't bother picking and choosing. The more, the better. Then they can come back here and we'll choose somewhere else for the same treatment.' 'There's that boxing match coming up on television.' 'Yes, there'll be a lot refuse to budge once that gets started. Off you go, then. Do your best. I want another five hundred names off this list before nine o'clock.' 'You'll be lucky!'

Nick stood with Philip at the bar counter in the smoke room of the Blacksmith's Arms near the Town Hall. It was a little after nine o'clock. The polls were closed, the ballot boxes sealed and probably already on their way to the count. The result from the ward Philip had contested was not expected to be declared until nearly ten and they had left Labour Party Headquarters with an arrangement to see Whitehead and his colleagues again later, on the floor of the Town Hall. Philip had removed the red rosette from his lapel before coming into the pub, to avoid comment and unwelcome conversation, and they spoke little to each other over their first pint of beer.

'Has it taken it out of you?' Nick asked, when their glasses had been refilled.

'What?' Philip said. His response was sluggish as he appeared to drag himself out of his thoughts.

'It must be a bigger strain than many people realise.'

'Oh ... Yes, I'm a bit tired.' He had rested his half-smoked cigarette on the ashtray while he counted out change for the drinks and now, that one forgotten, he took out the packet and lit another.

'I'm scared, Nick,' he said suddenly. The quick look he gave Nick with this confession was tentative, almost shy.

356

'That you won't get in?' Nick said, putting the most obvious construction on the remark.

'No, that I might ... That I shall have to make decisions, sort out what I really think and feel and swap the fine talk for positive actions. And I don't think I'm up to it.'

'Oh, come on ...' Nick said.

'No, Nick, it's true. I used to know what the score was; I had views on almost everything. I didn't imagine things were easy but I knew what I thought and felt and those things were true and honest for me. Now I don't know anything any more. I'm demoralised, afraid in certain moods almost to cross the street, let alone pass on messages to people like you and my own children. I wonder what I have to tell them. And if I can't sort myself out, what business have I making decisions that will affect the lives of others? I've got till I feel like a personification of all the wet heroes you've ever read about.'

'I've always loved that retort Johnson made to Boswell,' Nick said. 'It's in the *Life*. Boswell is remarking on some action and he says, "That, Sir, was great fortitude of mind." "No, Sir," says Johnson, "stark insensibility".'

Philip smiled. 'All right. Thank you. There's that parody of Kipling, too "If you can keep your head when all about you are losing theirs, then you just don't understand the situation".'

'Well, come on, then,' Nick said chidingly. 'I'm surprised at you.'

'It's just,' Philip said after a moment. 'It's just that you sometimes feel that there, just across a gap you can almost reach with your hand, there's sanity and freedom and an enormous liberating joy. And because it's not tangible, not a jewel, or money or a magic grail; because it's inside you, growing out of your own feelings and emotions, out of everything you are and what you need, you wonder that it has to stay there, just out of reach, that you can't produce it out of what you've got already, which is no different from anything else you'll ever find.'

'You mean the rainbow ends in everybody's back yard

and it's only a question of knowing to dig there for the pot of gold?'

'I'm not saying anything so folksy and simple,' Philip said. 'I'm really trying to judge what's weakness and what's strength. It seems to me there's a kind of strength which, unless it's super-human, just topples over into weakness. And there's another kind of strength, an ability to act according to one's nature which, while people might deplore certain aspects of it, is seen as somehow inevitable and natural and in tune with the universe. We don't *like* Heathcliff. He's a bastard in more ways than one; but we stand in awe of his passions, of the man possessed, and the last thing we can do is deny him.'

'But Heathcliff never felt the need to be liked,' Nick said.

'Oh, God.'

'To be approved of, then.'

'Worse still.'

'All right, he had no desire to change the world for the better, to perform any action which would improve the lot of his fellow men. Heathcliff loved but he was never ... never tender. And he didn't care.'

'But he was there. He existed. His justification was the size of him. He blocked out a piece of the sky while the world looked straight through lesser men.'

'So did Hitler. You couldn't be like Heathcliff if you lived for a thousand years.'

'No ... He wished Catherine in purgatory until he could go to her.'

'And if he'd fallen out of love with her he wouldn't have given a damn about her any longer.'

Philip nodded morosely. 'H'mm.'

'And if Emily hadn't told us about him we should never have known he existed.'

'You mean it's all the same in a hundred years' time? Don't you believe that good and evil, kindness and malevolence are qualities which are never lost, that they accumulate in the ether, creating atmospheres for mankind now and in the future? Don't you know about Heathcliff when the wind sighs in lonely places and your heart is filled with some nameless feeling of anxiety and dread? I think you can make out a case for the positive effect of a meritorious public life outweighing the negative effect of an inadequate private one. Many great men who've bestowed benefits on mankind have been blameworthy in private and theoretically you could cite the case of a man who, say, found it necessary to commit murder to free himself for his mission in enhancing the welfare of men in general. I say theoretically because it brings us to our old friend the problem of means and ends. But apart from that, a private life is all most of us, including Heathcliff, have got and to say that it won't matter in a hundred years is to absolve us of all duties and responsibilities.'

'Well, your virtue, for instance,' Nick said, 'is that you're a good teacher.'

'But if that's so it comes from what I am as a man. I can't separate the two things. A doctor might discover something of enormous benefit to the human race, something that could save millions of lives, by performing cruel experiments on living subjects. That was the excuse the German doctors in the concentration camps gave to themselves and their judges. We're back to ends and means again, I know. But the point is that what I teach and the way I teach are inseparable from my thoughts and feelings and attitudes as a man. I am me, an indivisible whole.'

Philip shrugged and looked at his watch. 'I'm sorry. We seem to have strayed a long way from the original point.'

'I didn't think we had.'

'Well, maybe not. But we shan't get anywhere standing here and talking in riddles.'

'Have we time for another drink?'

'Not really. I'd like to get stinking maudlin drunk tonight, but duty calls.'

'They surely won't be ready with the count yet.'

'No, but Kate's coming in. I said I'd meet her over there and I don't want to leave her hanging about on her own.'

They emptied their glasses and then on impulse Nick

359

stuck out his hand. 'Anyway, the best of luck with it.'

Philip hesitated for a second, his look pleased but again with that strange diffidence in it.

'Thanks, Nick.' They made for the door. 'The trouble with the system is that somebody's bound to lose.'

27

Andrea rode down into the town in Mr Simpkins' car, with Mrs Hargreaves and Mr Learoyd. They went straight to the Town Hall, where people were already making their way up into the public gallery from the main entrance. A policeman stood at the door to the public hall where entry tonight was restricted to officials and those responsible for counting the votes, the candidates and their scrutineers and persons with special authority. Through the open doors Andrea could see the tellers standing about between the long trestle tables under the bright overhead lights. Mr Simpkins' party lingered in the foyer while he spoke to a broadly built elderly man with an enormous paunch.

'If you go upstairs,' Mrs Hargreaves said, 'you'll find a room next to the mayor's parlour where you can tidy up and leave your coat. Come back down here when you're ready. We shall be about.'

Andrea went up the wide steps and on to the big landing. A corridor led off it, running the length of the building. Along there she found the heavy oak door with 'Mayor's Parlour' cut into the ornamental glass of its upper half and went into the cloakroom next to it. She had hung up her coat and was repairing her lipstick, using the mirror in her compact, when the door opened and closed behind her as someone came in. It was the odd lengthening silence which followed this that finally brought her round to see Philip's wife standing there.

'Oh.' It came out stupidly, involuntarily.

'I didn't recognise you at first, with your hair done differently,' Kate Hart said and it seemed for one ludicrous moment that she was about to pass an opinion on it. Andrea took a deep breath to try to calm her racing heart.

'I suppose if I were a man I could get some satisfaction from knocking you down.'

'I can't blame you for hating me.'

'Oh, you accept that, then?'

'I have to.'

'If that's so, why have you never thought yourself into my shoes; stopped for one minute to think what you were doing to me?'

'I have, many times.'

'It didn't alter your behaviour, did it? That night in the pub; you could laugh and joke and look me straight in the face, knowing all the time what was going on, knowing that it was still going to go on afterwards.'

'I expect it does seem like brazen, barefaced duplicity to you, and I can't expect you to believe that it wasn't like that. It wasn't as easy as that at all.'

'I'm not interested in how much trouble your conscience has given you,' Kate Hart said scathingly; 'only that it made no difference to your actions.'

'Look,' Andrea said, 'I've spoken to him once in the last six months. Once. There's been nothing between us since you and he had it out.'

'Nothing? Is that what you think? Nothing except what he's carrying round in his mind, what's stopping him from coming back to us as he once was, what's going to drive him into a nervous breakdown or something worse if nothing's done about it.'

'Oh, God, how he'd hate it if he knew, us talking about him like this.'

'*I* hate it,' Philip's wife said. 'I don't want to talk to you. I don't want to look the side you're on. I don't want even to know you exist. I wish you never had existed and then he'd never have let you get your claws into him and ruin his life as well as mine.'

362

Andrea flinched before the torrent of Kate Hart's bitterness but could not let what she'd said go unanswered. 'Can't you just for one moment think of him as a person in his own right and not an appendage of you?'

'I'm his wife.'

'Yes, you are. And you have certain rights that you can expect, certain demands you can make. But he's still a person in his own right; you haven't absorbed him, body and soul, into yourself. He still has choice. He could leave you.' She held up her hand. 'I say *could*. After all, people do part. It happens all the time and it doesn't mark the end of their lives. Some of them make new lives.'

'I suppose you've said all this to him. What a pity for you it didn't work.'

'I've never tried to take him away from you. Oh, you won't believe that, but it's true. I've never said a single word to try to persuade him to leave you for me. I don't think he ever would for that. If only you knew how safe you were, and if only you knew how much danger you put yourself in by insisting that what he feels for me can't be anything but contemptible. But it's got to be contemptible, hasn't it, because it's something outside you? Why don't you look at the danger to yourself as one thing and his feelings as another? Why can't you just hate me but give him the credit for feeling as he does? For being able to? He doesn't want your forgiveness. He wants your understanding.'

'Oh, I understand. He loves you, all right. More than he ever loved me—or differently, anyway. And what can I do to help him? If I put out a hand to him he thinks I'm forgiving him, and he can't accept that. Then I feel rejected and I start to resent his unhappiness.'

'He's terrified of being a hypocrite,' Andrea said. 'If we could both accept him for what he is, take what he can give us, he'd give us everything he has, without stint.'

Kate Hart shook her head. 'You're crying for the moon, you two. The only happiness you'll ever get out of this is what you had before I found out. The damage is done now.

We're all three scarred and nothing will ever be the same as it was before. I sometimes think I could accept this for myself, but not for the boys. He's rejected them, too, you know; and I've had to watch that as well. They see me in tears more than they should. Their father loses his temper over something which could be put right with a word. This is all part of it. And what can I do for them except turn them into Mummy's boys? They need him and they need security. To give security you have to have it, and we're without it now. You must have known some of this before you started. Why did you let it happen? Why didn't you stop it before it was too late?'

'Because I'm not perfect. Just a human being looking for a little happiness like anyone else. It was too late by the time we realised it. Then the rightness of what we felt for each other cancelled out the wrong of our actions. There was no question of my taking him from you—you must believe that for your own sake. He loved you; I never had any doubt about that. But I loved him and I was prepared to make do.'

'I wish I could shift time somehow and give you perhaps a couple of years together,' Kate Hart said. 'You've held all the cards: the excitement of secret meetings, the knowledge that parting was never far away. No worries about money, no nappies in a bucket under the sink.'

How could she? Andrea thought. How could she invest desperation with glamour? The nagging fear that it would disintegrate under them, the precious hours they had wasted because they were burdened not with excitement but the knowledge that they were stolen and the next ones might not be theirs to choose. Did she know what it was like to love someone to distraction yet have no place at all where she could have him to herself, completely safe from outside interference if not from the prick of conscience? Were these the cards in a winning hand?

'Philip thinks I moralise,' Kate Hart said, 'But that's because I have to use moral terms. My reasons are the reasons *for* morals and for laws. He really does believe that the freedom of the individual should be sacrificed to the common good but he can't apply it to his own situation. He hates the very word "expediency" and yet he's busily trying to apply it to his own life.'

She walked a few steps round the room, turning her back on Andrea before she took out a handkerchief and touched it to her face. Andrea waited. She was surprised that they had not been interrupted and her nerves were taut with both the strain of this encounter and the expectation that someone would at any moment, open the door and walk into the middle of it.

'Do you...' Kate Hart said, almost choking on the words. 'Do you still love him?'

'What do you want me to say?'

'The truth.'

'Yes ... I do.'

'Enough to leave him in peace?'

'Is that what he's got now? I've told you, I've made no move towards him, except for working in the election. I've spoken to him once in six months.' And it hurts, she wanted to add. Don't you know how much it hurts?

'You won't go right away and give him up altogether?'

'I can't ... I ... I promise you that I won't approach him. But...' She shook her head and put her hand to her face as her tears came.

'You can cry, then?' Kate Hart said in a moment. 'I was beginning to wonder if you could.'

'Oh, I can cry,' Andrea said. 'But I usually manage to keep it for when I'm on my own ... Oh, God, I'm sorry there's so much hurt in this for everybody, but I love him. I do love him. And I've got to be where he can find me if he needs me. Don't you see that? Don't you see?'

'All I can say, then,' Philip's wife said, 'is that I hope you'll one day find a man you can both love and be happy with and that one night you'll sit alone with the certain knowledge that he's with someone else; and when he comes in he'll look at you without love, scarcely with recognition. When that time comes I hope you'll think of me.'

Andrea turned away and, blindly fumbling in her hand-bag, said nothing. There was nothing to say that would make sense to both of them. In a moment she heard the door open and close. Then, as earlier, she was alone.

Simpkins stood with Baden on the floor of the public hall. He saw Andrea Warner come in and noticed her distracted look. He doubted that it was for the same reason he was feeling apprehensive. They were witnessing a small landslide. Labour were holding their own seats and they had taken two others in the results already declared. It was enough to give them a majority. Walter Whitehead was frankly jubilant and came to Simpkins and Baden to rub in the victory.

'Now we shall see something.'

'We shall, that,' Baden said sourly. 'Them that were daft enough to vote for you will an' all. It'll be a different tune this time next year. All you need is enough rope to hang yourselves.'

'You begrudging old so-and-so,' Whitehead said. 'Don't you wish you could take your bat and ball home and stop the game?'

Baden said 'Agh!' and turned away, ramming his hands into his trousers pockets.

'Got the old butterflies going, have you, Tom?' Whitehead asked, ignoring Baden's ostentatious back.

'Why?'

'There's been a couple of upsets. It could be your turn next.'

This brought Baden round again. Aloofness was never as satisfying as argument. 'It takes better men than you've got to topple Tom Simpkins.'

'Oh, we've got a good man against him. An excellent man.'

'A learner,' Baden said. 'You daren't put your old hands against Tom. You know you'd likely lose 'em.'

'I wouldn't underestimate him if I were you.'

'It's not up to me. It depends on the voters.'

'They've shown what they feel in West and Valley.'

'We shall see what we see.'

'Aye,' Whitehead said. 'You'll happen be wishing you'd accepted that offer of mine before long, though, Tom.'

'What offer?' Baden said.

'To cross over and get on the right side, where he really belongs.'

'Tom Simpkins among you lot?' Simpkins thought he'd rarely seen Baden more taken aback.' You must be out of your mind.'

'You don't see what's under your nose,' Whitehead said.

'I doubt if I'll live to see that day, at any rate,' Baden said. 'And apart from anything else, there's never been a turncoat in politics who's ever made owt in this town. Nobody trusts 'em.' He cocked his head back and looked up into the gallery as a group of spectators began to sing ' "Why are we waiting, Wha-y are we wai-ting?" ' 'Some of your lot getting impatient.'

'Why our lot?' Whitehead said.

'Same lot that's been heckling the speakers. It's not the floating vote, it's the lunatic fringe.'

Harry Tidyman, mayor this year, and returning officer for the election, came up to them. 'We'll open the boxes if you're ready, Tom.'

Simpkins stepped forward with Baden, finding himself beside Philip Hart and Whitehead. When the slips were out on the tables he looked round for Nick and saw him standing back, talking to a youngish fair woman whom he took to be Hart's wife. He motioned to him.

'Nick, I thought your mother and Shirley would be here by now.'

'They're up in the gallery. I met them as I came in. Mother said to tell you she'd sit up there and see you afterwards.'

It would have been her first appearance with him at a public function in the town and she had not been happy about it. It was perhaps as well. Let both her and them get used to the idea gradually. He turned his attention back to the tables where the voting slips were being collected in bundles of fifty for each candidate, with Baden and Learoyd, Hart and Whitehead prowling about before the tellers. A few more minutes and it would be over. He would either return to the council chamber and the committee rooms he knew so well or find himself rejected from public life for the first time in eighteen years. He wondered at both the strength and nature of his apprehension. It was not simply that he saw this as the toughest contest he'd fought in years; his natural uncertainty about that was mixed with another feeling which was almost anxiety. It was close to the strange disquiet which had nagged at him on the morning he heard about Sid's accident; only then he'd been able to trace its source in overheard remarks of the previous evening. Now there was nothing like that he could put his finger on, but just a vague, disquieting sense of unease, a sixth sense that all was not right.

Nick watched him light his pipe, puffing on it till his head was wreathed in smoke. The action was usually a calm, reflective one and Nick knew he was agitated. So was Kate Hart, drawn in on herself and communicating in nothing but monosyllables. He stayed beside her for some time as the count progressed then strolled along the floor, his approach seen by Andrea, who had taken a seat under the balcony with Mrs Hargreaves and as far away from Philip's wife as possible. She'd had no sign or look from Philip. She didn't know if he was even aware of her presence as he stood with his back to her, watching the count and nodding occasionally as the man next to him spoke.

Nick Moffat inclined his head at them and looked as though he would turn away. Then his face lit up with shy pleasure as Mrs Hargreaves addressed him.

'I haven't seen your mother and sister, Nicholas.'

'They're upstairs.'

'They know they're expected for supper afterwards, don't they?'

'I don't know. I expect so.'

368

'I suppose you'll be waiting to see which way the cat jumps before you say whether you'll come or not?' Nick shrugged awkwardly as Mrs Hargreaves said to Andrea, 'Nicholas is a young man with principles, you know.'

'I always think it's refreshing when people think for themselves and don't just blindly follow the herd,' Andrea said and Nick's quick glance thanked her for her words.

'Oh, yes,' Mrs Hargreaves said, 'I'm not criticising him. You'll be coming, of course?'

'Oh, I hadn't thought——'

'Of course you must come, and have a drink and something decent to eat. You've been existing all day on cups of tea and sandwiches.'

'Well, thank you.'

'That's right. We shall soon know whether it's to be a celebration or an inquest.' She leaned forward as the people near the table came together as if in conference. 'Something's happening, Nicholas. Will you see what it is?'

'They seem to have finished,' Andrea said.

'Yes, we shall soon know now.'

Andrea watched Nick speak to Philip, who turned his head and answered him briefly over his shoulder. Kate Hart beckoned him across and he went and exchanged a word with her before coming back to them.

'What is it?'

'I think there'll be a recount.'

'A recount. How many——?'

'Eight votes. It's in Tom's favour.'

Mrs Hargreaves relaxed beside Andrea. 'Well . . .'

'Can it make any difference?' Andrea asked.

'I doubt it. They'll probably allow the recount, but I should say it's as good as settled.'

'Eight votes,' Nick muttered.

'It's enough,' Mrs Hargreaves said. 'Less than that can decide it.'

'He took him to a close decision, though, didn't he?' Nick was addressing Andrea now. She nodded.

'Yes, he's done well.'

Nick's eyes lingered on her face for a moment. 'Yes. Yes, he's done well.'

Eight votes. Only eight. If she had missed just a few of the people she had brought in would someone else have caught them or would it have swung the result in Philip's favour? No, no, there were too many imponderables for her to blame herself. She had done what she'd agreed to do and done it as well as she could. The trouble lay in the tangled web which trapped her feelings and prevented her from declaring her real loyalty. She put her head down and looked for cigarettes in her bag as hopelessness suddenly bared its ferocious teeth to her heart. Oh, God, what a grotesque and desperate farce it was! Two women, both eating their hearts out for the same man; and him in the middle. She saw very clearly that however it might turn out for them it was too late for Philip to win either way; that distress in some form was now for him a permanent condition.

'Trust them not to concede it,' Baden grumbled to Simpkins.

'Oh, come now, Baden, Would you?'

'It can't make any difference. It's just wasting everybody's time.'

Baden's lack of graciousness irritated Simpkins. He suddenly, for one moment, was sorry that he'd won; that he couldn't leave the argument, backbiting and manoeuvring to young Hart, who seemed genuinely keen and concerned, and settle down contentedly himself to a life that was surely full enough with Norma, Shirley, Nick and the running of the Works. For a moment. Then he knew that his pride would have been badly hurt by failure today. The closeness of the contest was wound enough. Voluntary retirement was one thing, forcible rejection another.

'By shots, lad, but you've run him close,' Whitehead was saying to Philip as Nick went up to them.

'But not close enough.'

'It's nothing to be ashamed of, a performance like that.'

'And you've got your majority, anyway,' Philip said

wryly.

'Aye, we've got it at last.'

'Bad luck, Philip,' Nick said.

'Yes. It's not your fault, anyway, Nick. You've worked hard enough.'

'It makes you wonder, though, whether just a bit more effort...'

Philip shook his head. 'No, don't start playing the "if only" game. There's no end to it and it's driven men mad since the beginning of time.'

They went forward as the mayor, who had conferred with the tellers, signalled to them.

'There's nine difference on the recount. 1,441 for Simpkins, 1,432 for Hart. Are you prepared to accept those figures?'

'Yes,' Philip said, 'I'll concede it.' He turned to Tom and held out his hand. 'Congratulations.'

'Hard lines,' Tom said. 'You've run me closer than I can ever remember.'

'A miss is as good as a mile.'

'Not in this game,' Tom said. 'You've made a good impression. It might be a different story next time.'

'Ah,' Philip said enigmatically. 'Next time.'

Those observant members of the public who had seen Philip approach Tom knew what the result must be and there was a stir of interest in the gallery as the party trooped up on to the platform and the mayor, important in his chain of office and his duty here today, stepped forward and began to read.

'Elections in the County Borough of Cressley, 6 May, 1965. I, Harry Tidyman, declare the votes cast in the election for the North Ward to be as follows: Hart, Philip Leslie—1,432; Simpkins, Thomas James—1,441. As returning officer I declare the said Thomas James Simpkins duly elected.'

There had been some 'Oohs!' from the gallery as the closeness of the vote was revealed and now some half-hearted booing and stamping of feet was added to clapping as Simpkins came forward. The approaching wail of a fire engine's siren penetrated into the hall as he was about to speak and he waited until it rose in a crescendo to fill the street outside, then died away into the distance.

'Ladies and gentlemen—friends: I'm grateful for the confidence you've shown in me by giving me your votes and returning me for another term as councillor for the North Ward. This has been a clean contest and I must congratulate my opponent on putting up such a good fight and coming so close to victory in his first election. Which brings me to a sour note and since it's meant for people who are presumably not present now I hope the press will report what I have to say. The poll in this ward was about fifty per cent; that means that half the people eligible to vote didn't bother to do so. I know for a fact that many of those votes would have been cast in my favour. Whether it was plain apathy or a misplaced confidence in a foregone conclusion, I don't know. What I do know is that it could easily have gone the other way and if it had that result would have been the fault of those people who found it too much trouble to turn out and exercise their right to elect their representatives. The right to vote isn't just a privilege, it's a duty; and if the people don't get the local government they want then it's their own fault for not voting when they have the chance. That's all I want to say about that. To those who did support me, I say once more: thank you. I shall do my best, as I have over the past eighteen years, to serve you and look after the interests of all.'

'I'm glad he's told them,' Mrs Hargreaves said. 'A bit of plain speaking now and again does nobody any harm.'

But Andrea was hardly listening, intent as she was on the drawn and serious lines of Philip's face as he moved up to speak in his turn.

'I believe it's considered unsporting for the loser on an occasion like this to say anything argumentative. He's supposed to make a few polite noises and take his defeat like a man. Anything else suggests that he doesn't like being beaten. Well, of course I don't like having been beaten;

372

after all, I shouldn't have stood as a candidate if I hadn't wanted to win. I'm grateful to all who voted for me and made it possible for me to come so near to winning. I agree with my opponent's disappointment at the low poll. Where I disagree with him is in his assumption that the missing votes would have widened the gap between us, making his victory more decisive. There are other lessons to be drawn from this election and I'd say the obvious one for him is that to be returned to his seat by a mere twenty-five per cent of the electorate is no sign that he can rest on his laurels. The size of my vote—only nine less than his—indicates that there's a fair body of people in this ward who, after his eighteen years in power, are ready for a change. I met some of those people when I was canvassing and many of them have genuine grievances and a feeling that nobody cares about them . . .'

'Shame!' said someone in a loud voice. Andrea thought it was the man with the paunch, who was standing down near the platform.

'Yes, *I* thought it was,' Philip shot down at him. 'And I hope my opponent is man enough and human enough to know—unlike some of his supporters—that he isn't perfect and there might be a lot of things he's missed during his long time as a councillor. If he likes, I'll brief him on some of them . . .'

Why, he isn't even listening, Andrea thought incredulously as she saw Simpkins, his back half turned, in conversation with the mayor. Then, as he moved across the platform behind the standing group, she noticed the police constable who had appeared on the steps. He bent down and listened to what the constable said before throwing a quick look back at Philip and hurrying down off the platform and out into the corridor through the side door.

'I wonder what all that was about,' Mrs Hargreaves said. 'It isn't like him to appear so rude.'

Seeing his opponent disappear, Philip, the expression on his face containing both surprise and embarrassment at being left virtually talking to himself, wound up with a few formal phrases. In an atmosphere of anti-climax the party left the platform, Philip making his way towards his wife until he was halted in his path by Nick Moffat who burst in through the side door and almost cannoned into him.

'There's Nick,' Andrea said. 'He looks a bit hot and bothered.'

'If he doesn't come and tell us,' Mrs Hargreaves said, 'I shall have to go and ask him what's going on.' She added testily, 'I can't bear not to know what's happening. Can you see him now?'

'He's coming,' Andrea said as Nick moved between the people now standing round the doorway and approached them at what was almost a run.

'Nicholas,' Mrs Hargreaves demanded, 'what on earth is all the——?'

He cut in on her, his eyes bright with the excitement of important news, his hands moving in unconscious gestures of agitation.

'The police rang here for Tom. It's the factory. They say it's on fire.'

28

Apart from black smoke streaming out from where the oil store was located the main building of the factory seemed untouched. Jets from the two appliances already on the scene drenched the bay from end to end. Simpkins understood that they were reluctant to open the big doors to gain better access for fear of letting in a dangerous draught. Lightfoot turned from Simpkins' side as headlights lit the standing group and moved on. 'Will you clear that street of vehicles,' he roared to his men. 'The Dewsbury brigade's coming in that way.' He left them, muttering under his breath, to stride purposefully up towards the road where spectators, drawn by the sirens of the fire appliances and the pall of smoke, dark against the pale night sky, had gathered to view the destruction.

'There's nothing much for them to see,' Simpkins said to no one in particular. Then, even as he spoke, they heard the muffled thump of ignition, and flame ran along behind the windows of the bay like lights switched on in sequence. Norma and Bess, standing on either side of him, gasped simultaneously and echoed the spectators' unison 'Oh!' He took the hands of both of them, drawing their arms through his, and they stood in silence, held together like that, as the fire gained a grip along the length of the building. Now that he was faced with the actuality of the disaster his mind, freed of that uncanny premonition of earlier, was curiously calm, observing the fact of the fire and grasping its implications, yet unable to translate it all into feeling. It was Shirley who was showing the most emotion, uttering little cries of 'Oh, isn't it terrible? Isn't it terrible?' with tears streaming openly down her cheeks. Simpkins released Norma and pulled Shirley in between himself and her mother.

'Easy, love,' he said. 'Don't take on so. It's not the end of the world.' He could stand the loss of ten factories knowing that she cared and in her caring became his.

'Why don't they stop it?' she said. 'There's enough of them.'

'They're doing their best. They'll not rest till they've got on top of it.'

Nor would they; but what had seemed a little while ago to be no more than partial damage now looked like almost total destruction. They might save the shell of the building but most of what was inside would be damaged beyond repair.

'I only hope your insurance is in order, Tom,' Lightfoot said from behind them.

'Oh, that's all right,' Simpkins said. 'But it doesn't allow for the people thrown out of work and the time needed to build it all up again.'

'You won't get anything from whoever's responsible.'

'What?' Simpkins turned his head.

'You don't think it started itself, do you?'

'Well, how do I——?'

'They've got your night watchman, Chadwick, down at the other gate. He says he could swear he heard somebody inside the place about half an hour before he smelled the smoke and gave the alarm.'

'Somebody inside? But——'

'He says he went to look but he couldn't see anything out of order. He thought it was imagination then.'

'Oh, God,' Simpkins said.

'Well, I mean, look at it, Tom. It's not like a rag warehouse, is it, something that's ablaze all through in no time? I think you'll find the fire officers have the same idea.'

'But who the hell would want to do a thing like that?'

'Let's hope we can find out,' Lightfoot said. 'It might

376

stop the same thing happening somewhere else.'

'A fire raiser?' Simpkins said. 'Somebody who lights 'em for fun? Nay, Ned.'

'That, or somebody who's got it in for you.'

'I can't see it either way,' Simpkins said.

'Because you can't see yourself doing it? You've been on the bench, Tom. You've dealt with a lot of offences you could never imagine yourself committing.'

'Yes, but . . .'

Nick, standing a little apart from the group, turned as someone came up behind him. It was Philip.

'Hello, Nick. This is a right mess.'

'Yes. They seem to think it was deliberate.'

Philip whistled. 'Do they!'

'Tom won't have it,' Nick said. 'I think he can imagine it happening, but not to him. He's a nice man.'

'I had a friend who was a National Serviceman in Cyprus during the troubles,' Philip said. 'He told me that the first time he was fired on his predominant feeling was astonishment. He wanted to stand up and shout, "Hey, fellers, there must be some mistake: this is *me* you're trying to kill." '

They stood in silence for a minute or two, then Nick said, 'I haven't really had a chance to say how sorry I am about today.'

'Oh, I shall get over that. It's funny, though, because in a way it's the same feeling. I mean, to be rejected in favour of somebody else. I really haven't the temperament for that kind of contest. I want to offer my services only in circumstances where there's no chance of their being refused. Unjustifiable pride, I suppose, but there it is.' He was looking round as he spoke. 'Did Andrea come up here?'

'She was here a minute ago. Yes, look, over there.'

Philip made as if to go to her then stopped. 'Tell me something, Nick. Do you think I'm a bit of a bastard?'

Nick shrugged in embarrassment. 'No, of course not. I'm sorry, though. I think it's a shame.'

'Yes, isn't it? I don't take anything back, you know; anything I've ever said to you. It just turns out to be all a bit harder than I thought it was.'

He lingered for another moment, as though he wanted to say more, and Nick, searching for something he could say, came out with, 'Heathcliff would never have bothered to ask me.'

'No,' Philip said. 'No . . .' He turned and trudged away over the rough ground to where Andrea was standing alone.

She did not know he was there until he was right beside her. He slipped his arm through hers and found her hand where it rested in the pocket of her coat.

'Hello.'

'Hello.' She twisted her hand and tightened her fingers round his to let him know that her prosaic acknowledgement of his presence was no indication of her overwhelming pleasure in his suddenly being here. 'Isn't this awful?'

'Yes . . . I suppose I should have gone to Simpkins first and offered my sympathy. There's a pretty solid group of them there, though. It looks as though he's lost a factory and found a family.'

'Should you be here? I mean, is it wise?'

'I don't know. I took Kate home and said I'd better come back and see if there was anything I could do. I expect she guessed what I was really up to but I didn't care just then.'

'You know she and I had . . . that we had a confrontation tonight?'

'I didn't, but it explains one or two things. Was it awful?'

'Yes, for both of us.'

'You didn't savage each other, did you?'

'Not exactly. She asked me to go away and leave you alone.'

'It figures. It would be fine for her. Or at least, she thinks it would.'

'Wouldn't it solve things for all of us?'

'Do you think it would? For you and me?'

She had been working out how she might put it to him and now she said carefully, 'The trouble is that what I feel for you isn't just a selfish want; it involves me in a respon-

378

sibility towards you. I mean, I have a responsibility as a human being towards your wife and your marriage; but overriding all that is my concern for you, for what you want.'

'I know,' he said. 'I know, I know. And don't you, when you really stop and think about it, don't you hear a still small voice that says it's so ridiculous, that somehow we've got it all wrong and we're kicking against myths and customs and taboos that people accept as the final word, whereas somewhere there must be a rationale that would solve it all. It's all ... all a waste of time in the life of the world. When I get really worked up all I can feel is outraged bewilderment; and I don't think it's simply a childish refusal to accept the facts of life, that this toy is simply too expensive and I can't have it. I mean, there are people all over the world at this moment pulling triggers and *killing* people.' His voice had run up in keeping with the emotions he was describing. Now it subsided as he sighed and said. 'Of course it all presupposes that you'll blithely give away years of your life, spoil yourself for other relationships, when I've no future to give you.'

'I wish you'd stop that,' Andrea said. 'I've told you about it before.'

'It's still true.'

'You're talking exactly in *their* terms. There *is* nobody else I want. I love you. It's the fact of my life. I'm bound up with you whether I go or stay, whether I see you or I don't. Of course it would have been heaven if we'd both been free but since we're not I honestly think that just the promise of seeing you once a year would be worth more than nothing, worth more than my so-called freedom to turn to other people and make another life. I've just spent six months without hope, with every incentive to turn away and forget, and it didn't work.'

'Nor with me ... Half a year of awful deprivation, and every sleep a small suicide ... I saw a man on television the other night and he had the faint mark of a long and terrible scar on his forehead. He was smiling, making jokes, speaking lucidly about his subject, and I wondered how often he remembered the circumstances in which he received that wound, if he relived them, was partly shaped by them, or was it just the mark of some almost forgotten misfortune. A few nights later there was an attractive woman on, the innocent party in a recent celebrated divorce case. She was smiling, making jokes, speaking lucidly about her subject, and I wondered, though there was no outward mark, whether she had wounds inside which hurt her all the time, or whether they had healed over like the scar on the man's forehead and she'd learned to live with them and found another kind of happiness ... My subject,' he went on after a pause, 'is survival'.

A third appliance had arrived, the blue light spinning on its roof as it rocked gently down the lane and into the factory yard. Andrea watched a window burst outwards and a tongue of yellow flame lick up the side of the building. A jet of water swung in and began to play on it.

'Kate thinks I don't love her any more,' Philip said; 'that the most I feel for her now is a kind of pity. But she's wrong. Apart from the state of being in love, there's a special kind of concern that grows gradually between two people who've lived together for ten years in affection and tolerance. And I want that to be there for as long as she needs it, because giving it is a part of my life as well.' He paused. 'I don't bring you much for your comfort, do I?'

'I don't think that lies, and promises you couldn't keep, would help me more,' Andrea said. 'I know I love you. I know you love me. But without honesty it wouldn't amount to much. With it there are times when I know, I just *know*, that it can't all be for nothing; that somehow, somewhere, there must be something for us.'

'Not everything,' Philip said, 'nor nothing; but something.'

'Yes.'

Her eyes were drawn to a piece of black waste which had floated up out of the burning factory and was hanging above the highest tips of flame like some great idling bird.

Then the draught lifted it higher and the breeze caught it, bearing it away, rising all the time, till it was lost to view in the darkness of the sky over the valley. Something, some aspect of it that she couldn't define, released in her a powerful trembling wave of joy and Philip, feeling her shudder beside him, asked if she were cold, drawing her closer as she said no.

'Your letter to me is in those flames,' she said after a time.

'It was full of despair, anyway,' he said. 'I'll try to write you one with hope in it.'

'Just a little,' she said. 'Just enough for truth, and to tide me over.'

Nick took his gaze off them and made his way to his mother and Tom, who turned his head at his approach.

'Nick? I'm going to run your mother and Shirley home. Are you coming?'

'Unless there's anything I can do here.'

'No . . .' He seemed to lose himself again for a time in contemplation of the burning factory. 'I don't think there's anything any of us can do just now.'

They all walked together up the slope to the road, where the car stood. Seeing them, one of Lightfoot's constables spoke to Simpkins about the best way out, then went off along the road to clear a way for him.

Who? Simpkins wondered. And why? It was going to haunt him; haunt him and hurt him. But he must not let it destroy his peace. They had won through and nothing must spoil that. He became conscious as he looked round to see that everyone was in the car and settled, that Bess was crying quietly. He spoke to her gently.

'I was thinking about Father,' she said. 'How he built it all up, how proud he was of it all.'

'We'll build it up again,' Simpkins said. 'We've still got our goodwill left, and that's more important than bricks and mortar.' That, he thought, and the love you had for people and the love they had for you; the warmth round you when the people you loved were all together as now.

381

Bess herself; Norma, Shirley and Nick. He would build it again and when he had done that it would be his own, not something of his father's held in trust. He was still young enough; there was still time.

He said on a sudden thought, 'Aren't we forgetting Miss Warner?'

'She's talking to Philip Hart,' Nick said. 'I expect he'll give her a lift.'

Lightfoot appeared at the window. 'Will you be coming back, Tom?'

'In about half an hour.'

'Right you are.'

He straightened up beside the car as the young constable came up to say the way was clear.

'Straight ahead, sir. Steady as you go.'

'Thank you,' Simpkins raised his hand; then, letting in the clutch, he put the car in motion and took his family home.

THE END

A KIND OF LOVING
The best-selling first novel
by STAN BARSTOW

Written in the early sixties, *A Kind of Loving* is recognised with *Room at the Top* and *Saturday Night, Sunday Morning*, as one of the most important novels of that era—novels in which the ordinary, unhandsome and conventional young man and his way of life were first investigated and portrayed in the modern idiom.

Now, in the seventies, Stan Barstow's powerful novel emerges as one that surpasses all others of that genre; for in *A Kind of Loving*, the young Vic Brown, his attitudes and those of his family, his problems and the background against which he comes to resolve them, still have relevance to life today as many people know it. Moreover, Barstow tells his story with a realism and honesty that is rare and that put this, his first novel, into a class of its own.

0 552 09274 6—40p   T38

JOBY *by* STAN BARSTOW

To Joby Weston that summer, the world was surely a strange and brutal place. It was the summer when he should have been swollen with happiness at the knowledge that he was going to Cressley grammar school in September but which was clouded by his mother going into hospital. It was the summer when he tasted the bitterness of injustice. And it was Joby's last summer of innocence in which, slowly and painfully, he learnt the hard facts of life and discovered the world of adults was also full of tragedy . . .

'In *Joby* Barstow has pared everything down to essentials, the essentials of reality. It is a considerable work of art.'
THE SCOTSMAN

0 552 09278 9—30p   T39

A SELECTED LIST OF FINE NOVELS THAT APPEAR IN CORGI

☐ 08458 1	ANOTHER COUNTRY	*James Baldwin* 35p
☐ 09274 6	A KIND OF LOVING	*Stan Barstow* 40p
☐ 09277 0	THE DESPERADOES	*Stan Barstow* 30p
☐ 09278 9	JOBY	*Stan Barstow* 30p
☐ 09156 1	THE EXORCIST	*William Peter Blatty* 40p
☐ 09544 3	THE TERMINAL MAN	*Michael Crichton* 40p
☐ 09759 4	CRASH PROGRAMME	*J. R. Daniels* 40p
☐ 08963 X	CAPE OF STORMS	*John Gordon Davis* 40p
☐ 08108 6	HOLD MY HAND I'M DYING	*John Gordon Davis* 50p
☐ 09436 6	THE ODESSA FILE	*Frederick Forsyth* 65p
☐ 09121 9	THE DAY OF THE JACKAL	*Frederick Forsyth* 65p
☐ 09230 4	BUGLES AND A TIGER	*John Masters* 40p
☐ 09452 8	THE RAVI LANCERS	*John Masters* 45p
☐ 08887 0	VIVA RAMIREZ/	*James S. Rand* 50p
☐ 07954 5	RUN FOR THE TREES	*James S. Rand* 60p
☐ 08716 5	THE LONG VALLEY	*John Steinbeck* 30p
☐ 08459 X	THE PASTURES OF HEAVEN	*John Steinbeck* 30p
☐ 09356 4	THE RED PONY	*John Steinbeck* 30p
☐ 08325 9	THE WAYWARD BUS	*John Steinbeck* 35p
☐ 08326 7	TO A GOD UNKNOWN	*John Steinbeck* 30p
☐ 08327 5	CUP OF GOLD	*John Steinbeck* 30p
☐ 08993 1	ONCE THERE WAS A WAR	*John Steinbeck* 25p
☐ 09108 1	THE BRAVE CAPTAINS	*Vivian Stuart* 30p
☐ 09323 8	HAZARD OF 'HUNTRESS'	*Vivian Stuart* 35p
☐ 08866 8	QB VII	*Leon Uris* 60p
☐ 08091 8	TOPAZ	*Leon Uris* 40p
☐ 08384 4	EXODUS	*Leon Uris* 60p
☐ 08385 2	MILA 18	*Leon Uris* 40p
☐ 08389 5	ARMAGEDDON	*Leon Uris* 60p
☐ 08521 9	THE ANGRY HILLS	*Leon Uris* 40p
☐ 08676 2	EXODUS REVISITED (Illustrated)	*Leon Uris* 50p
☐ 09460 9	THE WORD	*Irving Wallace* 75p
☐ 09753 5	THE DAY OF THE LOCUST	*Nathaniel West* 50p

All these books are available at your bookshop or newsagent : or can be ordered direct from the publisher. Just tick the titles you want and fill in the form below.

CORGI BOOKS, Cash Sales Department, P.O. Box 11, Falmouth, Cornwall.
Please send cheque or postal order. No currency, and allow 10p per book to cover the cost of postage and packing (plus 5p each for additional copies).

NAME ....

ADDRESS ....

(OCT 75) OP4

While every effort is made to keep prices low, it is sometimes necessary to increase prices at short notice. Corgi Books reserve the right to show new retail prices on covers which may differ from those previously advertised in the text or elsewhere.